The Heretic of Granada

David C. Edmonds

Published by:
Southern Yellow Pine (SYP) Publishing
4351 Natural Bridge Rd.
Tallahassee, FL 32305

www.syppublishing.com

ISBN-10: 1-59616-065-9
ISBN-13: 978-1-59616-065-1
ISBN-13: ePub 978-1-59616-066-8
ISBN-13: Adobe PDF 978-1-59616-067-5
Library of Congress Control Number: 2018939300

Front Cover Design: David R Martinez

Printed in the United States of America
First Edition
March 2018

Dedication

In loving memory of
MARIA NIEVES EDMONDS
Who came into my world in the summer of 1994
And flew away with the angels in the winter of 2017
May God rest her beautiful soul.

After Galileo was convicted for heresy by the Spanish Inquisition for his theory that the earth revolved around the sun, he replied, 'Still, the earth is moving.'

Junichiro Koizumi

Other Titles by David C. Edmonds

The Girl in the Glyphs

Lily of Peru

Yankee Autumn in Acadiana

The Guns of Port Hudson—The River Campaign

The Guns of Port Hudson—The Investment, Siege and Reduction

The Conduct of Federal Troops in Louisiana

The Vigilante Committees of the Attakapas

Journal of a Voyage through the Spanish Main

A Personal Account of my Escape from the Inquisition

In the time of the War of Jenkins Ear

And my

Encounters with Hurricanes, Agents of the Holy Church, English Warships, Flame-throwing Zambos, and Spirits of the Underworld,

and my

Adventures with Pirates of the Caribbean

Father Antonio Escofet, S.J.

Diari d'un Viatge a través del Carib — Un Compte Personal de la meva Escapament de la Inquisició en el Temps de la Guerra de l'Orella de Jenkins i la meva Trobada amb els Huracans, els Agents de l'Església, Llançaflames Zambos, Vaixells de Guerra Anglès, i Esperits de l'inframón i Aventures amb Pirates del Carib.
Pare Antonio Escofet, C.J.

CVBA
Atlantic Ocean
HISPANIOLA
IAMAICO
P. Rico
Caribbean Sea
1st Voyage
2nd Voyage
NICARAGVA
COLOMBIA
Father Antonio's Voyage along the Spanish Main

CHAPTER 1

The Alhambra—Granada, District of Nicaragua
Sunday morning, August, 1741

In the eleven months since I'd been locked up in the Alhambra, no one talked about freedom. Not the jailer. Not the other prisoners in the sunshine yard, and certainly not the old Indian woman who cooked for us. Yet there she stood outside the door with my breakfast of boiled eggs, bread and cheese, mumbling "*libertad*" as if it were a commandment from heaven.

"They come soon," she said in her broken Castilian.

"Who is coming, Abuelita?"

"Pirates. I see it in the moon last night… a circle… a sign."

"A sign of what?"

"Freedom. They free you when they come."

"Why would pirates free me? They're English. I'm a Spaniard, a priest, a Catholic."

"They blow down building. You run… hide on islands with my people." She handed her tray through the little window that served as my only way to communicate with my jailers. "Eat. Get back strength. They come soon."

I rolled my eyes. The only way I was going to get out of this place was to finish my sentence. I thanked her anyway, limped to my little table, and started to peel one of her eggs when a loud boom shook the building. Doors rattled. Dogs barked. Dust filtered from the overhead. Then came a second blast and another, echoing through town in the gloom of early morning. Could this be it, a pirate invasion?

I waited—hoped—for the screams of terrified bystanders, the commands of the officers, the volleys of musketry, but there was only the stir of people and wagons, the barking dogs, and the shouts of the street criers making their rounds on horseback:

"*Oigan! Oigan*! Assemble in the plaza!"

I struggled up with my walking stick and took an uneasy step toward the window bars, almost knocking over the chamber pot. Since my arrest and imprisonment, I'd heard cannon fire and the shouts of criers many times. Only twice had there been three blasts in sequence. The first, about two months ago, was to announce the hanging of a notorious English pirate and the second, only a week ago, for the burning of Doña Seisdados, the village witch.

Would some other poor soul be executed today? I reached the tiny balcony and clutched the iron bars for support. In the plaza below, where the god of corn had once been worshipped by the natives, there now stood the menacing stakes of *La Inquisición*, freshly stripped of bark and pointing toward heaven like the Egyptian obelisks of Rome. Off to the side, where only yesterday a poet had been reading love sonnets to the girls, there now rested a pot of smoking coals.

A vision of the burning witch flashed through my mind: her shrieks, the smell of burning flesh, the explosion of her head.

Why would anyone want to see such a horrible thing?

Even as I watched, people hurried out of side streets and buildings—young and old, white and Indian, even women with toddlers. The executioners were there too—Samson and El Moro in their black hoods and leather vests—the same two men who'd taken a club to my leg. The leg was healing, but I was still passing blood.

"Who are they cooking?" yelled a man from a balcony.

Samson looked up from the brazier. "*El Cantante*!"

My heart seemed to stop. *El Cantante*? Surely he was mistaken. The Inquisition had sentenced me to two years confinement, then exile to Chile. I crossed the room, my leg no longer troubling me and pounded on the door.

"Jailer, where are you? We need to talk. César?"

He didn't answer. I pounded some more. "Abuelita!"

No one came. No one answered. It was as if they didn't want to face me, to tell me the truth. Had they known all along? Or had the bishop suddenly decided to silence me?

The outside commotion was getting louder with people shouting and singing, horses clattering along the cobbled streets, wagons creaking and rumbling.

Slowly, dreading what I might see, I made my way back to the window. The plaza was now more crowded than ever—women fanning themselves in the August heat, girls dancing as if today were the festival of the Virgin of the Assumption, dirty-faced children scaling trees. Even the vendors were out, peddling mangos and papaya juice, and one old man, crippled by age, was selling sacks of eggs and rotten bananas from a cart.

"*Proyectiles*!" he cried. "All the better for pelting."

Pelting? Hadn't the Church banned pelting? Bystanders could be injured. Women would have their dresses ruined. Pelting was allowed for only the most heinous crimes. All I'd done was try to protect an Indian holy site from the fury of the priests.

"Look!" someone shouted. "It's him… up there on the balcony."

"Burn him!" shrieked a woman. "*Quemelo*!"

The crowd picked up the chant: "*Quemelo*! *Quemelo*!"

I retreated into the shadows, unable to comprehend the hatred, the passion. These people used to be my friends, my parishioners, the same townsmen who'd come to watch me perform on stage and hear me sing. It was one thing to see a witch burned. But a priest? A Jesuit priest? *El Cantante*?

Be brave, I told myself. Hadn't Jesus faced the same ordeal?

I crawled into my hammock and clasped my hands in prayer. Why had God led me to that cursed cave with its strange writings and symbols? What crime had I committed?

Footsteps sounded in the hall. Loud footsteps, like the clop of a soldier's boots. I closed my eyes: "The Lord is my shepherd; I shall not want…."

The footfalls stopped at the door. Security bolts clanked.

"He maketh me to lie down in green pastures…."

There was a rattle of keys and the click of a turning lock.

"He leadeth me beside the still waters. He—"

"*Quemelo! Quemelo! Quemelo!*"

The door opened, slowly, creaking on its strap hinges.

Someone entered the room; a dark shadow fell over me.

"It's time, Father."

I expected to see the ugly face of Captain Gonzalez, the man who escorted prisoners to the stake, but it was César the jailer, a dark little fellow with pigtails, earring, and scarred face, carrying a pitcher of water. Like me, he was a Catalán from Barcelona.

He set the pitcher on the table. "I'm sorry," he said in the language we shared, "that's the way it is with these cursed Castilians. They lie, they—"

"How much time do I have?"

"They'll be here soon."

He put an arm beneath my back and helped me sit up. "My God, Padre, you're burning alive. We've got to get something in you."

"Why trouble yourself? I'll be dead soon."

"But why suffer?" He marched to the door and yelled down for the cook: "Abuelita, bring a mug of your fever juice."

From outside came the clatter of passing cavalrymen. One of them yelled up, "Hey Padre, are you going to sing us a song?"

"Bastards," César said. "They're as bad as the alcalde. You know what he told me when I first came in? Said if anything went wrong he'd have my head. Ordered me not to bring food or water. Said it's to avoid… well… accidents in front of the ladies."

"I can't eat anyway."

"You can drink fever juice. These Indians have better medicine than we do."

The door opened and in came Abuelita, all stooped and wrinkled, smelling of onions and peppers and dressed in the red and white of her Chorotegan tribe. The amulet of her superstition dangled from her neck. Only minutes before she'd been promising freedom. Now she nodded sadly, handed me a mug, and quit the room.

"It's vile as horse piss," César said, "but it'll kill the fever."

"Will it kill the pain?"

"If you drink enough."

I stared at the mug. "They offered Jesus a drug. Saint Mark, 15:23. 'And they gave him to drink wine mingled with myrrh, but he received it not.'"

"All they did was nail Jesus to the cross. You they'll burn."

"His suffering lasted many hours. Mine will be short."

"Are you going to drink it or talk about Jesus?"

I drained the mug. It filled my mouth and throat with bitterness and burned right down to my stomach.

"*Madre de Dios*," I said, wincing. "This is worse than fever."

"Drink enough, and it'll put you in a coma. I've seen Indians who wouldn't wake up."

"What a blessing if I could fall into a coma."

"Then do it. You saw what Samson did to the witch. Poked fire in her face. Don't give him that pleasure." Again he yelled down to Abuelita. "Bring up the entire jug!" Then he threw a blanket over me. "Is there anything else I can do for you, Father? Anyone to notify?"

I straightened up. "I'd like to send a message to Father Paolo."

"Tell me what to say."

"It has to be written."

His eyes widened. "I'm sorry, Father. The alcalde said no contacts with the outside world. Been that way since the Hebrew escaped. Any words have to be by mouth."

"It has to be written, César. Please. I'll need paper and quill."

"Didn't you hear me? Don't you know what they did to me after the Jew escaped? Look at these scars. See what they did? If they catch you with paper and quill, it'll be the end of me."

"Father Paolo will pay you."

"What good is gold if they lop off my head? I've got a wife and children."

I opened my mouth to say I once had a wife and children too but was interrupted by the appearance of Abuelita. She shuffled in with her jug and set it on the table. César waited for her to leave, the space empty of words. For a moment it seemed as if he might relent, but then he marched to the door. "I'm sorry, Padre, I can't take the risk. Drink your juice."

He stepped into the hallway and closed the door. The key in the lock turned. The bolts closed with a loud clank. I listened to his fading footfalls, then reached for the jug of fever juice.

CHAPTER 2

I gulped down a third cup and a fourth and was trying to down another when I noticed my heart beating faster. A heady sensation reached into my limbs, dulling the pain. The shuddering was gone. So was the headache. My mind became sharper, more alert. I even remembered the words of a letter I'd written years ago:

The priests call it 'Indian fever bark' owing to its palliative qualities, but it also has a reputation for prolonging carnal pleasure. When used judiciously, it brings to the infirm a sense of strength and wellbeing, followed by torpidity and sleep. If used to excess, it induces apparitions, hallucinations, coma, even death....

I looked at my cup. Empty. The jug was also empty. Dear God, what had I done? What if I fell into a coma and died? Wasn't self-induced death a violation of God's holy commandment?

"Yes," said a voice from the balcony.

I struggled up from my hammock.

The room flashed white. Bells clanged. My head spun, and as if the gateway to heaven had opened, there stood my childhood priest, Father Sebastiano.

How could that be? Father Sebastiano died years ago.

He took a step toward me, his eyes boring into mine with the same intensity as when he admonished me for childish pranks. "Antonio," he said, waving a bony finger in my face. "Do you not recall the cowardly death of Judas by his own hand?"

When Father Sebastiano spoke to me like that, I was twelve years old again. "Yes, Father."

"The teachings of St. Thomas Aquinas that God alone is the master of life?"

"Yes, Father."

"Then why are you trying to kill yourself? You must purge that devil juice from your insides."

I grabbed a pitcher of water and gulped it down. I slapped my face. I stuffed a finger down my throat and puked into the chamber pot. Then I dropped to my knees and begged forgiveness for every drop of Indian bark I'd imbibed.

Please, dear God, keep me alive until I reach the stake. Let me suffer no less than Jesus suffered on the Cross. Please, dear God, please, hear my prayers.

I begged forgiveness for the lies I'd told under oath at the *audiencia* of the Holy Inquisition, and for my part in the massacre that followed. And I was praying for the souls of my beloved Saraatepe and our two children when Father Sebastiano laid a hand on my head.

A shock ran through me, as if I'd been struck by lightning. It burned down to my neck and heated my chest. Again he spoke: "If I grant you a wish, Antonio, what would it be?"

"My wife and children. I want them back."

"Only in heaven will you see them, *mijo*."

"Then give me power to avenge their deaths."

"Vengeance is mine; so sayeth the Lord."

"Then give me my freedom."

"To do what, Antonio?"

"To flee this place. To worship the Lord elsewhere."

Again he reached down and touched my head, but this time it had a soothing effect. "Father Antonio of Barcelona, late vicar of the Island of Ometepe, *El Cantante* of Nicaragua, by these words and by the sign of the cross, I grant you your freedom. *In nomine Patris, et Filii, et Spiritus Sancti. Amen.*"

He made the sign of the cross over me, then walked across the room and right through the wall, leaving me in a state of disbelief. Was it possible? Had Father Sebastiano really granted me freedom? If so, why was I still kneeling on this wretched floor?

I pulled myself up and stumbled to the door.

Locked.

I looked above me and below, searching for an exit.

Nothing.

I felt along the wall where Father Sebastiano had disappeared.

Solid.

This made no sense. If Father Sebastiano was real, I should be able to walk right through the wall. Or open the door. Or pass through the bars. If only I could make myself small. Or turn into a bird. Yes, a bird. Wasn't that what Saraatepe used to say in my dreams?

"Turn into bird, my love. Fly through bars. Meet on the islands."

I crawled back into my hammock, closed my eyes, and tried to shut out the commotion in the plaza.

Focus, Antonio. Make yourself small. Turn into a bird.

My body seemed to shrink. Smaller and smaller. Small enough to fit through a keyhole. Light enough to levitate. Yes, now I was floating across the room and onto the balcony. Through the bars. Into the sunlight and over the yelling mob. Flying like a bird.

Thank you, Father Sebastiano.

But when I opened my eyes, I was still in my hammock and the mob was still yelling.

So that was it: a hallucination. Father Sebastiano was as phony as gypsy gold.

I picked up the empty jug and stared at it. Magic in a jug, full of fantasies. The only freedom for me was leaving this life at an earlier age than Jesus. They'd dress me in the outfit of a dunce and parade me around the plaza, pelt me with goat turds, taunt me, and beat me senseless. There'd be no forgiveness, no offer to recant, no final confession, and no freedom.

Only a wooden stake in the plaza and a painful, fiery death.

The sound of drums brought me to my feet. Again I found my way to the balcony. Amazing how much stronger I felt, how my hearing had improved. Even my eyesight was better.

Through the bars I saw a band of Gypsies snaking through the plaza—all head bands, boots, earrings and red scarves—the men circling the stakes and somersaulting through the air, the women dancing seductively, creating a great uproar with their kettledrums and pots.

Romans. These people were no better than ancient Romans, having fun before the lions ate the Christians. Where was the loyalty, the protests, the anger? Where were my friends, my flock, my admirers? I'd officiated at their ceremonies, christened their children, sang at their funerals and weddings. They said I had the voice of an angel, of a nightingale, a voice so deep and sonorous that it could make a statue cry.

Now, there wasn't a woeful look among them. No agony, no shame, no remorse.

But hadn't Jesus been denied by His flock?

The thunder of galloping horses came to my ears. Across the plaza a dozen or more cavalrymen rounded the corner from the cathedral, with pikes, plumed helmets and ceremonial uniforms, lashing at bystanders with their riding crops.

"*Muevense! Muevense!*"

People scattered, dogs barked, and as they came closer, I recognized the military chief of Granada: Captain Bonifacio Gonzalez y Perez, a vile little man with a fierce reputation, now mounted on a massive black war horse named *Relámpago*. Lightning.

Until that moment, the smell of horses and leather had always made me feel at home. Now I associated it with the thing I most hated: Gonzalez. It was he who'd led the cavalry against the women and children on the Island of Lizards. He who'd carried out the massacre on Isla Ometepe. He who'd ended the life of my dear Saraatepe and our two children. More shameless still, he was carrying the palms of victory as if he'd won a great battle against the Moors.

My blood surged. How I ached to burst through the bars and pounce on this evil man, choke him until he turned blue, drag him to the stake and light the fire myself.

Forgive me, Father, for I cannot turn the other cheek.

They drew to a noisy stop beneath the balcony. I eased back into the shadows, shamed by my impotence. "Where is he?" Gonzalez asked his troopers.

"That balcony up there. Can't you smell the shit?"

They howled with laughter. It wasn't every day they had the pleasure of burning a priest. Not just any priest, but one of those Indian-loving Jesuits.

"Hey, Padre, prepare yourself for hell! You'll get to reunite with your little Indian whore."

Heat rose to my face. Without thinking, I stepped to the bars and flung the empty mug at him.

It shattered on the cobbles. Relámpago whinnied and reared. Gonzalez pointed a gloved finger and had his mouth open to reply when an egg spattered on his dress uniform.

He wheeled about. "*Hijo de puta*! Who threw that egg?"

A ragged little Chorotegan boy stepped out of the crowd—Mateo, a goat shepherd from the Island of Lizards, the only survivor of the massacre. He'd hidden in a tree and seen it all: the rapes, the torture, the pillaging and murders committed by the soldiers.

"*Asesino*!" he cried and flung another egg.

Mateo darted away. Gonzalez spurred his horse forward. Vendors and spectators jumped aside. Mothers grabbed their children. Shouts of protest rose throughout the plaza.

"Run!" I yelled to Mateo.

A woman grabbed the reins of the captain's horse. Even from the balcony I recognized her—Rosa Morales, the painted madam of The House of Seven Veils.

"Stop it!" she cried. "He's just a boy."

Gonzalez kicked her, knocking her to the ground. Mateo dove beneath the skirts of a Chorotegan woman. The captain dismounted, grabbed the boy's legs, and was trying to dislodge him when the cathedral bells began tolling.

Gonzalez released him and turned to listen. Mateo scrambled away. "Time for the procession!" someone yelled.

CHAPTER 3

Bugles blew, drums beat, and out from the great cathedral marched the boys' choir of Granada, a procession of white cassocks, candles, crosses, and effigies of the Holy Virgin. The notes of *Te Deum* crossed the plaza, followed by the boys' youthful voices.

Te Deum laudémus. We praise Thee, oh God.

Te Dominium confitémur. We acknowledge thee to be Lord.

The boys skirted the plaza, still singing. Behind them came a brother carrying the green standard of the Inquisition, then the vicars, prelates, and prefects with their dangling crucifixes and long sacerdotal robes. Next came priests, brothers and friars from the surrounding villages, places with Indian names like Masatepe, Apoyo and Diriamba.

At the head of this assemblage, swinging a censer and dressed in the scarlet and purple of authority, marched a man even more feared and despised than Gonzalez: The Inquisitor-General of Nicaragua, Bishop Diego de Ureña.

Bystanders knelt faithfully as he passed, knowing their failure to do so would endanger themselves or their family.

An even greater rage bubbled up from my chest. Here was a man noted for his cruelty. A man who maintained a stable of young boys and girls for his pleasure. Yet it was I, an honest priest, who was condemned to the stake.

It wasn't right. Why didn't God punish the wicked the way He did in the Old Testament? Why didn't He bring down the city on the bishop's head?

The boys rounded the second corner and were now marching toward me. In front rode two cavalrymen, snarling at bystanders.

Hooves clattered. Horses snorted and pranced. Then the boys were directly beneath me, grouped in the rigid caste system of the colonies—Europeans to the front, followed by half-breeds, the mixed bloods, Indians, and, finally, a few boys of color, as if God would group them that way in heaven. There was Pablo, the baker's son, holding a candle. Beside him marched Ignacio, the blacksmith's boy, eyes straight ahead.

Why wouldn't they look up? Why were they ignoring me, their old choirmaster? Didn't they understand the injustice that was about to befall an innocent man?

Did they care?

They wound into the plaza and gathered around the stakes, still singing. On an elevated platform sat the invited guests, the hacendados, hidalgos and alcaldes, even a long-haired representative from the Viceroy in Guatemala, all with boots, sashes and embroidered waistcoats. The executioners, Samson and El Moro, pushed back the common folks with metal pokers. The bishop handed white roses to the widows and mothers of the slain soldiers.

What an indignity, the perpetrator comforting the victims.

The singing stopped. Effigies and banners were laid down or staked to the ground. Then the drums came to life, the same dismal beat that was normally reserved for the Day of the Dead.

Every head turned toward the balcony where I stood.

I glanced around desperately—at the heavy door with its metal straps and hinges. At the wooden floor and walls. At the ceiling with its exposed beams. Wood everywhere, thick and heavy, an entire building made from stone and ships' planking.

No way to break in or out.

But hadn't Jacobo the Jew escaped from this very room—on the night before the burning? They said he'd gone to the balcony and flapped his arms like a chicken, crowing and cackling, yelling he was going to turn into a rooster and fly away.

And sure enough, when Gonzalez came for him, the room was empty, the door locked from the outside, the walls and bars intact, a pile of feathers next to his clothes.

I slammed a fist against the wall. There was only one rational explanation: Jacobo's friends.

Where were my friends? Why had they not come to my rescue?

The drums stopped. The chants faded.

I figured they'd be coming for me any second. Instead, Bishop Ureña, on the platform with the guests, held up his arms for silence.

"Fellow Spaniards," he began in a clear voice that resonated of a Salamanca education. "Brothers in Christ…, townsfolk of Granada." He opened his Bible. "Listen to the words of our Lord Jesus Christ, John 15:6." He paused. "'If a man abideth not in me, he is cast forth as a branch, and is withered, and men gather them, and cast them into the fire, and they are burned.'

"The man we condemn today, Father Antonio, was our friend. We loved him as we love all our brothers. Yet, sadly, Father Antonio abideth not in his Lord. He has done great iniquity. He bringeth forth bad fruit. Therefore we must do as commanded: cast him into a furnace of fire!"

The bishop closed his Bible and sat down. Then Father Menendez, Fiscál of Granada, a man noted for cohabiting with six Indian girls, marched to the lectern and cleared his throat. His voice was high-pitched and dry, like an old man's.

"What sins, you may ask, have brought Father Antonio before the Holy Office of Inquisition? There are many. First, Father Antonio has been charged and found guilty of providing aid and comfort to English pirates who attacked the island where he worked as a priest…. This in a time of war with the English."

Liar. My only sin was not fleeing into the mountains.

"Second, for breaking his sacred vows by taking into his bed an Indian harlot."

"Fornicator! Fornicator! Fornicator!"

I shut out the chants and let my mind take me back to my beautiful Saraatepe, my bride with the long dark hair and olive brown skin. Because of her, I loved God more. Because of her, I loved her people. Because I loved her people, I worked that much harder to bring them to Christ. How could loving Saraatepe be a sin?

"Third, for siding with the heathens at a place of devil worship."

"Burn him!" the crowd chanted.

Father Menendez held up his arms for silence. "Let me tell you the story. It began on a holy Sunday almost a year ago. Father Antonio came to me with a tale so wild I assumed he'd been imbibing spirits with the ignorant savages whose company he prefers…."

"Fornicator! Fornicator! Fornicator!"

"According to Father Antonio, he was led by the Indian hunchback, Tomás, to a cave on the Island of Lizards. And in this cave, by light of torches, he claims to have seen mysterious symbols and paintings. And these symbols, according to Father Antonio, tell the story of a Moses of the Americas."

Murmurs of disbelief rose throughout the plaza.

"Not the Moses we know from Exodus and Deuteronomy, but a female Moses."

"Moses is a man," someone shouted.

Father Menendez's voice rose with indignity, as if he'd been personally insulted. "And furthermore, Father Antonio stated that this woman Moses, this Indian harlot, came down from the mountain with a divine slate of laws from God Himself."

A young boy hurled a banana toward the balcony. There were cries of "Blasphemy!" People pumped their fists and shouted insults. Even a donkey brayed. The outrage could not have been greater if I had burned an effigy of the Holy Mother.

Father Menendez returned to his chair with the satisfied look of a prince who'd slain the dragon. The bishop took the podium again, rapping his staff for silence.

"When this assault on our Holy Scriptures came to my attention, I ordered our soldiers to the island with orders to destroy this cave of the devil, but when these courageous men landed, they were set upon and brutally murdered by Father Antonio's Indian friends."

The bishop pointed to the group he had adorned with roses. "What are we to say to the loved ones of our fallen heroes? Do we now say forget this cave of the devil?"

"No!" the crowd answered as one.

"Do we say forgive the man who brought about this tragedy or do we cast him into the fire?"

"Burn him! Burn him!"

The speech ended; the drums started again. Off to the right the cavalry was skirting the plaza and rounding the corner toward the Alhambra, banners flying.

I pushed against the bars. Was that a cart in the rear? Yes, a two-wheeled oxcart. And behind that cart, pushed along by four soldiers with fixed bayonets, was my dear Chorotegan friend, Hunchback Tomás, filthy and bleeding. "No," I cried. "Dear God, no."

They had dressed him in a yellow penitential garment on which were painted demons, stars, the flames of hell, and the word, Sorcerer. His mouth was gagged; his hands tied and attached to the cart by a tether. On his head rested a five-point bonnet, also painted with stars.

He waddled sideways, dragging his twisted leg. Priests in black walked on either side, their faces buried deep in black hoods, each holding a small crucifix. Street ruffians spat on Tomás. They cursed him, pelted him with eggs, rotten bananas, and the droppings of horses. Even from a distance, I saw the pain on his face, the terror.

"Stop it," I yelled through the bars.

No one listened. A young boy with a stick began thrashing Tomás as if he were a dangerous dog. The hunchback stumbled and fell; the cart kept rolling, dragging him through mounds of manure. Other boys joined the fray, stomping, kicking, laughing.

At last, Father Paolo Prieto-Baró, my childhood friend and the one man in the diocese I respected, rushed over. "Stop this cart. I order you to stop it now!"

Curses and insults rained down from the balconies. Captain Gonzalez marched over to Father Paolo as if to give him a tongue-lashing. Father Paolo stood his ground and shooed away the boys. Then he unleashed the hunchback from his tether, helped him stand,

and guided him as gently into the plaza as if he were helping Jesus to the Cross.

The drums fell silent.

Father Paolo placed a hand on the hunchback's shoulder and spoke to him. I knew exactly what he was saying, for I, myself, had spoken the same words to victims of the Inquisition: "Breathe deeply the moment the fire is lit, breathe in the smoke before the flames reach you. Do not struggle. The smoke will put you closer to God."

A bailiff stepped forward to read the sentence: "Hunchback Tomás, you have been tried in the Court of the Inquisition of the Royal District of Nicaragua and found guilty of the crimes of sorcery, sedition, heresy, conspiracy, perjury, and murder. For these crimes, the court sentences you to death by burning. May God have mercy on your Indian soul."

The drummers picked up the beat.

The soldiers dragged the poor man onto the woodpile and tied him to the stake. They piled wood up to his neck and stepped away. The executioners stood by their braziers. Then the gamers began placing bets at a table that had been set up for that purpose.

I saw the glitter of gold and silver and imagined I could hear the chatter of the gamers. Would the hunchback's head explode with a loud pop? Or a gentle pop? Or end with a sizzle?

I wiped away tears. Why were men so callous, so cruel? They'd soon be betting on my head as well. But hadn't Romans cast lots for the robe of Jesus?

The bishop raised his crucifix and lowered it. The drumbeat stopped. In the silence that followed, I cried, "Spare this poor man! He is innocent!"

Every face in the plaza turned toward me.

A bearded man I recognized as a shoemaker yelled up, "Sing, Padre! Sing for your Indian friend! Sing him to hell!" Others picked up the cry: "Sing, Padre, Sing!"

The fear left me. I felt as if I'd been transported to a stage at a Zarzuela, the crowd waiting for my performance. Yes, why not sing for my friend? Sing him to heaven.

CHAPTER 4

The melody I chose—Giulio Caccini's *Ave Maria*—was the most beautiful tune I knew. It also had a reputation of bringing good to all who heard it. Estranged lovers would make up. Old grudges would be forgiven. Dogs would howl, and dry cows would lactate. There were even reports of it bringing the dead back to life.

I sang it now, with improvised lyrics from a poem about a woman looking for her lover:

Lashed to the stake, he is crying,
Everyone will say it is fear of dying,
But I know in his heart, he is singing, Ave Maria....

From the Gypsies came the accompanying strains of violins. Then a Spanish guitar. It was followed by castanets, a native flute and the slow beat of a drum.

Men removed their hats. Women dabbed at their eyes. One of the dons came to his feet and placed a hand over his heart as if recalling a deep personal tragedy. Others around him stood.

A change came over me. No longer was I singing to a rag-tag mob. Now, as if by magic, I stood in the glitter of a grand theatre, performing for an audience of royalty, and my song wasn't just a song; it was a prayer, a cry, a plea to intervene in the great injustice that was unfolding on the stage before me. I pointed to poor Tomás, helpless on the stake:

What evil has done this man that we slay him,
On the soil of his birth and ours? Ave Maria....

Never had my voice been so strong, so melodious. It seemed to sparkle, to ring with the clarity of a silver spoon against crystal. Adagio flowed to andante and then to allegro as smoothly as poured honey. I was Moses on the mountain, reciting the Lord's commandments. I was Jesus on the mount, preaching to my followers. I was the voice of scripture.

My voice grew louder, more powerful, and when I reached the coda, it was as if an arrow pierced my chest. The final Ave Maria lingered like the scent of fine perfume. One last flourish from the violinist and it ended in a magnificent crash of castanets and Gypsy drums. I bowed, but when I looked up again, my imaginary candles were flickering and going out. My grand theatre faded to black, and suddenly I was back on a barred balcony.

No one applauded. Yet there was no doubt their hearts had been softened. Men and women wiped at eyes. The dons and the boys and the priests and cavalrymen were nodding to each other.

Even the hunchback looked up and nodded.

Only the bishop seemed unmoved. He had a conference with Father Menendez, then shuffled back to his position. A drum-roll echoed across the plaza, loud and steady, announcing that death was at hand. The arrow in my chest sank a little deeper. El Moro and Samson lifted their brazier, waited for the drums to fall silent, and heaped their burning coals onto the brush.

Smoke rose around the hunchback. The Chorotegan women began pounding their breasts, wailing and shouting in their Indian tongue. "This is what the white man brings: misery and death."

They danced a circle around the burning stake, then squatted on the ground in stony Indian dignity. It grew so quiet I heard the spit and crackle of the flames. So quiet I could hear the flutter of angel's wings, and the departing soul of the hunchback.

"Go with God," I whispered.

And then I heard footfalls in the hallway.

For the second time that morning, I went through the agony of sliding bolts, jangling keys, and a turning lock.

But again it was César holding a leather pouch. He stepped into the room. "Santa Maria, you were magnificent." From the pouch, he produced two leafs of paper, a quill, and a small bottle of corked ink. "For your message to Father Paolo."

I was stunned. "Why are you doing this, César?"

"*La musica,*" he said, admiringly. "The song, the voice. What you did for your friend."

"Thank you, César. Father Paolo will reward you handsomely."

"My reward will be in heaven. But hurry, time is short." He patted me on the back and quit the room, locking the door behind him.

I pulled up my stool, uncorked the ink, dipped the quill, and began writing:

> *Esteemed brother in Christ: By these letters I send you greetings and farewell. My time on earth is short, but before I go to my God, I must share with you the location of the cave...*

A loud pop sounded in the plaza, followed by cheers, groans and the renewed wailing of the Chorotegan women. The unspeakable horror of what had just happened broke my heart. Gold and silver were changing hands, and now they were betting whether my head would explode.

I crossed myself and hurried my writing and was nearing the end when from downstairs came the dreaded sound of a slamming door, followed by the voice of the alcalde.

"Jailer, is the prisoner ready?"

I stuffed the letter, ink and quill under the blanket. Another door slammed, then it was the alcalde's voice again: "Holy Mother of Christ. Why are you dressed like that?"

There was a crash, followed by yelps, curses, and what sounded like a scream from Abuelita. Then came silence, a terrible moment that was empty and confusing.

What was going on? César fighting the mayor. Impossible.

I stepped to the balcony and looked out. Captain Gonzalez was still in the plaza. The band had struck up an animated martial tune. Children danced. The Gypsies swayed. Nothing awry. Not a hint of the drama that was playing out in the lobby.

I took out the letter again and ended it with my innermost feelings: In these final moments, I remember the laughter of my children and the warmth of Saraatepe and the smells of the lake, and I remember music in the night and the joy these things brought me. Now I sit in my cell alone, imprisoned by sadness and memories, awaiting footfalls and the stake in the plaza....

I blotted the letter on the blanket and was putting it away when for the third time I heard movement in the hallway. Not the loud clop of César, but the shuffling feet of Abuelita.

She opened the door and swept inside. Her eyes were wide, her face ashen. In her arms was a bundle of Chorotegan clothing.

"Take off robe and put this on," she said in her broken Castilian.

I stared at the bundle, unable to comprehend. "Why?"

"Make you look Indian."

I still didn't understand. Condemned prisoners were usually made to wear a yellow penitential garment. She grabbed me by the shoulders. "Listen, Padre, must leave now. Go free. Libertad."

Was I hallucinating? Was it the fever juice?

"Hurry," Abuelita said. "Must go before soldiers come."

My soul sprang alive. I yanked off my cassock and reached for the clothing. "But, but what about the alcalde?"

"Dead. César chop off head with sword."

I almost tripped over the knee britches. The alcalde dead?

Over my head went a white cotton pullover. Then I fumbled with the cord at my waist, tightened it, and reached for the poncho. No time to enjoy how clean and fresh it smelled. Or worry about the alcalde. The only thing that mattered was escape.

I stuffed the letter into my pocket, put on the wide-brimmed straw hat, and was at the door when Abuelita began pulling feathers out of her apron and tossing them into the air.

"Now they think you bird," she said, cackling like a witch. "Fly away like Hebrew."

So this was how the Hebrew escaped.

I took one final look at the room that had been my home for eleven months—the hammock, the balcony with its bars, the chamber pot, the juice jug, and the little table on which I'd penned my letter—and hurried out the door. Freedom at last. Was it possible?

CHAPTER 5

Abuelita locked the door and set the bolts. Then it was down the hall at a trot. At the top of the stairs she took my arm. "No, I can make it," I said, and bounded down the stairs. No pain, no fear. I was so energized I could have flown.

The last time I'd been in the lobby, I'd been chained, broken, and bloody, Captain Gonzalez dragging me across the marble floor as if I were an English pirate, causing a great stir among the crown's civil employees. Now, the place was as empty as my cell. Only the potted plants and crystal chandeliers, the paintings of Spanish royalty on the walls, and the double entrance doors that might burst open any moment. "Where is César?" I asked Abuelita.

"Here," he answered, and stepped out of the alcalde's office.

Earlier that morning, he'd been wearing the tattered clothing of a jailer. Now he was dressed like a Spanish gentleman, with shiny black boots, long jacket and cocked hat with a turned-up brim. He shut the alcalde's door and locked it behind him, but not before I caught a glimpse of a headless corpse. "Why?" I asked, staring in horror.

He ignored me and trotted across the lobby toward the front entrance, boots clopping on the floor, face fixed in grim determination. "This way. We're going out the front."

"Are you crazy? Why not the back?"

"Locked, everything locked. Can't find the keys."

He unbolted the front door and eased it open a crack. The sound of music swept in. "Good," César said, "nobody but Indians bunched up on the steps. Here's the plan: Abuelita, you go first. Turn right and keep going. Don't look back and don't run. Understand?"

She nodded.

"Then you, Padre, but you turn left. Understand?"

"Where are we going?"

"Out of here, that's where! And stop asking questions!" He peeked out again. "*Joda*, the captain's coming." He opened the door wider. "Go, Abuelita!"

Out the door she went.

"Go, Padre, *Marchate*!"

I slipped out the door and fell in behind a knot of Chorotegans on the steps, uncertain if I was heading for freedom or a short cut to the stake. The air was fresher, the music louder. No one seemed to notice. I was just another Indian in a sea of dark faces, straw hats, and red ponchos. Off to my right, Abuelita was pushing through the crowd. Behind me César was shoving through the door.

"Stay right there," he hissed. "Shield me while I lock up."

He had scarcely finished his sentence before the captain and two soldiers burst onto the steps, pushing aside men, women and children.

"Make way for the Captain! *Muevense! Muevense!*"

One of the soldiers carried a yellow robe and pointed dunce's hat. Behind him walked the same two ghoulish-looking priests who had escorted Hunchback Tomás, their crucifixes extended as if warding off the devil. Their long black robes and hoods that before had seemed so ridiculous now seemed terrifying.

The crowd parted, but not fast enough for Captain Gonzalez. He grabbed a feeble old Chorotegan by his shoulders and sent him sprawling. They were now coming straight at me—three cavalrymen and two priests. Panic clutched at my heart.

"Run," said the voice in my head.

But I couldn't. Behind me, César was still fumbling with the keys, muttering to himself, cursing, trying to lock the door.

"Out of the way, Indio!"

César dove aside at the last moment; I was too slow. The captain grabbed me by the shirt and britches and slammed me into one of the massive stone columns that fronted the Alhambra.

A light flashed in my head. I cried out in pain. My hat went flying, and if any of the soldiers had looked, they'd have recognized me by my shaved head and European features.

But they didn't look; Indians weren't that important.

The cavalryman carrying the dunce's outfit, a lieutenant named Vasquez, drove his shoulder into the door as if he expected it to open inward. It didn't. He pulled on it. It didn't budge.

"Locked," he said to Gonzalez.

"Of course it's locked, you idiot! It's supposed to be locked. It keeps these *mendicantes* from shitting on marble instead of the streets." He unsheathed his sword, reversed it in his hand, and pounded on the door with the hilt.

"Open up, jailer! We're here for the heretic!"

I grabbed my straw hat and pulled it low over my face. Rage burned in my breast. If only I had a knife. How easy it would be to plunge it into the captain's back, end his murderous rampage, avenge the death of Saraatepe and my children.

César grabbed my arm. "The hell you waiting for?"

I wiped blood from my lip and followed him into the crowd.

Martial music played. Bugles blew. Drums beat, and children danced. Behind us, the shouts and the pounding were growing frantic.

"Open up, jailer! Open up now or I'll have your head on a stake!"

At the corner, César turned left onto a narrow side street. I paused and glanced back toward the plaza. The bishop was still on the platform, chatting with the dons as if an execution were nothing more than a sporting event. The cavalrymen stood by their horses, waiting to mount up for another trip around the plaza. The priests and the boys' choir were also forming, moving toward the street with their effigies and banners, preparing for another burning.

And that was when I saw her—Saraatepe.

My breath caught. The music faded away. Could it be? Yes, I knew that walk, that face, that hair. It was her: my queen, my love, the mother of my children, standing on the street and staring toward the Alhambra with all the other Indians.

But was she real or a product of the fever juice?

"Saraatepe," I yelled, and went after her.

César grabbed me. "The hell you doing, Indio?"

Saraatepe turned in my direction. Had she heard me? Yes, she was scanning the crowd, moving toward me. Not an apparition.

I waved my hat. "Saraatepe! Over here—at the corner!

"Damn you to hell," said César, tugging on my arm.

I tried to yank loose. César held tight. Spectators gathered around, among them a carter I'd known for years. "*Caballero*," he said to César, "do you need help with that Indio?"

"He's drunk," said César, feigning a laugh. "I can handle him."

Saraatepe was just across the street now, still looking.

"*Cuidado*!" someone yelled. "Look out,"

A war horse thundered by—no rider and no saddle. I pivoted sideways to keep from getting trampled. Behind it came four or five more. And still others: an entire herd of loose horses, hooves clattering, bringing with them a cloud of choking dust.

Bystanders pressed against the walls. Women screamed for their children. The music stopped. The priests and the boys' choir retreated into the plaza. The cavalrymen mounted up and gave chase. Then Gonzalez was in the street, ranting like a madman, his face red.

"Why are those horses loose?"

"Fire! The convent is on fire!"

I glanced toward to the Convent of San Francisco. It was one of the oldest and most historic churches in the Americas, dating back two hundred years. The most famous Jesuit in history, Father Bartolomé de las Casas, had been posted there. It had paintings that dated back to the 13th century, and now it was on fire.

Columns of smoke rose from its rear, spiraling into the sky. How could that be? The entire cavalry was garrisoned nearby. Didn't they post guards?

Cathedral bells began ringing—loud, discordant peals. A cry for buckets went out. Gonzalez and his men dashed toward the convent, swords slapping at their sides. Then it seemed as if everyone in the plaza was running.

"Mother of Christ," César said, "they told me there'd be a diversion, but this?"

"Who told you there'd be a diversion?" I asked.

"Father Paolo. Who else?"

"Father Paolo wouldn't set the convent on fire."

"Somebody did."

I darted across the street with a surge of Chorotegans, looking desperately for Saraatepe. But the madness was boiling out of control—people racing around me, wagons rumbling this way and that, drivers collecting buckets, running toward the convent.

Where is she? One minute she was here; now she's gone.

César raced up beside me. "What is wrong with you?"

"Saraatepe, she was standing right here."

"It's the Indian juice. Now come on." He pointed up the narrow street that led away from the Alhambra. "I'm going that way, and I'm going now. You stay here and look for your ghost if you want."

He stalked away. I stood there in a daze, staring at debris, at a few dogs, at an empty platform and the smoldering stake. If Saraatepe had been real, wouldn't she have waited for me?

I trotted after César.

He set a quick pace, hurrying past wagons, buggies and draft animals that lined the street, putting the madness behind us. I was silent, vigilant, glancing into shadows as if death lurked in every doorway, numbed and bewildered by all that had happened.

Worse, the nausea that had started earlier was spreading to my bowels. "Where are we going?" I asked César.

"You'll see, and don't walk next to me. You're an Indian."

By then we were on the street behind the Alhambra, passing beneath a row of palm trees. Here and there a driver stood by his coach, or an old man looked down from a balcony. The smell of horse manure and urine drifted on the air, blending with the more pleasant smells of peppers and onions cooking over open fires.

A red fire wagon rumbled by, bells clanging, the driver lashing the mules mercilessly. Behind it ran a small Indian boy, holding his straw hat to keep it from falling off. He stopped, stared at me, and ran into my arms. "Father, Father, is it really you?"

It was Mateo, the boy who'd tossed the egg.

"I did it," he said, speaking in Chorotegan. "It was me. I did it."

"Did what, Mateo?"

"Set the fire. It was me."

I pushed him away. "Mateo, do you realize what you've done? That convent was more than two hundred years old. It was God's house, a place of worship."

"No, Father, not the convent. It's the stable behind the convent. The soldiers keep their horses there. I freed the horses and set fire to the hay. It spread to the barracks."

"Not the convent?"

"No, Father, the convent is not on fire."

I patted him on the head. "God bless you, my child."

César stepped up to Mateo. "Where is she, *mijo*? What's taking her so long?"

"She's coming. Said to wait here."

"She, who?" I asked.

"You'll see."

Thunder rumbled. The sky was turning black. The turmoil in my stomach worsened. I leaned against the wrought iron fence and was wondering how long I could hold it when a shiny black coach pulled by a pair of magnificent white horses came rolling down the street. Its wheels were red, the driver dressed in purple livery, the drapes drawn.

The door sprang open. "Get in," said a female voice. "*Apurense*."

César and Mateo dove inside. I eased in behind them and sank into the luxury of leather seats and perfumed cushions. Not until then did I recognize her—Rosa Morales, the rouged madam of the House of the Seven Veils. This escape was nothing but surprises.

Away we went, taking the same street back toward the plaza. At the corner where I'd seen Saraatepe we turned left and followed a dirt street that paralleled the road to the lake. My hands shook. Every pothole stirred up my stomach. Every turn made me sicker.

Madam Rosa patted my knee. "What a lovely voice you have, Father. So rich and melodious. Why did you become a priest instead of a *cantante*?"

"My parents didn't give me a choice."

"What a shame. What a waste of talent. Too bad I can't offer you a job at my place."

"Where are you taking us?"

"Ysese landing. To a merchant ship, *Nuestra Señora de las Palmas*. She sails with the tide at noon. That's a half hour from now."

"Where is the ship going?"

"Santo Domingo. From there you can book passage to Spain."

CHAPTER 6

Lake Road to Ysese

Spain? I wasn't going to Spain. Santo Domingo either. Not until I found out if Saraatepe was alive and not until I drove a stake into the captain's heart.

"One more thing," Rosa said. She reached into her bag and took out two drawstring purses. "Thirty gold escudos for each of you, compliments of Father Paolo."

I could have cried in gratitude. Thirty gold escudos was almost four ounces of gold, enough to live comfortably for a year.

César grabbed his purse and shook it. "Wonderful," he said. "Now I can go see the world. Live like nobility. All those pretty señoritas just waiting…."

"What about your wife?" Rosa said. "And your children?"

"They can take care of themselves."

I looked at him in disgust. What kind of man would abandon his wife and children? I started to say something, thought better of it, and instead took out the letter I'd written to Father Paolo in my cell and handed it to Rosa. "Would you please give this to Father Paolo?"

"I'll do it," Mateo said. "I'll do it now."

He took the letter and was about to jump out when I stopped him. "Wait, Mateo." I drew in a deep breath. "Did you see them kill her?"

"Kill who, Father?"

"My wife. Saraatepe. She was in the village that day."

"I was hiding in the woods, Father. They killed everyone."

"Did you see her body?"

"They dumped the bodies in the lake, then burned the village."

An image of the shabby little village flashed through my mind—thatched huts, naked kids, wash on the line, surrounded by towering stone statues of grotesque creatures, the remains of an earlier civilization. "But is it not possible there were survivors?"

"Anything is possible, Father, but wouldn't we have heard?"

In the silence that followed, Mateo jumped out with the letter and waved goodbye. Rosa reached over and touched my forehead with her palm. "Are you all right, Father?"

"I don't feel well. I might need to—"

"Can you hold it? We're almost out of town."

We rumbled on, passing blacksmith shops, leather tanners, wheelers, and other crafts. The smells were vile enough to drive out witches and demons. I held a hand over my nose and mouth. Things sloshed around inside me. My hands shook. If we didn't get out of this place soon, I was going to vomit all over Rosa's beautiful coach.

"Why are you doing this, Rosa, putting your life at risk?"

"Why? Remember Doña Seisdados, that so-called witch they burned last week? She was my sister, a good woman, an honorable woman, yet they burned her alive. And do you know why? Because she refused to pay them protection money, that's why."

"Who is "them", Rosa? Who was she refusing to pay?"

"The bishop, that's who. Also, the captain and the alcalde. They're crooks. Murderers."

"You can stop worrying about the alcalde," César said. "I finished him with his own sword."

"You what?"

"Killed the bastard, chopped off his head."

They fell into a heated discussion, Rosa saying there wasn't supposed to be bloodshed, César arguing it couldn't be helped. I wished they'd just shut up and get me out of town.

Rosa parted the velvet curtains on her rear window and looked out. "God help us all. They'll turn over every stone in this village." She turned back to César. "Look, I'm driving you to the edge of town only. From there you'll have to take a passenger carriage to Ysese."

"Why can't you take us all the way?"

"Are you crazy? Everybody knows my coach." She reached beneath her seat and took out two long-barreled flintlocks, together with priming flasks, balls, and leather belts with a dozen powder charges. "Already loaded," she said. "All you have to do is prime."

"Why do we need these?" I asked.

"Why? Because you're a dangerous criminal, that's why. And don't forget, you've got to pass through a military checkpoint. Pray to God they haven't been alerted."

I took a musket and strapped the belt around my neck. The coach stopped at the edge of a sugar cane field. A light rain was falling. The air smelled of damp earth. Rosa pointed to a narrow dirt path. "Follow that trail up to the main road. A coach is waiting. I figure you've got a fifteen-minute head start."

I mumbled a weak thank-you, stumbled down with my musket, and dashed for the cover of the cane patch. And it was there, surrounded by tall stalks of cane, that it all came out—the jug of fever juice, the headless corpse of the alcalde, the awful burning smell of Hunchback Tomás. Oh, the misery. How I wished I could dive into the lake and wash away the vileness.

"Come on," César yelled. "We don't have all day."

I cleaned myself in a rain ditch and followed him up to the main road where we found another driver and two-horse coach, the driver pretending to examine a wheel. He motioned us into the coach and took us off with a lurch. Sugar cane fields on one side, banana groves on the other, fresh air through an open window. Not until then did I feel we might actually get away.

"Tell me about the Jew," I said to César. "Did he escape or not?"

"Jew? You're worried about that damned Jew? I'm worrying about the checkpoint."

I sat back and rubbed my stomach. It was better, but weariness was creeping over me. First a sense of strength and wellbeing, followed by torpidity and sleep.

So that was it: I was entering the torpor stage. But I dared not fall asleep. Not until we were safely on the lake. I shook my head. César pulled out a goatskin flask and handed it to me. "Rum," he said. "It'll keep you awake."

I wasn't so sure but took a drink anyway. Warmth spread down my chest and into my stomach. César examined the muskets and pulled the hammers back to half-cock. "I may have to shoot one of the guards. You'll have to reload. Can you do it?"

Before I could reply, the lake came into view, spreading to the horizon, a lake as vast as a small country. Hundreds of tropical islands on which to hide. Friendly natives. Fish, fruit and wildlife in abundance. I'd choose an island—probably the Island of Lizards—secure the cave, then go looking for Saraatepe.

We turned right and approached the military checkpoint. By then rain was drumming on the roof. César looked out the window. "How many soldiers they usually have?"

"Two."

"I count four." He took out his pistol and primed it.

The checkpoint was little more than a gate and wooden shack. Soldiers sat on a bench beneath an overhang. Their horses stood back near a stand of mango trees, mere blurs in the rain.

"Two passengers for Ysese," the driver called out, pulling to a stop near the gate.

One of the soldiers stood and pulled on an oilskin. César cocked the hammer on his pistol.

A soldier I knew as Cojo limped toward the coach. I pulled my hat over my face and sank a little lower in my seat.

"Damn rain," Cojo grumbled to the driver. "That's all we get in August: rain, rain, rain. They must be having a tough time back in Granada, trying to burn El Cantante."

"I saw the smoke," said the driver. "You'd think they were burning the whole town."

"Shame. That padre was a good man. Didn't do nothing wrong." Cojo splashed to the door and opened it. "What is this?" he said. "Since when do you haul Indians?"

"He's drunk," César answered. "We're running late. Didn't have time for the Indian wagon."

"That may be, but rules are rules. He's going to have to—"

César handed him a silver real, almost two days' pay for most workers. Cojo stuffed the coin into a pocket. "Better hurry," he said. "The last rider said they were setting canvas."

The driver snapped the reins, and we drove on, passing into a swampy forest of tropical vegetation and giant trees. Spanish moss hung down like the beards of old men. The smell of decay and dampness permeated the air. It grew darker. The windows fogged, and I must have nodded because César slapped me on the shoulder.

"Don't you go to sleep on me now."

I slid open the window. "How much longer?"

"Five… six more minutes." He took a long swig from his flask and handed it to me. "You asked about the Jew. It's a sad story. Do you know what he did for a living?"

"They say he was a shopkeeper."

"Shopkeeper, my ass. He was a big man at La Casa."

"Where?"

"*Casa de Contratación*. He was *jefe*, top man in the finance branch, keeper of the codes. That's why they arrested him, not because he did anything wrong. They wanted those codes."

"Codes?" I suppressed a yawn.

"Personal account codes, something you set up with the bank for security purposes, say, your birth date or name of your dog. Only two parties know that code: you and the bank."

My arms and legs were growing heavy. Even my tongue felt like lead. "Who wanted the codes?"

"Gonzalez and the alcalde."

"For what reason?"

"The hell you think, Padre? To steal money. Suppose you walk into a bank and say, 'Hey, I'm Padre Antonio. I've got an account here and I want to take out a thousand escudos.' Think they're going to give you the money? Hell no, not without the code."

I shook my head and blinked my eyes. "Whose money were they going to steal?"

"Just the rich folks: Rosa Morales, the don, even the bishop."

"The bishop? You can't be serious. He's the inquisitor-general. He'd roast them alive."

"Not if he can't find them. They were going to Chile with the gold. Buy some land. Live out their lives as wealthy dons."

"But why would the inquisitor-general have money?"

"Oh, Father, what an innocent you are. He's one of the richest men in these parts. Who do you think does the collecting when someone leaves property to the Church? Who collects the money when the dons make a donation for a favor? That money is supposed to be for the Church. Instead it goes into his account."

Our coach pulled to the side. I wasn't sure why until I stuck out my head and saw a coach coming from the opposite direction. The rain felt good on my face. The drivers exchanged greetings. "Better hurry," said the other driver. "They'll be sailing any minute."

We drove on. My eyelids were getting heavier. Beside me, César was still talking.

"He was one of those girl types."

"Who?"

"The Hebrew, Father. Aren't you listening? He was a *mariposa*, a butterfly. Had this walk like a woman, this high-pitched voice. Well, guess what? The alcalde was one of those types too. Just didn't show it. So guess what he did to Jacobo?"

"What did he do?"

"Sodomized him, two, three times a week. Boom, boom, boom. I could hear them groaning, bumping. Afterward, I'd take water for Jacobo to clean up. What a sight he was, lying on the floor, crying. That's why he went crazy. I never had sympathy for Jews before, figured they caused their own problems, but I changed after that. Jacobo was a good man."

"You helped him escape?"

"He didn't escape."

"But I thought—"

"Look, here's what happened. He started yelling like a mad man, saying he was going to turn into a bird and fly away. Also said he was going to expose the alcalde. I heard them fighting, yelling. When I went up to see, Jacobo was lying on the floor, blood gushing from his throat."

By then I was wide awake. "The alcalde killed him?

"It was murder, plain and simple. Only thing I did was bury the poor soul. He's back there in the gardens of the Alhambra. The alcalde made up the story he escaped, but guess who got blamed? Damn near tortured me to death. And you ask why I killed the bastard."

"Did you notify his relatives?"

"Hell, no, Padre. They'd have gone to the alcalde, and he would've known it was me who told them." He grinned and patted his coat pocket. "But in the end, guess who got the codes?"

"You mean—"

"That's right, Padre. Jacobo wouldn't give them the codes, but he gave them to me—codes, account numbers. Said if anything happened to him he wanted me to ruin the bishop and Gonzalez, destroy them. But I need your help, you being a priest."

"Me? But how?"

"Simple. I get fake papers in Santo Domingo. Pass myself off as the captain. I was in the army. I look the type. I can do it, but I can't do the priest part. That's where you can help. You get fake papers and pass yourself off as the bishop. We drain their accounts."

"But it's God's money. It belongs to the Church."

"That's right, Father, and you can give your share back to God."

He roared with laughter and took another swig from his flask. I sat there trying to absorb what he'd told me, fighting weariness at the same time. And I had just closed my eyes when there came a shout that almost stopped my heart.

"Make way for the cavalry! *Muevase! Muevase!*"

CHAPTER 7

César muttered under his breath and whipped out his pistol. The coach angled to the side. An oilskin-clad cavalryman galloped by on a war horse, spattering mud against the coach's windows.

Then came another and two more—four altogether. They kept going, rounding a curve and melding into the mist. "What was that about?" I asked.

"You can wager it's not good."

We rounded the curve and came within sight of the ship, *Nuestra Señora de las Palmas*, a ghostly blur of canvas and masts against the clouds, barely visible through trees and mist. She lay a good distance out in deeper water, seven or eight minutes by tender.

I wiped condensation from the window. Where were the soldiers? Everything else was there: the great waterside trees with vines trailing into the lake; the overturned hulls and half-sunken vessels; the rock-strewn shoreline. Only one boat was docked at the quay, a large tender on which laborers were moving about like worker ants, unloading barrels and crates.

But no soldiers. "Where are they?" I asked César.

No sooner had I said it than the driver rapped on the partition that separated him from us. "*Soldados*! They've got us blocked!"

The coach slowed. I slid back the window and stuck out my head. César did the same on his side. There they stood: four riders abreast, sitting on their snorting war horses like the horsemen of the apocalypse in the fog and mist. One of the horses was as black as polished obsidian, as dark as the heart of the man who rode him.

Relámpago. Gonzalez's horse.

César cocked the hammer on his pistol. His face had the same grim look I'd last seen back at the Alhambra. "Get ready to hand me a musket," he said, his voice cracking. "The moment I shoot one of the bastards you hand me another. Understand?"

The coach stopped. Ahead of us I heard Captain Gonzalez ordering the driver to step down.

"How many passengers?"

"Only two: a caballero and an Indian."

A cavalryman urged his horse to the side on which César sat. The same man who had tried to force open the door at the Alhambra. César recognized him too. "Lieutenant Vasquez," he hissed. "Mean as a snake and twice as stupid."

Vasquez dismounted and rapped on the door. "Outside!"

César pushed the door open. "Is there a problem, Lieutenant? We're in a hurry."

"I gave you an order. Now step out of that coach! Both of you!"

César fired his pistol directly into the lieutenant's face. There was a flash, a loud report, the lieutenant falling backward into the mud, his horse rearing and galloping away. Then César sprang out the door with one of the long barrels, yelling at Gonzalez like a madman.

"Dismount! Get down now!"

But the captain, either panicked or following sound military logic, spurred his horse to the opposite side of the coach. "*Vamos*!" he shouted, and away they went in a fury, heading back toward the checkpoint, kicking up mud.

César ran after them like a dog chasing a wagon. He dropped to one knee, took aim and fired. Relámpago sagged and went down on his haunches. The captain hit the ground running but lost his balance and tumbled into a ditch.

The other two cavalrymen dismounted and rushed to his aid.

César trotted back to the coach. "Get this thing moving! Hurry!"

We raced away, splashing through mud holes and deep ruts, horses galloping, the coach bouncing. I gripped my seat in terror. No longer was I the innocent party. I was an accomplice to murder. The breath of hell was on my soul.

A minute or so later, with muskets reloaded and primed, we drew to a stop beneath the giant trees that bordered the shoreline. Lightning streaked the sky. A red flag of caution snapped and fluttered from a pole. It was getting darker. Below us, the lake raged against the breakwater with waves erupting into white spray before falling back into a creamy surf. César bounded out.

"Don't move this coach," he barked at the driver.

One of the laborers, a dark little man with earrings and strong Indian features, dashed over and pointed to a small boat tethered to a tree. It was the only passenger boat in sight, a flat-bottomed affair manned by four Chorotegan oarsmen. "They take you to ship," he said in broken Castilian. "Other boats gone, hiding from soldiers."

I struggled down with my musket. My legs felt like lead. The fatigue that had set in earlier enveloped me like a mist. I took one step, stumbled over a tree root, and went sprawling.

César tried to pull me up. One of the oarsmen rushed over to help, and they were walking me toward the boat when a panicked shout rang out: "*Soldados*!"

I whirled about in time to see the cavalry coming through the portal at a full gallop, not three riders, but thirty or more—the entire cavalry from the *auto da fé*.

And at their head, mounted on Vazquez's horse, rode Captain Gonzalez. The ground rumbled. In spite of César's orders to the contrary, the coach driver lashed his horses into a gallop, taking away our barrier.

The oarsmen frantically pushed away from shore. I found my legs and dove into their boat. César piled in behind me. The oarsmen jumped in and began rowing, and that was when I noticed Father Sebastiano, sitting at the bow, glaring at me.

"Antonio, how is it you cannot stay out of trouble?"

I shook my head. Was he really there? Maybe this whole thing was an illusion. Maybe I was still back in my cell, asleep.

"Row!" César cried. "Row like the devil is after you!"

One of the cavalrymen drove his mount right into the shallows, coming within a paddle stroke. César shot him off his horse. Father Sebastiano wagged a finger as if I'd fired the shot.

Balls splashed in the water around us. One took a splinter out of an oar. Another buzzed by my ear like an angry hornet. I slumped low, but César, ever the soldier, grabbed another long barrel and stood to fire. "No," I cried. "Get down! We'll soon be out of range."

"Not to worry. With those short muskets they couldn't hit a—"

A ball slammed into his chest, knocking him backward. The soldiers cheered. The oarsmen kept rowing. I ripped open César's shirt and looked in horror at the hole. It was directly in the center, oozing blood. He tried to lift himself up.

"Codes," he stammered, coughing up blood. "Use the codes, Father…, do it for me… for Jacobo."

"Where are the codes?"

"Here, inside… leather canister. Take it. Also take the gold. Give… to my family."

I took the canister and purse and tied them to the drawstring about my waist. A swell elevated the boat and sent us into a sickening plunge. The bow nosed under. Water cascaded into the bilge. I made the sign of the cross over César and was about to administer the last rites when Father Sebastiano said, "No, Antonio, you can't do that. You've been excommunicated."

"Then you do it."

"Dead priests can't administer last rites."

I placed a hand on César's head. "Almighty God, have mercy upon thee. Forgive thee thy sins and bring thee to everlasting life. May the Almighty and merciful Lord grant thee pardon, absolution, and remission of thy sins."

He clasped my shirt. The light in his eyes was growing dim. "Listen, Father, that song you sang for the hunchback…, Ave Maria. Sing it for me. Sing me home."

I held him and sang the Ave Maria. Sang it while rain cut into my face like tiny pebbles of sand—sang it while we rose and fell and the wind howled and the oarsmen struggled to keep us afloat. And I was still singing when a wave smashed into the hull like a cannon ball, plunging us into the water and turning our little boat upside down.

CHAPTER 8

In desperation, I grabbed a rope that secured the oars to the boat and tried to pull myself atop the hull, only to slide back into the water. Swells washed over me. The weight of the gold was like an anchor, tugging, trying to drag me under. Around me, my Choro friends were also struggling, praying to their gods.

The world spun. Wind howled. I even caught a glimpse of that cursed priest, sitting atop the overturned hull. I was growing weaker by the moment. Everything I wanted was slipping away—Saraatepe, my freedom, even the desire to live.

A swell lifted us higher, and there, looming out of the water like an angel from heaven, was *Nuestra Señora de las Palmas*, crewmen along her railing, pointing and shouting.

Please, dear God, not another hallucination.

Ropes came down, and somehow by the grace of God, one of the Choros attached it to our boat. More ropes were thrown, but it wasn't until the storm passed that the five of us were lifted to safety and laid out on the deck like the catch of the day.

How long we lay there, coughing, spitting up water, I do not know. In time, the noise of wind and slap of water turned to voices. I rolled over and tried to focus on my surroundings—shrouds and masts, the smell of tar, officers in dark blue, crewmen in canvas and striped shirts, marines in red and blue.

"*Coño*," said one of the marines, "that one looks white."

"He's as Indian as Moctezuma," said another. "Look at his clothes." He poked me with his boot. "You there, Indio, do you speak Christian?"

"Bandidos," I croaked. "They were chasing us, shooting. The storm caught us."

Someone pulled me to my feet. I held a mast for support and looked back at the landing. To my horror Gonzalez and some of his men were in the freight tender, rowing toward us. Worse, the semaphores were waving their mysterious flags.

"Distress signals!" barked a voice from the quarterdeck.

"Alert the captain, you idiot!"

Despair crept back into my soul. I turned to the nearest officer, a bearded man who seemed to be in charge. "Can you help the Choros with their boat, get it turned upright?"

He looked at me in my soaked Indian clothing, and when he spoke it was in the accent of a Galician. "And who might you be, your highness, giving orders aboard a Spanish vessel?"

"I'm appealing to your Christian charity. Can you help those Indians?"

"First you answer the questions: who might you be?"

On the stage I'd often played the role of court emissary. Now I bowed like the dignitary. "I am, kind sir, Monsignor Francisco Olivares de la Vega y Reyes, special emissary of the Viceroy in Guatemala to the Court of his Royal Highness, Felipe Cinco, King of Spain by the grace of God. And I am carrying an urgent message from the viceroy to the king."

"An emissary to the king, you say? A monsignor dressed like an Indian? Ha." He bowed right back. "And I, Monsignor, am Don Miguel Cervantes, creator of *Don Quixote de la Mancha*."

"Do not jest, kind sir. I am what I say."

"Then why are you dressed like a savage?"

"To remain incognito. It didn't work. The brigands came out of the swamps anyway. They chased us… killed my assistant. The cavalry drove them away."

I followed his gaze out to the lake. The freight tender was closer, the men rowing, Gonzalez waving his arms. Then I saw a sight even more frightening—El Moro and Samson with their leather vests and shaved heads, standing at the bow.

"Are you going to help those poor Indians?" I said. "Or must I petition your captain?"

He turned and gave the order. The capsized boat was ratcheted from the lake, turned upright, and lowered back down. The Choros plunged into the water like frightened frogs and climbed into their boat. "Are you coming?" one them yelled up in his Indian language.

"Bring the boat in closer!"

The Galician grabbed my arm. "The hell you doing, Monsignor?"

"Waving goodbye to my friends."

"Well, finish it up and come with me. Captain wants a word."

Panic again clutched my chest. I figured I had about five minutes before Gonzalez came within shouting distance.

"Must go now!" the Choros yelled. "Hurry! They come!"

"Row to the other side," I hollered back. "Wait for me."

The Galician glared at me. "How is it you speak the tongue of those savages?"

"They're not savages; they're a proud people… and I speak many languages. It's my job."

I followed him across the deck and up a ladder to the forecastle where the captain stood with his bullhorn, staring at me in my wet Indian clothes. I introduced myself, thanked him for plucking us from the water, and told him the same story I'd told his first officer. "I have papers," I said, "but they were lost in the lake."

"No papers. No clothes. How do you plan to make your presentation to the king?"

"It's an oral message… for his ears only. Besides, he knows who I am."

The freight tender was now so close I could hear their shouts, see their frantic arm waving. I couldn't make out the words, but I had a pretty good idea what they were yelling.

Worse, the Choros were rowing away. Fast. Not that I blamed them. Samson and El Moro would beat them to death. Or Gonzalez would hang them from the nearest tree. Again, my hopes faded. The only possibility now was to jump into the water and swim for one of the islands. I'd never make it, but death by drowning was better than death at the stake.

The captain pointed to the tender. "What's that shouting about? Are those your friends?"

I cupped a hand to my ear. I still couldn't make out a word, but said, "They're asking if I'm safe. Is there any way to let them know… so they can return to port?"

"Not unless they understand semaphores. Stand over there and wave."

I did as he ordered, and was standing next to the Galician, wondering if I should plunge into the water, when the captain yelled, "Tide's turned!"

The shrill notes of a whistle set the crewmen to their positions. The Galician trotted away, shouting orders. Up came the anchor. Yardarms swung and yawed. The canvas caught the breeze, and then we were gliding in the water on the starboard tack, putting Gonzalez, the Choros, and the great waterside trees of Ysese behind us.

CHAPTER 9

Cartagena de Indias

The voyage to Cartagena, on the north coast of the South American continent, took seven days. Seven days of pirate alerts, foul weather, seasickness, and talk of war with the English. Seven days to mourn for César and the hunchback and Saraatepe.

Seven days to scheme.

I spent most of that time in my cabin, venturing out only to exercise my legs. My body began to heal. I even had the pleasure of peeing without the horror of seeing blood in the chamber pot. I might actually survive. But my life from now on would be in the shadows, and it would be weeks, maybe months, before I could go back for Saraatepe.

Which is why I decided to debark in Cartagena and change my identity.

We dropped anchor in the bay, beneath the towering walls and fortresses that had repelled an English invasion only a few months earlier. The remains of their vessels lay all around, skeletal reminders of the might of Spain. I dressed in clothing the captain had provided and took the first tender across the bay, looking more like a commoner than a priest; but as we approached the landing, the old dread came back. What if through the magic of the semaphores Gonzalez had sent an alert to the local diocese? What if Gonzalez was here already, waiting?

The tender tied up alongside a massive wooden pier, next to the hulk of a burned-out English ship. Seagulls swarmed around us, squawking as if to say, "Heretic! Heretic!" and by the time the gate opened and I worked my way up to customs, I was taking short, tight breaths.

The officials sat at their tables with open registers, recording the names of debarking passengers. Nothing to worry about, I told myself. They were looking for smugglers and English spies—and people who speak Castilian with a Catalonian accent.

I was fourth in line… third… second. Please, dear God, get me through this.

A uniformed official raised his eyes to my face, slowly, seeming to take notice of my six-day stubble. "Name?"

"Francisco Olivares de la Vega y Reyes."

"Destination?"

"Santo Domingo."

The questions went on: Had I recently been exposed to fever? No. Was I transporting goods for debarkation? No. Was I carrying a firearm? No.

He recorded the information, handed me a copper token to surrender on my departure, warned me to be alert for pickpockets and gypsies, and said to keep my eyes open for chupacabras.

"Chupacabras?"

"Bloodsucking vampires. They say the English brought them over during the invasion."

I thanked him and hurried out the exit, passing through a mob of shouting, pushing, pulling-at-clothing people that frequented such places—whores, coachmen, beggars, peddlers, shoeshine boys, and people waiting for loved ones, all wanting my attention.

"This way for a coach."

"What's the news from Granada?"

I strolled around, enjoying the fresh breeze off the water, listening to music and laughter, watching the pretty girls—the milkmaid with her pails. The butcher girl with her bloodied apron.

The Gypsy fortune tellers. Rouged señoritas offering "comfort" services.

"*Caballero*."

I turned about and stared into the smiling face of a young woman who was selling walking sticks. "Only two *reales*," she said. "Take your pick."

I needed a walking stick for my bad leg, so I chose one made of brass. Heavy. The kind that could smash a skull. For Saraatepe, I bought a gold and emerald necklace; but when I imagined myself placing it about her neck, I almost cried.

Was she alive, or was she an apparition?

By midmorning I'd filled a travel bag with the garments of a Spanish *caballero*. But I'd also drawn a crowd—children, beggars, and cripples tugging at my sleeves. Moreover, I was growing weary, and the gold at my waist was getting heavy. I checked my bag of purchases into the debarkation center, took a coach into the city, and lumbered into the Jesuit Office of Finances.

The clerk stared at me in my commoners' clothing. "This facility is only for the priesthood."

I plopped down two purses of gold. "I'm a priest in transit. I have an account here." I explained that my bags had been misplaced, and I hadn't yet had time to purchase a new cassock. He took my account number and disappeared into the back. While I waited, I glanced around like the fugitive I was, taking in the massive doors, the painting of the pope on the walls, the stout guards at the entrance. Maybe this wasn't such a good idea.

At last he returned, but with a ledger and an elderly priest in sacerdotal dress.

"Is there a problem?" I asked.

A troubled look came over the old priest. "*Pues*, according to the information in our files, you were excommunicated back in November of year Forty. Is that correct?"

A knife seemed to twist in my stomach. I felt like running out of the place. Instead, I feigned anger. "That was a mistake; I've since been reinstated."

"It also says you were condemned by the Inquisition for heresy."

One of the guards stepped closer, a big man with a name tag that read, ENRIQUE.

I forced a smile. "But, Father, you know how it is with the Inquisition. Anyone can denounce you. They put you through an *audiencia*, and then they… forgive me for saying this, but they use persuasion. I've since been found innocent. I'm now on sabbatical, recovering."

"I understand, Father, and I'm so sorry, but your account has been closed. It's the rules of the Inquisition. And that's not the worst part." Again he paused. "Your funds, almost four hundred escudos, were confiscated by the Church."

He showed me a notation in the ledger—By the authority of Bishop Diego Francisco de Ureña y Montes, Inquisitor-General of Nicaragua.

I couldn't speak, could scarcely breathe. Everything Saraatepe and I had accumulated in ten years of marriage was gone, confiscated by the man who'd condemned me to the stake.

"Are you all right, Father? I'm sure you can explain it to the bishop."

I turned away and limped across the lobby, past the guards, out the door, and onto the street.

CHAPTER 10

How long I wandered about the city, I do not know. How could Jesuits break the sacred trust it held with its depositors? Even if I were guilty, they should at least return the money to my family.

I sat on a bench and opened the canister César had given me. The edges were water-faded, but everything else was there—account numbers, secret codes, titles, and names.

Bishop Diego de Ureña, Inquisitor-General of Nicaragua.

Captain Bonifacio Gonzalez y Perez, Military Commander.

Father José Antonio Menendez y Valle, Fiscál of Nicaragua.

What Philistines they were. They didn't deposit their gold in the Jesuit bank; they sequestered it in the much larger *Casa de Contratación*, away from the prying eyes of the Church. Could I steal their money? According to César, all I had to do was dress the part, walk into the bank with the codes and account numbers, and walk out with their gold.

But gold was heavy. Better to open my own account in a fake name and transfer their gold into the new account. I hailed a passing coach and was about to tell the driver where to take me when I noticed a man sitting on a bench across the street, staring.

Enrique, the guard from the bank.

Why would he be following me?

"Go," I said to the driver. "Hurry!"

"Where to?"

"*Casa de Contratación.*"

We rolled away, passing beneath the branches of flowering jacarandas. I glanced back, expecting to see him loping after us, but he remained on the bench, not even looking. *A coincidence*, I told myself. It was mid-day in Cartagena, the hour of siesta, and like all places Spanish, the city had shut down. Enrique was probably taking his noon break.

La Casa was closed for mid-day, so I found a place near the water, ate a divine lunch of chicken, corn, and potato stew, bought a Bible, and was at the bank when it opened. I limped into its massive interior, found the finance section, shook out my coins, and told the clerk I wanted to open a new account with fifty escudos.

"The minimum requirement is a hundred."

"I understand, but I'll be making a larger deposit in a few days."

"*Un momento*," he said, and went off to consult with his superior. They both stared at me, and again I felt the old dread. "That's him," I imagined they were saying, "the escaped priest."

The other man nodded, then the clerk returned with the news. Yes, they'd provide open provisional account for six months. He wrote down the fake name I gave—Don Antonio Arteaga y Flores—and told me I'd need a secret word for security.

"*Jorobado*," I said.

"Hunchback?"

"*Sí, Señor*, hunchback."

He wrote down the word and asked if I had questions.

"What is your process for withdrawal?"

"We'll need three items—your account number, secret code, and a *cédula* personal."

"A *cédula*?"

"An official document that establishes identity, residence, occupation, and date of birth. We're very careful."

I tried to hide my disappointment. There was only one way to get a *cédula*, and that was from a forger, which would mean more delay and another trail to follow.

"I'm pleased you're so careful," I said. "Has anyone ever defrauded an account?"

"Not since Drake sacked the city."

I took a secluded walkway back toward the landing, thinking to retrieve my bag and find a place to stay for a few days. At least I had an untouchable account. I was also rid of my burden of gold. But more importantly, I now knew exactly how to bring financial ruin to my enemies.

"Father Antonio?"

I whirled around and stared into the face of the bank guard.

"My apologies, Father, but the inquisitor-general wants a word with you."

I fought down the impulse to flee. To jump into the bay and drown myself. The inquisitor-general of Cartagena would hold me until news of my escape came on the next ship.

"Why?" I asked.

"They didn't say, but I imagine it has something to do with your account."

He stepped closer as if to take my arm.

I backed away. "How much are they paying you, *mijo*?"

"Are you trying to bribe me, Father?"

"Of course not, *mijo*, but I'd dearly love to buy that musket and cartridge box from you."

"How much are they worth to you?"

I pointed to a bench on the sidewalk, beneath a shade tree. "One gold escudo if you'll just put your pistol on that bench over there and walk away, tell the bishop you couldn't find me."

"Well, well, Padre, so you really are on the run. I knew it the minute you limped out of the bank. What did you do, seduce a nun? Violate a little boy?"

"I'm not guilty of anything other than being honest." I took out a gold escudo—more money than a bank guard earned in two months—and held it up for him to see. "You interested or not? With this you could buy four or five muskets."

"It's going to cost more than one escudo."

"One is all you're going to get." I placed the coin on the bench and stepped back.

He scooped up the coin, smiled, and stuffed it into his pocket. Then he turned to face me, his eyes narrow and mean. "How much more gold do you have in that little pouch?"

"I thought we had an agreement. Now, go, *vete*, *vete*."

"I'm an honorable man, Father. I was injured in the war. I was an officer, a lieutenant. Now I'm a merely a guard trying to support a wife and kids." He took a step toward me, palm up, fingers wiggling in a give-me-more gesture. "Come on, cojo, help a disabled veteran."

I stood my ground, holding the brass cane in front.

"Come on, cojo, let's—"

The swing of my cane caught him on the wrist. He staggered back in pain, crying, cursing, saying I was good as dead. Then he fumbled for his pistol.

I whacked him again, this time on the knee.

My third blow caught him on the head, knocking him to the cobbled walkway.

By then I was in a fury, ready to kill, to exact revenge for all the injustices inflicted on me by the Church in the name of God. And I had my stick in the air, ready to smash his skull with one final blow, when from somewhere came Father Sebastiano's voice:

"*Ya, basta*, Antonio!" Enough.

I glanced around, but there were only the cawing seagulls, the ships in the bay, my racing heart, and a groaning, bleeding man at my feet. "You should have taken my offer," I said, and dragged his limp body into a thicket of flowering acacias. I took his pistol and powder box, a dagger, and the escudo.

He groaned and reached for my leg. "Help me, Father."

"Why should I help you? You tried to rob me."

"I meant you no harm, Father. Please. I need…."

"Need what, *mijo*?"

"Forgiveness…, I'm dying." His voice lowered to barely a whisper. There was dread in his face and voice. Blood ran from the wound on his head. "Please, Father. Give me the sacrament of Last Rites, the viaticum."

I knelt beside him. "I'm an ex-communicated priest. I'm not allowed—"

"Please, Father. You're all I have…."

I used his dirk to fashion a bandage from his shirt and was propping him against the trunk of a mango tree when I heard laughter. A group of four or five nuns were strolling along in their billowing robes and habits, chatting among themselves.

I clapped a hand over the guard's mouth. The nuns stopped in front of the shrubs that shielded us.

"Is that blood?" one of them asked.

"Oh, my God," said another. "It might be chupacabras."

They raced away, their footfalls fading. I finished dressing the wound. "Listen," I said. "You must renounce Satan and his evil ways, and when you recover you must go to your priest and ask for a sacrament of penance and reconciliation."

"But I might not recover. Help me renounce Satan now. Please."

I made the sign of the cross. "*Abrenuntias Satanae*?"

"*Sí, Padre*, I renounce Satan and his evil ways."

"Then I absolve you of your sins *in nomine Patris, et Filii, et Spiritus Sancti.*"

Thus discharged of my Christian duty, I gathered my things. But I could not bring myself to take this contrite man's possessions. I'd already broken his arm and crushed his knee-cap. Probably broken his skull. So I tossed his musket and dagger into the bush beside him, told him to sin no more, and limped away in disgust. Now I'd have to leave Cartagena. How stupid of me to have gone to that Jesuit bank.

But where to go? *Nuestra Señora de las Palmas* wouldn't sail for another day, and another day would give Enrique time to tell his story.

I followed the walkway back to the landing, past the storage buildings and the empty tables where the customs men had sat. There were other ships in the bay, some of them setting canvas. I limped into the passenger office. "Where are those ships going?"

"Santo Domingo. That one, *Nuestra Señora de Sevilla.*"

He stopped in mid-sentence. "Is that blood on your shirt?"

"Wine. Spilled it at lunch. When does the *Sevilla* sail?"
"On the tide. If you hurry, you might be able to get aboard."

CHAPTER 11

Cartagena to Santo Domingo

The officer of the deck, a wiry little man with bad teeth and foul smell, wanted to know my port of origin, why I was limping, and why I'd boarded at the last instant.

"They're demanding information on every passenger," he said.

"Who is demanding?"

"The customs captain of every port."

"Why?"

"Who knows, *Caballero*? Do I hear a Catalonian accent?"

I cringed. "It is."

"They don't like Catalonians in Santo Domingo. I wouldn't wear a beret if I were you."

He motioned for the steward, an old man named Sanchez, and a few minutes later, I was in my cabin, listening to the stir of a ship getting underway.

The first six days passed without incident. But on the seventh day, as we approached Hispaniola, the clouds turned ugly. Each ring of the ship's bell took us deeper into the gloom. Top gallants were ordered down. The ship came alive with the creaking of timbers and the whistle of wind. There was talk of a dreaded *huracánes*, and by four bells—ten in the morning—we found ourselves in the midst of a violent tempest.

"Into your cabins," ordered the steward. "Stow all gear!"

The ship rose and plunged, leaving my stomach in the air. Wind shrieked through the rigging like an insane chorus. There were shouts and curses, things banging about, and I vowed if I survived this voyage, I'd never board another ship.

Day turned to night, and still the storm raged. Men raced up and down the passageways with glimmering lanterns. I smelled vomit and things worse. Water dripped from the decks above, and I rolled and swung in my hammock like a barrel, praying for deliverance. Surely God did not save me from a fiery stake, a shootout at the landing, a near drowning, and a nasty encounter with a bank guard only to send me to the bottom.

At some point, I realized the ship was no longer rolling. A ray of light filtered through cracks around the cabin door, and I heard the welcome cry of seagulls. I grabbed my cane for support, left the cabin, and dragged myself up the companionway to the upper deck.

Sunlight. Calm seas. The sails drawing low and aloft. The blessed sight of land off the port bow. I trudged back to my cabin, cleaned up at the washbasin, and began pulling on my new clothes. The *pantalones* and ruffled shirt. The buckled shoes that gave me an extra inch or two of stature. The waist coat and crimson sash.

As a final touch, I put on a plumed hat and had a look at myself in the mirror.

Perfect. My pursuers would be looking for an emaciated priest with a shaved head, pale as a maggot. But the man staring back at me had a beard, dark hair, and sun-browned face.

"Don Antonio," I said, and bowed to the image.

At three bells of the fore-noon watch—nine thirty by the clock—we drifted into Santo Domingo on the tide and dropped anchor at the mouth of Rio Ozama.

The sensation of swinging back and forth wouldn't go away. But wrongs had to be righted. Papers had to be forged. So I bade farewell to the *Sevilla*, took the first tender to the landing, lumbered up the steps like a drunk, and formed a queue with other passengers.

The ground seemed to move beneath my feet. Dizziness swept over me. I grabbed a post for support. The world turned giddily before my eyes, and in the moment before I collapsed, I could have sworn I saw Father Sebastiano.

A customs officer in a crimson jacket helped me up. "Sea malady," he said. "You should eat. Get some rest." He escorted me to the front of the queue. The official at the table merely wrote down the fake name I gave him, asked a few questions, and waved me through.

It must be the clothes, I thought, and a minute or so later I was outside the building, shielding my eyes from the sun and trying to fight my way through beggars, fortune-tellers, boot-blacks and thieves. The air was filled with the most wonderful aromas of outdoor cooking, reminding me of my empty stomach. A rouged woman smiled, licked her lips and took my arm.

"Good morning, *caballero*. Would you like company?"

"I'm a happily married man."

"I can make you even happier."

"Can you tell me where the market is?"

"Over there, *caballero*, where all those people are gathered."

I thanked her and set off toward the market. A knot of ragged children followed, tugging at my waistcoat and begging for coins, looking at me with the most piteous expressions.

"*Por favor, caballero. Una limosna*?"

One of the Gypsies tagged along as well, a pretty girl with hoop earrings, scarves, jangling bracelets, and a long purple skirt. Her white-toothed smile and the fragrance of jasmine brought back pleasant memories of Saraatepe.

"I know all about you," she said in an angelic voice.

"What do you know about me?"

"I know you are a man of God."

I stopped in the shade of a stand of coconut trees. I'd never consulted a fortune-teller before. To me they were little better than the witches and soothsayers of Isaiah and Deuteronomy. Yet here was this young woman who couldn't have been more than sixteen, and who looked more like an angel than a witch.

"Aren't we all children of God?" I said.

"You do not have to deny who you are with me."

By then we were well away from the landing. I took out a few coins, handed one to each child and sent them on their way. Then I turned back to the Gypsy and offered her a coin.

"No, Father, I do not want your money."

"Why do you call me Father?"

"Do you not believe in the power of what you cannot see?"

"I believe only in Jesus, God, and the *Espiritu Santo*."

"Only a priest would say that."

"Who are you, *mija*? What do you want?"

She studied me with dark probing eyes. "You have suffered."

"All people have suffered. It doesn't take a diviner to know that."

She reached out as if to place a hand on my forehead.

"Please," she said, "I will not harm you."

Her hand on my face was as warm as her voice. The warmth burned down to my neck and heated my chest. For a moment I was as helpless as if I were lying in Saraatepe's arms.

She closed her eyes as if in a trance and mumbled in her Gypsy tongue, and when she opened her eyes again, she stated my deepest desire—to be with my wife again—and she said it in my native Catalán." *El seu desig és per reunir-se amb la seva muller. No*?"

What a clever young woman she was. She'd heard me discoursing with the prostitute about my wife. As for Catalán, many people spoke the language, and anyone who heard my accent would know. But suppose she was genuine?

"What do you know about my wife?" I asked.

"Only that you do not know if she is alive or dead."

"Who are you, child? What do you want?"

"I came to warn you about the men who wish you ill. They will come sooner than you think."

"How soon?"

"The answer is in the tides, Father. Go now. Hurry."

She turned as if to leave. "Wait," I said. "What else do you know about my wife?"

"Do not despair, Father; your friend in black will help you."

"Father Sebastiano?"

"There he is now, beneath the mango tree, waiting in the shade."

I gazed at the tree, into the shadows and foliage. Father Sebastiano was not there, and when I turned back to ask the Gypsy, she was gone.

CHAPTER 12

An icy chill raised the hairs on the back of my neck. How could she just disappear, leaving not a trace of her perfume? And how would she know about Saraatepe? I turned this way and that, looking. The wind blew steadily off the water. People and stray dogs flowed around me. Music and the smell of cooking came from the market. And over at customs, a second wave of passengers was emerging from the doors, pushing past beggars and Gypsies.

The girl was not there.

Maybe she'd never been there. Maybe it was the fever juice, still playing tricks in my head.

"*Oye, cabrón*!"

My heart almost stopped. I swung around and stared into the face of a customs officer. Back at customs I'd been a *caballero*, a gentleman; now I was a lowly *cabrón*—a goat, a boy, a bastard.

He peered into my eyes, his expression hostile. "You didn't tell us where you're lodging."

"No one asked me."

"I'm asking you."

"Where would you recommend?"

"Catalonians stay at the Posada Barcelona."

I sighed in frustration. Was I such a poor actor that I could not hide my origins? Could he see I was Father Antonio, the heretic of Granada, playing the part of Don Antonio?

He stepped closer. "The first officer tells me you boarded with blood on your shirt."

"It was wine, not blood."

"Is the shirt there, in that bag?"

I opened the bag and showed him. "See, there's nothing."

"How long are you staying in our city?"

"Only a few days. Then to Spain."

"The sooner the better. We don't want troublemakers in our city. You people should be grateful we allow you to be Spaniards, not spit in our faces with demands for independence."

He dismissed me with a wave of his hand, and as I limped away it seemed important not to look back. Damn him anyway. The next ship from Cartagena would bring news of the assault on the bank guard. Why, dear God, does everything have to be so difficult?

Once inside the market with its bustle and exotic smells, I stepped behind a stall and peered back. The captain was still there, conversing with two other soldiers, pointing in my direction, probably saying, "Keep an eye on that Catalonian."

I groaned. Now I'd have to change my looks again. I pushed deeper into the stalls, weaving past tables stacked with fruits and vegetables, passing beneath lines strung with headless chickens. Workers stepped aside, gentlemen tipped their hats, and it seemed as if every merchant in the market was shouting for my attention:

"Over here, *caballero*!"

"Best prices on amber!"

"Bracelets! Earrings! Pendants for the señora!"

I gave my old travel bag to a beggar and purchased a shoulder bag from a leather merchant. Into it I stuffed my plumed hat, the waistcoat and crimson sash. Next, I rolled up my sleeves and unbuttoned my collar, trying to look different, and was smoothing back my hair when the two soldiers who'd been talking with the captain stepped into the alley.

They looked straight at me and kept going.

By then my hands were trembling, my head spinning. What I needed was something in my stomach, so I purchased two kebabs from a sidewalk vendor, found a wooden bench beneath a mango tree, and devoured the food like a ravenous dog.

How wonderful to be free again. To taste exotic foods. To breathe wonderful aromas and listen to the music and sounds around me. But

I wasn't free—yet. And I'd never be free until the men who destroyed me were themselves destroyed.

I washed down the last of my food with a concoction of papaya and mango juice and asked the woman who prepared the juice where the *escribantes* had their tables.

"*Escribantes*?" she asked.

"Men who read and write for those who cannot read and write."

"You don't look like the type who cannot read and write."

"I need to have something printed."

"Ah, then you should go to the Hebrews." She pointed down a side alley. "They're down that way, near the water. You can spy them by their clothing, but they'll charge you a pretty peso."

I hurried on, passing tables stacked with fish, wheels of cheese, and baskets of mangos, rehearsing what to tell the scriveners. Aside from Jesuits, they were the most scholarly men around, and earned a living mainly by translating and writing letters for the illiterate. But they also replicated documents, filled out forms, wrote wills and trusts, and served as notaries.

Most importantly, they had a reputation as forgers.

At last I came to a block where the air stirred with a cool breeze off the water. And there, beneath the shade of towering palms, sat the Hebrews, all beards, dark hats and dark robes. On the tables before them were the tools of their trade—writing boards, paper, quills and ink. A sign read:

ITCHAK LEVY AND SONS
ABOGADOS AND MEN OF LETTERS

Strange, I thought. Today was Saturday. Why would Jews be working on a Saturday? And why would they be dressed in traditional clothing? Back in Nicaragua the inquisitor-general would have them on their knees, worshipping the Cross.

A solemn old man with a face weathered by deep lines motioned me onto a crude wooden stool. "*A sus órdenes, caballero.*" How may I help you?

Again, I looked over my shoulder like the convicted heretic I was, half expecting to see the customs captain in the shadows. Or soldiers. Eleven months in a cell waiting for the stake does that to a man. I drew in a deep breath. "This is a delicate matter."

The scratch of pens on paper slowed to a crawl. Everyone looked up. The old man tugged at his beard. I smelled the sharpness of ink in his clothing, and when he spoke it was in a voice that sounded as if he'd swallowed gravel. "Not to worry," he said. "Scriveners are like priests in the confessional. Besides, my eyes are bad, my ears worse, and I easily forget."

I smiled. He probably hated the Inquisition more than I did. So I told my story about the near drowning in the lake, said I'd lost my papers, and that I needed three *cédulas*. "One for myself, one for a priest and another for a captain of cavalry."

He tapped a bony finger on the table. "Where are the other men?"

"On their way from Cartagena."

"You realize that the three of you could merely present yourself at the House of Accountancies and request replacement documents."

"Well, that's the problem. I'm serving as their agent. They expect the documents to be ready when they arrive. It puts me in a… well, difficult position."

"Are you saying these men are not the forgiving types?"

"We live in troubled times, señor."

His dark eyes seemed to bore right through me. "The law requires the presence of all parties."

"I understand, and I apologize, but it's of the utmost importance."

He stood and motioned me to follow. One of the other Hebrews, a younger man, barked something to the old man in their Ladino language. I didn't understand the words but understood the harshness, as if he were saying, "Take heed of strangers."

I followed him across a wooden bridge and around a thicket of palmettos, stopping at a dirt intersection that was blocked by a fallen coconut palm. The air smelled of fish and decay. Out in the river, a vessel under a yellow and red flag was dropping anchor.

The old man sat on the trunk and motioned me to sit beside him. Again he pulled at his beard. "Let me explain, *caballero*. The governor demands two things of us. First, we must work on Saturdays like everyone else. And second is that we not engage in anything extra-legal. As long as we abide by those rules, they promise not to persecute us."

"All I'm asking is for replacement *cédulas*. Is that illegal?"

"No, *caballero*, to ask is not illegal. To honor your request is not illegal. What is illegal is if you use the identities to defraud, deceive, impersonate or engage in any act that brings harm to another person."

"I would never harm an innocent party."

He wagged a finger. "But your friends, are they innocent?"

I shrugged but said nothing. The old Hebrew went on: "Listen, *caballero*, what you do with the *cédulas* is your affair. But what concerns me is this: how do I know you're not an agent for the Inquisition? Their offices are well known for underhanded methods."

I almost laughed at the notion. "See that ship out there? It's the *Sevilla*. I just came off her. This is my first visit to Santo Domingo."

"How do I know you just came off the ship?"

I reached into my pocket and pulled out my travel document. "See, they stamped it at customs. It shows the date."

He examined the paper and handed it back. "How soon do you need the *cédulas*?"

"Two days. Sooner if possible."

"Impossible. My work I can finish in no time, but then I have to… well… take it to other parties. *Cédulas* must be stamped. They need signatures, seals, approval. Money has to exchange hands. And don't forget tomorrow is Sunday."

His words were punctuated by the tolling of church bells across the city, the announcement of the midday siesta. The Hebrews at the tables began gathering their things. One of them came crunching across the shell path in our direction.

At the bridge, he halted and gestured behind us as if to say, "Beware!" I turned around in time to see two soldiers coming out of the palmettos.

CHAPTER 13

The beefier of the two, a soldier with old pox scars, looked as if he wanted to roast us on the spit. He took a menacing step toward the Hebrew, the threat of harm clear in his eyes. "What kind of toxic brew are you Jews stirring up?"

I tightened my grip on the walking cane. If I'd learned anything from my fight with the bank guard, it was to strike without warning. "Watch your tongue!" I said, trying to disguise my accent.

"And who might you be, your highness?"

I puffed myself up like an indignant hidalgo. "I am Don Diego Francisco Ureña y Montes, personal assistant to the governor, and I demand to know why you are sniffing around in the bushes like dogs in heat?"

He stiffened but did not answer.

"I asked you a question, soldier."

"The captain sent us here to—"

"To what, soldier?"

"To look for a Catalonian in a plumed hat."

"Do you see a Catalonian in a plumed hat?"

"No, *caballero*."

"Then why are you harassing innocent citizens?"

He looked over at the other soldier and back to me. "Well, sir, I wasn't really harassing, you see. What I wanted was to ask is if you've seen the man we're looking for. He had a dark beard like yours… and a limp, and he was wearing a crimson sash."

"A sash? What kind of man wears a sash?"

"Well, that's exactly what I said to Chino. Maybe he's one of those…."

"Those what?"

"You know..., one of those butterfly sorts, like a woman. He was also carrying a bundle like a woman, like he was going shopping."

The old Hebrew glanced at my leather bag beneath the tree trunk, then threw me a look of alarm. Beads of sweat ran down the inside of my arms. I had to act fast, before the soldiers noticed the bag. "Did you look for this Catalonian in the market?"

"Yes, sir, we just came from there."

"Then I suggest you look again. I saw a man of that description in the jewelry section."

"Well, that figures. Where else would a *maricón* be?"

I slapped my hands together. "Now go! Do your duty. *Vete!*"

They saluted and took off at a trot. As soon as they were out of sight, the old Hebrew sank onto the tree trunk and breathed deeply. I uttered a silent prayer of thanks and also begged God's forgiveness for telling another lie. After at least a minute, the old man turned to me. "You're not really a friend of the governor, are you?"

"I don't even know his name."

"What would you have done if they challenged you?"

I answered with a swing of my cane.

"But there were two of them."

"In that case I'd have expected you to take down the other one."

He clutched his stomach and laughed so hard he almost fell off the tree trunk. I laughed with him. Laughter turned to wheezes, and after we settled down, I said, "What is the earliest you can get the work done?"

"Four days. Wednesday."

My heart sank. The news of my fight with the bank guard would arrive long before Wednesday. "I'll pay you double if you can get them done by Monday."

"Impossible."

I kicked the tree trunk and picked up my shoulder bag. My face felt hot, as if I'd been too long in the sun. The old Hebrew trekked back to his table. "Why are those soldiers after you?"

"Because I'm Catalonian. It's a curse."

"A greater curse is to be Jew."

"Jews aren't the only ones who suffer from the Inquisition."

"Christians suffer selectively. We suffer as a people. How do I know I can trust you?"

I rolled my eyes. What was wrong with this old man? Couldn't he see I was also an outcast? Hadn't he heard about the royal decree that prohibited Catalonians from speaking our own language? "Surely you're not suggesting I'd tattle to the bishop?"

"No, *caballero*, what I'm suggesting is that sooner or later you might end up in a dungeon. How would you then explain three *cédulas*?"

"I'm not planning to end up in a dungeon."

"None of us plan on evil, but evil happens."

"Look, I'm going to ask you to put the *cédulas* on well-worn paper. Make them appear as if they'd been issued years ago. In Spain. They would never suspect a forgery."

He put a hand over both ears. "I did not hear you say that word."

"And I did not say it."

He wanted six escudos for the work. I bargained him down to five and paid two in advance. I wrote down all the information. We agreed to meet again on Wednesday noon, and then he asked where I'd be lodging in case he had questions.

"Where would you suggest?"

"Catalonians usually stay at the Posada Barcelona."

CHAPTER 14

Dreams can play us false, but the dream of Saraatepe in bed beside me was so real I never wanted to wake. Saraatepe, my beautiful Saraatepe, so close I felt her warmth. So close I smelled gardenias in her hair, so close I felt the beat of her heart.

"Fly away," she whispered in her Indian tongue. "Turn into a bird and fly back to me."

"But you are here. Stay with me forever?"

"I will stay until you wake, then I must go."

Her presence stirred me the way it always did. My breath caught, and I was feeling the promise of pleasure when the Gypsy floated into the room. "Evil is on the tide," she said in her girlish voice. "They will be here sooner than you think."

The dream receded. My eyes opened, and I heard church bells tolling the end of midday siesta. The pillow that had been Saraatepe was now just a pillow, crumpled and lifeless. The Gypsy was gone, but her words still played in my head.

"They will be here sooner than you think."

What did that mean? Who would be here? Surely not Captain Gonzalez. I was at least two or three weeks ahead of him.

I bounded out of bed anyway, dressed, and eased down the stairs to the lobby. The works of Catalonian artists hung on the walls. Even the signs were written in Catalán: *Benvingut* for Welcome, *Menjador* for Dining Room, *Sortida* for Exit.

No one stared, but the sounds of my native tongue came to my ears like the soft notes of a lute.

I took the door marked *Sortida*, followed a tiled walkway to Calle de las Damas, and flagged down a coach. No one followed, but just to be certain, I asked the driver to take me to a part of the city where I had no intention of going, then took another coach.

At last I stood before the local *Casa de Contratación*, a building that bore an uncomfortable resemblance to the Alhambra from which I'd escaped. It was as massive as a fortress—an entire city block of cut stones, ornate balconies, and black metal doors with protrusions and strap hinges. Here was the place where taxes were collected, where records were kept and commerce regulated. Here was the place where the wealthy stored their gold, people like Captain Gonzalez and the inquisitor-general of Nicaragua.

And here was the place I was going to destroy them.

I marched inside as if I were just another well-off citizen of the crown, strolled into the section marked Accountancies and Fiduciaries, stepped to the counter, and drew in a deep breath. "I have a question," I said to the clerk, trying to keep my voice steady.

"*A sus ordenes, caballero*. How may I help you?"

"Next week I'm going to transfer a large quantity of funds from one account to another. Gold escudos. I need to know the procedure so I can come prepared."

He reached for a quill and dipped it into an ink well. "How large of a transfer?"

"Does it make a difference?"

He put away the quill and looked up. "All we require is documentation—account numbers, codes, and proof that you are who you say you are."

I breathed easier. The clerk back in Cartagena had told me the same thing, and it was comforting to hear it again. I thanked him, tipped my hat, and was about to leave when he said, "Oh, and one more thing. Are you a local resident?"

"No, just passing through."

"Well, in that case you will also need a travel document—a *pasaje*—with your name. It's an extra layer of security."

I thanked him again and strolled out the door. "Damn! Damn! Damn! A travel document in the name of Captain Gonzalez. Now I'd have to go back to the Hebrews for more documents.

I sank onto a bench and tried to calm down.

"Antonio."

Father Sebastiano stepped from behind a tree and sat on the bench beside me. Same white hair and black cassock, same pasty skin and sour smell, as if he hadn't bathed in years.

"Antonio, what are you plotting now?"

"You know very well what I'm plotting."

"Have you considered the consequences?"

"Yes, Father. I know the danger, but it has to be done."

"I'm not talking about danger; I'm talking about your soul. Your soul, Antonio. Do you not recall the Lord's commandment—Thou shalt not steal?"

"Is it wrong to steal from thieves and murderers?"

"Is the motive to gain personal fortune?"

"I have put aside all considerations of personal fortune."

"Is it vengeance?"

"I'd be lying if I denied it."

"Vengeance is mine; so sayeth the Lord."

"But wait, Father, it's not only vengeance. It's also for the helpless Indians on the islands. They'll never be free until Captain Gonzalez and the bishop are ruined."

A wagon rattled by. Another bell tolled, reminding me that I had other duties to perform, and when I turned back to finish my argument, there was only the breeze, a passing dog, and a young boy staring as if I were just another homeless drunkard, conversing with the wind.

My next stop was on Calle Las Mercedes, at a place that sold surplus military goods. I swaggered in like a wounded warrior and was welcomed by a scrawny little fellow with greasy hair pulled back in a ponytail. I told him I needed a cavalry captain uniform. "Also, campaign ribbons and a French dagger."

"Are you a captain of cavalry?"

"Why else would I be buying a uniform?" I related the story of the overturned boat and lost luggage and wondered how many times God would forgive the same lie.

"How did you come by the limp?" he asked.

The dungeon of the Alhambra came back in a painful rush—the stench of unwashed bodies; El Moro and Samson, leather-clad and sweaty, standing over me with a club. "Savages shot my horse from under me," I said. "Broke my leg."

"I hope you made the bastards pay."

"They paid."

After that, he followed me around like a dutiful aide de camp. Yes sir and no sir, taking measurements and showing me my options. "Do you wish us to deliver?"

"No, I'll pick up the uniform Wednesday, but I'll take the dagger now."

I bagged the dagger and holster, and as I was leaving, the clerk snapped to attention. "Were you in the king's service?" I asked.

"First Grenadiers. We fought at the Battle of Dos Pasos."

I had never heard of the battle but patted him on the back anyway. "Go with God, soldier."

The smile faded. "Trooper," he said. "Grenadiers are horse soldiers. We're called troopers."

I slapped myself on the head. "Of course, what was I thinking? Go with God, trooper."

"And you as well, *capitán*."

He watched me go, suspicion in his face, and even followed me out of the shop.

Means nothing, I told myself, but just to be safe, I flagged down another carriage, rode around the block, and a few minutes later purchased a bishop's purple cassock with all the trimmings at a clerical shop across from a Jesuit church. No questions were asked. People did not question a bishop in the time of the Inquisition.

Finally, I stopped at a second-hand garment shop for *marineros* and purchased a dark blue sea jacket, a sailor's pullover, a captain's hat and a well-worn sea-bag.

Bells were tolling for evening Mass by the time I was back on the street. The sounds of music drifted down from shuttered windows, and the air was filled with the most wonderful aromas of cooking. The smells sharpened the hollowness in my stomach, and I was thinking of the Catalonian dinner that awaited me in the Barcelona when I heard a woman's voice. An angel's voice, singing Claudio Monteverdi's *L'Orfeo*. In Italian.

"*Pretade, oggi e amore, triunfan ne l'inferno....*"

How many times had I stood on stage and sang that very number? How many times had I acted out the drama of Orpheus ascending from hell with his lovely Eurydice?

Brass and percussion played in the background, so clear I could sort out the harpsichords and contrabass violins, and the double harps. And the cornets and trombone. The lyrics came to my ears like a siren of Greek legend, and for a moment I felt certain this unseen woman was singing for me. For me, *El Cantante*, on a mission to rescue the beautiful Saraatepe.

I followed the sounds like a mariner of old, lured along the cobbles by her seductive voice, the words tearing at my soul. Acoustical magic in the late afternoon, here on this narrow street beneath the balconies and flower pots.

"Worthy of eternal glory is only he who has victory over himself...."

I hurried to the next street, listening. Now the song was coming from behind me. Now from above. Now from another direction, as if hanging on the wind. But where was she?

Nymphs and shepherds danced around me. Drums beat, bugles blew, and snakes slithered across the stage. Helplessly, I leaned against a wall, closed my eyes, and let the sounds consume me. I was Orpheus. I was *El Cantante*, and I could not help myself. I sang:

E la virtute un raggio, degno d'eterna Gloria.
Vanne Orfeo, felice a pierno....

How long I stood on that narrow street, singing, imagining I was Orpheus on the stage, saving my lovely Saraatepe from hell, I do not know. But when the lamps dimmed and the curtain closed, I opened my eyes and saw that a crowd had gathered. Women with baskets on their heads. Negro servants with their lords and mistresses. People looking down from balconies.

Shouts of "Bravo!" and "Encore!" rang through the street.

I bowed, flourished my hat, and hurried away. What was wrong with me? I needed to get to the market and find the Hebrew, ask him to make travel documents. This wasn't the way to remain incognito either. My pursuers would be looking for a man with a Catalonian accent. A man with a limp.

A man who could sing Monteverdi's *Orfeo*.

I reached the next block and was looking for a passing coach when I heard footfalls on the cobbles behind me. Light footfalls, like a woman's sandals. But it was her fragrance that gave her away. The sweetness of jasmine.

She fell into step beside me, a dazzling sapphire with her swirling skirt, scarves, hoop earrings, and jangling bracelets, her dark eyes flashing, hair awash in the glow of late evening light. "Did I not warn you evil is on the tide?" she said in her wispy voice.

I stopped and stared into her teenage face. "Who are you, *mija*?"

"I am who I am, and I am here to warn you."

"About what?"

"How many days did it take you to travel from Cartagena to Santo Domingo?"

"It took ten days."

"And how many days does the voyage normally take?"

"I don't know… a week, I suppose."

"Your ship was delayed by the *Huracán*. Another ship from Cartagena will be here tonight."

A cold gust blew across my heart. "What ship, child, and who is on it?"

"For that you must see for yourself. Go, Father, hurry. You do not have time for the Hebrew."

She did a rapid volte-face and headed away. "Wait," I called out.

She turned the corner and was gone, as if she'd never been there.

CHAPTER 15

I flagged down a *coche* and was back at the Barcelona within minutes. Rushing inside, I asked the clerk about the tides. Everyone knew about the tides. The colonies of Spain lived on their ebb and flow. "Almost high tide," he said. "Ships are still coming in." He pointed out the open back door. "See how the river has risen."

I took the stairs two at a time, a knot gripping my stomach. The room that had seemed so luxurious before, with a real bed instead of a hammock, now seemed like a deathtrap. The Barcelona would be the first place they'd look.

Off came the old clothes and on went my mariner's clothing. Everything else fit into my sea-bag. No, better to leave a few things to give the impression I hadn't fled. Back into the armoire went the ruffled shirt, waistcoat, and sash. As an afterthought I ripped the feathers out of the plumed hat and flung them into the air the way Abuelita had done at the Alhambra.

Abuelita. Was she on the run like me?

A minute or two later I was back on the street in the fading light, just another bearded mariner heading to sea. By then, the air was scented with the possibility of a thunderstorm. I flagged down a passing *coche*. "The landing," I said to the driver.

He cracked the whip and away we went, rumbling over the cobbles and passing alongside the oldest European structures in the Americas—the Cathedral of Santa Maria de Menor, the Monastery of San Francisco, the Fortress Ozama with its soldiers and cannon.

The closer we came to the landing, the faster my heart beat. Along the river a ghostly mist was forming, thick here, lighter there.

In the gathering darkness the locals were pulling kerchiefs over their noses and mouths as protection against the dreaded night dew—the *sereno*—on which witches and demons were said to carry sickness.

"That your ship?" said the driver, pointing out to the river.

"What ship is that?"

"*Nuestra Señora de las Palmas*. She just arrived."

I stared into the gloom. Yes, no doubt about it. The same ship I'd escaped on from Nicaragua, the ship I'd have been on now if not for the bank guard in Cartagena.

We clopped on, the driver telling me to watch out for chupacabras, saying he'd heard stories of throats ripped out and bodies drained of blood, as if I didn't have enough to concern me.

The customs house loomed up like the gate to Hades, bathed in the dying rays of light. The usual crowd of coachmen, luggage handlers, boot-blacks, Gypsies, whores and mendicants, had gathered in front, waiting to fall on the arriving passengers.

I paid the driver, jumped out with my sea-bag, and half ran, half tripped to a wooden fence overlooking the landing. Sure enough, a tender was coming in from *Las Palmas*, close enough to hear the splash of the oars. I peered through the slats.

Dampness seeped into my clothes. There was a flash of lightning. The night deepened, bringing with it the smell of decay and rotting fish. I pulled a kerchief over my mouth as if I too were concerned about the *sereno*. All the better to conceal my identity.

"Oars up!"

The tender landed with a watery thump. Gates swung open. Passengers debarked with their luggage: a man holding a dog, a woman with two children. A soldier with a lamp to guide them up to the customs house. I breathed easier. Nothing out of the ordinary.

Until someone yelled, "We need help with this passenger."

A soldier hurried down to help. There were grunts and movements in the darkness, and into the light came a passenger on a crutch, his head and leg bandaged, left arm in a sling. Was that Enrique, the bank guard from Cartagena? There was only one reason for him to be here—to identify me. Bastard. What an ingrate. I should have busted his skull.

I pushed through the crowd to the customs door, watching him. Officials sat at their tables. Lanterns hung from the rafters, turned up for maximum light. Moths and other death-defying insects swirled around them. The Captain of Customs—the man who'd made my life miserable—stood back in the shadows in his crimson jacket, arms folded across his chest.

"*Por Dios*," said a voice beside me. "Look at those monsters."

I followed his gaze to the admitting gate. And there, to my horror, came Samson and El Moro, tromping into the room as if they owned the place, all tattoos, muscles, and earrings, their stubble-covered heads as scarred as Roman gladiators. As if that wasn't bad enough, Captain Gonzalez, Father Menendez, and six or seven cavalrymen marched in behind them.

Once done with customs, Gonzalez led his companions out the door and into the darkness, pushing through the waiting crowd and brushing so close I could smell their unwashed bodies.

Behind them came the Captain of Customs with a lantern. "*Oigan! Oigan!* Important announcement! Everyone, gather round!"

I stayed back in the shadows, ready to take flight. Captain Gonzalez hopped onto a bench for his announcement. Samson and El Moro took up position on either side, looking like bodyguards for a Turkish Sultan. The whores, luggage handlers, and Gypsies moved in closer, as did soldiers and debarking passengers.

"Citizens!" Gonzalez shouted in his gruff voice. "Fellow Spaniards. I need your help!"

It grew quiet enough to hear the slap of water against the dock.

"We're looking for an escaped fugitive from Nicaragua, a priest!"

"What kind of priest?"

"A Jesuit, mind you. Hid his crimes behind the Cross. Escaped a day ahead of us, but by the grace of God and power of winds, we were able to hail a freighter and give chase."

"What does he look like?"

"About my height. Walks with a limp. Speaks with a Catalonian accent. I've got sketches." He held up a drawing and put it close to the light of a lantern.

"Madre Maria," said one of the whores. "That's the man I saw this morning."

"Worse than a chupacabra," said the captain. "Shot one of my officers in the escape. Also chopped off the alcalde's head. Left a trail of blood from Nicaragua to Santo Domingo."

"Why was he in jail?"

"Because he's a rapist, that's why. Slashes the throats of his victims and drinks their blood. Innocent girls, mind you. Your wives and daughters are not safe."

There were murmurs and angry nods. Gonzalez pointed to Enrique. "Just look what he did to this poor fellow. Beat him senseless. Left him for dead. And why? Because this bank guard, this hero of the war against the English, caught our desperado in the act."

"Act of what?"

"Do I have to draw a picture? He had a young girl, forced her into the bushes."

"Is there a reward?"

The captain held up a drawstring purse and rattled it for effect. "Thirty Pieces of Eight."

A stir went through the crowd. Thirty Pieces of Eight was the equal of fifteen gold escudos, more money than a blacksmith earned in a year, enough for a hundred head of cattle. A rough looking man stepped into the light. "You want him alive or you want him skinned?"

"Alive. It's important he go back to face his victims' families. Then we're going to turn him over to these two gentlemen." He pointed to Samson and El Moro.

The crowd whooped their approval. Gonzalez hopped down from his bench.

I slipped the dagger out of its holster. Now was the time to act. To stop this man who'd murdered more than a hundred innocent villagers on the Island of Lizards. This man who'd murdered Saraatepe. *Get him now. In the darkness. In the confusion.*

El Moro and Samson paid me no heed. Neither did the whores and mendicants or anyone else. A coach pulled up and drew to a noisy stop. Gonzalez and Father Menendez struck off with the Captain of Customs. I hurried to catch up.

Ten paces. Five. I raised my dagger to strike.

"Antonio!"

Father Sebastiano stepped from the shadows, a luminescent glow in the darkness. He pointed a bony finger. "What is wrong with you, Antonio? How will you explain yourself on the day of judgment, when the book is opened?"

Gonzalez hopped into the *coche*. The driver snapped the reins and away they went, probably heading for the Barcelona. I turned back to Father Sebastiano. "But you heard what he said."

"All I heard were words, Antonio. Words, nothing more. Before you raise your dagger, you should consider other roads."

"What other roads?"

"Ask the Gypsy. My only concern is your soul."

He made the sign of the Cross and faded into the night.

By then the crowd was getting worked up—arguing, yelling, cursing. "Let's go find him!" shrieked the whore. "Collect the reward! He's probably hiding under the bridges."

"But what if he's a chupacabra?"

"Then you shoot him, you idiot! Right between the eyes."

They set off at a trot, a mob of angry voices and swaying lanterns, their feet beating along the road, coming straight at me.

CHAPTER 16

Dogs barked. The shouts came closer. I dashed into a grove of mangos, heart in my throat. *Run*, said the voice in my head. *Go into the countryside and keep running. Go all the way to the French side of the island.* In the darkness I tripped over a log and was struggling to get up when the Gypsy appeared at my side, another luminous glow in the darkness.

"Poor Father Antonio," she said. "Come with me."

"Where?"

"Back to the river, down the levee, a stroll beneath the trees."

"Are you crazy? That mob will skin me alive. I need a horse."

"There are other roads to travel."

"That's what Father Sebastiano said."

"Father Sebastiano looks after your soul. I am for your safety."

We tarried until the mob faded, then followed a dirt path into the mist, our way illuminated by fire-flies and a pale half-moon. By then the night air had grown heavy. Flashes of lightning lit the sky. Frogs croaked, things splashed in the river, and every few heartbeats an animal or some other creature dashed into the underbrush. Worse, every shadow loomed as an armed vigilante, every sound an approaching soldier.

At last, we reached the quays where a multitude of ships lay at anchor, a forest of masts and figureheads. Lanterns glowed through open portholes. Fragments of foreign discourse came to my ears, and the smell of tar, salt and rotting wood brought back memories of other voyages.

"What is that ship over there?" asked the Gypsy.

I followed her gesture to a three-mast ship in the river, a ghostly blur in billowing lakes of mist. A light flashed on the aft deck and moved forward until it too was swallowed in the fog, leaving only the slap of water. "The *Sevilla*," I said. "The ship that brought me here?"

"Where did they tell you she would be going next?"

"To San Juan Bautista."

"And when did they say she would sail?"

I left the Gypsy in the mist and trotted back to the embarkation center, my excitement growing. The *Sevilla* would be sailing tonight, on the tide. A three-day voyage to San Juan Bautista. Three days to get there and three days back. In time to pick up the *cédulas* from the Hebrews. Thank you, Gypsy.

The waiting room was poorly lit by two smoky lanterns. A small knot of passengers huddled in the dimness: the men smoking pipes, the women with kerchiefs over their mouths. No soldiers, though, and no one from the street mob.

I stepped to the counter with my sea-bag, conscious of eyes studying me, and told the clerk in a faux Italian accent that I wanted a private cabin to San Juan Bautista.

"That would be eight *reales*," he said. "French mirror, bunk and hammock, curtained privy closet, and cabin service."

"When do we board?"

"Who knows, *caballero*? Could be an hour."

An hour. I didn't have an hour. I might not have ten minutes. I handed him a Piece of Eight anyway and glanced at the entrance, at the exit to the landing, at the passengers. A burly, bearded man sitting in a corner eyed me suspiciously. Had he been in the mob outside?

The ticket master wrote out a *pasaje* in the name I gave him—Claudio Monteverdi—and placed my sea-bag with a pile of other luggage and boxes. "Have a seat and relax."

Relax. How could I relax when half the citizens of Santo Domingo wanted to flay me alive?

Each time the door opened, my stomach did a little flip. What if Gonzalez came in? Or El Moro? Or some of those crazies?

When I could bear it no longer I plodded to the back door, careful not to limp, and stared through the gloom down at the river, only thirty or forty paces away. Yes, I could make it, jump in if I had to. Better to drown than burn at the stake.

A flash of lightning drove me back inside. More passengers came in with trunks and boxes, and one old man plopped down next to me. "I can smell it," he said in a booming voice.

"Smell what?"

"SPEAK LOUDER, SON, I CAN BARELY HEAR."

I leaned closer. "I asked what you can smell."

"That *huracán* we had the other day..., why, it's going to turn around and come back at us. Mark my word. IT'S THAT TIME OF YEAR." He pointed to a weather glass on the wall. "Glass is going down, sinking. JUST LIKE US IF WE SAIL INTO A STORM."

Other passengers turned and scowled as if to tell the old man to shut up, that it was scary enough just going on an ocean voyage in pirate-infested waters.

Not wanting to bring more attention to myself, I stood and ambled into the shadows, wondering what was worse: another hurricane, pirates, or the sight of Gonzalez coming through the door. Gonzalez, I figured, and stepped to the entrance for another look.

A heavy rain was falling, spattering on the cobbles and dripping from the roof. Flashes of lightning lit the street. Wind howled, and the air was heavy with the smell of dampness. Back in my island paradise with my family, the patter of rain had been the sweetest music; but here in this colony far from home, where the locos could fall on me any moment, the sound grated on my ears like a plague of locusts.

"Tender coming in! Prepare to board!"

I raced back inside and followed the other passengers out the rear and into a driving rain, down a cobbled path and onto the tender. The gate slammed shut behind us, oars splashed in the roiling water, and in spite of the storm we were soon alongside the *Sevilla*.

Rain bit into my face. Wind whistled in the rigging. The tender slammed back and forth and up and down. How we got aboard without falling, I do not know, but at last we were all there, on a wet, slippery deck, clinging to anything that would support us.

The steward, an old man I recognized from my earlier voyage, guided us across the deck and down the companion.

"Listen up!" he cried, holding a lantern aloft. "Get to your cabins and stow loose items. Secure chamber pots and washbasins. Smoking lamp is out. Douse your lanterns soon as you're settled in. Then get into your hammock and wait."

More crewmen came down with bags, boxes and trunks. They guided us to our cabins, and when I stepped into mine, I realized it was the same cabin I'd vacated earlier that morning.

A sudden lurch tossed me against the bulkhead. Another caused me to bump my head on a beam. From somewhere came the shout of a crewman informing us the weather glass was still dropping. I stowed my gear, doused the lantern, and crawled into my hammock. The ship's timbers creaked and groaned. Something clattered on the deck above me. Then a crash sounded from the next cabin, followed by a string of vile curses.

Back and forth I swung in my hammock. In the darkness. Back and forth and up and down. The cabin swirled. My stomach knotted. I retched. Bile came into my mouth. I jumped up, felt my way to the curtained closet, and barely made it to the chamber pot.

How long the storm raged, I do not know. Sometimes it grew more intense. Then it would ease. And it was during one of those slacks that there appeared the glimmer of a lantern through the doorway cracks, followed by a sharp knock. "*Oiga*, you in the cabin!"

"I'm here," I answered weakly.

"Did you stow your gear and douse the lantern?"

"Stowed and secure. Lantern is out."

"Captain says we have to check anyway. Open up, *por favor*."

Grumbling, I padded across the deck in bare feet, heading toward the light like a moth to a burning candle. I unlatched the door and was pulling it open when the man—or men—on the other side gave it a hard shove and tromped into the cabin.

El Moro, the executioner and Father Menendez.

CHAPTER 17

I couldn't breathe, couldn't speak. My legs felt as if they'd give way. How could they be here already? I backed away, clutching the cord of the hammock for support.

Father Menendez took a menacing step toward me, holding the lantern aloft. The light spilled out, catching his pinched face and black cassock. El Moro pushed in behind him, all tattoos and scars, his massive, stubble-covered head pressed against the ceiling between the deck beams; and when he spoke, I could have sworn I caught a whiff of sulfur.

"Identify yourself," he said in a voice as coarse as a grinding stone. "What is your name?"

I glanced from one to the other, willing my breath to slow down and my heart to stop thudding. Some part of my mind was still functioning, because I realized they hadn't yet recognized me in my mariner's clothing and growth of beard.

"No, you identify yourself," I said, putting an Italian inflection to my speech.

El Moro raised his massive fist, but Father Menendez stepped between us. Again he held up the lantern. "My friend asked you a question. You have one more chance before he starts breaking bones. Now tell me your name. We don't have all night."

"Monteverdi. Claudio Monteverdi."

"*Italiano*?"

"*Sí, Padre*, I'm a buyer of produce—cotton, indigo, tobacco."

He sniffed the air and clopped around as if he were the inquisitor-general, taking in my sea-bag in the corner, opening the locker door, peering into the mirror and even rearranging the hat on his head. What a hypocrite he was, this man who'd denounced me at the *audiencia.* This man who had accused me of breaking my vows even though he lived openly with five Indian wives.

The *Sevilla* took another sickening plunge. I used the movement to fall onto my sea-bag in a corner, from which place I could reach my walking stick. Not that such a weapon would be of use against El Moro. Against him I needed a cannon.

Father Menendez hung his lantern on an overhead bracket. "You say you're Italian?"

"*Sí, Padre*, from Sorrento."

"*Ah, Sorrento. Provenite dalla città bella di Sorrento.*"

He continued his speech in Italian, a language I knew in the words of its music, and which I spoke, although not well enough to fool a fluent speaker like Father Menendez. He told me in a lyrical Roman accent that he'd served in the Vatican for five years and had traveled many times to *bellissimo* Sorrento by the bay. And had visited the Cathedral of San Francisco d' Assisi, and did I happen to know if Father Pietro Gioia was still among the living.

"Certamente, conoscete Pater Pietro. Tutto lo conosce."

All I could do was shrug. So this was my test. I knew it and he knew it, and for all I knew Father Pietro was as fictitious as the fake gold they sold in the market. "*Non ricordo il nome*," I answered in a voice that sounded phony even to my ears.

"How can you not know Father Pietro?"

"Maybe he was before my time. Or after."

He stared at me in the murky light, shaking his head as if to say how stupid I was for not having a better excuse. The smell of my vomit grew stronger, sloshing around in the chamber pot, as bad as the stench of Father Menendez's breath.

"Tell me more about yourself," he said. "Let's hear the flavor of that Sorrentino accent. *La poesia, la musica* of the speech. *Non è bellissima?*" He raised his palms, Italian fashion, to make his point.

By then I knew he was toying with me. Probably waiting for the storm to pass so he could get me ashore and have El Moro break my leg again. Beat me senseless.

I slid my hand down to the walking stick. There was no hope of escape, but I could at least go down with a fight.

"So," said Father Menendez, switching back into Castilian, "it seems you're not Italian after all." He glanced up at El Moro. "*Qué te parece*?" What do you think he is?

"I think we just caught ourselves an escaped rat."

"Worse than a rat, Morreno. This man is a murderer, a rapist, a heretic." He fixed me in his glare. "Who helped you escape? We know the jailer had a hand in it."

I said nothing.

"Why did you kill the alcalde?"

I kept my silence.

"Same old Father Antonio. See no evil, hear no evil."

He turned to El Moro. "When Father Antonio first came to Nicaragua… fresh out of the seminary, he'd never had a woman. Didn't know how they use their wiles to trap a man. But then our padre here, this young novitiate, gets transferred to this shithole of an island out in the middle of Lake Cocibolca."

A flash lit the cabin, followed by a sharp crack of thunder.

"Next thing you know he meets this dark-eyed little Indian beauty named… oh, what was that girl's name? Sara? No, Saraatepe. *Sí*, that's it. She's got this walk, this sway of the hips, this seductive flash of eyes… as if she grew up in a Parisian brothel. What an Indian beauty. She has these big luscious melons. And wears these short little wraparounds that show flesh."

He rubbed his crotch. "*Coño*, I'm getting stiff talking about her."

A burning rage came over me. How dare this grinning snake talk about Saraatepe in such intimate terms? This man who represented every cruelty I'd suffered in the past year.

The candles inside the lantern flickered; the cabin became darker. Menendez re-lit the third candle and plopped down onto the bunk. "Here's the best part. What our young padre didn't know was that his sweet little Indian thing, this Saraatepe of the islands, was anything but innocent." He howled with laughter. "She must have spread those brown Indian legs for every white man in Nicaragua. Oh, how she loved it. Why, I've had her myself more times than—"

"Liar! She'd never get near you."

"Poor Father Antonio, then I guess you didn't know we captured her and she's been living with me for a year, sharing my bed. As for your two boys, they're now living with Bishop Ureña, the inquisitor-general. And you know what that means?"

Pain coursed through my body like the venom of a snakebite. Surely he was lying. But what if he wasn't? Better that I'd perished at the stake. As if in answer to my agony, the *Sevilla* rolled sharply to port, knocking me off my sea-bag. Father Menendez clutched the bunk for support. El Moro grabbed the hammock. Then came a grating sound, as if we were dragging chains beneath the keel, followed by a loud pop.

"*Madre de Dios*," said Father Menendez. "We're drifting. Must have slipped the anchor. "

El Moro bent over to look out the porthole.

And that was when I struck.

If I'd been slower, El Moro would have grabbed the stick from my hands, laughed at my puny efforts, and tossed it aside; but I wasn't slow, and El Moro wasn't quick. He never saw it coming, and the swing of the cane caught him squarely on the back of his neck.

Down he went, hitting the deck with a thud.

Then I was on him like a beast of prey, slamming him again and again. Oh, the pleasure of hearing the thunk on his skull, of seeing the spatter of blood. And I must have laid four or five solid blows on his head before Father Menendez slammed into me from the side.

The violence of his assault knocked me off my feet. The cane flew from my hand and clattered against the bulkhead, just another racket in the storm. Then we were rolling and tumbling across the deck, slipping in El Moro's blood and the vomit of an overturned chamber pot, cursing, fighting like street cats.

I landed a punch between his upper lip and nose. Flesh and cartilage tore under my fist. Blood gushed from his nose, but still he fought—he who had been well nourished by his five wives while I had withered in a cell—and before long he had me on my back.

"Die!" he screamed. "Die and go to hell!"

He straddled me like a woman on a man, cassock spread over me, his hands around my throat, choking the life out of me.

I thrashed and tried to roll away, but it was as if he'd fastened me to the deck with nails. I tried to pull his hands away, but he was too strong. I tried to reach the dagger that was still in its holster at my waist, but it was pinned beneath his naked leg.

His grip tightened. I could not get air into my lungs. How could I defeat a giant like El Moro only to fall to a weasel like Father Menendez?

Darkness came over me. His curses, so loud before, faded to silence. My whole body seemed to go warm and relaxed, as if I were floating on water. Was this the end? After all I'd gone through, was I going to die at the hands of this evil man? It didn't seem right.

From somewhere came a blue light and the tinkle of chimes. And I was floating in the lake on a warm tropical day, a woman coming toward me, walking on water, her white robe flowing.

Saraatepe, I thought, an angel to take me to heaven.

But as she came closer she became the Gypsy, as radiant as a bride at the altar.

"Why are you giving up? Do you not wish to punish the wicked?"

"If it is God's will."

"Then you must not succumb."

Her words gave me strength. Somehow, I managed to grab Father Menendez's testicles with my left hand and squeeze. Hard. He released my throat. Fresh air filled my lungs. My vision returned. I reached for the dagger with my right hand and yanked it free.

Then, with all my remaining strength, I thrust it into his stomach.

Another flash of lighting lit the cabin, and if I live to be a hundred I shall never forget that parting glimpse into the face of evil—the bulging eyes, the open mouth as if in a silent scream.

His body stiffened. He tried to speak, maybe to ask God's forgiveness for his sins, but the words spilled out in a torrent of blood that rained over my face.

Then he fell limp.

For the longest time I lay beneath him like a corpse, too exhausted to move, unable to comprehend. How could I, a weakened priest who'd never lifted a hand in anger, have beaten two of my strongest enemies? I, a man of peace whose greatest joy was in music and family. Was it God's work that those anchor chains snapped or random good fortune?

"God had nothing to do with it," thundered a voice above me.

I crawled from beneath the corpse and pulled myself up by the hammock. Father Sebastiano stood near the porthole, a ghostly figure in black. He gestured at the two bodies. "Antonio, Antonio, what have you done?"

"It was them or me."

"Are you now a soldier? Are you now to toss aside your beliefs and turn to bloodshed?"

"All I want is my wife and children."

"A wife, Antonio. The shame of it. You should never have taken a wife. Should not have fathered children either. You broke your vows. Now you are paying. Didn't you hear what Father Menendez said about your Indian wife, about her affairs before you met her?"

"He was lying."

"How do you know he was lying? Indians are different. They're not like us. Their women have no Christian values. No morals. They're deceitful. They steal. They lie. They—"

"Saraatepe isn't like that."

"Really, Antonio, how naive you are. Look at it from her side. She needs companionship. You're out of sight, out of mind, and along comes Father Menendez."

I pointed a finger. "Get out of here!"

"You can't order me out. I'm your priest, your headmaster, your spiritual adviser."

"You're nothing but a bad vision. I created you, and I can destroy you. Now get out. Go!"

He turned and gestured toward the porthole, through which I caught a glimmer of light. "In case you haven't noticed, Antonio, your ship is afloat in the channel. Out of control. Going this way and that. You could crash into one of those other vessels any moment. Or end up on the rocks. I would advise you to fall on your knees and beg forgiveness for your sins."

"Not until you're out of my life."

He threw out his arms as if in disgust, then turned and walked right through the bulkhead, leaving me alone on a runaway ship with two dead bodies in a raging storm.

CHAPTER 18

No sooner had Father Sebastiano departed than the storm finished its fury. I heard curses and shouts, the boatswain's whistle, the pop of sails, the bustle of feet on deck.

Could it be? Were we out of danger?

I stumbled to the porthole and looked out at the fading lights of Santo Domingo. Yes, God had spared me once more. Or had He? What if Sampson was also aboard? And even if he wasn't, how was I going to explain the bodies?

I held up the lantern. Blood and vomit everywhere, on the deck, all over the locker, on the bulkhead and door. In my hair and on my face. The spilled contents of a slit stomach. The bashed head of El Moro. The open eyes of Father Menendez.

And the stench.

I didn't have the strength to haul two bodies up the ladder and dump them into the sea. And even if I did, I couldn't do it without being seen.

"Use your imagination," said the Gypsy.

I spun around and searched the shadows. "Where are you?"

"Here, Father, in the air."

"I need help. How do I get rid of these bodies?"

"Maybe you should become a priest again."

Priest? What was she talking about? I glanced at the corpse of Father Menendez. He was about the same size as me. Same hair color and a week's growth of beard. Yes, I could be Father Menendez, at least until we reached San Juan Bautista—assuming he didn't have friends aboard. And he could be me. Escaped heretic, killed by El Moro in a struggle to the death.

"The key?" the Gypsy said. "See if he has a cabin key."

I dropped to my knees and went through Father Menendez' clothing. No key, but I relieved him of his silver crucifix and money pouch. The key I found on a cord around El Moro's neck. I wiped off the blood and held it up to the light. Cabin number 3, two doors away.

"But what if their friends are in the cabin?" I said to the Gypsy. "What if Sampson—"

"What other choice do you have?"

None. So I stripped off my mariner's clothing and was pulling off Father Menendez's cassock when footfalls thudded in the passageway. The glimmer of a lantern bled through cracks in the door. Then came a sharp rap. "You in there. Are you all right?"

"I'm here. Just a little sick."

"Passengers in the next cabin say they heard screams."

"I heard them too. They were coming from the deck above."

"That your vomit I smell?"

"Didn't I say I'm sick?"

The light disappeared, the footfalls faded. By then my hands were shaking so badly I could barely function. Somehow I managed to dress Father Menendez in my bloody mariner's clothing and straddle him atop El Moro as if they'd been fighting.

It was bad enough having to look at their open eyes and slack features, but the worst was when I placed the dagger into El Moro's hand and sank it back into Father Menendez's stomach. Blood and gore oozed out, thick, black and so vile-smelling I had to hold a hand over my mouth.

Now I had to cleanse myself. But how? I'd make a mess if I used the basin. Dead men didn't make a mess at the wash basin. Maybe there was another way.

Rain was still falling, so I eased open the door and stuck out my head. Yes, the water that had accumulated on deck was cascading over the ladder like a small waterfall, barely visible in flashes of lightning. I grabbed a bar of lye soap, hurried into the passageway in my bare skin, and scrubbed for as long as I dared, washing away the stench, the sin, the memory.

A light appeared down the passageway. Someone was coming, swinging a lantern. In an instant I was back in my cabin, dripping water, praying they hadn't seen me.

The footfalls came closer. A glimmer of light appeared in cracks around the door. Had I left a trail of blood? The footfalls passed, leaving me alone with that awful odor of death.

"Gather all his belongings," said the Gypsy. "Leave nothing."

"I thought you were gone."

"No, Father, you're too unnerved to think. Hurry, get out of here."

A few minutes later, dressed in fresh clothing, I scooped up Father Menendez's money pouch, crucifix, and cassock, grabbed the lantern he had brought, and eased into the passageway like a murderer leaving the scene of his crime.

Fresh air from the open hatch filled my lungs. Flashes of lightning lit the ladder and the little waterfall that was now a trickle, and from above came the clang of water pumps. Oh, to be back on my island paradise. Cool lake breezes, the cries of seabirds, the smell of honeysuckle.

Again I glanced right and left. Which way to cabin number three? I turned right, hurried along the corridor, and lifted my lantern to check the number on the next door.

Seven. Why couldn't anything be easy? Back I went, forcing myself not to limp, praying no one else was in the passageway. As I passed my door again, I sniffed the foul air and made the sign of the cross. I could not help myself. I was still a priest.

"You there! What are you doing?"

My heart seemed to jump right out of me. A man stood in the open hatch above, silhouetted against flashes of lightning. "I'm not well," I said, easing deeper into the shadows. "I thought it best to get some fresh air."

"Everybody needs fresh air, *caballero*. Get back to your cabin. And douse that lantern."

"*Vale*," I said, and hurried into the darkness.

The echo of his voice followed me. The bulkhead seemed to close in from both sides, shadowy and sinister. Had he seen my face? Noticed my accent?

At last I reached cabin number 3. Cold fingers gripped my heart. What if Sampson was inside? I looked for the glow of a lantern in the cracks around the door. Nothing. No sounds either. I pressed my ear to the door and listened. Still nothing. Finally, I set down my bundle and rapped on the door. "*Oigan*, you in there."

No answer, not a sound. Only the creak of timbers. I inserted the key and turned it in the lock. "God give me strength," I muttered, and pushed open the door.

It creaked, loud enough to alert anyone who might have been sleeping. I stepped inside and lifted the lantern, slowly.

"Anyone here?"

No answer. Nothing stirred. The two hammocks were still folded in their places, and the only sign the cabin had ever been occupied was a pistol and charge belt on the deck.

Idiots. They'd been in such a hurry to get me, so sure of themselves, they hadn't bothered to bring a pistol. I waited for my heart to calm, for my breathing to return to normal, then I retrieved my bundle, latched the door, and hung the lantern on a bracket.

The cabin was larger than mine, though the amenities were identical. No smell of vomit and entrails either, only the usual smells of dampness, tar and decay. The locker doors hung partially open, no doubt jarred loose by the storm. I yanked open the doors and pulled out two traveling bags, one leather, the other cloth.

The leather bag stank of sweat and evil. El Moro's, I figured, and wouldn't have been surprised if it had been full of vipers. I shook the contents onto the deck and stared at dirty clothing, a thick leather belt studded with silver stars, a large hunter's knife, and a cudgel.

Cudgel. Was it the same instrument he'd used to break my leg back at the Alhambra? The throb in my head came back. So did the memory of El Moro hovering above me in his black leather vest, the cudgel in his hand. Where is the cave, Father?

The vision so inflamed me that I wanted to go back and deliver a few more blows. I set the cudgel aside and opened Father Menendez's bag. At the top was a half loaf of onion bread. I bit off a chunk and then pulled out a beautifully engraved wooden box.

Inside was his Bible, a personal journal, writing material, identity papers, and copies of wanted posters. And there it was:

Wanted by the Inquisitor-General of Nicaragua
Father Antonio Escofet, S.J., heretic, rapist and murderer

Bastards. The bishop's name should be on a wanted poster. Not mine. Why was it that the innocent suffered and the wicked prevailed? Where was God's justice?

"Justice is in the hereafter, Antonio, not on this earth."

"I thought I told you to leave me alone."

"Someone has to look after your soul."

I ignored Father Sebastiano and kept digging in the bag until I found what I wanted—an extra cassock, sandals, and a priest's hat. Yes, my little scheme might work after all.

I stripped off my clothes and changed into the cassock. Oh, to feel the cloth around me again, to hold a crucifix in my hand, to be a servant of God. I bit off another chunk of onion bread.

"For shame, Antonio. First you kill a priest. You take his money like a common thief. You take his identity. Now you eat his bread."

I spun around, my face growing warm, thinking to engage this intrusive old priest in a debate about morality and survival. But when I realized I'd just be debating myself, discoursing with the walls like a homeless *borrachón*, I checked to see that the door was bolted, then blew out the candles inside the lantern, and was crawling into the hammock when a watchman came plodding along the passageway, dragging his night stick along the bulkhead.

"By the grace of God, the storm has passed… the seas are calm… stars are shining… sails are full drawing. Stay in your cabins until first light dawning. *Tan tranquila es la noche…*"

His song faded, and there were no further disturbances, only the creaks and groans of the timbers, the strikes of the ship's bell, and the images of Saraatepe that kept flashing through my mind: Saraatepe, with the dark almond eyes that melted my heart, Saraatepe, with the fragrance of gardenias in her hair.

Saraatepe, lying naked beneath the body of Father Menendez.

CHAPTER 19

The strike of four bells brought me out of my dream—six a.m. by my reckoning—and it all came back. The storm, the fight, the bodies in the cabin. The realization that for the remainder of this voyage I was Father Menendez.

My stomach twisted. The air around me seemed to convey the scent of death—vomit, blood, and other things vile.

Father Menendez's cassock, I figured, still wadded up on the deck. Maybe I could push it through the porthole. But suppose a crewman on the upper deck saw me? Or a passenger? Best to take it topside in the chamber pot.

I eased out of my hammock and opened the tiny port hole to let in fresh air. The morning was still misty and dark, but with enough light to tell me the sea was calm and we had not yet put the island of Hispaniola behind us. Through the fog, I caught glimpses of trees, a rocky shoreline and craggy hills.

Oh, to be back on my tropical island with Saraatepe.

I dressed in my priestly garb and was contemplating how to survive the day as Father Menendez when the steward came plodding along the passageway.

"Candles! Fresh candles and fire for your lanterns!"

I drew in a deep breath and stepped into the passageway. The steward, an aging man with a white beard and leathery skin, turned out to be the same crewman who'd helped me to my cabin the evening before. He held up his lantern. "Good morning, Father."

Not a hint of confusion. He handed me candles and was turning to go when I said, "Where can I report a missing passenger?"

"Who is missing, Father?"

"My cabinmate. El Moro. Big man with shaven head."

"Oh, him. When did you last see him?"

The clang of the galley bells interrupted him. Other passengers began stumbling out of their cabins, all ghastly and pale, heading for breakfast. The aroma of frying bacon wafted in the air around me.

The steward dismissed me with a wave. "Probably found himself a woman," he said in his ragged sailor's voice. "Happens all the time. You might find him in the galley."

I hurried back into the cabin with my candles, closed and latched the door, and grabbed El Moro's pistol. Through the doorway, I could hear the steward telling the other passengers to be sure and try a new refreshment in the galley called café. "Comes from the isle of Martinique. Not as tasty as chocolate, but it'll light a fire under you."

Yes, that was what I needed: something to keep me going all day.

I folded Father Menendez's blood-stained cassock, shoved it into the chamber pot, and stepped back into the passageway. It was now lit by sconces along the bulkhead, but I still had to pass my old cabin with its memories of violence and death. As I approached, I caught a whiff of foul air, but there were no bloody footprints. No blood seeping from beneath the door either.

I made the sign of the cross and was about to climb the ladder when the steward came plodding down. "Begging your pardon, Father. Find your missing friend?"

"Not yet. It's not like him to disappear."

He stepped closer with his lantern. "Are you ill, Father?"

"I'm not used to storms at sea."

"You'll get over it." He sniffed the air as if wondering what was stinking up the place, then glanced at my chamber pot. "I'll take it," he said. "You're a *Clase de Oro* passenger."

"No, no, I'll take it topside. I need the fresh air anyway."

He helped me up the ladder, into the morning mist and fresh air. The *Sevilla* rolled steadily, her bowsprit dipping, and I could tell by the billowing sails that God had blessed us with a good wind. "Dump spots on the aft deck," he said. "See the little flag on the bulwark? But test the breeze and watch your step. Deck's slippery as bat dung."

I trod carefully to the place he'd pointed out. The aft deck was bathed in spray and mist, and the crew was busy with repairs—hammering, sawing, and shouting. A quick look around, and I emptied the slops along with Father Menendez's cassock. It spread on the water, bobbed a couple of times, and disappeared into the wake.

"Good morning, Father. Steward tells me you've got a problem."

I almost dropped the chamber pot. The officer standing there was the same wiry little man with bad teeth who'd questioned me when I first boarded the *Sevilla* in Cartagena, the man who'd asked about the blood on my shirt. Had he seen me toss the robe? And even if he hadn't, he could probably see right through my cassock to my deceitful heart.

Why hadn't I done more to alter my looks? Stuffed cotton between my cheeks and gums. Whitened my hair.

But he showed no sign of recognition, not a hint of suspicion, and led me to the hatch that led down to the ladder, away from the breeze and the noise of pounding hammers.

"I'm told your cabin mate is missing. What happened?"

"Don't know," I said, trying to raise the pitch of my voice to the annoying level that was Father Menendez's speech. "He left the cabin last night but didn't return. This was during the storm. Said he was going to check on a suspicious looking passenger."

"Suspicious?"

"A man we've been chasing from Nicaragua."

"Wait a minute, Father. Who are you people?"

"I'm sorry, I thought you knew." I bowed my head and offered my hand. "I am Father José Antonio Menendez y Valle, Fiscál of Nicaragua. At your service."

"Fiscál?"

"Personal assistant to the inquisitor-general."

He pulled back his hand and swallowed hard. Obviously, he was as terrified of the Inquisition as I was. The thought emboldened me, so I puffed myself up the way Father Menendez would do. "The man we're chasing is a priest. He murdered the alcalde of Granada. Chopped off his head. Then killed two of our men in the escape.

We're told he boarded your ship in Cartagena, after he almost killed a bank guard. Maybe you recall him—about my height. Walks with a limp. Carries a walking cane. Catalonian accent."

"*Por Dios*, I remember him well. Had blood stains on his shirt. I suspected he was up to no good. Damn Catalonians. You think he's still aboard the *Sevilla*?"

"Yes, *Capitán*. That's exactly what I'm saying."

"Lieutenant, I'm first officer, not captain."

"Lieutenant. Captain. Anyhow, we sighted him aboard the ship. Dark beard. Dressed in mariners' clothing. I'm pretty sure it was him. I wanted to report him to the captain, but El Moro—that's the name of my cabin mate—wanted to confront him."

"Did he?"

"That's El Moro for you. I told him to wait until after the storm, but he wouldn't hear of it."

"Why didn't you go with him?"

"Couldn't. I was throwing up my innards. Besides, El Moro is huge. He can break a man in two with his hands."

"Why didn't you report him missing last night?"

"It was storming. We were told to remain in our cabins. Besides, I was too sick to do anything but crawl into my hammock. I fell asleep… and when I awoke this morning, El Moro's hammock was empty. That's when I reported to the steward."

He slammed a fist into the palm of his hand. "This is exactly what we don't need. It's bad enough with talk of pirates. Any idea which cabin this escaped convict is in?"

"I'm pretty sure it was in first class section, near the galley."

He rubbed his beard and took a step backward. "Listen, Father, why don't you go down to the galley and wait? Make yourself comfortable. We'll have a look and report back to you."

"Thank you, Lieutenant, but tell your men to be careful. Father Antonio is a desperate man."

"*Vale*," he said, and marched away.

Satisfied with my performance, I watched him head for the forward deck ladder. But then he wheeled about and retraced his steps. “Have we met before?”

My heart skipped a beat. “Not that I recall. Why do you ask?”

“Well, you look familiar. Were you on this vessel before?”

“No, Lieutenant. Perhaps you saw me in Santo Domingo, when I came off *Las Palmas*.”

“That must be it,” he said and marched away.

CHAPTER 20

It was too late to change my countenance. All I could do was pray he wouldn't place me, so I hurried back to my cabin, put on my saintly hat, and was about to head for the galley when I noticed Father Menendez's journal. Last night had been too dark for reading, but now, with morning light streaming through the porthole, I opened it to the first page and scoffed when I saw the Latin script—Latin being the secret language of scoundrels and educated priests. The heading noted that it was a duplicate of a letter written by Father Menendez to the inquisitor-general. I sank onto the bunk and read.

> *With respect to the parties who aided in Father Antonio's escape, I urge your Grace to incarcerate them at once and sentence the lot to death. Should you fail in your efforts, I urge your Grace to choose an equal number of Indians from the island of Ometepe, whose simple minds were poisoned by the teachings of said Father Antonio. May God curse his name.*

My face burned with rage. What madmen they were. The letter was probably already in the hands of the bishop, and he'd be rounding up suspects, torturing them for information. The trail would lead to all the good people who'd helped me—Father Paolo, little Mateo, the madam of the House of Seven Veils, the innocent oarsmen.

A bell sounded the final call for breakfast. The gnawing in my stomach told me I should go, but I kept reading anyway, flipping through the pages and looking for anything about Saraatepe. Then I found a passage that both heartened and sickened me.

With respect to Father Antonio's two bastard children, they are now housed at my residence. If for any reason I am delayed on this voyage, I urge your Grace to take them into your care. My gift to you.

My boys were alive! But for how long? What horrors would they suffer at the hands of that sadistic madman? I had to return. Gonzalez and the inquisitor-general had to be stopped, and the only way to stop them was to wipe them out like an infestation of rats.

I stuffed the pistol into my side pocket and stormed out of the cabin, slamming the door behind me and marching toward the galley as if I were captain.

The galley fell silent when I entered. Everyone looked up. Obviously, word had gone out that a dreaded fiscál was aboard. I stood there a moment, breathing in the smells and surveying the room the way Father Menendez would do, taking in the crowded wooden tables with their first-class passengers. No soldiers and no Sampson, and no one else who looked like a threat.

A server behind the counter grabbed a tray for me and piled it with boiled eggs, ham, bacon, and fresh fruits. Another poured a mug of this new refreshment called café and added a spoonful of bee's honey. Then they led me to the only table with an empty space, across from a matronly woman with a large, ugly dog at her feet.

Her dog bared its teeth as if it sensed the evil in Father Menendez's cassock. "Señora," I said, "if you do not control that cur, I shall have it fed to the sharks."

The woman jumped to her feet and practically ran toward the exit with her dog, leaving her food uneaten, the galley in silence, and me alone at the table.

In time the stir of discourse resumed. Plates clattered. Everyone who entered made a show of blessing their food, the Holy Father and the king. There was talk from the next table of the War of Jenkins' Ear. The loud-talking old man who'd frightened everyone at the ticket office with his talk of hurricanes was also there.

"Worst thing about sailing the Main," he said, "is PIRATES."

Passengers glanced out the ports as if a ship flying the skull and crossbones was bearing down on us. The chatter went on. No one joined me at my table, and I was on my third mug of café when the steward burst through the door and trotted over to me, his eyes wide.

"Captain wants to see you. Now!"

I drained the mug and followed him out of the galley, down the passageway, and toward the cabin that contained the bodies, forcing myself not to limp. My hands trembled. My head swam, and I had the same restless sensation as when I'd drank Abuelita's fever juice.

"Hope you've got a strong stomach," said the steward.

The door was partially open. Beside it stood the lieutenant I'd spoken to earlier. Three or four marines waited with him, grim-faced and sickly looking. The smell of spilled guts, vomit and death hit me from at least ten paces away. "Captain's inside," said the lieutenant.

I crossed myself and stepped into the cabin.

"Mother of God," I uttered. "What happened here?"

The captain, a large bearded man in crimson and blue, stood near my sea-bag, holding a kerchief over his mouth. He gestured toward the bodies. "Which is your friend?"

Flies buzzed about them. My stomach revolted, and I wanted to run out of the cabin. Instead, I pointed a shaky finger at El Moro. "The big one. He was my cabin mate."

"What about the other one? That the man you were chasing?"

My impulse was to say yes, but since Father Menendez was slumped face down across El Moro, features hidden, and the lieutenant was in the cabin, I said, "I can't see his face."

The captain yelled for a marine. In marched a rough looking fellow who rolled Father Menendez onto his back, exposing the wounds in his stomach. Flies rose up in protest. A portion of intestine protruded from the body, oozing blackness and creating an even greater stench. "That's him," I said, holding the neck of the cassock over my nose. "He escaped the fire of the Inquisition, but he'll get his due in hell."

The lieutenant kneeled down and took a long look at the body. "That's not the Catalonian."

The knot in my stomach tightened. "Why do you say that?"

"Because I remember him well. Limped aboard the *Sevilla* in Cartagena. Had blood stains on his shirt. Catalonian accent, a week's growth of beard. Dark hair. I suspected him the moment I saw him. Even reported him to the Captain of Customs."

"That corpse has a dark beard, doesn't he?"

"He does."

"And we can't very well watch him limp, can we? Or listen to his Catalonian accent?"

"No, but…"

"But what, Lieutenant?"

"All I'm saying is something's not right." He pointed at the door. "Notice the door handle. Blood all over it, like somebody in a hurry to leave. Then you've got smudge spots over there, somebody trying to clean up. And if that's not enough, consider what Sanchez said."

"Sanchez?"

"The steward. Says one of the passengers heard screaming in this cabin, so he—Sanchez—knocked. Someone answered through the closed door, told him everything was fine. Now how could dead man say things are fine?"

The captain looked at me. I shrugged.

"There's more," said the lieutenant. "Like that man I saw in the passageway last night. Passengers were supposed to be in their cabins. But here was this dark figure at the bottom of the ladder, in front of this very cabin. I saw him through the hatch."

"Did you recognize him?"

"Too dark. I challenged him, but he scurried off like a scared rat."

The captain turned to me. "What do you think, Father?"

"I can think of a dozen explanations for everything the lieutenant just pointed out."

"Maybe you can," the lieutenant shot back, "but there's more to this story. Somebody else has to be involved."

"That's enough," said the captain. "You can present your theory to the bishop when we get to San Juan Bautista? And one more thing. I want this kept quiet. Passengers are already panicked by the thought of pirates. We don't want them thinking we've got a killer aboard."

Once in the corridor, in the blessed fresh air from the open hatch, the captain led me away. I did my best to walk with a steady gait.

"I'll have to log this," said the captain. "God willing, we can put this behind us, but I'll need your thoughts on what happened. Regulations. Then we'll have to report it to La Casa when we land."

"La Casa?"

"*Casa de Contratación.* Everything has to be reported to them."

"What about the bodies?"

"Burial at sea. Bodies are already getting ripe."

I could scarcely contain my glee, and was thanking the saints, when that cursed lieutenant came hurrying after us. "Captain."

"What is it now?"

"Shouldn't we get the other passenger to identify the bodies?"

"What other passenger?"

"The one who was traveling with them."

My heart climbed into my throat. Another passenger? The captain turned to me. "Who else was with you?"

Before I could answer, there came a shuffling movement from the shadows, followed by the grunt of a man in pain. Then the thunk, thunk of wood on wood, like a blind man tapping a stick on the deck. "That's him," said the lieutenant. "I sent the steward to fetch him."

Everyone turned to stare, and there he came on his crutches, all bandages and bruises—Enrique, the bank guard from Cartagena.

CHAPTER 21

If the captain had not been standing near the ladder, I'd have dashed for the upper deck and jumped overboard, but there were no avenues of escape, nothing but a captain waiting for an answer and a bank guard who could identify me.

Enrique stopped and leaned forward on his crutches. A bloody bandage covered his head; other bandages covered a knee and left arm. An eye was almost swollen shut. But from the way he stared, there was no doubt he recognized me. I had to do something, so in desperation I turned to the captain.

"Just look what the heretic did to this poor man."

Enrique looked me squarely in the eye. "That's right," he said to the captain. "Pounded me with a heavy walking stick. Left me for dead. Would have killed me, except…."

"Except what?"

"Went weak at the last moment. Maybe the priest in him."

"What is your name?" the lieutenant asked.

"Enrique Octavio Iturriategui-Careaga, at your service."

"Basque?"

"*Sí, Teniente*, from the north of Spain."

Another seed of hope blossomed in my chest. Basques of Spain hated Castilians and the Inquisition as much as we Catalonians did.

"I want to show you something," the lieutenant said. He guided Enrique into the cabin where the bodies lay. The captain and I followed, but we didn't enter the cabin.

"*Por Dios*," Enrique said, and crossed himself. "Look what they did to El Moro."

"Which one is El Moro?" the lieutenant asked.

"Big one in the leather vest. They called him El Moro. He was the executioner. Poked fire in his victim's faces."

"What about the other body? Is that the heretic?"

How long the silence lasted, I do not know, but it was long enough to hear the pop of sails. Long enough to feel the pounding in my head. I even had time to remember a Gypsy spiritualist in Barcelona who claimed she communicated with people through her mind. How I wished I could communicate my thoughts to Enrique.

"Well," said the lieutenant. "Is that Father Antonio or not?"

"*Sí, Teniente*. El Moro must have killed him."

I sank onto the lower step and breathed in the stifling air with the delight of someone freed from slavery. My injured leg throbbed. Enrique hobbled out of the cabin on his crutches, caught my eye, and nodded as if to say he'd heard my unspoken plea.

I nodded back. The lieutenant marched stiffly out of the cabin, bellowing at crewmen. "Get that mess cleaned up! Wrap the bodies in canvas and get them topside. And be quick about it."

I arose with as much dignity as I could summon, felt myself go lightheaded, and only by the support of the cane saved myself from tumbling to the deck. Enrique took my arm, and the two of us set off in a slow stalk to my cabin, well aware of the lieutenant's eyes on us. He had to know we were hiding the truth.

At the door, I fumbled with the key, opened the door, and pulled Enrique inside. "God bless you," I said. "You could have earned yourself a hefty reward."

"My soul is worth more than thirty pieces of silver."

He sank onto the bunk with a sigh. "They forced me to come with them. Didn't even give me a chance to say goodbye to my family. I wasn't going to give you away no matter what, not after the way you helped me. But there was another reason."

"What reason, Enrique?"

"I heard them talking about you, laughing, bragging about what they did to those villagers, talking about Indians like they were animals. What I didn't tell them is my wife is Indian… a Chibchan. We have two children."

I reached into my purse and took out two gold escudos, the equivalent of more than thirty Pieces of Eight, probably more than he earned in two years as a bank guard.

"No, Father, you don't owe me anything."

"Yes, I do, Enrique. Take it. I might need your services again."

We heard no more from the lieutenant. My confidence grew. I was "dead," buried at sea. I'd given a statement to the captain for his log, and also used Father Menendez's letterhead to write a detailed report for Bishop Ureña back in Granada.

It also helped that I had someone to talk to, and by the time we dropped anchor beneath the bluffs of San Juan Bautista, I was in such high spirits that I sang a verse of Caccini's *Ave Maria.*

"Why are you singing?" Enrique asked from the wash basin.

"What's not to sing about? We'll soon be off this cursed vessel."

He tossed his towel on the bunk and turned to face me. His health seemed to be improving by the hour. He'd even thrown away the crutches and was now using the cane I'd used to kill El Moro. "You're not worried about that lieutenant?"

"Nothing to worry about. We'll be on another ship before he realizes we're gone."

We set our bags out for the steward and were plodding along the corridor with other passengers when the lieutenant came plunging down the companionway. "There you are," he said. "Captain wants to know when you're reporting to La Casa."

I beat down a strong desire to pull out my pistol and shoot him. "When is the captain going?"

"Soon as we clear customs. You're going with us?"

"I have other items to attend to."

He arched an eyebrow. "The captain expects you to be there."

"I understand, Lieutenant. I've got my report right here." I tapped the pocket that held my pistol. "Tell your captain I'll meet him at La Casa by mid-morning."

"*Vale*," he said, and took his leave.

As soon as he was up the companionway and out of sight, Enrique turned to me. "Please tell me you're not going."

"Of course not. This changes nothing."

A bellowing voice announced the arrival of a shore tender. We climbed aboard with other passengers and landed a few minutes later beneath the massive fortress of San Felipe del Morro.

CHAPTER 22

San Juan Bautista de Puerto Rico

Banners snapped and fluttered. Armed marines stood around in their crimson and blue uniforms. We collected our bags and as soon as we entered the building with its smoky interior, I spotted the lieutenant at the desk of the Captain of Customs, pointing us out. By then, I'd had enough of this meddlesome little man. I was, after all, a fiscál of the Inquisition.

"I'll be right back," I said to Enrique.

The lieutenant stiffened at my approach. The Captain of Customs, dressed in his brilliant uniform with blue epaulettes and golden sash, came to his feet and touched the brim of his hat. "Good morning, Father. How may I assist you?"

"Would you be kind enough to tell me where I might find the inquisitor-general?"

"I imagine he's at the hanging."

"What hanging?"

"English pirate, Billy Chupacabra. They're stringing him up this morning."

The name echoed in my head. Billy Chupacabra was the name of the pirate they'd hanged in the plaza of Granada.

"Did you say Billy Chupacabra?"

"That's what he calls himself, the goat-sucker. He's been here only three days, and dead animals are already showing up, every single one of them drained of blood."

By then, everyone within earshot was listening. An official at a nearby table turned in his chair. "Not only animals," he said, raising his voice. "They found a dead woman with bite marks on her chest. Blood sucked right out of her."

Mothers shouted for their children. Passengers demanded details, and pretty soon the name Billy Goatsucker was spreading through customs like the stench of a spilled chamber pot.

It took another minute or two for things to settle down, and by that time I was grateful for the distraction of a hanging. There'd be speeches and music and an *auto da fé*. The captain and lieutenant would be occupied at least until noon, and long before noon Enrique and I would be on another ship, safely out to sea.

"Where is this hanging to take place?" I asked.

"The plaza. Just follow the mob."

He waved us through customs without a search. We pushed through the usual crowd, entered the embarkation building, and headed straight to the ticket counter. "When's the next ship for Santo Domingo?" I asked the clerk.

He consulted his chart. "*Toledo's* leaving at dark… on the tide."

"Tonight? Why not earlier?"

"Pirates, Father. Thicker than fleas on a dog. Nothing leaves out of here in sunlight… nothing but warships and seagulls. It's that stupid War of Jenkins' Ear." He took a puff on his pipe. "Guess you're as anxious to get out of here as everyone else. This chupacabra business is stirring up a panic. This morning they found three more women."

"Dead?"

"Hanging upside down. Not a drop of blood in them." His story went on—throats ripped out, a hairy beast leaping across rooftops, virgins disemboweled.

"Enough," I said, and held up a hand. "I have a report for Nicaragua. It's for Bishop Ureña. Would it have to wait for tonight to go out?"

"A warship is sailing today. It can convey your papers."

I was about to hand over the report when another idea struck. The bishop was one of the most superstitious men I knew. These stories of chupacabras would keep him up at night.

I borrowed paper, quill and ink, sat at a nearby table, and composed a postscript to my other report: in Latin, all in one long paragraph without spaces between words. I wrote about the dreaded chupacabras and how they'd brought terror to the city, adding the fiction that I—Father Menendez—had seen the evidence with my own eyes.

> *Already the demons have taken the lives of six of our brothers. The local bishop was himself attacked. There are rumors that the beasts are migrating from this colony to the next, spreading terror, and their victims are members of the clergy. I urge your Grace to take all necessary precautions...*

Feeling pleased with myself, and not troubled by another lie, I signed as Father Menendez, sealed the report, and handed it to the ticket-master along with a few coins. We then checked our bags into the luggage hold and hailed a coach for the ride into the city.

"Where are we going?" Enrique asked.

"The plaza. Don't you want to see a hanging?"

The road took us up a sharp embankment and alongside the massive fortress of San Felipe del Morro with its battlements and banners. Soldiers drilled in an open field, all crimson and blue in the early light, and for a moment I caught a glimpse of a warship heading out at sea, its sails full of wind. "I don't like this," Enrique grumbled. "We should stay out of sight."

"That's the worst thing we could do."

"I don't want to see a hanging."

"You don't have to watch. There'll be lots of drinking and eating and carrying on. Then you've got siesta. By the time it's over we'll be on another ship."

Door after door went by the window, most of them with signs indicating their purpose: Mamacita's House of Pleasures. The Inn of the Happy Mariner. Even a play-house that brought back happy memories of my days as a stage actor.

In time, the street became narrow and cobbled. It was also filled with people on their way to the hanging—men, women, and children. Some carried axes. Others wore strings of garlic around their waists. Men carried muskets as if going to war. Virtually all had prayer beads or crucifixes, but unlike the rowdy mobs that had come out to see me burn in Granada, these people shuffled along like a parade of zombies, so quiet I could hear the thud of footfalls.

"Well?" Enrique said. "Why aren't they dancing and drinking?"

I ignored him. We slowed from trot to a walk. The air that before had been fresh and clean now became stifling hot, reeking of horse dung and garbage.

At last we rolled into the plaza and found ourselves in the midst of a familiar scene: a cathedral on one side and convent on the other, a plaza filled with spectators. Street vendors making their rounds with pig cracklings and blood sausages.

"*Chicharónes! Morcellos!*"

But no music or laughter. No stake either. Instead, there loomed in the center a low braced crossbeam with a swinging noose. On the platform behind it sat the dons, the important priests, military officers and representatives of the crown, all in their glittering finest.

Enrique nudged me. "Which one is the bishop?"

"Fat one in purple and lace. See him there, square biretta on his head, leaning on his cane."

Enrique shaded his eyes with his hands. "He doesn't look very festive either."

"Would you just shut up?"

"Don't get mad with me. You're the one who said they'd be carousing."

The sun rose higher, creating a glare, and it grew oppressively hot. People fidgeted and grumbled, fussing at children and munching their pig skins. Enrique complained about his leg, and I was looking for a place to sit when the cathedral bell tolled nine.

The bishop raised his right arm. From somewhere came the low roll of a drum. Then the creak and rumble of wheels over the blue cobbles. The crowd parted, and there they came: four soldiers on horseback followed by four on foot. Then the executioner in his black mask. And finally, a single horse pulling a two-wheeled cart in which stood Billy Chupacabra himself, blonde and tall and proudly erect.

I stared in disbelief. He was the same pirate who'd led the invasion of my little tropical island.

The memories flooded back—pirates rushing ashore, the locals fleeing with their goods, women screaming, chaos on all sides. And now, even on a cart, he cut the same fine figure—knee breeches and stockings, ruffled shirt that was open to the waist, hair tied back with a red ribbon, wide shoulders and a tanned face.

"*Coño*," Enrique said. "I didn't expect him to look like that."

The cart rolled to a stop beneath the noose. A deathly silence fell over the plaza. The executioner, a man as muscular as El Moro, hopped aboard the cart and adjusted the noose around the prisoner's neck. He jerked on the rope to test the strength, then took out a hood.

"No!" the pirate cried and kicked the executioner off the cart.

Murmurs of disbelief shot through the crowd. I, who despised executioners only slightly less than inquisitors-general, barely suppressed a desire to shout "Bravo."

The executioner picked himself up. "That the way you want it, Englishman? Fine. But I'm going to make it a slow choking death."

Three or four bystanders, perhaps emboldened by the executioner, hollered in agreement.

"Hang him!"

"Make him suffer!"

Billy stood there in stony English dignity. The pirate they'd hanged in our plaza had begged for his life. The executioner stalked to the front of the cart, next to the mule.

A drum roll sounded. All eyes turned to the bishop. He attempted to stand but couldn't because of his obesity, and finally rose with the help of assistants. He waddled a few steps forward, stomach leading the way, and grasped the railing for support. His neck, if it existed, was hidden beneath his collar, and the features of his face were almost lost between apple-colored jowls.

"Fellow Spaniards," he said in a high-pitched voice. "Citizens of San Juan Bautista. Brothers in Christ. This Englishman you see before you, this man who calls himself Billy Chupacabra has been condemned by the court of the Inquisition as a murderer, a pirate, a heretic, and a demon that practices the dark arts of the underworld. And for that reason—"

"No!" shrieked a woman behind me. "Spare him!"

CHAPTER 23

She rushed forward and fell to her knees beneath the bishop. Her dress, a simple black garment without ornamentation, was as frayed and rumpled as the pirate's shirt.

"Spare him," she said in a strange accent.

She looked familiar, so I pushed closer. Was she the same girl who'd raided my little island in Nicaragua with the pirates? Yes, no doubt about it. Same fair complexion, same golden hair that fell to her shoulder in tresses, and a face that was above the common order.

The bishop smiled down at her like a kindly grandfather.

"Tell me, child, why should I spare this man?"

"Because he is the devil, your Grace."

The bishop's smile vanished. I listened in disbelief. No one in their right mind would say that to an inquisitor-general. Yet she kept talking, her voice growing stronger. "If you put this man to death, this colony will be visited by plague. Children will come down with the evil eye. Those that survive will be devoured by chupacabras. The scourge will spread…"

One of the other priests, probably the fiscál, hurried down from the platform and pulled the girl away. But instead of dragging her to a dungeon, he seemed to be reasoning with her.

I turned to a nearby priest, a man with his face buried in a dark hood. "Why are they tolerating that girl?" I asked.

At first he didn't answer, and when he did it was in a voice that sounded as if his throat had recently been cut. "Look at her, Padre. Pretty, is she not?"

I saw what he meant. She couldn't have been more than a teenager, probably a captive, and now she'd be further victimized by the bishop. Until he tired of her, and then she'd either be hanged or condemned to some place like Mamacita's House of Pleasures.

The drums started again. The girl's protests grew frantic. The bishop raised a hand and quickly brought it down. The executioner struck the mule with his lash.

The cart rattled away, and Billy Chupacabra was left kicking and swinging in the air.

What happened next made no sense, and if I hadn't known better, I'd have sworn the gates of hell had opened. First, a dead goat came flying through the air, knocking down spectators and creating panic. This was followed by dead chickens, dropping from the sky like leaves from a tree, along with a shower of feathers. Dead dogs came next—two, three, four.

And then a horned creature appeared on the roof of the convent, shrieking and cursing.

"Chupacabra!" someone yelled. There were screams and shouts. The mule that had carted the Englishman to the gallows fell dead near my feet—as did the executioner.

Everyone with a gun began shooting: a volley here, a single shot there, until the entire plaza was filled with an ungodly collision of shrieks, gunfire, smoke and acrid smells. Panic turned to stampede. The whole place exploded with the roar of bodies shoving past other bodies; and when I looked back where the pirate had dangled, there was now only a swinging noose.

The panic struck me as well—I, who did not believe in chupacabras—and yet, there I was, on the verge of running like a frightened rabbit, until I heard the cries of the girl.

"No, leave me be!"

My eyes swept the place. Where was she? I dashed up the steps of the platform, bounding over a body, and saw her no more than thirty paces away, struggling with the fiscál.

She clawed at his face. She kicked. She yelled foreign words that made no sense.

Stay out of it, my mind said. But my heart said otherwise. That girl could be Saraatepe. I turned to Enrique. "Toss me your cane."

He pitched it to me—my old brass cane that had never failed. I caught it in midair, leapt off the platform, and set off after them. Just one blow, I told myself, not enough to kill.

Ten paces… five. I tightened the grip on my cane and was about to make the final dash when from behind came the clatter of a galloping horse.

"*Cuidado*!" Enrique yelled. "Look out!"

A horse and rider galloped past. Then another, followed by four or five others, hooves clattering on the blue cobbles, heading across the plaza and fading into the shadows of a side street. At first I thought it was cavalry, but when one of the riders came back, reining his horse to a stop beside the struggling girl, I saw the cowl.

A hooded priest on horseback?

This made no more sense than flying goats.

The rider bounded off his horse and knocked the fiscál to the cobbles. Not until then did I understand. Those people weren't priests; they were Billy's friends. They'd been in the crowd, their English faces buried in cowls. They'd created this distraction. Probably used a catapult to toss dead animals from the convent. The girl would be rescued, Billy would escape, and my conscience would be clear.

Or so I was thinking until the girl began fighting her rescuer.

The fiscál saw it too. He struggled to his feet and jumped the pirate. Out came a dirk. There was a glint of sun on metal, and right before my eyes the pirate buried his knife in the priest's neck.

Down went the priest, flailing like a chicken whose neck had been wrung, blood spurting. The pirate then grabbed the girl and dragged her toward his horse.

Again she fought, screaming as if a chupacabra had bitten into her throat. It made no sense. Why would she be fighting her friends?

Maybe it was my sense of fairness. Or maybe it was the priest in me. Whatever the case, I fell instantly upon the villain from behind, and with one swift blow from my cane laid him to the cobbles. He tried to push himself up. I throttled him again. His horse whinnied and trotted away. The girl skittered backward on her hands and knees, staring at my cassock and crucifix, terror in her eyes. “Don’t be frightened,” I said. “I’m trying to help.”

“You’re not one of them?”

“No, child. I’m not going to harm you.”

Tears ran down her cheeks. “They kill me,” she said in her strange-sounding accent. “Your people, they want to burn me alive at the… *como se dice*, the, the pole.”

“The stake, child. We call it a stake.”

She came to her feet and fell in beside me, and from her jerky motions, the way she kept looking back, I figured she wanted to get away from that cursed place as much as I did.

“Is Jack dead?” she asked.

“Who?”

“Jack.” She pointed back to the pirate. “Is he dead?”

“I don’t think so.”

“You should kill him, you should.”

“There’s been enough killing. Let the soldiers hang him.”

“They’ll not hang Jack, they won’t. Only way to kill Jack is cut off his head.”

That sounded a bit drastic, so I took her hand and led her away. Enrique rushed up beside me, glancing from me to the girl.

“Are you crazy, Father? Are you trying to get us hanged?”

“I’m helping this girl. You don’t like it, go back to the landing.”

By then there remained only the wounded and the dead in the plaza, the overturned carts, cast-off items, and people staggering about as if looking for loved ones. I scooped up a discarded shawl and handed it to the girl. “Here, cover that hair.”

She pulled it over her head, and the three of us set off toward the nearest side street, passing alongside the convent.

“Why were you fighting the pirate?” I asked her.

“Wicked man, Father. He tries to make me Billy’s woman. Better I die on the pole.”

So that was it. I’d risked my neck to save the virtue of an Englishwoman. “That makes no sense,” I said. “You were begging them to spare Billy.”

"Oh, but kind sir, do you think me the fool?" She pointed toward the roof of the convent. "La. Up there. They have muskets, they do. They threatened to shoot me."

Instinctively, I moved closer to the wall, out of view of anyone on the roof. So that was the reason the mule had dropped dead. And the executioner. And if Billy hadn't been swinging between the roof and me, they'd have shot me as well.

"What happened to Billy?" I asked.

"Who knows, Father? They do not tell me, they don't."

Within minutes, we were back with the masses on Calle del Morro, putting the plaza behind us. Earlier that morning I'd thought the people looked frightened. Now they looked terrified—women sobbing and praying, men glancing over their shoulders.

The girl tugged at the sleeve of my cassock. "Kind sir, where are you taking me?"

"A bathhouse. We'll get you fresh clothes… fix your hair."

The street grew hotter. It stank of sweat and fear and bodies packed together. Some of the women reached out to kiss my hand or ask my blessing. Enrique's leg was troubling him again, and we were about to stop for a rest when I noticed a sign over a door:

CASA DE BELLEZA: BAÑOS PUBLICOS, PELUQUERÍA Y TALLER DE ROPA

Perfect, a bath, hairdresser and clothing shop, all in one place.

I rapped on the door with the brass knocker. On both sides were horseshoes, hoops, and other symbols to ward off evil spirits. A peephole opened. The face of a light-skinned Negro woman appeared, a pretty woman with green eyes and a slave wrap on her head.

"Bath," I told her.

She glanced out, didn't perceive us threatening, and began unlocking and unbolting. While we waited, I turned back to the girl. "What is your name, child?"

She answered in a small voice. "Molly Mulvaney."

Enrique glared at her. "English?"

"Irish, señor. My family comes from the country you call *Irlanda.*"

CHAPTER 24

I'd met Irishmen before: a few priests, deserters from the English navy, even Father Sebastiano, but I knew little about them other than that they were good Catholics and good friends of Spain.

The door creaked open. The woman with green eyes motioned us in. She glanced into the street, looking both ways, and then bolted the door behind us. "Is it true?" she asked in a voice that sounded as foreign as the girl's.

"Is what true, *mija*?"

"Chupacabras, Father. The devil incarnate."

I did my best to explain there were no such things.

"Oh, but Padre," she said in that strange sounding accent, "where I come from we have the loogaroo vampires. And the zombies, and witches that scream at night."

"Where is that, *mija*?"

"Hispaniola, the French side of the island. A place called Ayti."

"You were a slave?"

"Was. Now I am *femme d'coleur libre*. Free woman of color."

She introduced herself as Marie Bernadette Green Eyes, repeating the last name in French—*Yeux au Vert*—then led us up a stairway and along a balcony on which lounged a dozen or more cats, all black as the heart of Satan. A courtyard below teemed with activity—women stirring their sticks in cast iron pots, girls bending low over ironing boards, wash flapping on the line—and the air reeked of burning wood, soap, dampness and sweet flowery smells.

"Here," said Green Eyes, and directed us into a waiting room inhabited by more cats. Molly sank into a wicker chair. Fear showed in her face. She kept glancing this way and that as if expecting the pirates to burst in. Green Eyes saw it too.

"Not to worry," she said. "It's safe here."

She rattled off a long list of services I'd never heard of—facial oiling, pedicure and eyebrow plucking, delousing—and the list went on for so long that I finally held up a hand. "Look, I want you to darken this girl's hair and give her anything else she needs."

"What about you, Father?"

"A good scrubbing and a hair trim, also a change of clothing."

"*Vale*," she said, and hurried away.

While we waited, I turned back to the girl. "Why was the bishop protecting you?"

She remained silent. I told her she didn't have to explain, but she seemed to want to get it off her bosom. "He took me to his chambers, he did, and said he would protect me if I would be good. I inquired of him his meaning of good, and he answered by taking off his clothes."

She pointed to her cuts and bruises. "I made known to him that I was a married woman—though it was a stretch of veracity—and argued that the institution was a sacred bond in the eyes of our Lord, but he said I was a foreign wench without rights and fell to—"

Green Eyes appeared at the door. She stepped over to Molly and examined her like a surgeon, mumbling in French about parched skin and long eyebrows, about her broken nails and dirty toes, the hair on her legs, the bruises and scratches.

"Poor child," she said in French. "What have they done to you?"

Molly didn't answer, though I suspected she understood French as well as I did. "How long is this going to take?" I asked.

"For the two of you, not long. But for the girl, oh… four hours."

Enrique rolled his eyes as if to say he'd never heard of such madness. Four hours was fine with me. Five would be better, considering we needed to keep Molly out of sight until dark.

"One more thing," I said to Green Eyes.

I led her onto the balcony and closed the door. From the courtyard below came the splash of water. "It's important no one knows we are here. Can I trust you?"

"Please, Father, in this house we hear nothing, see nothing, speak nothing." She stepped back inside and led Molly away.

As soon as their footfalls faded, Enrique said, "This is crazy, Father. She's a pirate's woman."

"Was a pirate's woman. Now she's in our care. Besides, she might be able to help us."

"Help us do what? Go to the gallows?"

We were still arguing when from downstairs came a loud rap. A servant hurried down. We heard voices, the sounds of the door being unlocked, opened and closed. Then the shuffle of footfalls along the walkway. We faced the door, holding our breath, listening to the footfalls that were now on the stairs, coming up, getting closer.

The handle turned, the door opened, and into the waiting room stepped that nosey little lieutenant from the ship.

In all the excitement, I'd forgotten about him. His request that we meet at La Casa no longer seemed important, yet there he stood.

"Did you forget your appointment?" he said.

"Are you crazy? Didn't you see what happened in the plaza?"

"That's no excuse. The captain reported to La Casa anyway. Now he has to report to the inquisitor-general. He's already at the Alcaldia, waiting for you."

"Don't you think the bishop has more important matters?"

"Makes no difference. Regulations require us to make a report—and to bring the witness."

I closed my eyes and gritted my teeth. He was right, the little bastard. A murder aboard one of the king's ships had to be reported, even if a *terremoto* brought down the entire city.

"How long is this going to take?"

"No more than an hour. Then you can come back for your bath."

He backed out the door and glanced down at the porch of cats, staring in the direction Molly had taken. Yet he said nothing about her. Damn him. Had he seen her?

I stepped over to Enrique and lowered my voice. "If I'm not back in an hour take Molly and get out of here."

He nodded, handed me the cane as if to say I might need it, and a few minutes later I was back on the street with that cursed lieutenant, heading into the plaza with its dead bodies and the bouquet of death. "How'd you know we were at the bath house?" I asked.

"Because I followed you."

Soldiers with muskets and fixed bayonets were going from building to building, pounding on doors. Cathedral bells tolled non-stop. The Carmelite nuns in their brown habits were there too, tending the wounded, and there were priests praying over the fallen, and men with mule carts and wagons, picking up the dead and shooing away the vultures.

"This is crazy," I said to the lieutenant again. "All these dead people, pirates on the loose, a chupacabra panic, and you think the inquisitor-general has time for us."

"Oh, come now, Padre. Surely you're not afraid of the bishop?"

I ignored the comment and followed him into the center of the plaza, passing the spot where I'd clubbed the pirate. He was not there, but the fiscál lay where he had fallen, his body covered with a blanket. Around him stood five or six priests, hands clasped to chins.

"*Domine, Iesu Christe, Rex gloriae, libera animas omnium fidelium defunctorum….*"

I made the sign of the cross and followed the lieutenant beneath the gallows where Billy had swung on a rope. The executioner and his mule still lay there, surrounded by vultures with their red heads and hideous naked necks.

"Disgusting creatures," the lieutenant said. He clapped his hands and hissed like a snake, trying to drive them away, but all they did was flop along the cobbles before us.

I knelt down and took a long look at the mule.

"You going to pray over a dead mule?"

"No, Lieutenant." I pointed to the entry wound behind the poor creature's right eye. "See that hole. Just as I suspected. They shot him from the roof."

"Who shot him?"

"Pirates. They were up there. They shot the mule, shot the executioner and shot a few priests. You're lucky they didn't shoot you, dressed in that pretty uniform."

"How do you know that's what happened?"

"Because I'm a fiscál. It's what I do. I investigate crimes."

A wagon with three or four corpses on it rattled by. We resumed our walk across the plaza, passing beneath palm trees and alongside flowering hibiscus, shooing away vultures. The pistol in my pocket bumped against my hip; the cane felt solid in my hand, yet I still felt sweat running from my armpits down my ribs. Was the lieutenant leading me into a trap?

At last we reached an imposing one-story structure near the cathedral. Armed soldiers stood at the doorway, staring. So did a half dozen or so priests, all grim-faced and solemn looking.

No one paid us the slightest attention. Priests and soldiers were going this way and that. Candles burned, prayers buzzed in the background, the smell of gardenias and incense hung in the air like a funeral wake.

The lieutenant stopped a passing priest. "Excuse me, Father, but who is in charge?"

"That would be the *Calificadór*. He's busy."

"We'd like to see him. It's important."

We sat on an uncomfortable wooden bench beneath a window. More soldiers came and left. A woman holding a bloody bandage to her face burst in and loudly demanded to see someone about her missing children. Words like chupacabras and pirates came to my ears, and then the lieutenant turned to me. "What is a calificadór?"

"Third man in charge, after the bishop and fiscál. He's also the ecclesiastical censor of books and all other things prohibited by the Inquisition."

"And you're a fiscál?"

"Is that a problem for you, Lieutenant?"

Before he answered, a priest as corpulent as the inquisitor-general waddled into the room and introduced himself as the calificadór. He looked tired, with bloodshot eyes and broken veins, and when he spoke, I smelled wine.

"You from the *Sevilla*?" he asked the lieutenant.

"I am. We're supposed to meet the captain here."

"Your captain is gone. He said to get back to the ship."

The lieutenant didn't budge. "Did he meet with the bishop?"

"Haven't you heard?"

"Heard what?"

"The bishop is dead."

CHAPTER 25

A rambling explanation followed, but the calificadór's words were so slurred I wasn't sure if the inquisitor-general had died of heart failure or a musket ball. Not that it mattered. He deserved it for what he did to the girl. He looked from me to the lieutenant.

"What is your business here?"

"Killing aboard the *Sevilla*," said the lieutenant. "Two dead."

"*Ay, bendito*, can't this wait? We've got pressing matters."

"But I'm talking murder, Father."

"Are you serious? Can't you see—" He put a hand to his chest as if he were in pain. He stumbled and grabbed the wall for support. "Would someone please bring me a drink?"

A small man with dark Indian features hurried out of a side room, carrying a tray on which rested a silver goblet. The calificadór grabbed the goblet, took a long drink, smacked his lips, and turned back to the lieutenant. "Were you here during the panic, during the attack on the Holy Church and our citizens?"

"*Sí, Padre*. I saw it all."

"And you're suggesting we just stop what we're doing to concentrate on one little killing?"

"It was more than a killing." He gestured toward me. "This priest here claims to be a fiscál—from Nicaragua—but I have reason to believe he's not who he says he is."

I threw out my hands in feigned disgust. "You're an idiot, Lieutenant. A moron. One more accusation and I'll have you thrown into a dungeon. You'll be sorry you ever—"

The lieutenant turned to the calificadór. "Can he do that?"

"He can if he's a fiscál."

The lieutenant opened his mouth to reply, seemed to think better of it, and retreated toward the door. I taunted him, my confidence growing. "Come on, Lieutenant, show me evidence."

He said nothing, and when I turned back, the old priest was in discourse with an army officer, waving his arms and ranting about Englishman. "We'll catch those devils if it's the last thing we do. This island is small. All those red English faces. Where can they hide? We're already checking ports and roads." He slammed a fist into his palm. "Fifty Pieces of Eight for Billy Goatsucker. Five for any of his friends. Dead or alive."

"How much for the girl?" asked the lieutenant from the door.

"What girl?"

"The pirate's woman, the Englishwoman."

The defiance I'd felt only moments before deserted me. Had he seen Molly go into the bathhouse? The calificadór yelled down the hall for someone named Paco. Out of a side room hurried the same little man who'd brought the goblet. "Father?"

"What's the reward for the witch?"

"Eight, but Father Alonso wants to make it ten."

"Make it ten, and have someone check the whore houses."

The lieutenant said nothing, but he had to be adding it up in his head. Ten Pieces of Eight was probably more than he earned in six months. Leave now, said a voice in my head. Get to the bath house and warn them.

I turned to the door and was reaching for the handle when the calificadór took my arm. "If you're from Nicaragua, then you must know Father Menendez."

My heart seemed to stop beating. "I'm Father Menendez."

The calificadór stepped closer, bringing with him a strong smell of wine. "When this business settles down, why don't you stop back for a visit? You can tell me what happened on that ship."

I promised I would, and hurried out the door, stepping back into the plaza with its death and buzzards, hastening my progress.

At each step I expected to hear the clop of soldiers running after me. Damn that lieutenant. I should have whacked him on the head back in the bathhouse. Now I was going to spend the rest of the day worrying if he'd seen Molly.

By the time I reached the bathhouse, I'd convinced myself that the entire Spanish army was after me. They were already going door to door, checking on the bawdy houses. My lungs burned. My leg hurt. My cassock was drenched in sweat, and a headache was coming on. I pounded on the bathhouse door. It seemed to take forever for the peephole to open. A woman I had not seen before looked out. And that was when a pair of soldiers came trotting in my direction, waving their muskets. "Father! Father!"

The peephole slammed shut. The soldiers came closer, holding their muskets as if afraid I'd turn into a chupacabra. Neither looked older than sixteen, skinny, red-cheeked, and sweating in the heat, mere children in ill-fitting uniforms.

"What is it?" I asked, trying to sound indignant.

The taller of the two stepped close enough to feel heat from his body. "Begging your pardon," he said in the peasant accent of northern Spain. "It's just that, well, we've been told the pirates are dressed like priests. We have to—"

"Do I look like an Englishman to you?"

He snapped to attention. "No, sir, I mean… no, Father. We're just doing our duty."

"I understand, son, and well you should."

"We're also looking for a pirate woman. Blonde hair, *muy linda*, speaks Castilian with a funny accent. There's a reward."

He glanced at the sign over the door. "They told us to check whorehouses."

"This isn't a house of sin, son. It's a bathhouse. Now run along and look for pirates."

He thanked me and turned to go but turned back. "Begging your pardon again, Father, but may I ask a question about chupacabras? Are they real?"

I forced a laugh and gave him a fatherly touch on the arm. "No, *mijo*, all that talk about chupacabras is only a ruse."

"*Ay, bendito*," he said, which seemed to be the most common expression on this island. He thanked me a second time and trotted away. I yelled after them to go with God, then I pounded on the door again. It opened in seconds, as if the woman on the other side had been waiting.

"I need to see Green Eyes," I said. "It's urgent."

She led me up the stairs, along the gallery with the cats, and around a corner, stopping at a door painted a deep hue of green.

"Wait here, Father."

When she opened the door, I caught a glimpse of a room dimly lit with candles. Molly Mulvaney sat in a tub, facing me. She glanced up and caught my eyes but was slow to cover her breasts. French women were like that, I'd heard. But I thought Irish women were modest.

Green Eyes stepped out with a towel in her hand, bringing with her a sweet soapy smell.

"The soldiers," I said. "They're on the street. Going door to door."

"We have nothing to hide."

"But you have the girl. Her husband could—"

"Not to worry, Father. Soldiers come, soldiers go. See nothing."

I stared at her, still not understanding.

"Come," she said. "I show you."

She led me back around the corner, past the cats, and into a room decorated with floor to ceiling tapestries, telling me in her soft way of speaking that this was the entry to the Pleasure Room, a place with the biblical weight of the Promised Land. Even in the dim light I could make out the bright colors on the walls, the greens and reds, and dancing nudes in the tapestries.

She lifted a tapestry and pushed on the wall. A portion of it swung open, revealing yet another room.

"Poof, house of magic. Here you are safe."

I stepped into her secret room, a place lit with scented candles and furnished with a copper tub. A fan hung in the overhead, operated by a rope and pulley, and the walls were lined with paintings of nude women in the most suggestive postures.

"Where is Enrique?" I asked.

"Please, Father, we do not use names."

I sank into a chair to let my heart stop pounding, to accept that soldiers weren't going to beat down the door. But what about the reward of ten Pieces of Eight for Molly? That was enough to tempt anyone. I took out a gold escudo and held it up for Green Eyes to see.

"I have two more of these when you get us safely out of here."

Her face lit up. She hugged me and tugged at my cassock, and a few minutes later I was submerged up to my neck in a tub of warm, aromatic water.

How many girls came and left, I do not know. They were all young and pretty and scantily dressed and had exotic names like Pineapple, Jasmine, and Moonflower. One brought a plate of heavenly smelling empanadas. Another came with a platter of sliced pineapples. And yet another shaved my beard, trimmed my nails, and even massaged my aching feet.

For a long time, I lay in that tub dreaming of Saraatepe and the times we used to run naked along the beach and dive into the lake waters. Saraatepe with the long dark hair and shapely legs, the moonlight glistening off her wet skin.

My excitement grew, the blood in my body redistributed itself, and before long I found myself shamelessly thinking of Molly Mulvaney in the next room.

She was probably on the other side of the wall next to me, lying naked in a tub of warm water, long golden hair and firm breasts. My breath quickened. Would God forgive my wicked thoughts?

The peal of church bells shocked me out of my dream. Two o'clock in the afternoon. Or maybe three. Darkness would be only four hours away. Four hours until I could finally board a ship and get away from this cursed island with its chupacabras and pirates and beautiful women.

I climbed out of the tub. What to do for the next four hours? The only thing certain was I couldn't stay in this Garden of Temptation. But where to go?

Then it struck me. Of course. Why hadn't I thought of it before? I wrapped a towel around myself and pulled the attendant cord. A few moments later, Green Eyes came into the room.

"You look like a different person without the beard," she said.

"Would you please order a coach for me?"

CHAPTER 26

As soon as we rolled away, passing along the deserted streets in the direction of the waterfront, I took out the list César had given me. On it were seven names, but only three interested me:

Bishop Ureña, Inquisitor-General of Nicaragua.

Captain Gonzalez, military commander of Granada.

Father Menendez, Fiscál.

The first two I couldn't touch until I returned to Santo Domingo and retrieved the *cédulas* from the old Hebrew. But Father Menendez was a different matter. His *cédula* was in my pocket.

I memorized his account number and looked at the secret code—Malinche.

"Checkpoint," the driver announced.

We rolled to a stop. The door opened, letting in a whiff of horse manure. A soldier stuck in his head.

"Why are you stopping us?" I asked.

"Pirates, Father. Some of them are dressed as priests." He hopped onto the sideboard and looked at the top of the coach; other soldiers looked underneath. Then a young lieutenant came over and saluted. "Sorry to inconvenience you, Father, but please to step outside?"

"Why?"

"One of the pirates is a woman. She'd easily fit beneath a seat."

"*Ay, bendito*," I said, and stepped outside.

The air was cooler now, with threatening clouds and a nice breeze off the water. Thunder rumbled in the distance. I asked the officer if they'd arrested any pirates.

"Not a one. They must have flown."

They finished their search. I hopped back into the coach. The driver snapped the reins, and we rumbled along the cobbles again, following an ancient seawall that had been built to keep out the likes of Hawkins and Drake. Out the window I saw only soldiers and a few skinny dogs. Maybe this wasn't such a good idea. Not when the city was on full alert.

We rounded a long sweeping curve and stopped in front of my destination, *La Casa de Contratación*, a massive building that could have been the palace of a Moorish caliph. By then, a few drops of rain were falling. Across the street stood a row of Malinche trees, crimson and in full bloom, limbs whipping in the wind.

"God give me strength," I muttered and stepped down.

Armed guards stood atop the seawall, eyeing me in my cassock. More guards stood on turrets atop the building, and the heavy metal doors with their strap hinges looked as if they could withstand an assault by Vikings.

I paid the driver and marched into the building as if commanded by God Himself. The interior was better lit than the Alcaldia, thanks to a Moorish skylight that cast a soft glow across marbled floors. A guard directed me up the stairs and down a long corridor of offices marked with their functions—Taxes and Collections, Cartography, Ship Registration and Licenses, Fees and Fines, and finally the banking section, *Negocios de Banquero*.

Sentinels stood along the columns. Customers in stockings and plumed hats waited in long lines or sat on marble benches. A skinny little clerk with a pipe asked my business.

"Personal transaction."

He took in my freshly groomed looks, sniffed the air as if to say how regal I smelled, then gave me the number 26. "Take a seat over there," he said, smoke escaping from his mouth and nose. "Might take a while. Never seen it this crowded."

Sitting was the last thing I wanted to do. How could I sit and relax when I was about to defraud the account of a fiscál?

"Nineteen!"

I sat anyway and fidgeted with the canister in my pocket, reciting the account number and waiting for my number to be called. Other clients came in and were given numbers. From the outside came a clap of thunder.

"Twenty and twenty-one!"

The numbers rose, but not fast enough. What was going on back at the bath house? Where was that damned lieutenant? Had he given up or was he still making his case to the calificadór?

"Twenty-five!"

A man in the uniform of a high-ranking naval official pointed me out to his friend, and they both stared. Was it my cassock? Had they heard about pirates disguised as priests? But the worst of it was when a pair of soldiers marched into the room with a wanted poster. They looked around, then pasted their poster on the wall.

Four of five people sauntered over for a look. Suppose my name was on the list? Father Antonio Escofet, S.J., wanted for heresy, murder and theft. I stood and was about to make my way to the poster when an elderly gentleman with thick white hair and bushy mustache stepped out of a cubicle.

"Twenty-six."

He introduced himself as a licensed accountant—I didn't get the name—and led me into his cubicle, away from the eyes of the crowd. He motioned me into a chair and leaned forward. Not until then did I notice that only one of his eyes focused on me; the other looked off in a different direction. "How may I help you, Father? Hmm?"

"A personal transaction. I'd like to transfer—"

"*Ay, bendito*, that's all I've been getting today. People wanting to leave, to escape."

I told him about my long voyage from Nicaragua and said I was here to attend an ecclesiastical conference, but when I mentioned the bishop, he interrupted me.

"They say his throat was ripped out. Blood drained from his body. The sign of the devil cut into his chest. How do you explain such things? Hmm?"

"Well, I was at the Alcaldia this morning, and—"

"Then you've got all those women hanged upside down, blood drained from their bodies. It's scary, Father." Again he leaned forward. "It's the woman."

"What woman?"

"Pirate woman. They say she's a… *bruja*, a witch. Hmm?"

If I'd learned anything these past few weeks it was to never disagree with anyone in a position to help, especially if they were ignorant and superstitious.

"Yes," I said, "that would certainly explain it."

His tirade went on—pirates and Englishman should rot in hell. Billy would never have escaped except for the incompetence of the executioner. The problem with society was that the young had no moral values.

"I'm in a bit of a hurry."

"Another problem of society—everyone in a hurry. You said a personal transaction?"

"Correct. I'm purchasing property in Nicaragua. For the Church, of course. What I'd like to do is transfer some of my funds into the owner's account as payment."

"Why didn't you do your transfer back in Nicaragua? Hmm?"

"The conference with the bishop. It came up suddenly."

He rocked back in his chair. "What did you say your name is?"

"Father Jose Antonio Menendez, Fiscál of Nicaragua."

He swallowed hard. "Oh, my. I had no idea."

"Not a problem. I assume you'll need identification."

"That and your account number and code."

I used his ink and quill to jot down the information. He looked over what I'd written. "Malinche?" he said, frowning. "Wasn't she Cortez's mistress?"

"The same, but it's also the name of a beautiful tree with crimson flowers."

"Every time I hear that name I think of betrayal. Deceit. Like Judas in the Bible. Hmm?"

My mouth seemed to go dry. "I'm not sure I get your meaning."

"Oh, never mind. What ship did you say you came in on?"

"The *Sevilla*."

"Ah, yes." He stood and headed toward the back, taking the card.

The minutes went by. From outside came the rumble of thunder. Then the buzz of discourse from the rear. What was taking so long? Why did he need the name of the ship?

At last he came back with a ledger. "How much do you want to transfer?"

"Most of it, but I'm not sure of my balance."

"Most people know their balance down to the centavo."

"I'm not most people, sir. I have a clerk to handle these matters."

He squinted at the ledger. "Well, assuming you have no debits against your account, your balance is a bit more than nine-thousand gold escudos. Hmm?"

My breath caught. Nine-thousand escudos was more than a thousand ounces of gold, the equivalent of almost 150,000 *reales*. A common laborer earned a half real per day.

"Father?"

"Yes, yes, that sounds about right."

He asked to see my travel document as an extra layer of security. I surrendered it and sat there in a daze while he put together the paperwork. Nine thousand escudos was a fortune. Enough to go away with Saraatepe and the boys and become a powerful *hacendado* in Chile or Argentina. Grape vines and servants. A big house and carriage. Workers tipping their hats.

Don Antonio.

The door behind me opened, and in walked the skinny little clerk with his pipe clenched between his teeth, bringing with him a strong smell of tobacco. "Here it is," he said to the banker. He stared at me a moment, said, "Father," and quit the office.

"What is that?" I asked, suddenly alarmed.

"Latest report from the *Sevilla*. All captains have to file reports with us. This one was filed at—hmm—looks like nine by the clock this morning, about the time of the hanging."

My big hacienda in Chile became smaller. The banker looked over the report. "*Dios Mio*. Two passengers killed." He stared at me with those unfocused eyes.

"Why didn't you sign the addendum?"

"What addendum?"

"The one written by the first officer." He waved it in my face as if it were a death sentence.

"I didn't see that one."

An eyebrow lifted. Suspicion showed all over his wrinkled face. "Well, let me read the last couple of lines... and these are the lieutenant's words: 'I believe the evidence supports my contention that the man who calls himself Father Menendez is an imposter.'"

I almost came out of my chair. "That lieutenant is an idiot. He made the same accusation this morning... at the Alcaldia. The calificadór threatened to arrest him."

It must have been the right thing to say because the banker settled back in his chair. "You were at the Alcaldia this morning?"

"Indeed, I was."

"And you know our local calificadór?"

"We go back years."

"Ah, then there's the solution. If you'll be kind enough to get him down here and vouch for you, we can take care of this matter in minutes. Hmm?"

"Are you saying I can't transfer my own money?"

"I'm sorry, Father. I'm sure you are who you say you are, but we owe it to our depositors to protect them. Hmm?"

He stood as if to say this meeting was over.

I slammed the door on my way out and hurried through the waiting room, my mind telling me to get out before something worse happened. At the exit, I noticed another wanted poster on a column, with people standing around. I glanced behind to be sure no one was following and paused long enough to read.

Wanted, Dead or Alive
English pirate, Billy Chupacabra—50 Pieces of Eight reward

The girl pirate known as Molly—10 Pieces of Eight reward
Other common English pirates—5 Pieces of Eight reward

My name was not there. But these posters were probably all over the city. The servants at the bathhouse would see them. So would Green Eyes. And they'd be wondering about the girl with the golden hair. And dusk was still two hours away.

CHAPTER 27

Rain was still falling when we reached the bath house, everything gray and gloomy, but no soldiers. I paid the driver, hurried over the wet cobbles, and rapped on the door. It opened, and there stood Moonflower, the young girl who'd earlier massaged my feet.

"Have the soldiers been here?" I asked.

"No, Father."

She led me up the wooden stairs, past the cats, and around a corner to the balcony that overlooked the garden. I looked left and right and into the overhead. If soldiers were here, now was the time for them to strike. But there were only the meowing cats, the soapy smells, the patter of rain, and Enrique sitting in a wicker chair.

"The devil you been?" he asked.

I almost didn't recognize him with his slicked-down hair and new clothing. The swelling in his face was gone, and the only sign of the wounds I'd inflicted on him was a bandage. I sank into a chair, waited to catch my breath, and told him about the wanted posters.

"Ten Pieces of Eight for Molly. We have to get her out of here."

"Are you crazy? Best thing is leave her here."

"A good priest does not his flock abandon."

"Look, you can stay here and fry with her if you want, but I'm going to the landing." He picked up his cane and headed for the door.

"Hold on, Enrique. It's raining. Give me a minute to think."

He went back to his chair, still grumbling. I closed my eyes and let my mind wander back to all the plays I'd performed, all the dramas of damsels in distress:

Andromeda, chained naked to a rock.

Griselda, of Chaucer's Canterbury Tales.

Rain beat against the window, and before long damsels were swirling around like flying ghosts: Eurydice. The Spanish Lady. Even Don Quixote's Dulcinea of La Mancha, whose eyes are sun, her lips coral, her hands ivory, her fairness snow…

Her fairness snow?

Suppose she wasn't fair at all? Suppose she was as dark as Green Eyes? "You're right," I said to Enrique. "I'll tell her."

In time, the rain gave way to a misty foggy gloom. And finally darkness, which brought out the most infernal hoots, croaks, coos, and a high-pitched chirr that Green Eyes called the music of coquis. Dogs howled. Roosters crowed. Even the cats sounded restless.

I shed my cassock and changed into the clothing of a gentleman, and at the stroke of seven, Green Eyes appeared with news that our coach had arrived. We followed her out the back and along a forested path that came out on a side street where two coaches waited, lanterns lit and doors open. "What's the other coach for?" Enrique asked.

"It's best you not know."

We rolled into the night. Dampness seeped into the coach. The darkness was broken by an occasional yellow glow in a window. Other coaches followed, lanterns swaying, springs creaking, wheels rumbling on the cobbles, carrying passengers to the landing.

Enrique leaned over and sniffed my clothing. "Why do you smell like chocolate?"

I was wondering if I should tell him when the driver slid back the partition. "Checkpoint."

I didn't see Enrique make the sign of the cross, but I felt the motion. A soldier with a lantern swung open the door, letting in fresh ocean air. Behind him, Fortress El Morro loomed up like a medieval castle, lit by torches along the ramparts.

"Speak to me," said the soldier, waving the lantern. "Say something in Christian so I know you're Spaniards."

"How fares the search?"

"Not good. It's like they flew away on broomsticks." He gestured at Enrique. "You, *Cabro*. Do you speak Christian?"

"Watch your tongue, soldier. I'm not a *cabro*. I'm Basque. It's also a language."

"Basque is not a Christian tongue."

"It's as Christian as that dog shit of a language you call Castilian."

I jabbed Enrique with an elbow. Another soldier stepped into the light. "They sound Christian enough." He twirled his finger and told us to go ahead. As soon as the door shut, I said to Enrique, "Sometimes you have to swallow your anger."

"No, Father, a Basque the other cheek does not turn."

We rattled on, traversing a steep bluff down to the embarkation building. Waves crashed against the breakwater, sending up clouds of spray. The usual crowd had already gathered, as well as passengers pushing to get inside. There were also cows and sheep for boarding, horse-led wagons carrying crates of chickens, and mountains of bags, boxes, bundles, and chests.

We collected the bags we'd left that morning and pushed into a dimly lit waiting room. All around were other travelers trying to escape the madness—men with smoking pipes, women with kerchiefs over their faces, entire families with children and dogs. Even a caged monkey. Smoke drifted to the ceiling, swirling like fog in a swamp. My eyes stung. My stomach churned.

"What do you think will happen to her?" Enrique asked.

"Don't tell me you're developing a conscious."

He was trying to explain when a bearded man in a maritime uniform stepped forward and rang a cow bell. "*Oigan, oigan*! Tenders for the *Toledo* ready for boarding! First class only!"

We fell into line, and that was when Enrique grabbed my elbow and pointed toward the section reserved for Negroes and Indians. "*Coño*, is that Green Eyes?"

I didn't have to look. I'd seen her come in with Molly: two *femmes d'coleur libre* chatting in French. Big hoop earrings, crimson scarves, and enough jangling bracelets to do a Gypsy proud.

"Stop pointing," I said. "Just settle down."

"But that's Green Eyes. She's with a colored girl who—"

"If you don't shut up, I'm going to shoot you with my pistol."

He was still gawking when a bright flash lit the room, followed by a loud boom. Not the boom of thunder, but the boom of cannon. There were more flashes and more booms. The building shook. The word "Pirates!" flew around like shrieking bats.

Then everyone was running for the exits.

Molly rushed forward, and the three of us surged through the embarkation door with a mob of pushing, cursing passengers.

"What happened to Green Eyes?" Enrique asked Molly.

"She's not coming."

Three or four flat-bottomed tenders lay at the dock, their oarsmen staring at the fortress above us. The guns on the ramparts fired in sequence, one dull thud after the other. Streaks of light arced into the heavens, casting a pulsating glow, illuminating ships, water, and faces. "Flares!" cried an oarsman. "They're looking for pirates."

"There they are," someone shouted. "In a sloop."

I followed their gestures to a single-mast ship in the bay, barely visible through fog and smoke, its sails catching the wind, heading for the open sea.

"They won't get far," said another voice.

The guns on the ramparts went off with a deafening roar, their barrels shooting out long tongues of flame. The pressure almost blew off my hat. The smell of gunpowder drifted down like a whiff of hell. Plumes of water mushroomed around the pirate ship, and I imagined Billy Goatsucker at the bow, urging on his pirates.

Molly squeezed in so close I smelled the chocolate we'd used to darken her face. Everything around us sparkled and glowed, and we were watching the pirate sloop, expecting it to disintegrate, when the dreaded words, "Fire ship!" exploded all around.

Whistles blew. There were shouts and curses, sails unfurling, anchors coming up, cables casting off. "Let's go," I said, and pulled Molly onto the nearest tender with other passengers.

Ropes were cast off. Everyone scrambled into a seat. The oarsmen rowed like the devil was after us, and we were putting the dock behind when the entire horizon lit up in a series of brilliant red flashes, as if a hurricane had unleashed its fury all at once.

"Broadside! Must be our warships."

Even before we heard the boom, there came the terrifying whoosh of cannon balls over our heads. A ball landed atop the fortress. Others went no telling where—maybe all the way into San Juan Bautista. "Why are they shooting at us?" yelled a passenger.

"Because they're English, you idiot."

The gunners in the fortress turned their attention to the fire ship. The entire place lit up in blinding flashes, as if lightning were striking all around. Their booms rippled the water.

And still the fire ship drifted straight toward us.

A ship loomed ahead, with crewmen in the rigging. They were waving their arms and yelling to hurry when another broadside lit the horizon. A splash of water blossomed off to starboard, sending spray over the tender and spinning us to starboard.

Molly grabbed my arm. The pilot at the rudder corrected our drift, and a moment or so later, we thumped against a ship.

In the flashes I could clearly read the name—*Nuestra Señora de la Sevilla*, the same ship on which I'd killed El Moro and Father Menendez. The lieutenant's ship.

"Our tickets are for the *Toledo*," I said.

Everyone but me burst into nervous laughter. "You want to swim to the *Toledo*," said an oarsman. "Go ahead. She just took a hit."

"Where is the *Sevilla* going?"

"Out of here, that's where."

A rope ladder came down. The oarsmen scrambled up like monkeys, helping with bags and boxes, cursing, urging us on.

I helped Molly over the gunwale, climbed over myself, and almost bumped into the lieutenant. There he stood, this little misfit, following the progress of the fighting. He'd seen me in my bloody shirt, seen me as a priest, and would soon see me as a gentleman.

"Wipe that chocolate off your face," I said to Molly. "Do it now."

"Fire ship's coming straight toward us!"

It was larger than I imagined. A captured warship, maybe, with gun ports and two masts. Englishmen were still aboard, stoking the fires, opening ports, guiding her toward their targets. Even as I looked they began jumping overboard and climbing into smaller boats.

A yardarm came down with a thundering crash. Debris and sparks flew in all directions. This set the lieutenant in a retreat toward the forecastle, cursing, waving a pistol. “Are you people crazy?” he yelled at the passengers. “Get down! She’s going to blow!”

CHAPTER 28

I pulled Molly below the gunwale with other passengers. Rosaries came out. There were whimpers and prayers, signings of the cross. The reflection on our canvas grew brighter, turning into a reddish glow. "Oh, God," someone said. "She's going to hit us."

By then, the fire ship had drifted so close I could feel the heat, hear the pop and crackle of the flames. Then I saw the name beneath the bowsprit: *Nuestra Señora de la Concepción.*

A Spanish ship, captured by the English.

The cables gave way. Jets of flame shot from the hatches. Sparks ascended into the heavens like thousands of little stars. Tongues of fire crawled up her rigging.

Then she drifted past.

Crew and passengers cheered. I felt a breeze, and that was when I realized we were moving, sailing into the open sea. Thank you, dear God. Thank you.

The sounds of battle faded; the glow melded into fog and smoke. And I was beginning to relax when there came a blinding flash followed seconds later by the explosion.

Sails fluttered like sheets on a wash line. The blast sucked the air out of my lungs. All around were expressions of awe and dread.

It took a long time for the flickers to die. No one spoke, not the crewmen and not the passengers. But I could sense their agony. The hated English had once more diminished the greatness of Spain. They could be behind us this very moment, out there in the darkness.

The gloom darkened, and somewhere amid this despair, a man began reciting the Lord's Prayer. Others joined in. And even I, disgraced priest that I was, added my voice to the chorus.

"Stand by for the captain!"

The captain's voice, powerful and clear, cut through the darkness: "Fellow Spaniards. What you saw tonight was a great insult to our country. To our king. To our flag…"

There was no moon to illuminate his face. Only intermittent flashes of heat lightning, but as he spoke, I remembered him from my other voyages—a large bearded man in crimson and blue. He went on, saying how proud he was of the men and officers.

"You saved the ship. You are truly the best of Castile. I thank you. I salute you. May God bless Spain, and may God bless his Most Royal Highness, King Phillip the Fifth."

His words set off a clamor, with stomping feet and clanging bells. "*Viva España*!" echoed from bow to stern and into the rigging, followed by chants of "Death to the English!"

I did not join the demonstration. Why should I, a Catalonian, care if pirates raided the ports of these religious fanatics who would gladly burn me at the stake?

"Why do you not chant?" Molly asked.

"I should ask you the same question."

In time, the chanting gave way to a rousing version of *Que Viva España*. Then a fiddler struck up *Ave Maria*. As bad as it was, I felt myself choking with emotion. Would I ever sing it again?

Yes, I told myself. At the funerals of Captain Gonzalez and the bishop.

Molly snuggled closer. "Pray tell, if God is a Spaniard, why He let the pirates escape?"

"What makes you so sure they escaped?"

She placed a finger to my lips. "Later," she whispered, and pulled my hand to her lips.

"What was that for?"

"Because you are my protector, kind sir, and I am in your debt."

I couldn't see her face, but I felt her warmth. A sinful spark ignited inside me. How easily, I thought, one could step off the path of the righteous. God might forgive murder—if murder be done in self-defense. He might forgive theft—if theft be for noble reasons.

But would He forgive adultery?

"Are you afraid?" she whispered.

Before I could answer, there appeared in the companionway the faint glow of a lantern, followed by a voice I recognized as the old steward who lit the morning candles.

"Listen up, passengers! We're heading below. Move this way."

We groped our way in darkness, around poles and cables and stays and Lord knows what other obstructions, eventually reaching the companionway hatch.

"Come on, folks. Move it! We don't have all night."

"Where are you taking us?" asked a voice from the darkness.

"The galley."

Down the ladder I went with Molly, grasping the railing, following a line of shadowy figures until I was back at the same spot where I'd showered off the blood.

In front of the cabin where I'd killed El Moro and Father Menendez.

The warmth I'd felt only moments before turned to ice. The horror flashed through my mind. The savage blows to El Moro's head. The spatter of blood. The look on Father Menendez's face when I drove the dagger into his stomach. Even more troubling was the fear the old steward would recognize me. How was I going to explain how a priest named Menendez was now a gentleman named Gonzalez?

"Come on, folks, keep it moving. Galley's this way."

We followed his lantern like a crew of drunks, holding onto each other, ducking beneath beams until we entered the galley where I'd had my first taste of café.

The portholes were closed, locking in an unpleasant stuffiness and the smell of burned oil. The ship rose and fell. It seemed to have a permanent cant to larboard. We held on to anything we could grab—columns, the counter, the low-hanging beams.

The steward hung his lantern from a beam. "Listen up, folks. What we're going to do now is get your names. Eh? Make sure there's no pirates among you."

We stayed back in the shadows, grateful for the poor light. When my turn came, I pulled my hat low over my face and handed him the *pasajes*. With hardly a glance, he gave me the key to Cabin 3—the same cabin I'd occupied with Enrique.

"Our best," he said.

Enrique was assigned the cabin across from us. The steward lit candles, passed them around, and told us in his gruff seaman's voice that we were sailing under blackout conditions. "At three bells of the First Watch—soon—you must be in your cabins, gear stowed. Do not open ports until all candles are doused. Eh? And no wandering about the passageway."

"Where is this ship going?" asked a rotund man with his equally heavy wife.

"Who knows, *caballero*?"

He headed for the door. "I'll be making my rounds after the bells. If I see a glowing candle… or a lit pipe, I'll take it that you're signaling pirates. Eh?"

We found our bags and stumbled down the passageway to our cabins. I pulled Molly inside, closed the door, and paused to take in the familiar surroundings.

Molly plopped onto the bunk and swept her eyes over the place.

"Don't get used to it," I said. "You're staying in Enrique's cabin. He'll be staying here."

"I'll not stay by myself, I won't."

"Why not, child? You'll have privacy."

"The darkness. It scares me, it does." She jumped up and wrapped her arms around me. "Please not to make me to stay by myself. Please." Tears welled up in her eyes. She pressed against me, her face next to mine. "I pray you, kind sir, relent."

Normally I wasn't nervous around beautiful women, but Molly was no ordinary woman, and there was nothing ordinary about the circumstances. Worse, she possessed a powerful allure, this pirate girl who smelled of chocolate and cinnamon, and I'm not sure what I'd have done if Enrique hadn't chosen that moment to limp into the cabin. He glared at Molly, who was bathed in a little pool of light next to the candle, her long hair falling to her shoulder, tears in her eyes, looking like an angel in need of comfort.

"We need to talk," he said.

I followed him out the door and into his cabin, ducking my head to enter. His single candle barely disturbed the darkness. "Say it, Enrique. Get it off your mind."

He sank onto the bunk. "She's a pirate, Father. That lieutenant will sniff her out."

"She's not a pirate and stop calling me 'Father.' I'm an official with La Casa."

"You'll not fool the lieutenant."

"Last time he saw me, I was a priest with a beard. Now I'm a gentleman with a mustache. All I have to do is avoid him."

"You haven't avoided him yet."

"Stop worrying. Let's talk about it tomorrow?"

"You like her, don't you?"

"Not in the way you think."

"Please, Father. I'm not stupid."

I used the wash basin, waited a few minutes to give Molly privacy, and eased back into the passageway. The only light came from cracks around cabin doors. From all around came the pop and groan of timbers, and maybe it was my imagination, but even in the passageway I caught a whiff of chocolate and cinnamon.

I knocked. Molly said, "Come in," and I stepped back into the cabin in time to see her undoing the ribbons on her blouse.

My heart raced. Her smile seemed to increase the warmth in the cabin. I latched the door and turned back to see her taking off an earring. Oh, the loveliness of those eyes that were locked onto mine. The moist lips. The way her darkened hair fell to her shoulders, shimmering in the candlelight.

"There's something I should tell you," I said.

The ship plunged into a trough. We grabbed each other for support and ended up on the deck. Our lips found each other. She ran her hand beneath my shirt and nibbled on my ear, her breath hot on my cheeks. The very air seemed to ignite around us, and I was kissing her neck and shoulders, and her breasts, when from the outside came the clang of a bell.

"Stand by for lights out!"

We both jumped up as if we'd been caught. Molly muttered a foreign word I did not understand. Then she wrapped her arms around me from the back.

"Are you angry?"

"No, *mija*, but we've got things to do before the bells." I shoved our bags into the locker, yanked off my shoes, laid out the pistol and dagger for easy access, and was pulling off my stockings when three bells sounded, followed by the cries of the steward.

"Lamps out!"

I blew out the candles and opened the port to let in fresh air. Beside me, I heard the rustle of clothing, and Molly climbing into her hammock. She reached for my arm. "Father?"

"Stop calling me 'Father.' We're supposed to be married."

"What should I call you?"

"Any endearment you'd like."

"Are you really a priest, dulce?"

I climbed into my hammock. "I'll answer your questions if you'll answer mine."

"Ask me, kind sir. I have nothing to hide, I don't."

I had a hundred questions for her, but before I could form the first one, the steward came down the passageway again, rattling his nightstick on the bulkhead.

"By the grace of God, the seas are calm… sails are full a-drawing. Lights are doused… and all a-snoring. Stay in your cabins until first light dawning. *Tan tranquila es la noche…*"

His song faded. I turned back to Molly. "Tell me about Billy."

CHAPTER 29

She hesitated, and when she finally spoke, her voice was lyrical, poetic, even in her broken Castilian. She said Billy's real name was William Youngblood, an English officer, a sometimes privateer, which was another name for pirate under the English flag. And like all pirates he'd adopted a fearsome nom de guerre, Billy Goatsucker.

"Vampire Jack gave him that name, he did."

"Vampire Jack?"

"The pirate you clubbed in the plaza. You should have killed him, you should."

"Why?"

"Because he's the devil, he is. Kills women and marks them with the sign."

"If your friend, Billy, is an English officer, why doesn't he stop this Vampire Jack?"

"Only the devil controls Jack."

She tried to explain the difference between the Royal English navy and privateers, but the more she talked the more they all sounded like pirates. They all raided ports and cut off ears and destroyed Spanish shipping and scared the wits out of old women and little children. And now they had me on the *Sevilla* instead of the *Toledo*, in a hammock with one of their women beside me.

"Something else I should tell you," she whispered.

"What, *mija*, tell me."

"They didn't capture me in New Orleans. I went with Billy of my own accord, I did."

The ship's bell sounded four times. I asked her why she ran away with Billy.

"First I want to know if you're a priest."

I sighed, and there in total darkness, with no sounds but our voices and the protests of the ship, I owned up that, yes, I was a former priest on the run from the Inquisition, and I'd survived by changing identity from port to port, and now the three of us had the misfortune of being on the same ship as a fanatical lieutenant who was determined to haul me back to the stake.

"I knew it," Molly said. "Knew it when you saved me in the plaza." She lowered her voice to almost a whisper. "What are you going to do about the lieutenant?"

"Nothing. He's not going to find us out." I reached over and took her hand. "Why did you run away with Billy?"

"It's a long story."

"We've got all night."

She drew in a deep breath and told me about swamps and mosquitoes and poverty and sickness, so when Billy came along she gladly packed her bags and ran away to what she thought would be a life of romance and adventure.

"And a sorry choice it was. I thought Billy would be true, but we had not lived long in our intimacy before I realized he was given to drinking and whoring." She choked up. "I prayed to Mother Mary, and I don't know if she rightly heard me, so finally what I said to him was this: 'Kind sir, I value my pride, and I will not abide your whoring.'"

"And?"

"Rebuffed me like a dog, he did, so I went pit a pat."

"Pit a pat?"

"Left him. I thought it was over, but Billy sent Jack to fetch me to his chambers. I went, thinking Billy had altered his behavior. He had changed all right, but for the worse."

She broke down in long bitter sobs. I rubbed her shoulder and told her how sorry I was and agreed that most men were cheating dogs. After a few minutes, she said, "The worst of it is Jack will be coming for me again, and this time he'll want to kill you."

"He'll have to get in queue. Besides, Jack is probably dead by now."

"Only way to kill Jack is cut off his head."

A flash of lightning lit the cabin, and I lay there thinking it was bad enough that I had the lieutenant to worry about. And Sampson and Captain Gonzalez. Now I'd been marked for grievous harm by a pair of lunatic pirates whose woman I'd saved from misery, and I hadn't even lain with her yet, at least not in the biblical sense.

The ship bell struck six times—eleven by the clock. Weariness overcame me. I pulled the blanket over myself and closed my eyes. And the next thing I knew, Molly was in the hammock with me, tugging at my clothes.

The cabin should have been dark. It wasn't. I could see every feature in that lovely face—her freckles, her brown eyes, her seductive smile. I said this was wrong, that I was a married man, that she should get back into her hammock, but she responded by pulling off her gown. Raw desire consumed me. The desire of a man who had not known a woman's touch for more than a year. She kissed my lips, my shoulders and chest, and when I thought I would explode with pleasure, she whispered in that strange accent, "Not here."

"Where?"

"Across the water. Beyond the mist."

We climbed out of the hammock, and in the kind of logic that makes sense only in dreams, I followed her out the door, up the ladder, across the deck, over the water and back to the bathhouse in San Juan Bautista, where we immersed ourselves in the warmth of the tub. Candles glowed. Music played. The nudes on the walls became Pineapple, Lemon Rose, Jasmine and Moonflower. They danced around us, swirling, smiling, clapping their hands like Zarzuela performers. The beat of drums filled my ears.

"Now," Molly whispered.

She straddled me in the tub, and pulled me into that wonderful, velvety warmth I'd first experienced with Saraatepe. I smelled her perfume, felt her breath against my face. The cries that escaped her lips became my cries. The drums beat faster. And just when I reached the point of no return, that damn steward came plodding down the corridor with his nightstick, rapping on cabin doors and singing his morning song about fire for candles and first light dawning.

A hand shook my shoulder. "Dulce, wake up."

I sat up, and as my head cleared, I realized I was back in the darkness of my cabin, and the tub of water in which I'd been immersed with Molly was fading. And the hand on my arm belonged to a girl with whom I'd committed adultery only in a dream.

"It's the steward," Molly said. "Don't we need candles?"

I pulled on breeches, hurried out, and found myself in the midst of five or six other passengers, most of them as barefooted, half-dressed, messy-haired, and as sleepy looking as I felt. The rotund man was there too, demanding to know where we were going.

"All I know is we're on a westward bearing," said the steward.

"Tell the captain I'd like to see him," said the man. "In my cabin."

"The captain doesn't take orders from passengers. You can speak to the first officer if you'd like. His name is Ramos. Lieutenant Ramos."

The man took a candle and waddled back to his cabin, slamming the door. The smell of frying bacon sharpened the hollow in my stomach. From the deck above came the crow of a cock.

"Roosters on the ship?" asked a sleepy voice.

"The captain's dinner."

Everyone laughed. The steward passed around candles and told us in his broken mariner's voice that the lieutenant wanted everyone in the galley in a half hour. "No exceptions."

"For what?" I asked.

"He didn't consult me, *caballero*, but if I had to venture, I'd say it's about our destination."

I retreated into the cabin in time to catch the first rays of light streaming through the open porthole. Molly was standing barefoot next to the hammock, a blanket around her, staring with those big brown eyes. "Did I hear him say the lieutenant wants to see us?"

"Not just us. Everybody. Better get dressed."

Not long afterward, the three of us crowded into the galley with other passengers. The lighting was poor, the air heavy with pipe smoke and cooking smells, and it seemed as if everyone had an opinion about the meeting. Most agreed it was about destination, but the heavyset man claimed otherwise.

"Isn't it clear?" he said. "Pirates are on the loose. He wants to know we're all Spaniards."

Molly shrank against me. She had changed her dress and done up her hair Spanish fashion, with *peineta* and a lacy *mantilla*, but her expression told me she was as worried about the lieutenant as I was. "Do I look foreign to you?" she asked.

"No, Molly, you look like my beautiful señora."

"Then why are those people staring?"

"They're admiring you, dulce, saying what a lucky man I am."

"Enrique doesn't look very happy."

"Enrique never looks happy."

"What if the lieutenant questions me?"

"Spanish men don't question other men's wives."

She glanced around. "Oh, no."

"What?"

"That man sitting next to Enrique. Blue eyes and light hair. He could be one of Billy's men."

"Just because he's light complexioned doesn't mean he's English."

We ate. We drank café until my head was spinning. People around us grumbled about the lieutenant. Molly kept insisting the light-haired man was an Englishman, and I was trying to get her to hold down her voice when the room fell suddenly quiet.

Into the galley marched the steward and two armed marines.

Behind them came Lieutenant Ramos.

CHAPTER 30

Molly uttered an oath. I pulled a wad of cotton from my pocket and stuffed it between my cheeks and gums to give myself a fuller face. The steward rapped his nightstick on the counter. "*Oigan! Oigan!*" He opened the manifest in which he'd recorded our names the evening before.

"Alvarez!"

"Present."

"Santibañez!"

"Here."

The call went on. Only one person was absent, a passenger with the odd name of Golondrina. The lieutenant, all starch and polish in a crimson and blue uniform, looked perturbed. He got right in the steward's face. "Weren't you told to get everyone here?"

"Yes, Lieutenant."

"When I give an order, I expect it to be obeyed."

He laid so many words of scorn on the steward that I thought the poor fellow would dissolve in tears. "Don't just stand there like a helpless dog. Go find him! And be quick about it."

The steward scurried away. Then the lieutenant turned his attention to us. "I'll come straight to the quick. Last night we were supposed to verify your identity, but in the confusion all we could do was weigh anchor and set sail. We'll complete the process now."

A chorus of groans filled the room. Molly took my hand and held it in plain sight. Enrique shot me his I-told-you-so-look. The fair-haired man raised a hand, and when he spoke, it was in perfect Castilian. "They verified our identification at the checkpoint."

"So what? Anyone could have slipped past in the confusion."

"But didn't we see the pirates escaping last night?"

The lieutenant strode all the way to his table. "Let me ask you something, señor. Did you get a good look at the men in that sloop?"

"It was dark. They were too far away, but—"

"So what you're saying is you don't know who was on that sloop. For all you know, that sloop could have been nothing more than a diversion."

The man shrugged but said nothing. The lieutenant backed against a support column. "Can anyone here tell me what a pirate looks like? Anyone?"

No one uttered a word.

"Come on, folks, tell me how a pirate looks. Back at the hanging, they were dressed as priests." He paused as if to let his words sink in. "Priests, mind you. Men of God. Others wore regular clothing… just like you ladies and gentlemen in this galley. Imagine that."

He paced the deck like a restless dog, stopping here and there to peer into faces, coming so close that I smelled tobacco on his uniform. He paused to stare at Molly. And when he turned his eyes on me, I felt my heart in my throat.

"We've been told that two of the pirates got separated from the others. One was injured in the plaza. Eyewitnesses saw him staggering away like a drunk, blood running down his face."

"Vampire Jack," Molly whispered.

"The other was a woman, young and pretty. You might have seen her at the hanging."

Molly looked like she wanted to bolt, and I could feel panic building in me as well.

"So what I'm saying is we need to be vigilant. Look for anything suspicious. Listen for foreign accents. That's why I'm going to ask everyone to stand and say something in Christian."

He pointed to Enrique. "You, señor, let's begin with you."

Enrique struggled up with the help of his walking stick and glared at the lieutenant. Not a trace of fear showed in his face. "Would you like me to sing *Viva España* or quote a passage from Cervantes?"

The place burst into laughter. A smile crossed the lieutenant's face. "Well, well, well," he said. "If it isn't the bank guard from Cartagena."

Molly and I exchanged looks. If the lieutenant could sniff out Enrique, surely he could see through my disguise. He stepped closer to Enrique. "What happened to Father… uh…?"

"Menendez. Last I saw him, he was going to Bayamón."

"Interesting, and now you're going back to Santo Domingo to report the heretic's death?"

"I'm sure they'll want to hear my report."

"Convenient, wouldn't you say? The bodies buried at sea. Everyone goes home, the heretic still on the loose."

Enrique narrowed his eyes. "Maybe you could explain that in plain Castilian."

"You know exactly what I'm saying. You and that heretic… oh, what is his name? Father Antonio, isn't it? The two of you cooked up this entire thing, didn't you?"

"Father Antonio is dead."

"I think not. Father Antonio is still alive, pretending to be Father Menendez."

To my horror, he glanced at me. My mouth with the cotton in it felt as dry as the sands of Morocco. He turned back to Enrique. "How much did he pay you?"

"No one paid me anything."

"Oh, no? Then why are you lying?"

Enrique said nothing, but I could see fire in his eyes.

"This case is far from closed. When we get to Santo Domingo, we're going to discuss it with the Captain of Customs. Eh? Also, with that cavalry captain, Gonzalez."

He turned to walk away, and that was when Enrique slammed the cane on the table.

I jumped as if I'd been shot. So did Molly and everyone else in the place. The two marines trotted over with their muskets. I thought the lieutenant would arrest Enrique right there. Instead, he stepped back to Enrique's table, smirking, as if enjoying the moment.

"Is there something else you'd like to say?"

Silence ruled the galley. Everyone stared, listening. I had an awful feeling Enrique was going to use his cane on the lieutenant's head. Instead, he leaned forward and placed both hands on the table. His face was red, his mouth twisted in rage.

"What you're forgetting, Lieutenant, is that I'm the one who got the shit beat out of me…, and I'll be damned if I'm going to let you treat me the way you treated that poor old steward." He leveled a finger. "On this ship, you may be master of the deck. The *numero uno*. But when we set foot in Santo Domingo, we'll be equals, and I'll make bold you not cross my path."

"Are you threatening me, señor?"

"Call it a challenge. We'll see how brave you are without your bodyguards." He shot a venomous glance at the two marines and stormed out of the galley.

By then, Molly's hand was gripping mine so tightly her fingernails were biting my flesh. I sat there as gap-mouthed as everyone else. The buzz of discourse started up again. The lieutenant rubbed his beard as if nothing had happened, then stepped over to our table.

"Your turn, *caballero*. Please to stand and identify yourself."

A few minutes before, I'd been ready to run out of the place and jump into the ocean. Now, after the way the lieutenant had humiliated the steward and tried to bully Enrique, I felt like pulling out my pistol and shooting him between the eyes.

"My name is Gonzalez," I said. "And what might your name be?"

"I'm the one asking the questions."

"I don't recall anyone introducing you."

He drew in a sharp breath. "My name is Ramos. Lieutenant Porfirio Ramos-Calderón."

"And your position?"

"First officer. Anything else?"

"Is it your job to harass passengers?"

He gave an agitated snort, then made a complete circuit of the table, his shoes thudding on the oaken deck, glaring at Molly the way a lascivious man leers at a prostitute. This set my blood to an even higher boil. "My wife," I said. "Marie Bernadette Duval de Gonzalez."

"French?"

"From the French side of Hispaniola."

"And what is the purpose of your travel?"

"*Negocios*, Lieutenant. I'm with the *Casa de Contratación* in San Juan Bautista."

He took a step backward as if realizing he was in the presence of power. The *Casa de Contratación* probably owned the ship. He swallowed hard. "And your position?"

"Head of Ship Licenses and Registration."

A flush came over his face. I took a long sip of café, set down the tin, and squinted my eyes. "Is your captain's name Navarro? Big man with a beard?"

"Why do you ask?"

"Because I have a dispatch for him… from the Inquisitor-General's office. The calificadór delivered it himself. Tell me your name again?"

"Ramos. Lieutenant Ramos. *A sus órdenes*." He touched his hat.

"Ah, yes, Ramos. The calificadór mentioned your name."

The lieutenant looked suddenly ill, and I could only imagine his turmoil. First La Casa, now the Church; the two most powerful institutions in the colonies.

I puffed myself up and was about to deliver a final *golpe* when a young crewman came rushing into the galley, alarm showing in his face. He double-quicked to the lieutenant.

"Begging your pardon, sir. Captain says to report topside."

"*¿Qué pasó, hombre*?"

The crewman whispered something I couldn't hear. The lieutenant's eyes widened. He rushed to one of the scuttle ports for a look, then trotted out with the marines.

No sooner had they left than the entire place turned chaotic: benches scraping, passengers rushing to portholes, voices asking, "What is it?"

"Ship! It could be pirates."

Molly sprang to her feet. "Billy," she blurted. "It's got to be him."

CHAPTER 31

No one heard her. They were too busy rushing out, trying to get topside for a better view. Molly wanted to go topside as well, but I stopped at Enrique's cabin and pounded on the door. While we waited, we could hear shouts to lay on more canvas.

"Hear that?" Molly said. "We're in trouble if it's Billy."

The door swung open. Enrique stuck out his head. His eyes were bloodshot, as if he'd been crying. "Now I've done it," he said. "I don't know what came over me."

"You did the right thing," I said. "I've never been more proud."

"What's the excitement about?"

"Might be pirates. Why don't you go topside for a look?"

"I'm going too," Molly said.

"No, Molly, it's best the three of us not be seen together."

"Then I'll go by myself."

I took her arm. "Listen, Molly. Please. You heard what I told the lieutenant about a dispatch. I have to write a letter to the captain."

"That letter won't mean *mierda* if Billy catches us."

I pulled her into our cabin anyway and latched the door. She headed to the port for a look. From the closet, I took out Father Menendez's paper and quill and began writing—in Latin to make it more official, without paragraphs or spaces between words.

> *Esteemed Captain Navarro: By these letters, I hereby direct you and first officer, Lieutenant Porfirio Ramos-Calderón, to present yourselves in person in the Inquisitor-General's office, the purpose being to explain an unsubstantiated charge brought by said*

lieutenant against one of our most honorable and esteemed priests, Father José Antonio Menendez....

The shouts on the upper deck grew louder. Molly paced as I wrote. "You can't outrun Billy," she said. "He'll catch us, he will."

I signed as the calificadór, blotted the fresh ink, folded it, addressed it to the captain, and sealed it with red candle wax, using the seal of the Inquisitor-General. "Now we can go," I said.

Molly wanted to hurry, but something nagged at me. Not until we were on the ladder did I remember. "Wait here," I told Molly.

I retraced my steps to the cabin and opened the door. There they were, the three bags I'd hauled all the way from Santo Domingo: My old sea-bag. Father Menendez's bag. El Moro's smelly bag. The cleaning crew would recognize them.

I hung a *NO PERTURBEN* tag on the door.

When I returned, Molly was on the top rung of the ladder. "Enrique's over there," she said, pointing to the larboard stern where passengers had bunched up at the gunwale.

Lines and cables were being pulled this way and that. More sails were going up. A gun crew labored over a cannon at the stern, and the air was permeated with curses and commands, the pounding of hammers, and endless shouts between the crow's nest and the captain.

"Hull up. Laying on more canvas!"

"How many masts?"

"Three. Looks like a frigate!"

Molly mumbled a foreign word. "Do you know what hull-up means? It means they're on our side of the horizon. You can see the entire ship—top gallant to water line. That's less than twelve miles. Twelve miles! They'll catch us ere dark. I'll wager she's the *Vulture*."

"*Vulture*?"

"Billy's ship. Used to be *H.M.S. Thunder*, a ship of the line. Two decks of guns, forty-eight total. And how many do we have? One at the stern, another at the bow."

I foolishly asked, "What will they do if they catch us?"

"They're pirates, dulce. Fly the black flag. No prisoners."

"What about the women?"

"Only women they spare are young and pretty."

The same had happened on my little island. Back then, Billy had given us a choice—provision his ship or watch the village go up in flames. It went up in flames anyway. Women violated. Men killed.

"How long do we have?"

"We'll know in a few hours."

I made a quick reckoning in my head. If they were twelve miles away and faster than us by one knot per hour, that would give us twelve hours, and twelve hours would take us into the night. But what if they were faster by two knots? Or three?

Molly raised an index finger as if testing the wind. "This ship probably uses a Demi-cross," she said. "Or Davis quadrant. But a finger's just as good." She took my hand. "Here, hold your finger toward them… straight up and as far from your face as you can. Like that. Now, measure how tall the ship is on your finger."

"It covers the nails on my index finger."

"When it covers twice as much of your finger, they've cut the distance in half, so…"

Her words trailed off. I didn't ask her to finish. All I wanted was six hours to that first knuckle. Anything less and we were doomed. So we stood there with the shadow of defeat around us, listening to the sawing and hammering.

"Sails ho! Abaft the first one! Hull down! Top gallant showing!"

Some of the passengers claimed they could see this second ship. One old man said it was probably an English warship, and they'd be kinder to us than the pirates. Another said the second ship was Spanish, and she was chasing the pirates.

Molly shook her head. "Billy always travels in twos, he does."

We watched for at least an hour, then retreated back to the cabin. Even there, Molly paced the deck, mumbling, cursing Billy in her foreign tongue, saying we should already be tossing things overboard to lighten up. I told her to settle down, that God hadn't saved me from the stake only to let me perish at the hands of pirates.

We took sightings at each half-hour strike of the bells, but each sighting diminished my confidence. Some passengers prayed the Rosary on deck, others in their cabins, and all around I heard competing voices in Castilian and Latin.

"*Dios, te salve a María, llena eres de gracia…*"

"*Ave Maria, gratia plena….*"

At noon, the steward showed up in the passageway, ringing a cow's bell. "*Oigan, oigan*! Captain sends word that the approaching ships have not been identified. We do not know for certain they're pirates. He begs you not to panic."

At two bells of the afternoon watch—one by the clock—we gathered in the galley for black beans, boiled potatoes, and fried chicken. The serving crew had the long faces of men who had sailed their last voyage. Hardly anyone ate. The rotund man sat by himself, puffing on his clay pipe. So did the fair-haired man, and many of the passengers who last night had been singing *Viva España* were now reciting the Lord's Prayer.

Just when I thought the mood could get no blacker, the old steward shuffled back into the galley. "Anyone seen the lieutenant?"

There were shrugs all around.

He lumbered out, slump-shouldered and defeated. Everyone thought it odd that the first officer would be missing. "I'll wager he went looking for Golondrina," Molly said. "And helter skelter, hang sorrow, care will kill a cat. That's what Sister Agnes used to say."

A faint grin crossed Enrique's face, and I couldn't help but wonder if he, Enrique, had killed the lieutenant.

At five bells of the afternoon watch—two-thirty by the clock—the measurement reached the first knuckle of my finger. "There's hope," Molly said. "Six more hours will take us to nightfall."

"What about the moon?" I asked. "Will there be a moon tonight?"

She had her mouth open to answer when there came a pop like the sound of musket fire.

"*Cuidado*! Look out below!"

Lines and ropes fell to the deck. A seaman in the rigging yelled, "*Hijo de la gran puta*!" Then the lower sail of the mainmast went as slack as wash on a line, flapping sideways.

CHAPTER 32

I'd never heard of such a thing, except in battle. But there were no flying cannon balls. Not even a lightning strike. We were making fine speed, sails full drawing, the bowsprit dipping and rising in the swells. So why would the mainsail suddenly collapse.

The captain burst out of the roundhouse, yelling for the lieutenant. The lieutenant didn't answer.

He put the second officer in charge, a young lieutenant named Hurtado, and the cursing that followed was vile enough to burn a pirate's ear. Barefooted crewmen in knee breeches scurried around deck with new cordage. Bare-chested men crawled along the lines hand over hand or bounded from spar to spar like monkeys in a tree.

Two or three of the ladies on deck, making a great show of offense, retreated below. Molly, who wasn't troubled at all by foul language, nudged my arm. "Billy's men did this."

"But wouldn't an Englishman be recognized?"

"Vampire Jack is Gypsy. He'd fit right in."

A chill came over me. I glanced all around—at the crewmen in the rigging, at the praying passengers along the gunwales, at the chicken coops and canvas-covered lifeboats.

"What does Jack look like?"

"Swarthy and hairy, about your height. Smells like a goat."

"He have a last name?"

"Swallow. Jack Swallow."

"What does Swallow mean in Castilian?"

"How should I know? A swallow is a bird."

"*Golondrinas*?"

Her eyes widened. Before she could say anything, the crewmen and passengers erupted in loud cheers. I glanced up in time to see the mainsail filling with air.

Molly shaded her eyes and took another sighting. "*Mierda*!" she said. "That broken sail cost an hour." She pointed to the west, where dark clouds were building up. Already I could see sheets of rain and streaks of lightning. "That's our only hope."

Once more we watched and prayed, taking new measurements at each strike of the bells. A search party was sent out for the lieutenant but turned up nothing.

At one bell of the first dog watch—four thirty by the clock—the measurement on my finger reached the big knuckle. Molly shook her head. Despair showed in her face. And for the first time I noticed she'd removed her mantilla and tied a bandana around her head.

"How much longer?" I asked, dreading the answer.

"They'll be in shooting distance an hour before dark."

No sooner had she said it than lightening flashed around us, followed by a frightening crack of thunder. Passengers retreated below. I suggested we do the same, and we had just turned around when the captain himself hurried over to my side.

"You the gentleman from La Casa?"

"I am."

"You're aware your company owns this ship?"

"Of course. How may I help you?"

"Here, I'll show you." From his pocket he took a small section of tar-soaked cord. "Look at it. Perfect condition. But you can plainly see it's been slashed. Sabotage."

I took the cord, sniffed it as if smelling for rot. "Any suspects?"

"I can assure you it wasn't my men. Not our marines either. I know them all."

"How many men do you have?"

"Sixty, counting the lieutenant. And that's just my crew. Add twelve marines and twelve carpenters, and the eight oarsmen that came aboard last night. Then we've got how many passengers—twenty, twenty-one?"

"Why don't we call them to assembly? Hmm? Line them up, sort them out?"

"Not with pirates after us. I need them at their stations."

He led me across the quarterdeck, past a pair of armed marines, and into the roundhouse. Unlike the gloom of my cabin, his was well lit with skylights and ornate glass windows that overlooked our wake. He motioned me into a chair next to a large table cluttered with charts and instruments. Defeat showed in his face. "By my reckoning," he said, "we've got two hours, then I'm going to have to make some hard decisions. What do you think Don Ignacio would do?"

I had no idea who Don Ignacio was but couldn't admit it.

Another flash of lightning lit the room, followed by a loud roll of thunder. The captain went on: "My choice would be to fight. Problem is my crew. They're not fighting men. They've already told me what they want—strike the colors if it comes to faceoff, give up without a fight. They say there's at least a chance. God willing."

"Can't we lighten the ship, start throwing things overboard?"

"That the recommendation of La Casa?"

"That's what Don Ignacio would do."

He dipped his quill and began writing. I signed as Don Benicio Gonzalez, Head of Licensing, CC, and was putting away the quill when the first drops of rain splattered on the skylights. The clouds were darker now, more ominous.

"What about this weather?" I asked. "Will it improve our chances?"

"God willing."

"Do you have extra pistols? I'd like two, one for myself… another for my wife."

He lumbered over to a locker and took out two pistols along with flasks of balls and leather powder straps. "Belgium-made," he said, handing the pistols to me. "The best."

I made a show of examining them and stuffed them into my belt. "You should also arm yourself, Captain…, and keep the marines near you. Hmm? Whoever sabotaged that sail probably also got the lieutenant. He could come after you."

"I'll be ruined anyway if I lose this ship."

I didn't know how to reply to that, so I thanked him, picked up my powder belts, and was heading out to find Molly when one of the marines came rushing in.

"Sir, it's the lieutenant. We found him."

Out the door we trotted, across the quarterdeck to the starboard gunwale, past the overhanging longboat, and aft to the point where the roundhouse projected over the stern. There, below the projection, dangled the lieutenant by his ankles—naked and upside down. His throat had been ripped out, and an image of a horned goat carved into his chest.

"*Madre de Dios*," said the captain.

Lieutenant Hurtado, the young officer who had replaced Lieutenant Ramos used a grappling hook to pull the body within reach. He cut down the lieutenant with the help of another crewman, and when they laid the corpse out on deck, I caught a whiff of goat, bitter and repulsive. The captain tried to say something but couldn't get out the words. Lieutenant Hurtado vomited over the side. "This is the work of a pirate," I said. "He's aboard this ship. He's the one who sabotaged the mainsail. They call him Vampire Jack."

Lieutenant Hurtado turned around and wiped his mouth. "Vampire Jack?"

"*Sí, Teniente*. They say he's swarthy, about my height, speaks with a Romano accent."

"Romano?"

"Gypsy. Smells like a goat. And his body is covered in hair, like an animal's."

The sky darkened. The rain that had started with only a few drops turned into a downpour. Passengers ran for shelter. Wind thundered in the sails, and the ship tore through the swells at a fierce rate, pitching and straining, spray washing over us.

The captain turned up his collar and grabbed a shroud for support. Rain poured off his hat. "Get that body wrapped in canvas!" he barked, "And keep your mouths shut about what happened. Passengers are already panicked."

He hurried away, shouting for the helmsman. I followed him back into the roundhouse where I retrieved my priming flasks and charge belts.

"Pray the rain lasts," the captain said. "I'm putting this ship on a different tack."

I said I'd be in my cabin if he needed me and struggled down to the passenger deck where a crowd had congregated in the passageway. There were happy faces all around. The rotund man and his wife were drinking from an open bottle of port; the fair-haired man was playing a flute, and a woman who'd been crying hysterically was now twirling to the music. How easy it would be for Jack, I thought, to come up behind me and put a knife into my ribs.

A hand grabbed my arm. I swirled around and stared into Molly's face; Molly with a red bandana about her head. She handed me the towel. "Here, dry yourself."

I led her into Enrique's cabin, closed and latched the door, and gave them each a pistol and belts. "We found the lieutenant," I said, and explained the circumstances.

Enrique glared at Molly as if she were responsible for Jack. "So what are we supposed to do now?" he said. "Cower in our cabins until we reach Santo Domingo?"

"This ship will never make it to Santo Domingo," Molly answered. "Our only hope is get close enough to Hispaniola to run aground."

It grew darker and stuffier in the cabin. The only thing pleasing about it was how Molly stayed close, leaning into me as if we were lovers. We loaded our pistols and exchanged ideas on how best to protect ourselves: stay together, watch each other's back, avoid mixing in a crowd.

As darkness approached, all three of us transferred to my cabin, which was larger, and Molly was setting up the berth when there came the clang of the steward's bell.

"*Oigan! Oigan!* Captain says remain in your cabins. Doors locked. Douse all lights. Anyone caught outside will be clapped in irons!"

"We should get some sleep," Molly said. "My guess is we'll be up long before dawn."

We latched the door, climbed into our hammocks fully clothed, and listened to the protesting timbers, the roll of thunder, and the slap of sea against the hull. I said a silent prayer for Saraatepe and my children and was drifting into sleep when a tap sounded at the door.

"*Oigan*, you in the cabin!"

Molly tumbled out of her berth. "It could be Jack."

We took our pistols and opened the door slowly, only to find the steward, grim faced as ever. He motioned me outside with his lantern. "It struck again," he whispered.

"It?"

"The chupacabra. Got to the first mate… tore out his throat." He glanced into the darkness around us. "Captain says he could come after you…, you being owner of the ship."

"Any sign of the pirates?"

"Nothing, but we're on a different tack, a few points closer to the wind. Marines are on double watch. Captain says to stay alert. Never know what'll happen next."

I thanked him and again latched the door behind me. Molly jerked on it a couple times for good measure, then jammed a chair at an angle beneath the latch.

"You think that'll stop him?" I said.

"It'll give us a few more seconds."

"Surely you don't think he'll try to bust in."

"Problem with Jack is you never know until it's too late."

That kind of talk should have kept me awake, but I was so exhausted that no sooner did I close my eyes than I fell into a restless slumber. Once or twice a crack of thunder shook me awake. Enrique's snores didn't help either. I heard footfalls on the deck above, a prayer from the next cabin, and the strike of ship's bells. In a dream I saw Vampire Jack hovering over me with a knife. His swarthy face. The earring in the left ear. A rope in his hand to string me up.

I even smelled the stench of goat.

"Dulce."

The pressure of Molly's hand on my mouth woke me. I sat up, still half asleep. "What?"

"Shhh, keep your voice down. He's here. At the door."

"Who is here?"

"Jack."

CHAPTER 33

I struggled up with my pistol. Behind me, Enrique was climbing out of his hammock. The faintest glow of outside grayness penetrated the porthole. "Listen," Molly whispered. "You can hear him."

I crept to the door and listened. Yes, a faint rustle, like an object rubbing on wood. He must have inserted a knife in the seams between the planks and was working the latch.

Enrique eased up behind me, "Let's shoot him through the door."

"Too thick," Molly whispered. "It's stout oak."

"Which way does the door open?"

Molly said in, Enrique said out, and in the panic of the moment, with my pulse pounding and my breath coming in spurts, I couldn't remember which way either. I ran my trembling hands along the door jam, feeling for hinges. Yes, strap hinges inside, meaning the door swung inward.

"I've got an idea," I said. "But we've got to act together."

I told them in ragged whispers. They agreed. We cocked our pistols in unison, using a blanket to muffle the metallic double-click. Then we bunched up at the door.

"Ready," I whispered.

"Ready."

"Now!"

In one swift motion, Molly pulled away the chair. I popped open the door latch. Enrique yanked the door open.

Then I fired into the darkness.

There was a flash, a loud report, and I saw him as clearly as if a bolt of lightning had penetrated the deck. Not a hairy monster with horns and claws, but a man with a goatskin over his head, eyes and mouth open as if shocked by our sudden action.

Enrique, who was supposed to fire into the illumination, waited too long. The blackness returned. The man in the passageway made a furious dash along the passageway, heading toward the ladder. We did not see this, but we could hear his fading footfalls.

"Get him!" I shouted. "Don't let him get away."

Enrique stepped into the passageway and fired into the darkness.

In the flash, while the passage was perfectly lit, Molly fired her pistol. The pirate yelped like a dog that had been kicked. His knife clattered to the deck. And in the last instant of light I saw him go sprawling. "We got him," Molly yelled. "Come on. Let's finish him."

I grabbed her. "Are you crazy? He may have a—"

Before the word, "pistol," left my mouth, he fired back.

"*Mierda*!" Molly screamed and dove into the cabin.

My ears rang. Flashes of gunfire lingered in my eyes. I latched the door by feel. "Did he hit you?" I asked Molly. "Are you all right?"

"Jack couldn't hit the side of a barn."

I clicked my flintlock, giving them illumination to recharge their pistols. From the cabins around us came muffled voices and sounds of movement. "Let's give him another blast," Molly said.

She yanked open the door but was stopped by shouts from the marines. "What the devil is going on? What was that shooting about?"

They came tromping down the ladder, a line of marines, lanterns and muskets. Smoke lingered like a noxious fog, thick and eye burning. So did the stench of goat. Other doors were open, passengers peering out. I stepped into the passageway, expecting to see a crumpled body near the ladder. But there was nothing. No one.

"Pirate," I said to the marines. "He was trying to break in."

I explained the circumstances. The marine in charge, a stocky man with sergeant's stripes, sent one of his men on the double-quick to look for blood.

"It's here," he reported back from the ladder. "Goes off in that direction."

"Go find him," barked the sergeant. "Take Pablo with you. Use pistols instead of muskets."

They trotted away. By then, the other passengers were bunched up in the passageway. The sergeant held up his lantern. "Which one of you is the gentleman from La Casa?"

I stepped forward. "That would be me."

He touched his hat in a partial salute. "You're wanted topside." He waved his lantern. "As for the rest of you, get back to your cabins. Lock your doors. Now! *Vete! Vete!*"

The passageway cleared. Doors closed. I asked the sergeant why I was needed topside.

"It's best we not discuss it here."

The three of us followed the two marines past the bloodstains, up the ladder, to the weather deck, and into the fresh air. The rain had stopped, but the sky was still overcast, with only glimpses of starlight and flashes of lightning.

The sergeant shaded his lantern. "Watch your step."

"What time is it?" I asked.

"Last I heard was five bells of the middle watch. Two-thirty by your clock."

We struggled across the deck behind the marines, catching at lines and shrouds for support, climbing the ladder to the quarterdeck. Wind whistled in the rigging. Sails shimmered and popped. Here and there I caught a glimpse of moonlit sea, but the darkness around us was as impenetrable as the biblical plague of Egypt.

"Halt! Who goes there? Speak!"

"Sergeant Ortiz with three passengers. Stand down!"

A shadowy figure appeared at the door of the captain's quarters. The sergeant explained the gunshots and told him to watch for the other two marines. The guard pushed open the door and bade us enter, and it was clear from the smell of vomit that things were amiss. Curtains had been drawn. The only light came from low-burning lanterns. Lieutenant Hurtado sat at the captain's table, his eyes blank as a corpse. He looked up at us and then rested his head on the table.

"What's going on?" I asked the sergeant. "Where's the captain?"

"That's just it. We don't know. He went missing awhile back."

The outside guard stuck in his head. "See, here's what happened. He went down to the weather deck. I says to him, 'Captain, sir, don't you want me to stay with you?' But he says, 'No, *mijo*, you watch the cabin, I'll be right back.' And that's the last we saw of him."

"Did you search for him?"

"Turned the deck upside down."

"What's wrong with the lieutenant?"

"Drunk, sir. Been like that for hours, puking and praying. I says to him, 'Lieutenant, sir, we need you to take command.' All he did was grab his bottle and start swigging."

"Where are the other officers?"

"Aren't any. It's a *Casa* vessel. You've got the captain, the two lieutenants and first mate. But the first mate's… well…"

"Dead," said the other marine. "Strung up the same way as Lieutenant Ramos."

I sank into a chair at the table. "So who is in charge?"

"Looks like you are, sir. You own this ship, don't you?"

They stared as if waiting for my orders—three marines in red uniforms, Molly and Enrique with their pistols tucked into their belts. One of the marines helped the lieutenant into a berth. Another yelled for a seaman to clean up the mess. I lumbered outside and breathed in fresh air, trying to gather my wits. Less than twelve hours ago I was a fugitive, my mouth stuffed with cotton to give me a different look. Now, because I'd so cleverly disguised myself, I was captain, a heretical priest who'd never piloted anything larger than a rowboat.

No wonder I had a headache.

A muffled shot rang out, followed by two others.

The sergeant rushed out the door, pistol drawn, and trotted across the quarterdeck. At the ladder, he yelled back to the guard, "You, Flaco, keep them in the cabin!"

They faded into the darkness, leaving us in suspense. What if Vampire Jack had ambushed the marines? What if he had other friends aboard?

"Begging your pardon," said Flaco, "but it's best you not stand in the doorway. Pirates could be in the rigging with a musket."

We retreated into the cabin and began opening lockers and drawers. Molly pulled a pistol from a locker, stuffed it in her belt, gave another to Enrique and yet another to me. "Always best to have two pistols," she said. "Saves recharging."

I slumped into the captain's chair. Molly plopped down beside me. "Not to worry," she said in that sweet Irish accent. "Billy taught me how to sail, he did."

My headache grew worse. This could only have a bad ending.

Flaco stuck in his head. "Someone's coming."

We waited in the darkness, pistols at the ready. From below came thumps and curses, things moving about. Then a figure appeared at the top of the quarterdeck ladder, barely visible.

"Halt!" Flaco shouted. "Who goes there?"

"Sergeant Ortiz with three marines and a corpse. Stand down."

Up the ladder they came, dragging a body across the quarterdeck and into the roundhouse. The smell of goat rose up around him. The sergeant rolled the body over, yanked off his goatskin, and held the lantern to his face. "This your pirate?"

"*Coño*," Enrique said. "It's that fair-haired man, Santibañez."

Molly let out a string of curses. I stood there staring, trying to grasp the meaning. How could this frail little man have sabotaged the sails and killed three men all by himself?

"If he'd been in the rigging," I said to the sergeant, "wouldn't his hands be tarred?"

The sergeant knelt down for a look. "*Hijo de puta.* There must be a second pirate."

A couple of seaman showed up with buckets and mops. They dragged out the corpse and threw him overboard, and while they were swabbing up the mess, stirring up smells of lye and vomit, I motioned the rest of us outside.

"Does anyone know our location?" I asked.

"Westerly bearing," said the sergeant. "South of Hispaniola. Following the weather."

"How far from land?"

He shrugged, so I sent the sergeant to fetch the helmsman. Then I asked the marine guard for the latest news from the crow's nest. He cupped his hands. "Ahoy, lookout!"

No answer. Nothing but the pop and flutter of sails. Another marine came up beside me. "Ahoy, Correa! The hell's going on? Speak up or I'll report your sorry ass!"

Still no answer.

An uneasy feeling came over me. The sergeant returned with the helmsman and did his share of yelling. Then he ordered a seaman named Acosta to climb up and see what happened.

Acosta faded into the darkness. Then we waited, listening to his efforts. "Almost there!" he cried. "Just a few more rungs!"

"Any sign of ships?"

"Nothing, Captain, nothing but darkness!"

Captain. How strange it sounded.

"I'm here. Nest empty! No one home!"

Groans and curses erupted from one end of the deck to the other. I yelled up to stay alert and was digesting this bad news when Acosta cried out again.

"Captain, somebody placed a white streamer at the mizzen-mast topgallant!"

We backed away for a look. And there it was, flapping like a beacon, probably visible for miles. "Who the hell did that?" the sergeant demanded to know.

"Vampire Jack did it," Molly said. "A signal for his friends."

The sergeant ordered a seaman to cut it down. While this was going on, I directed the helmsman, a wiry little fellow with a bandana and sun-scorched face, into the roundhouse.

"What is our position?" I asked him.

He unrolled a chart on the captain's table and pointed to a large island off the southeastern coast of Hispaniola. "Isla Saona. Passed it about an hour ago. So we're about… oh, I'd say twenty miles from land, *más o menos*."

"Too far," Molly said. "We should be hugging the coastline."

"You heard her," I said to the helmsman. "I want this ship as close to Hispaniola as possible."

"It might put us in moonlight."

"Doesn't matter," Molly said. "I'll wager the pirates are already on our tail."

The words had scarcely left her mouth than there came the dreaded cry from above.

"Sails, ho!"

CHAPTER 34

The notes of the boatswain's whistle cut across the deck, followed by clanging bells, shouts, curses, and seamen climbing into the rigging. I ordered oarsmen, carpenters, and cleaning crew to start hauling up stores from the hold, then I took the captain's bullhorn and asked for attention.

"There's a pirate aboard this vessel. He could be anywhere. If you cannot see the man beside you, demand he identify himself. And one more thing. God willing, we're going to either lose the pirates or put this ship aground in Hispaniola. Can I count on you?"

They answered with shouts of *Viva España*, and the entire crew set to work in a fury, adjusting sails, tightening lines, and hauling up stores. Over the side went boxes, crates, trunks, barrels, sacks and excess sails, everything except water casks.

I turned to Molly. "Let's hope Billy is still bearing west."

"There's no losing Billy."

"How can you say that? It's dark. How would he know?"

"Vampire Jack. He's on this ship somewhere, sending signals."

I ordered Sergeant Ortiz to keep a sharp lookout for lights around the stern. He assigned two marines to the task. But no sooner did they hurry away than a brightness fell over us, a three-quarters moon that silvered the mainmast and shined white on the sails.

"Fook!" Molly said. There were curses from the rigging as well, and I was wondering how to handle this new challenge when we sailed back into darkness.

No one celebrated. No one said a word, and the question on everyone's mind was answered a few minutes later when moonlight fell on the pirate ship. "Still following!" cried the lookout.

"Distance?"

"Closer than before!"

Molly squeezed my arm, and for the first time I heard alarm in her voice. "We've got to keep lightening up. It's the only way." She yelled for Sergeant Ortiz. "Toss the anchor and chains. Also the forward cannon. It must weight a ton."

The sergeant looked from her to me. "*Perdóneme, Capitán*, but who is in charge?"

"I am, but she has experience. Do as she says."

The sergeant struck off to give the orders. I closed the door and turned to Molly. "Look, dulce, I'm not sure how to put this, but I'm supposed to be the one giving orders."

"Sí, *Capitán*. Can I get you some coffee?"

"Please, Molly. I need your cooperation."

It went like that for almost an hour. Tempers flaring. Men cursing and shouting. Splashes over the side. No sooner did one problem get resolved than someone stepped forth with another. Like when Enrique asked if we should scuttle the livestock. "We've got two milk cows, three sheep, six goats, a bunch of hogs and dozens of chickens."

The idea of drowning animals didn't agree with me, even if they were destined for slaughter. "Wait a bit longer," I said. "See if we're putting distance between us and the pirates."

Eight bells sounded—four by the clock. The watch shifted from middle to morning watch amid a great deal of fuss. The overcast grew thinner. We sailed in and out of another pool of light. The curses this time were louder. "Any sign of land?" I yelled to the lookout.

"Nothing, Captain!"

At one bell of the morning watch—four-thirty—the old steward showed up with a pot of café and platter of bread and cheeses. "Passengers are restless," he said. "Can I send them to the galley?"

"Send them. Are their bags ready?"

"Already scuttled. But your bags are here."

Our bags. Meaning the bags of Father Menendez and El Moro as well as my old sea-bag. We dumped the contents on the deck and selected a few items for taking ashore—priest garments, the letters and paper canister, and the string of emeralds I'd bought for Saraatepe.

"Land ho! Starboard and north!"

Crewmen cheered and thanked the Virgin. I stepped outside with my glass and saw what appeared to be forests shrouded in fog. "Ten miles," Molly said beside me, but we're sailing at an angle, so make it fifteen. I figure an hour."

We watched and waited. I used that time to write our circumstances into the captain's log. At two bells—five by the clock—the first shafts of morning light crossed the sky. Molly said if we could get past three bells we'd have a chance.

She was still speculating when they burst into the light behind us.

Men groaned and cursed. A few shouted obscenities at the pirates as if they could hear. Molly grabbed one of the captain's instruments, took another measurement, and shook her head. "We'll never make it. Not unless we get more speed out of this tub."

The carpenters scuttled all their lumber, every wooden door and even hatches, and then set to disassembling bulkheads. We kicked out the captain's skylight and scuttle ports. Over the side went his table and desk, safe, all his lockers, sand barrels, water casks and even barrels of port.

Molly asked about a bag marked *Postales y Correspondencia.*

"Leave it. My letters to the bishop are inside."

The gunners sacrificed forty of their cannon balls on the stern gun, leaving only ten to slow the pirates. I sent word to the galley to dump stoves, crockery, tables, pots and all their stores, and was wondering if we should dismantle the deck when Enrique said one word: "Livestock."

Again I glanced out the open window. Billy's ship loomed behind us, full sails, heeling to larboard. "Free the chickens," I said to Enrique. "Let them fly. Then sink the coops."

"What about the other animals?"

"We'll need something to eat when we get ashore."

The sky grew brighter. I gave permission to light lanterns. Not long afterward, I heard a commotion near the forecastle. "Captain's body! Inside a coil of rope!"

His throat had been slit, and an image of a horned goats carved into his chest.

"Jack," Molly said. "He'll kill us all if we don't snare him."

The marines prepared the body for burial. I made the notation in the log. Then we hauled him to the gunwale beneath an orange glow from the eastern sky. The sergeant informed me that under ordinary circumstances we'd lower the ensign, read from the scriptures, and fire a volley. But there was no time for niceties. So in plain view of the pirate ship, I read a verse from the captain's Bible, after which we committed his body to the deep.

Everyone made the sign of the cross. But before we could get back to our stations, a crewman found the lookout's body inside a piece of folded canvas. We had another ceremony, another splash.

"Second ship! Dead ahead! Short-sailed and anchored!"

We rushed forward, hoping to see a Spanish warship, but Molly's curses and the grumbles of men in the rigging told me otherwise.

"*Sea Viper*," Molly said. "Billy's other ship."

I stumbled into the roundhouse and slumped into the only chair that hadn't been scuttled. Not since El Moro and Father Menendez had burst into my cabin had I felt so helpless. I noted our particulars in the log and was still agonizing when Molly came into the roundhouse.

"We've got to stay the course."

"They'll just blow us to splinters."

"No, dulce, they're not going to broadside us." She knelt beside me. "They're pirates. They want this ship in one piece. That's how they make money. What good would it do to sink us?"

I wasn't convinced of her logic. Wasn't convinced of her loyalty either. But what choice did I have? So I stepped outside and ordered the helmsman to stay course. Then, with armed marines on either side, I picked up the captain's bullhorn. "We have two choices!" I shouted. "Either strike the colors and let the pirates hang us or dash for land."

"But they'll broadside us!" came a cry from the rigging.

"We can make it!" I yelled back. "It's not blood money they want; it's prize money. They want this ship intact! And they can have it far as I'm concerned… after we're safely on terra firma!"

No one answered, but there was no defiance either. Molly took my arm. Enrique came up on the other side, and we stood on the quarterdeck with twelve marines, drawing closer to the *Sea Viper* by the minute. "*Coño*," Enrique muttered. "She's running out her guns!"

"Bluffing," Molly said. "They're not going to shoot."

Land was now so close we could see coconut trees, and dark hills that rose up behind them, and boiling reefs along the shoreline. Gulls circled and squawked, some diving into water, others seeming to stand still in midair. Molly twisted around. "Billy's almost in range."

I ordered our gunners to stand by to fire. Already I saw black flags on both ships. And men congregating on the decks. And semaphores going up and down.

"What are they signaling?" I asked Molly.

"They're ordering us to heave to and strike."

"Signal back—tell them we don't understand."

She turned to the sergeant. "Red pennant. Three times up."

The sergeant yelled for a flagman. A minute or so later a red pennant went up the mizzenmast, one… two… three times. The *Sea Viper*, still to our starboard front, answered with a blast of stern cannon, followed by a mushrooming splash to larboard.

The hint of a smile crossed Molly's face. "What it really means is, 'Thank you, kind sir, but we'd rather not surrender,' which is a nice way of saying, Go fook your mother."

"Are you crazy? We shouldn't be provoking them."

"They're pirates, dulce. They're already provoked."

The distance between us and the *Sea Viper* closed. The chief gunner on our stern cannon, a sun-blackened fellow with a scarf on his head, rattled off the numbers every minute or so.

"Eight-hundred and closing!"

"Seven-hundred!"

How he divined distances without an instrument I do not know, and I was about to ask Molly when Lieutenant Hurtado stumbled out of the roundhouse. He was pale, his eyes hazy, and he seemed to be struck stupid by the sights and sounds around us.

"What is going on?" he asked. "What are those ships?"

The sergeant explained. The lieutenant stumbled back into the roundhouse.

"Five-hundred and closing!"

Already I could see pirates in the rigging and at the gunwales, and the muzzles of their projecting cannon. Please, dear God, let Molly be right.

"Three-hundred!"

If they were going to fire it would be now. I held my breath and prayed. Even the marines were crossing themselves.

"Under a hundred and sliding!"

We came alongside them, close enough to throw a stone. No broadside. Not even a warning shot, nothing but stares from the pirates and a few shouts in their crude language.

"What are they saying?" I asked Molly.

"They're wishing us a safe and happy voyage."

The marines laughed. I breathed again. But before we could celebrate, the *Sea Viper* began laying on canvas as if to pursue us. Worse, the *Vulture* fired a warning shot. The ball mushroomed to larboard, close enough to wash us in spray.

The chief gunner rushed up and saluted. "Begging your pardon, sir, but that ship behind us is in range and closing! Five-hundred or thereabouts. We're primed and ready!"

"Fire at will."

He rushed back and touched the wick to the pan. The blast jolted the ship. Passengers yelped as is we'd been struck. Smoke blew over the deck in spite of our forward motion, thick and acrid.

"Did we hit them?"

"No, but we gave them a bath."

By then, the sea was churning around us, angry and dangerous. Breakers were strewn about like boulders on the Spanish plains, the sea crashing over them in white spray. I asked Molly if we should stay on our present course or take the shorter route through the breakers.

"Breakers," she said. "It's our only chance."

I gave the order. An extra hand was put to the helm, and we were making the turn when passengers began dashing onto the deck from the open hatch.

"Fire below!" they shouted. "The ship's ablaze."

Smoke spilled out behind them. Bells clanged. The smell of burning tar permeated the air.

"Vampire Jack," Molly cried. "He's trying to slow us."

CHAPTER 35

Passengers crowded the gunwales as if ready to jump, crying and praying, and everything seemed to be going on at once—the whistle of wind, the roar of the churning sea, the helmsman yelling to shorten sails, shouts from the rigging, blasts of cannon fire, the cries from the lookout, and the smoke and stench of burning tar.

"Breakers! Steer to starboard!"

We sheared away, but not in time to avoid an ugly scrape, a vibration moving aft along the entire length of the ship. Spray burst over us like smoke from a cannon blast. I glanced back to see Billy's ship veering to larboard, putting the *Vulture* in position to fire.

A linesman began calling out the depth: "Six minus!"

Then the old steward came stumbling out of the hatch, coughing and fanning smoke from his face. "Tar barrels," he hollered up. "Entire hold's ablaze."

"Minus five and dropping!"

The fire crackled and fizzed. Smoke poured from hatches and ports, leaving a trail of ugly black clouds. The ship rose on a swell and then plummeted, giving me a view of a sandy white beach. Again we veered. Then the steward yelled to me again.

"Begging pardon, sir, but shouldn't we bring up the slaves?"

"What slaves?"

"Africans, sir. Six men and three women… they're in irons."

"Get them topside. Make it quick."

Over the swells we went, around the churning reefs, toward the shore that couldn't come fast enough. Smoke poured from open hatches, ugly and black. Behind us, in safe waters beyond the reefs, Billy's *Vulture* had dropped anchor and shortened sails.

"*Mierda*," shouted the gunner. "They're going to broadside us."

The gloom of defeat came over us again. Our ship was in flames. No longer of value to the pirates. Why not use it for target practice?

Our ship rose suddenly on the crest of a tall swell, and from this towering view I plainly saw them lowering their longboats.

"What are they doing?" I asked Molly.

"Coming after us."

"Why? This ship will soon be ashes."

"Maybe they're coming for Vampire Jack."

I yelled down to the sergeant, who was helping slaves up the ladder. He trotted over, saluted, and broke into a string of curses when he saw the pirates in the longboats. "We can ambush them on the beach," he said. "But we'll need to arm the crew."

"Do it. And don't forget Vampire Jack. We've got to find him."

"Leave it to me, sir."

He dashed away, shouting instructions. The leadsman called out a reading of three plus and dropping. Hands scrambled down from the rigging. Others gathered near the skiff and longboat. Molly said we'd be aground within three minutes.

"Brace for impact!" I cried through the bullhorn.

We sheered giddily though a cresting swell. The last of the sails came down. A column of fire broke though the mid-deck hatch. Molly grabbed my arm. "Those slaves won't stand a chance if we break up."

"They'll have to swim like the rest of us."

"They're shackled together. Look for yourself."

I struggled over the deck and surveyed them from the railing—six men and three scantily clad women, on their knees and holding each other for support, crying and praying in their African language. Unlike other slaves I'd seen coming off ships from Africa, they appeared well nourished, as if they'd been fattened for the market.

"Unshackle those Negroes!" I ordered. "Do it now."

"No," shouted the rotund man from the gunwale. He was now dressed in a silk greatcoat and fine clothing. "These servants are a gift to the governor. They'll escape if we release them."

"And they'll drown if you don't. Release them now. Be quick!"

"Do you know who I am, Sir? I am Don Fajardo y Soto, a friend of the governor."

"I don't care who you are. I gave you an order."

"I don't take orders from you."

I turned to a marine. "Take that man's key, then throw him overboard."

Don Fajardo yanked out his key. "You'll answer to the governor for this. You'll—"

The ship scraped bottom with such force that he tumbled sideways. Lines snapped. Everyone fell flat. Something crashed on the forward deck. Smoke turned to hissing steam, and there was so much confusion around me, with screams and shouts, the thunder of the wind, spray washing over us, that I could scarcely fathom what was going on.

Molly pulled me to my feet. "Are you hurt?"

I wiped blood from my lower lip and looked down to see Enrique with the key, unshackling the slaves, pulling the chain through the loops, freeing them.

Then, with a wild whoop, all nine Africans plunged into the sea.

Don Fajardo ran back along the gunwales, pistol drawn, cursing, shouting like a madman. "You ingrate scoundrels, you worthless *hijos de puta*! I'll see you strung up like dogs!"

He aimed his pistol as if to fire, but before he could get off a shot we again struck bottom, this time with a long scraping jolt that shook us like an earthquake.

More lines snapped. Things popped and cracked. The bowsprit lifted. The ship tilted sharply to starboard. One final shudder and, by the grace of God, we came to a crunching halt, in beautiful blue water not more than thirty paces from a sandy white beach.

I looked around for the bullhorn, couldn't find it, so cupped my hands around my mouth. "Abandon ship. Get to shore. Hurry!"

Crewmen sprang to the skiff and longboat. Molly and I lent a hand with the livestock, freeing them from cages and urging them overboard. Chickens that had taken roost in the rigging fluttered toward land. Passengers who could swim jumped over the side, and within seconds the water was teeming with people, pigs, sheep, bleating goats, and a milk cow.

The marines got a skiff in the water, loaded it with muskets, balls and powder kegs, and rowed it to shore. By then the flames were licking at our feet, the smoke choking us, and the pirates no more than fifty or sixty yards behind.

I made a final notation in the captain's log, then Molly and I, together with Enrique and the sergeant, piled into the waiting longboat.

I thanked God for getting us safely off the ship, and was breathing in the fresh, clean air, watching the coconut trees come closer, when an oarsman pointed back at our burning ship.

"What the devil?"

A man stood on the bowsprit like a statue—headscarf and chest strap. "That's him," Molly said. "Vampire Jack."

The sergeant raised his musket and fired.

"Waste of powder," Molly said. "Only way to kill Jack is cut off his head."

We landed and hurried up the beach, heading toward a jungle of palmettos, creepers, and palm trees. The sand hampered our progress, and animals were running every which way—squealing, squawking, bleating. Yet within minutes the passengers were in the foliage, and the marines had set up a defensive perimeter of three parallel lines, using rock formations for cover.

I didn't like it, exposed as we were to the guns from Billy's ship, and was making the case for moving farther back when Paco rushed down with news of a trail to the west.

"Let's take it," I said. "Get away from the beach."

"Not a good idea," said the sergeant. "They'll just pick us off from the rear."

"But they'll bombard us from the ship."

"I doubt they can even see us. Not with all this smoke."

Billy and his pirates, about seventy in number, landed their two longboats and quickly spread out along the beach, shouting in their crude language, taking cover behind boulders, plants and other obstructions. "Stand by to fire!" shouted the sergeant. "Aim low. Don't fire until I give the command!"

Hammers were pulled back. Bayonets fixed. Men took aim.

Black smoke drifted over the beach. Ashes fell around us like fine mist. Animals wandered about the beach. Chickens clucked and crowed, and still the pirates did not attack.

How long we waited, I do not know, but eventually a pirate advanced with a white flag, waving it back and forth. Behind him came none other than Billy with two other pirates.

I stepped into the open. "What do you want?" I yelled down.

"*Un parley*," answered the man with the flag.

"Parley for what?"

They kept coming, crunching through the sand until Billy Goatsucker himself stood no more than three paces to my front. Vest and leather boots, a crimson chest strap for his cutlass, hair tied back with a red ribbon, as tall and handsome as when I'd first seen him.

He doffed his hat and bowed like a *caballero*. His blue eyes seemed to sparkle. "To whom do I have the honor of *parlando*?" he asked in his tortured way of speaking Castilian.

"Captain of the *Sevilla*. What do you want?"

"Please, Captain, let us not to hurry." He mopped sweat from his face with a kerchief, then pointed to a fallen coconut tree. "*Porque* no the two of us step over there in the shade, take a seat and relax. Eh? You look like a... *como se dice*... man of reason. I'm sure we can work out our differences in a manner most cordial. *Ce que vous pensez, Capitaine?*"

"Would you prefer to speak French?"

"*Mais oui, Capitaine, s'il vous plait.*"

I looked sideways for Molly, but she had conveniently vanished, so I followed Billy into the shade and sank onto the downed tree. Wind rattled the fronds above us. Birds chirped, seagulls cawed, and the smell of burning ship and tar was heavy in the air. Billy again wiped sweat from his face. "Warm for this time of day. No?"

"What do you want?"

He glanced around as if looking for someone—Molly, I supposed—and finally spoke. Slowly, in perfect French, as if he too had grown up in New Orleans. "Look, Captain, allow me to first explain your circumstances. They are not so good. Eh? Out there is my ship. Its guns are trained on this place. One signal from my semaphores and most of you will die. No? Those that escape—if any—will have another problem. My other ship, the *Sea Viper*, is heading to the west, between you and Santo Domingo. They'll be waiting in ambush. Am I clear?"

"*Parfaitement*. So what is your point?"

"Point is this. You are trapped. You cannot escape. You cannot win. But"—he held up a finger—" if you cooperate, we'll sail away and leave you to lead a long, productive life."

"In exchange for what?"

He smiled as if enjoying this discourse. "In exchange for my Negroes, the *hommes de coleur libre*."

"Why do you want them?"

"Oh, please, don't play the game with me. Those nine Negroes are part of my crew. They were captured the same day I was captured by your Spanish marines."

"Last I saw they were heading into the bush. Take them, if you can coax them out."

"Thank you, Captain. You are most generous."

He stood as if to end our parley, walked a few paces toward his flag bearer, then turned back. "*Veuillez m'excuser, Capitaine*, but there is one more matter."

"What?"

"A woman passenger. I'm told you call her Molly."

CHAPTER 36

I should have known it would come to this but had been so bewitched by Molly's charms that I accepted her explanations that Billy was chasing us only to seize our ship. "Are you saying you've been after us all this time because of a woman?"

"Not just any woman. Molly is my *femme*, my wife, my love."

"Are you talking about the woman who abandoned you back in San Juan Bautista?"

"She did not abandon me. She was taken by priests."

I glanced back into the direction I'd last seen Molly but saw not so much as a hair. "It seems to me, monsieur, that if she wanted to be with you, she'd be out here now, in your arms."

"Perhaps you have chained and muffled her."

"She is not chained and muffled."

"Then bring her out. Present her to me." He cupped his hands about his mouth. "Molly! *C'est moi*, Billy. *Venez ici.*"

Molly remained silent. Not a word.

"There you have it," I said to Billy, "Isn't it obvious she doesn't want to go with you?"

"Oh, but please, *Capitaine*. Molly is a woman. Since when do women have a say in these matters? She took an oath to obey her husband. *Moi*. It is her duty. Surely you are not willing to sacrifice the lives of your crew and passengers to keep her from me?"

"No one has to die. All you have to do is walk away.... Call off your pirates, get back in your boats and row away."

"Never, not without Molly. Order her out now."

"Excuse me, sir, but I don't take orders from pirates."

He stood, stamped around a bit, managed a weak smile, and said, "*Monsieur le Capitaine. S'il vous plait.* Would you be so kind as to allow me to *parlez* with my wife? Alone. I will convince her of my affection. Surely you will grant me that courtesy. *D'accord*?"

"I'll ask her but tell me this. Suppose you convince her to go with you? She won't, but suppose she does? What assurances can you offer you wouldn't bombard us anyway?"

"Please, Captain, I'm an English officer. You have my word of honor."

"You are a pirate, sir. You have no honor."

I turned my back and headed into the bush, looking for Molly while he was still assailing me with words I mercifully did not understand. She was sitting on the ground with her back against a coconut tree, a pistol in her hand. She looked up, tears in her eyes.

"He wants me, doesn't he?"

"I told him it's your choice."

"Is that what you want?"

"No, Molly, it's just that…."

"Just what? Go ahead and say it. He gave you a choice, didn't he? Spare the lives of everyone in exchange for me. Well, I have a choice too." She stood, yelled something to Billy in English, then cocked her pistol and went after him.

I grabbed her. We struggled. The pistol went off next to my ear. I sank to my knees, thinking I'd been shot. Molly dropped down beside me, her voice frantic. "Are you hurt? Are you hurt?"

It wasn't until the sergeant and Paco came running that I realized the shot had gone wild. "What happened?" the sergeant asked.

"An accident. Get back to your post."

The sergeant looked from Molly to the smoking pistol.

"I'll explain later," I said. "Give us a minute."

As soon as they crunched away, I let Molly cry in my arms. She was part of me, of this place, this adventure, and I could no more give her up than I could sacrifice the crew. "Listen," I said, "I'm not going to trade you. Come out in the open. Let him see you."

She wiped her eyes and followed me out of the thicket. By then almost everyone was standing in the open: passengers, crew, even the pirates, all staring and waiting.

I marched straight over to Billy. "She doesn't want to go."

"*No me importa* what she wants. I am her master."

He tried to approach her. I blocked his path. He then addressed her in their language, speaking calmly. Molly answered in a heated tone, but the only words I understood were "fook" and "no."

Finally, Billy flung out his arms in disgust and turned on me. "This is your fault, Captain. You have corrupted her mind with promises. What did you offer her?"

"I offered her nothing. She is free to go or stay."

"Ah, so you are fucking her. No?"

Before I could answer, he began ranting in his broken Castilian, mixing in French and what I supposed was English, his voice growing louder, his face turning red. "You, *Capitán*, have condemned your people to death. *Pourquoi*? Because you have stolen my wife."

I pulled out my pistol, thumbed back the hammer, and aimed it in his face.

"Ah," he said, "so now you are going to shoot me? Me. The husband. The injured party."

"No, I'm going to hold you hostage, exchange you for safe passage to Santo Domingo."

He backed away. "We came under a white flag."

"Your ship is flying a black flag, monsieur. Under your plan, everyone dies. You said so yourself. Under my plan, no one dies. We hold you until we're safe, then release you."

Billy's flag bearer, who'd stood silently throughout our discussions, suddenly yanked out a pistol. Whether he planned to shoot or not I will never know because Paco, ever alert, fired a ball into his forehead.

There may have been gasps or screams or curses. I heard none of this because I stood there, dazed at another violent death, and when my senses returned, the smell of gun smoke and tar lingered in the air. The body lay motionless in the sand. The other two pirates were staring in disbelief, and the marines were pushing Billy at the point of their bayonets. "You'll pay for this," Billy screamed. "I'll have your bloody hide."

Paco stepped up to me. "Begging your pardon, sir, but why don't we hang him right now?"

Everyone nodded agreement. Someone cried, "Hang the pirates!" A rope came out, and within seconds it looked as if the matter was out of my hands. "No!" I shouted. "Don't you see the folly? They'll bombard us if we hang him. We need him for safe passage. Without him we won't stand a chance."

Molly and Enrique agreed. So did the sergeant. Reason prevailed, and we sent word to the pirates to get into their longboats and start rowing. "You've got one minute," I yelled.

The pirates held a parley among themselves. While this was going on, the Negroes came out of hiding and dashed down the beach. This brought out Don Fajardo, his face contorted in rage. "See what you've done. Do you know the penalty for helping slaves escape?"

Molly poked him in the chest. "You want your damn slaves. There they are. Go get them."

The sergeant pushed him away, but still he ranted, threats spilling from his mouth like grapeshot from a cannon. The pirates took to their boats, and we were preparing to march when there came the boom of cannon. Not from the *Vulture*, but farther west.

I scrambled atop a boulder and raised my glass. *The Sea Viper*, Billy's companion ship, was heading out to sea in full canvas.

Behind her came two Spanish warships, cannon booming.

Everyone cheered. There'd be no pirates behind us now, no one to impede our trek to Santo Domingo. Billy saw it too. "*Capitaine*," he said, "you are now safe. May I go?"

Without waiting for an answer, he and the two men with him set off on the double quick, heading down the beach and waving their arms, shouting at their departing confederates.

Marines and crewmen took aim with their muskets.

"No," I yelled, "let them go."

A crewman fired anyway. Billy stumbled, grabbed his right leg, and went down. "*Hijos de puta*!" he yelled back, shaking a fist. "You want war? I'll give you war!"

The Negroes rushed back for Billy, which sent Don Fajardo into another rage. They lifted him up, got him in a longboat, and shoved into the waves, rowing around the remains of the *Sevilla*, their semaphores running banners up and down the masts.

"*Mierda*," Molly said. "They're signaling to shoot."

Whistles blew. The sergeant began barking orders like a madman. Everyone grabbed their valuables, and up the rise we scrambled, running from Billy's guns.

There were shouts and curses, people tripping and pushing through a tangle of creepers, vines, brambles and palmettos, struggling to get beyond the crest. And we had almost reached it when Don Fajardo, puffing and red-faced, went sprawling.

Pieces of Eight, gold escudos and other coins scattered around him. I struck off to help, but before I could get there, four or five crewmen fell on him like vultures.

"Thieves!" yelled Don Fajardo, waving his arms. "Scoundrels!"

The men took their coins and dashed away, disappearing into the thicket. Don Fajardo's wife tried to pull him up, but the stampede of bodies sent her sprawling as well. No one stopped. No one seemed to care. And they were both struggling to regain their feet when the broadside struck.

Foliage disintegrated. Things hissed and whistled overhead. Dust and debris fell around us. Then the sergeant was on his feet again, waving his arms and yelling at us to find cover and lie low, saying we had less than two minutes before the next broadside.

"One minute and forty seconds," Molly said.

We waited, taking cover in low spots, amid boulders, and behind almond trees that loomed up on all sides. The smell of crushed bark and foliage rose up around us, mingling with smoke and dust. Meanwhile, the boom of cannons diminished, the noise of jungle returned, the seagulls resumed their caws, and even the goats and sheep began gathering around.

Molly snuggled up next to me. Her cheeks were flushed. Her breath came in short spurts. "It's been more than two minutes," she said. "Maybe they left."

I crawled through a thicket of sea grapes for a better command. Sure enough, Billy's *Vulture* was in full retreat, heading out to sea. But something else caught my eye—a movement beneath the coconut trees where I'd parlayed with Billy, a man leaning over the dead pirate. He glanced up as if he felt my stare, then hurried into the foliage.

Enrique and some of the marines saw him too. I raised my glass for a better look, but saw only trees, rock formations and the white banner that was still stuck in the ground. "Could be a deserter," Enrique said. "Didn't look like one of ours."

"Vampire Jack," said one of the marines.

A chill came over me. I turned to Molly. "What do you think?"

"I think we better watch our backs."

I thought so too, and we were discussing how to deal with this new threat when Don Fajardo grabbed my elbow. His eyes bulged. His greatcoat that had once been crimson was now the color of earth. Spittle flew from his mouth as he spoke. "They took all my *plata*. Surely you're not going to let them get away."

I shook loose. I had no sympathy for this man and his tainted money, yet as acting captain I could not ignore his complaints.

"Can you point them out?"

"I didn't see their faces."

"Can you describe them?"

"What kind of question is that? They're all dressed alike."

"So how are we supposed to find them?"

"Line them up and search them. Make them empty their pockets."

I rolled my eyes, making no effort to conceal my disdain. "And pray tell, kind sir, how can you say the *plata* in their pockets is yours? Some of these men have their own treasure."

"These men are scoundrels and misfits. They have no treasure."

A ground-shaking rumble interrupted us, followed by a cloud of dust and the appearance of a troop of cavalry in the depression below—fifty or more horses with a 6-pounder field cannon, wagons, and the fluttering gold-and-red standard of King Felipe V.

A bearded cavalry captain with two escorts rode within hailing distance. They were covered with road dust, their horses panting and slick with sweat. The captain spat out a wad of tobacco.

"Who are you people?" he asked.

Explanations followed. We learned they were from a *guarda-costa* station a few miles in the direction of Santo Domingo and had been drawn by the smoke and fury. At my request, the captain sent a squad of riders down to investigate our sighting of a straggler. Then I asked how we could get to Santo Domingo.

"It's urgent I get there as soon as possible."

"It's a fair trek, *Capitán*. Road's bad. Indians aren't friendly. You'd be better off resting at the station. Get a fresh start tomorrow. I'll provide an escort."

"How far to the *guarda* station?"

"I'd say two hours. Three if you have stragglers."

"Are there sloops at the station? Ships? I have dispatches for the inquisitor-general." I didn't, of course. The only people I wanted to see in Santo Domingo were the Hebrews.

"I can send a rider with your dispatches."

"No, Captain. It's for his eyes only."

He turned about and ordered a rider to the station. "Ask them to send wagons. And tell them to prepare a sloop for the captain."

A voice behind me said, "Tell them about the chupacabras."

Passengers and crew jumped into the conversation, spilling their stories the way old women used to talk about Blackbeard, saying chupacabras had already taken over San Juan and were spreading across the Spanish Main, that they'd stowed away on our ship, and the figure we'd seen on the beach could be one of them.

"See what I mean?" I said to the captain. "See why I need to get to Santo Domingo?"

"Can you ride a horse?"

"Of course. I also need a mount for my wife and assistant."

He ordered three of his troopers off their horses, and another three to escort us to the station. I thanked the marines and crew for their help and told them I'd see them at the board of inquiry in Santo Domingo—which I had no intention of attending.

I also turned over the captain's log to the sergeant and instructed him to write his own version of events. Then Molly, Enrique, and I mounted up and rode west. But not before catching a final glimpse of Don Fajardo complaining to the captain, pointing a fat finger at us.

CHAPTER 37

Hispaniola—Santo Domingo

We arrived in the gloom of night, aboard a *guarda-costa* sloop that had been provided by the station *comandante*. A three-deck warship challenged us at the entrance to the river. So did sentries along the levee. Torches flared around the customs building, and over at Fortress Ozama, I could make out entire encampments of soldiers.

"I don't like it," Enrique said. "I say we board the first vessel heading west."

I agreed. Captain Gonzalez would still be here with his wanted posters. So would that meddlesome Captain of Customs. They'd also want to drag me before a board of inquiry about the loss of the *Sevilla*, and Billy's spies would be prowling the waterfronts, but I needed at least a day to pick up my documents from the Hebrews and make another try at La Casa.

I put a hand on Enrique's shoulder. "Listen, friend, you've been a faithful ally. I appreciate all you've done, but it's time for you to go home to your family. Board the first ship to Cartagena."

"Don't tell me you're staying?"

"Only for a day or two."

"To do what?" Molly asked. "Get yourself hanged?"

"It's best you leave too. You can find passage for New Orleans."

She glared at me a moment, ducked beneath the shrouds, kicked the gunwale, said "Fook" loud enough for everyone to hear, then came back. Even in the poor light I could see the tears. "Is that it? After all we've been through, you're going to cast me overboard?"

"No, Molly; I don't want to put you at risk."

"That's for me to decide. I don't take orders from—"

A bell clanged. Crewman shortened sails and took to the oars. A few minutes later, we bumped against the quay. Lines went out, planks put down, and no sooner did we debark than we were surrounded by soldiers, all with night kerchiefs over their mouths.

An officer raised a lantern. "You folks from the *Sevilla*?"

I told him we were. This brought everyone in closer. The officer asked, "Is it true what they're saying about chupacabras, that they're spreading across the Main, killing women?"

"Not just women. They seem to have a particular affinity for priests and soldiers."

It grew so quiet I could hear the wash of the ripple.

More soldiers with lanterns came out, including the soldier with the pocked face. Someone shouted, "Make way for the Captain of the *Sevilla*," and the three of us were escorted into customs as if we were angels of death.

The last time I'd entered this building, seasick and weakened from a long voyage, I had stumbled and collapsed. Now, after a long chase across the Caribbean and almost no sleep, I felt like collapsing again. "This way," said the soldier with the pocks.

He led us down a corridor and into a dimly lit office where sat none other than the Captain of Customs, the same man who'd made my last visit so miserable. Same protruding yellow teeth. Same crimson coat with flakes of dandruff on the shoulders. Same vile-tempered look, and his expression didn't improve when he addressed the soldier who'd led us in.

"Get out there and arrange for a coach to the palace. Now!"

The soldier trotted away. The captain shuffled some papers on his desk, and while this was going on I noticed all the wanted posters on the wall—pirates, smugglers, thieves, and heretics.

And there I was, a reward of thirty Pieces of Eight.

"You the captain of the *Sevilla*?"

"Acting captain," I shot back, grateful for the poor lighting.

"So you're what, first officer?"

"No, I'm head of ship licensing for the *Casa de Contratación*."

My bona fides established, I sank into a chair. "Look, Captain, we've had a long voyage. Barely survived pirates, chupacabras, a burning ship. We're exhausted. Haven't slept for days. So if it's agreeable to you, we'd like to find a place to stay, wash up, get food in us and rest."

His eyes narrowed. "Perhaps you don't understand the gravity of the situation. We have a crisis. Right now we've got to take a ride over to the governor's palace."

"The what?"

"Governor-General's palace. He's waiting for your report." He stood and put on his hat, stirring up the air with the smell of an unwashed body. "We'd best be going."

The knot in my stomach pulled tighter. Was this a trap? "But we can't go to the governor like this. Look at us. Look at our clothes. We need to clean up, to change."

"Who said anything about we? It's you the governor wants, not your wife and assistant."

An image of Don Fajardo flashed through my head. Was it possible he'd arrived before us? "Who else will be there?" I asked.

"How should I know? The governor doesn't consult me. But since you ask, I'm told it'll be the inquisitor-general, the fortress commander and a few others. They want answers."

Molly, who stood behind me, pressed my shoulder as if to say it was time to shoot the captain and run. Instead, she said in her sweetest faux French accent, "I'd like to go as well."

"No, señora, there's an inn for mariners across the street."

I shrugged as if untroubled by this news and surrendered my shoulder bag to Enrique, keeping only a pistol and the letter I'd written to Captain Gonzalez on the sloop. Enrique nodded and wished me good fortune. Molly took my arm, whispered at me not to limp, and the three of us followed the captain out of the office and onto the street where a two-horse carriage waited.

The captain hurried ahead and opened the door, but Molly held me back. "There's something I have to tell you," she whispered.

"What?"

She pulled me close and kissed me full on the lips, a moist wonderful kiss that would have inflamed me had the circumstances not been so dire. "We can make a run for it," she whispered. "Green Eyes told me where to go. She has a sister here, a bathhouse."

She tugged at my arm. "It's only a block away."

Time was short. No time to consider options. I glanced all around, into the shadows and the fog that hung over the river. Should I run or go with the captain? Then it struck me. I stepped over to Enrique. "Can I count on your help one last time?"

"Just tell me. We can't leave before tomorrow anyway."

I handed back the letter for Captain Gonzalez and told him what I wanted.

"Come on," the captain barked. "The governor's waiting."

To annoy him further, I gave Molly a long, sinful embrace, assured her I'd be all right, and sauntered over to the coach, slowly.

The ride to the governor's palace took us through the market where I'd bargained with the old Hebrew, along the waterfront with its multitude of ships and soaring masts, and past the massive Fortress Ozama. Bonfires blazed along the levee. Soldiers stood in the glare, and the pleasant aromas of roasting onions, peppers and suckling pigs sharpened the emptiness in my stomach.

Mercifully, the captain talked more than he inquired, and was muttering something about the hanging of runaway slaves when we drove up in front of a magnificent two-story building that I recognized as *La Casa de Contratación.*

"I thought we were going to the palace," I said.

"This is it. La Casa occupies the left, governor's palace the right."

Guards with plumed helmets challenged us at the entrance. A pair of liveried servants admitted us through the front. But when they looked me over, taking in my tar-covered hands and smudged shirt, my torn stockings and dirty knee breeches, they showed me into a small room with a wash basin.

"Make it fast," said the captain.

"Maybe you should wash up yourself," I said, and slammed the door in his face.

I deliberately took my time, scrubbing my hands with lye soap and washing my face.

"The devil you doing in there?" he railed, pounding on the door.

When I came out, he was pacing the floor like a caged prisoner, his face as red as his coat, his yellow teeth protruding like a rabbit's. "Have you no sense of time? Do you not realize—"

"Where can I get something to dry my face and hands?"

The servants produced a cloth. I took my time drying, thanked the servants, then followed them down a long corridor toward a pair of open doors from whence came the lovely notes of a harpsichord sonata. How soothing, I thought, and was trying to identify the piece when something crashed in a side room, followed by the screams of a woman: "No, no! Please!"

An image of Samson and El Moro flashed through my mind. The sonata continued. So did the screams, but the courage I'd mustered for the captain diminished with every step.

Don't limp, I told myself. Don't speak with a Catalonian accent. Don't pull out your pistol and start running.

The buzz of discourse and clatter of dishes came to my ears. I smelled mouth-watering aromas. Servants scurried around with platters of food, and, finally, we were shown into a grand dining room where, at a long table with his guests, sat the governor of Hispaniola.

The sonata came to a ragged coda.

Everyone turned to stare—priests, soldiers and *funcionarios* in their finest, all boots, swords, crucifixes, sashes, and glittering medals. Beyond them, though open double doors that led to the Rio Ozama, stood more soldiers and priests, among whom I recognized the Inquisition's torturer, Samson, in his leather vest.

"Your Excellency," announced one of the liveried servants in courtly fashion. "I have the honor to present the Captain of His Catholic Majesty's ship, *Nuestra Señora de Sevilla*."

The woman screamed again.

A servant shut the door behind me. Governor Zorillo, dressed in a finely cut greatcoat and a powdered bag wig, pushed away his plate and stood, which brought everyone else to their feet. He turned a venomous glare on the Captain of Customs. "Did I not instruct you to show this gentleman here the moment he arrived?"

"My humblest pardons, Your Excellency, but the delay was caused by—"

"Enough with your pretexts. Get back to your station and start searching ships! *Vete*!"

The captain shuffled off like a beaten dog. There were nervous chuckles all around. Then the governor turned his attention on me. "And, you, sir, come on in and meet these gentlemen."

Introductions followed—the local inquisitor-general in his purple cassock, the fortress commander in crimson and blue, the fiscál in his sacerdotal robe, a cavalry commander in puffy pantaloons, an admiral in white, a scribe with his plumed quill and open book.

And Captain Gonzalez in the same dress uniform he'd worn for my execution.

His black eyes burrowed into mine. Would he recognize me now that I had a mustache, a full head of hair, and a few more pounds?

"Have we met before?" Gonzalez asked in his rough voice.

"Not unless you've been lately in San Juan Bautista."

"Not lately," he said, and moved on.

I breathed again. A maid thrust a goblet of wine into my hand. I drained it, then apologized to the governor for my wretched appearance, saying there'd been no time to clean up or change.

"Not to worry," he said, and waved me into a chair at the table.

A young servant girl prepared a plate for me.

"Eat," said the governor. "We've had our fill."

The harpsichordist picked up where he'd left off. Pipes were lit, filling the room with tobacco smells. Spittoons and ashtrays appeared. A large paddle fan above the table stirred the air. The governor and his guests politely went on with their chatter; and in spite of my discomfort, I gnawed a pheasant drumstick down to the bone.

At last, the governor clapped his hands for silence.

The scribe put on his spectacles and dipped his quill into the inkwell. Servants and maids stood against the walls and at the doors. Everyone else sat in their places, staring, listening. It grew so quiet I could hear the creak of the fan. Then the governor looked squarely at me. "Tell us what happened in San Juan Bautista. Did you, yourself, Captain, personally see one of those creatures?"

"Creatures, Excellency?"

"Creatures, Captain. Chupacabras. Loogaroos."

I shoved away my plate and stood, feeling more comfortable on my feet. "I saw something, Excellency. It was in the main plaza, top of the Carmelite Convent. We were there for the hanging of an English pirate, Billy Chupacabra."

"Wait! Are you saying they hanged that low-life scoundrel?"

"They hanged him all right, but he still escaped."

I explained as best I could, relating the large crowd, the hanging. "I've never seen anything like it. People started dropping dead around me: priests, soldiers, the fiscál, even the inquisitor-general."

The governor's eyes widened. "Bishop Landa is dead?"

"Dead, Excellency. The other survivors will confirm it."

Silence reigned. Everyone made the sign of the cross. So did servants and those listening at the open patio door. The clock chimed half past the hour. And just as I was about to resume my story, a servant stepped into the room. "Begging your pardon, Excellency."

"What is it, man? Speak."

"A survivor from the *Sevilla* is here. A wounded man. He says he has urgent dispatches from San Juan Bautista… and wishes an audience with Captain Gonzalez."

CHAPTER 38

Enrique appeared at the door, looking like the victim of a chupacabra attack—his arm in a red sling, Molly's red scarf beneath his chin and over his head, a "bloody" bandage around his knee, and yet another red wrapping around his waist.

The governor seemed as stunned as everyone else.

"Who is this man?" he asked Gonzalez.

"Bank guard from Cartagena, Excellency."

Enrique limped into the room, glancing from left to right like a frightened deer. The governor waved him into a chair away from our table, as if his presence would taint the air. A servant handed him a goblet of wine. The governor said, "Why are you so bandaged up?"

"It was that runaway priest, your Lordship. He—"

"Stop right there, young man. A governor is called Excellency."

"Begging your pardon, Governor, I mean, Excellency. Anyhow, it was that damnable priest. Beat me senseless. Bashed my head, left me for dead. Captain Gonzalez..., that's him right there. He took me into his employ, purpose being to—"

The governor held up his hand. "Stop right there. This inquiry is about chupacabras."

"But..., Sir, I mean, Excellency, you asked about the injuries."

"I know what I asked. I'm now asking about chupacabras."

"Oh, yes, Excellency. I seen them clear as day, galloping across the rooftops."

"Galloping?"

"Like horses, Excellency. Ugliest creatures I ever seen. Almost big as a human. Long fingernails. Horns like a goat. Why, one of them dropped down right in front of me."

"Well, go on. What did you do?"

"Flashed my red at him."

"Flashed your what?"

"Red, Excellency, like a bullfighter. They told us that at customs… one of the odd things about chupacabras is they shy away from red. So me and Father Menendez—"

"Father Menendez?"

"Fiscál from Nicaragua, Captain Gonzalez's friend. Anyhow, we acquired some red sashes. And sure enough, no harm came to us."

"Where is Father Menendez now?"

"Still in San Juan. He bade me tell the captain here"—he motioned at Gonzalez—"that he'll be delayed a few days."

Enrique reached into his pocket and pulled out the letter I'd written for Captain Gonzalez. "Everything's explained in this letter for the captain… death of the bishop and fiscál, the slaying of El Moro, the death of that damn heretic, Father Antonio."

"The heretic is dead?"

"Dead and buried at sea. I saw the body myself."

Gonzalez seemed to turn ill. Not that he ever smiled anyway. He took the letter and retired to a small table. Bastard. How I wanted to kill him with my bare hands, smash his head into the table, rip off his campaign medals and stuff them down his throat.

"Tell us about the inquisitor-general," said the governor."

"A terrible thing it was, Excellency. We went to his office after the attacks. You should have seen the mess, everyone in a panic, six or seven priests already dead, the bishop with a big chunk torn from his neck. Soldiers running this way and that, bells tolling, people praying, crying. Anyhow, the *calificadór*, well, he's the third man in charge. He suffered us to go where the bishop lay dying, and the bishop told us the most awful tales, and what he told us was…"

He paused, and for the first time I saw how I'd underestimated Enrique. He was enjoying his lies, delaying the suspense, speaking in the voice of a frightened *campesino*.

"What did the bishop tell you?"

"He said that for two or three days before the attack someone had been singing the *Ave Maria* outside his window. A beautiful voice. The bishop looked outside but seen nobody. Sometimes the singing came from his bedchamber, or up on the roof, even from under the bed. But the worst of it was the night before the attack…."

"Would you just get on with the story?"

"Sorry, Excellency, it's so scary I get these chills thinking about it. Anyhow, the bishop, well, he said a ghost appeared to him in the night, a man with one of them… cowls. You know, that hooded thing monks pull over their heads."

"We all know what a cowl is."

"*Sí, Excelencia.* Anyhow, the bishop, well, he recognizes the ghost. Said it was a Hebrew he'd put to fire for heresy. And this ghost, this Hebrew, well, he tells the bishop that evil is going to befall him, and evil will befall the Church, and evil will befall some of the priests, and evil will befall some of the soldiers because of…."

"Because of what?"

"Begging your indulgence to repeat the words, Excellency?"

"Speak, man. What did the ghost say?"

"It said evil would befall the bishop because of the Inquisition."

The admiral almost choked on his wine. Everyone exchanged uncomfortable looks. Then the governor raised his goblet. "Let us all drink to the bishop's soul."

"To the bishop's soul," we responded.

"One more question," said the governor. "Was this a dream the bishop had about the ghost?"

"Oh, no, Excellency. The bishop said he'd swear on a Bible."

The governor sat there for the longest time, saying nothing, and finally rose to his feet. "I need to look in on my wife. Let's take a few moments to collect our thoughts."

Servants came in with fresh carafes of wine. Pipes were relit. Smoke rose up around me. Guests went in and out, and when I looked around for Gonzalez, I saw him on the outside patio with Samson, showing him the letter and looking back at Enrique.

In time, the governor marched back in.

"It's a girl," he announced, looking disappointed.

The bishop raised his glass. "Congratulations."

Everyone hoisted goblets, and all around was a chorus of muttered approval. So that was it, the source of the screams. How could the governor be so indifferent to the birth of his child?

He took his place and asked me to tell him my experiences.

I told the story with all the drama I could muster—the chase by pirates, the horrid deaths of the lieutenant, captain, first mate and others. "We weren't sure who or what killed them, but there were rumors of stowaway chupacabras."

The governor began issuing orders: Inspect the holds of every incoming ship. Place extra guards on all the roads leading into the city. Alert the citizens. Wear red. He stood and paced around the room. "I want someone to bring me the corpse of one of those beasts."

"But Excellency," said his cavalry commander. "How are we to kill these beasts?"

Enrique raised his hand. "You chop off their heads."

"And pray tell," asked the admiral who had not spoken before, "how are we going to get close enough to chop off their heads?"

"Simple. I heard it from a *campesino*, one of them cane field laborers. They attack the *chupas* with these long knives they use to chop sugar cane. Machetes."

"Write that down," said the governor to his scribe.

The questioning went on. The servants refilled our goblets. My head spun. And by the time the interrogation ended, I was slurring my words and trying to hold down my food.

At last, the governor gave a little speech about how we should all wear red and arm ourselves with machetes. Then he thanked us for coming and dismissed us with a wave.

I struggled to my feet and would have collapsed except for Enrique. He grabbed my arm, and the two of us stumbled out the side door into the foggy night air with the other guests. And that was when Governor-General Zorillo came up behind me and took my other arm.

"I forgot to ask about my brother-in-law." he said.

"Who is that, Excellency?"
"Don Fajardo. I'm told he was on your ship."

CHAPTER 39

In spite of my swirling head, or perhaps because of it, images of Don Fajardo and his wife flashed through my mind. Where were they now, that obnoxious couple? "I recall the gentleman well," I said, trying to keep my words straight, "both he and his wife."

"That would be my sister, Pilár. Are they well?"

"Oh, yes, Excellency, a bit ruffled but uninjured."

The governor waved me into a chair and called for more wine. While we waited, the strains of Caccini's *Ave Maria* came to my ears. A woman's voice. What was wrong with me? The governor raised his goblet. "To you, Captain, for saving your passengers and crew."

"And to the marines and crew," I said. "For their loyal service."

I took a sip even though I knew I shouldn't. In the darkness behind me, somewhere amid the twinkling fireflies and fog and notes of *Ave Maria*, Enrique and Gonzalez were discoursing about my "death" and that of El Moro. I twisted sideways to hear better, but the governor reached over and punched me on the arm.

"I asked about the runaways."

"Runaways?'

"Didn't Don Fajardo tell you? Nine worthless Negroes."

"Oh, yes, Excellency, I had no idea they were runaways."

"The worst kind." He raised his goblet. "To their hanging."

"You're going to hang them for running away?"

"No, *Capitán*, before they ran away, they murdered my slave master. Commandeered a ship, and murdered half the crew, then sailed off and joined the pirates."

I almost choked. What would he say if I told him his slaves wouldn't be at the hanging?

The governor stood, put on his hat, thanked me again for coming, and left me sitting amid the croak of frogs. I twisted around, looking for Enrique, but my eyes couldn't focus. Worse, the ground beneath me seemed to be moving, the world spinning.

"No," I heard Enrique say. "You promised ten Pieces of Eight."

There were curses, the clink of money exchanging hands, and occasionally the rumble of Samson's voice—heavy, oxen-like, coming from a deep chest. Enrique muttered a curse in response, and if I hadn't been so nauseated, I might have marveled at his temerity. As it was, I stumbled to the levee in the darkness, fell to my knees and let it all out—the wine, the food, the misery.

I rested until the nausea passed, then made my way back to the table where I'd sat with the governor. Now I could see them, vaguely—Enrique, Samson and Gonzalez—at a table just beyond the patio, their faces yellow in the light of a low-burning lantern. Enrique was saying, "Saw the heretic with my own eyes. Dead as a smashed frog… guts hanging out."

"And El Moro?"

"Head smashed. They must have killed each other."

Samson stood and clomped around the patio. "Damn that heretic. He'll pay for killing El Moro."

"He's already dead. How are you going to make him pay?"

Gonzalez spoke up. "I'll tell you how. He has two bastard kids."

My hand went instinctively to the pistol in my belt. How dare this snake threaten the lives of my children, this monster who burned villages, who violated women and murdered the innocent.

He kept talking, his voice growing louder. "We should eliminate the little bastards the moment we get back, do to them what we did with their mother?"

I froze. Did he just admit he'd killed Saraatepe?

Enrique, who knew about my hopes for reuniting with her, asked, "You killed their mother?"

"She was an Indian. She resisted. Came at me with a knife."

"Slit her throat," Samson said, "after we sampled her charms."

Their laughter passed like a flame through my tortured ears. Forget logic. Forget the guards. Kill them now. I pulled out the pistol and was fumbling with the hammer, trying to pull it back, when a familiar voice spoke from the darkness: "No!"

Where the Gypsy came from I did not see, yet there she stood, a luminous glow in the darkness. Long white dress and hoop earrings, her hair catching the breeze off the water.

"The moment is not now," she said in Saraatepe's Indian tongue.

I shook my head. Why was she speaking to me in Chorotegan? "Is it true what they are saying?" I asked.

A look of sadness crossed her face, and I knew without a doubt that what Gonzalez said was true, that I'd been deluding myself. The image faded. The frogs came back, but even they seemed to be mocking me, croaking *Ave Maria.*

"Father, *estás bien? Qué te pasó?* Father?"

Enrique was standing over me. The table where Gonzalez and Samson had sat was vacant. Around me, servants were dousing lanterns and stacking chairs.

I struggled to my feet. "Where is Gonzalez?"

"Gone. Didn't you see them leave? You must have fallen asleep."

He took my arm, and the two of us stumbled through the darkness to a coach. I told the driver to take us to the mariners' inn, and as soon as we were inside the coach and the door closed, reality struck: I'd never see that lovely face again, never hear her voice, never feel her warmth. For eleven long months in my prison cell I had known she was dead, but the effects of the fever juice had given me hope.

Enrique put a hand on my shoulder. "Maybe they were lying."

"No, Enrique. Everyone except me knew the truth."

We rolled along the waterfront in silence, passing ships, the fortress, the market, and the Catedral de Santa Maria. A flash of lightning brightened an ugly cloud bank over the Rio Ozama and just as quickly left us in darkness. "Stop," I ordered the driver.

"What's wrong?" Enrique asked. "You're sick again?"

"No, just wait here."

I alighted from the coach, staggered into the cathedral, passed along the aisle where sat other lost souls on the benches, and fell to my knees in the shadows at the altar. There, beneath an icon of a candlelit Virgin, I lit a candle and prayed for Saraatepe's soul.

Take her into heaven, I begged. Make her an angel. Let her light forever shine. I prayed until my knees hurt, until I became aware of other supplicants beside me, and when I ran out of things to say, I staggered out into the night.

"Captain, is that you?"

It was Samson, all scars, shaven head and tattoos, his silver chain catching a glitter of torchlight. "Thought it was you," he said in his coarse voice. "What are you doing here?"

"Lit a candle for a friend. What about you?"

"*Oigame*, Captain. I may look like a bull. I may be an executioner, but I'm devout. Besides, that man they mentioned in the letter, El Moro. We were like… brothers."

He choked up and wiped at his eyes. It didn't seem right. Samson the torturer, the man who'd light the flames beneath my feet and burn me alive, now crying like a baby. What would he say if he knew it was I, Father Antonio, who'd battered his dear friend to death?

"What about Captain Gonzalez?" I asked. "Why isn't he here?"

"The captain wouldn't light a candle for his own mother." With those words, he clopped into the church, made the sign of the cross, and left me on the steps.

At last, we arrived back at the inn. "If it was me," Enrique said, "I'd sneak back to the cathedral now. In the darkness. Set up an ambuscade. Get him when he comes out."

"I've got other plans for him."

We woke the innkeeper, got our key, and lumbered up the stairs to the second floor where Molly had taken a room for us, where she was supposed to be waiting.

I knocked on the door. "Molly, it's us. Are you awake?"

She did not open it. No movement or sounds either. I fumbled with the key, got the door open and pushed inside with my lantern.

Her bed was empty, her things gone. Molly had left us.

CHAPTER 40

The creak and rattle of a passing wagon brought me out of a dream; and when I opened my eyes, the pillow that had been Saraatepe was just a pillow, crumpled and lifeless. Tears ran down my cheeks. If only I'd never gone to that cursed cave. If only I'd told them where to find it. If only I could make the pain go away.

But I couldn't. Not as long as my children were in peril. And not as long as the men who killed Saraatepe were still working their evil.

I rolled out of bed and shook Enrique awake.

"Come on. We've got to find Molly."

He struggled out of bed, groaning. "What's the hurry? She said she was going to that bath house up the street." He clutched his stomach, retched, and dashed to the chamber pot.

I didn't feel well either, so I opened the window and breathed in the early morning smells of fish and wood smoke. Below me, the city was coming to life—bells tolling, roosters crowing, a vendor hawking fresh bread from a platter. A three-mast ship was coming in on the tide, stirring up sea gulls. The usual crowd was gathering at the customs house. An even larger crowd was gathering around a poster. "What does it say?" I yelled down.

"A warning about chupacabras. Says to wear red and arm yourselves with machetes."

"Is that all?"

"No, it also says pirates attacked and burned the *Sevilla*, but the best news is that heretic priest from Nicaragua was killed. They buried him at sea."

"Did anyone collect the reward?"

"It doesn't say."

We washed at the basin, dressed in our rumpled clothes, and trekked down the stairs to the dining room. Ham hocks hung from rafters, along with strings of onions, garlic, and sausages. Pleasant aromas rose up around us. Frying onions and peppers. Bacon and sausage. Bread in the oven. Coffee. It was too much to pass up, so we each loaded a platter and found a table beneath a thatched roof on the outside patio, facing the street.

From our table, I could easily see the locals around the poster—women with babes in arms, tradesmen carrying axes and mallets, Gypsies, soldiers, and a flock of ragged children begging for handouts. A bearded man who looked like a ship's captain was reading the poster aloud for those who couldn't read.

"It's a sign," shouted a wrinkled old woman in black, her hair as scraggly as a wet dog.

"A sign of what, Grandma?"

"The end of the world. The Bible speaks of times like these… earthquakes and hurricanes, wars and plagues, beasts crawling out of holes. Everyone should read the *Book of Revelations*."

"What if you can't read?" asked a man in mud-spattered clothing.

"Get someone to read it for you."

Her rant grew louder: Jesus would appear in the clouds any day. We would all be judged. Many of us would be devoured by the beast. The only salvation was to repent.

"It'll all blow over in a month," I said to Enrique. "After they learn there's no such creature."

"What do you mean, no such creature?"

"Oh, please, don't tell me you've fallen for that nonsense?"

"It's not nonsense. I might have been stretching the truth to the governor, but I saw something. And how do you explain Vampire Jack? Molly says you have to cut off his head."

I rolled my eyes. Was this how vampire stories got started? Was it possible people would still be talking about chupacabras a hundred years from now?

We finished our breakfast and crossed the street just as a stream of passengers with bags and trunks was flowing out of customs, pushing through the locals and heading toward coaches.

Questions flew at them from all sides, and within minutes we'd learned of a Wayuu Indian attack in Cartagena, the hijacking of a gold-bearing wagon train near Portobello, and another Virgin appearance at Vera Cruz.

"See," shrieked the old woman. "The Holy Bible says…"

I'd had enough of her babble and was leading Enrique away when a familiar face hobbled through the customs door, a white-haired priest balancing himself on a walking cane.

Could it be? Yes, Father Gregorio of Masaya.

He glanced over his shoulder the way I often did, as if he too were on the run, and began answering questions. "I'm from Nicaragua," he said solemnly. "The news is not good. What we're having is an uprising… Indians resisting the bishop's edict."

"What edict is that, Father?"

"An edict to remove natives from their ancestral homeland."

"Everything is predicted in the Bible," cried the old woman.

How I wanted to ask about Abuelita and Rosa Morales, and little Mateo, Father Paolo and others, but I couldn't. I was "dead," buried at sea. But Enrique, who could never let an issue rest, said to the priest, "There's a wanted poster here for a heretic from Granada, a singing priest. They say he's a murderer and rapist."

"Lies," spat the old priest. "*El Cantante* was a good man, a faithful servant of God. All he did was try to protect the Indians from the unholy greed of the inquisitors."

He hobbled away and climbed into a coach. I watched him go, emotion welling up inside me. Had they confiscated his possessions as well? Excommunicated him? How brave he was. How good to know I was still held in high esteem among my friends.

I pulled Enrique into the departures building, marched to the counter, and got the clerk's attention.

"When's the next ship leaving for Nicaragua?"

"Wouldn't know, *caballero*, but we've got a ship sailing today for Cartagena. On the tide, three in the afternoon, *más o menos*."

Three o'clock. It was already going on nine. That left six hours to get my documents from the Hebrews, pick up my clothing at the shops, finish my business with La Casa, find Molly, and get back to the landing. I purchased tickets for Cartagena, then pulled out the latest letter I'd written to the bishop.

"Can you send this with one of the warships?"

"Not a problem, *caballero*. It'll get there before you do."

We thanked him and hurried outside. By then the old woman was standing on the same bench Gonzalez had used to warn the populace about me, now brandishing a Bible.

"Repent," she cried. "Sever our relations with the devil."

Enrique said, "I've had enough fire and doom. Let's find Molly."

"Molly can wait. Right now, I'm going to rob a bank."

"You're what?"

"You'll see."

By the time our coach stopped in front of La Casa, I was Father Menendez again, dressed in a cassock with hat, sandals and dangling crucifix. Church bells were tolling nine. A small knot of clients had gathered in front, waiting for the doors to open.

I paid the driver, then the two of us stood on the walkway with our bags, Enrique trying to talk me out of it.

"Doesn't it trouble you to steal?" he asked. "You being a priest?"

"Oh, please, Enrique, it was ill-gotten gains to begin with: stolen, plundered, extorted. Besides, I want it to go back to the Church… or charity, or the families of the victims."

He shook his head. "Excuse me for asking, but are we discoursing about the same Church that wanted to burn you at the stake?"

The doors swung open. Guards with plumed helmets began motioning people in. I stuffed a wad of cotton between my teeth and gums to give myself a fuller face, tied Molly's red scarf around my waist, and turned back to Enrique.

"Hail a coach the moment you see me coming out."

"What if you don't come out?"
"Then you should find Molly and get her out of town."

CHAPTER 41

La Casa de Contratación

I stepped inside with other clients, and followed the signs toward Accountancies and Fiduciaries, forcing myself to walk like a priest in a communal procession, hands clasped in front. A gentleman in the corridor said, "Bless you, Father." Other clients nodded and smiled. The clerk behind the counter asked if it was true what they were saying about the Second Coming of Christ.

"Only God knows the truth, *mijo*. Put your faith in Him."

I told the clerk my name and business, trying to emulate Father Menendez's high-pitched tone, and after a short wait was shown into an office where an older *funcionario* sat with a ledger in his hand. His belt was red. So was the handkerchief around his left wrist. He introduced himself as a *licenciado de contabilidad*, which meant he was a licensed accountant.

"I'm told you're a fiscál," he said, "from Nicaragua."

"I am. We've been chasing a heretical priest."

"Dreadful business. You must be relieved to hear he's dead."

"Not at all. He should have suffered for his sins. Should have burned at the stake."

He squirmed a bit in his chair. "Yes, I agree. A man like that should suffer."

I repeated my story that I was purchasing land and other properties for the Church in Nicaragua, saying the owner was a gentleman named Don Antonio Arteaga y Flores—the name on the account I'd opened back in Cartagena. "I'm paying nine thousand escudos. That should leave me enough to keep my account open."

"Nine thousand? It must be sizable property."

"Very large—cattle, horses, barns, storage buildings."

I laid out Father Menendez's *cédula* and travel documents on his desk, jotted down his account numbers, then told him the secret word—Malinche. He examined each document carefully.

"Interesting. Wasn't Malinche—?"

"Cortez's mistress. It's also the name of a tree."

He asked a few more questions, picked up his ledger, said he'd be right back and stepped out, leaving me sweating in my chair. Would he come back with a superior?

After a few minutes he shuffled back into the office. "Everything is in order."

Blessed relief swept over me, and I sat there, silently, watching him write out a copy of the transaction. He then stamped the document with an official seal, called in another clerk to witness my signature, and handed it over.

I rose to my feet, stunned at the simplicity. If it was this easy, maybe I could defraud Captain Gonzalez's account here as well, do it today instead of waiting to get to Cartagena. "I have a question," I said. "Have you met my partner from Nicaragua, Captain Gonzalez?"

"I have not had that pleasure, Father. Why do you ask?"

"Well, as I understand it, he has a problem with his account."

"What kind of problem?"

"I'm sure he'll tell you if he stops by, but it's something like this. His most trusted lieutenant, a man named Vasquez, was killed during the escape. Vasquez did all his banking for him, had all his numbers, codes, everything. The captain's worried that he—Vasquez—might have written down that information, or told someone else, and someone else could get his money."

"Oh, my. One should never entrust personal accounts to others. It invites fraud. He should change his code and account number."

"Can the captain do it here?"

"Absolutely. Tell him to stop by and ask for me."

"I doubt he can get here before the mid-day break. What time do you re-open?"

"Two by the clock, Father." He wished me a safe voyage and escorted me to the door. I thanked him and strolled out of his office, richer by nine thousand escudos. Richer than I'd ever been in my life. And about to get a lot richer if I came back as the captain.

The guards at the exit held the door for me. A cool breeze blew off the river. Birds sang in the trees above me, and I was so consumed by my success that I didn't notice the Captain of Customs until it was almost too late.

There he stood with Enrique, who looked on the verge of panic. With him were Chino and the soldier with the pock-marked face, the same soldiers who'd confronted me with the Hebrew during my last visit. Worse, they all looked up as if to say, "We know who you are."

My heart seemed to stop. The old dread came back. I angled away and kept walking. Two steps. Three. Don't look back. Don't run.

No challenge. Maybe they didn't recognize me. I picked up the pace and headed into the plaza where workers were hammering away on a gallows' platform. Another reminder of things gone wrong. By then my breath was coming in short spurts, my heart pounding.

I leaned against the trunk of a mango tree to catch my breath, but the workers seemed to mistake my action as interest in what they were doing. "What do you think, Father? Will it hold all nine runaways?"

"Looks sturdy to me. Bless all of you for your hard work."

"They say Jesus is coming soon. What do you think?"

"No one knows, *mijo*. Could be today. Could be tomorrow."

I hurried away, passing around the platform and turning back in the direction of La Casa. Behind me, the saws were buzzing again, the hammers pounding.

Enrique was still on the walkway, now by himself, glancing around, looking for me. I waved. He waved back, hailed a coach, and a minute or two later I was sitting in the coach beside him, rolling away from La Casa. "What did the captain want?" I asked.

"You. The governor is having another meeting. Now, this very minute. He wants you there.

"I told him you were inside La Casa, reporting to superiors. He went inside looking for you. And that's not the worst part."

"What, Enrique? Tell me."

"Some of the survivors from our ship arrived this morning. Remember Don Fajardo?"

"What about him?"

"Well, after we left him, he fell behind on the road. When they went back for him they found him strung up from a tree—neck slashed, blood drained, mark of the devil."

I closed my eyes and shook my head. "And his wife?"

"Safe. She says he went into the forest to relieve himself. Didn't come back. She claims it was the runaway slaves that killed him. And she's blaming you. So is the governor. He's mad as a rabid dog. Wants answers about why you unshackled his slaves."

He took a deep breath. "And you haven't heard the worst part."

"What, Enrique? Just tell me."

"The governor's been consulting with some high ups from La Casa. They say they never heard of you. They're at the meeting."

I groaned and shook my head. Now I didn't dare report to the governor. But to ignore his summons and go into hiding would be an admission of guilt. They'd send out search parties. And the first place they'd look would be the landing. "I've got an idea," I said.

"Every idea you have gets us deeper into *mierda*."

Four or five minutes later, we were back in front of La Casa. I sat on a bench facing the entrance, tossing bread crumbs to the sea gulls like a benevolent old priest. Passersby strolled around us. The coach with our bags waited a block away. Enrique stood in the shade of a spreading Flamboyán tree, crimson petals falling all around.

"I don't like your idea," he said. "I think it's best if we hide out until boarding time."

The Captain of Customs marched out of the building, his face a picture of torment. With him were the marine sergeant, the old steward, and his two soldiers.

"Don't panic," I said to Enrique. "They won't recognize me dressed as a priest."

The captain spotted Enrique and clopped over.

"Has he come out yet?"

"He came out all right. I told him what you said. Told him the governor wanted to see him pronto. He said he'd go to the meeting, but then a coach drove up with news about his wife."

"Wife? What are you talking about?"

"His wife. She was taken ill… needed him right away. He asked me to wait here to tell you. Says he sends regrets, but to tell the governor he'll be back soon as possible."

The captain's eyes bulged. His teeth protruded. He stomped around, shaking his arms and mumbling to himself. Then he got right in Enrique's face. "You let him go. You knew this was important, and you just let him go."

"Couldn't be helped. I'm not his superior."

"Where is he? Where did he go?"

"How should I know? I was just a passenger on the ship."

"Either you answer me, or you answer to the governor."

"Oh, yeah, and who's going to make me go see the governor?"

The captain reached for Enrique's arm. Enrique jerked loose and bawled up his fists. "You asking to lose them buck teeth?"

The marine sergeant stepped forward. "Begging your pardon, sir, but I know this gentleman. He was only a passenger. I could answer the governor's questions better than he could."

"That makes two of us," said the old steward. "He don't know more'n he's telling."

I felt color returning to my face. The captain glowered at Enrique a few seconds, then he and the four men with him struck off toward the governor's entrance.

We lingered until they were inside the building, then headed for the coach. Only four more hours to finish my business and get to the landing. "Where are we going?" Enrique asked.

"You'll see."

CHAPTER 42

Our first stop was at the shop to pick up the bishop's garb I'd purchased a week or so earlier. There were no questions and no problems, at least not until I climbed back into the coach. "A bishop's clothing?" Enrique said. "What the hell are you going to—"

"Don't ask Enrique, and I won't tell."

We changed coaches in case the driver got suspicious, then told our new driver to take us to the market. Along the way, we passed "bath" houses I had not noticed before—the Mysteries of the Orient, Maria's Palace of Pleasure, and *Les Belles Haitiens.*

"That's it," Enrique said, "*Les Belles Haitiens.*"

An image of Molly flashed through my head—the two of us on the street last night, tears in her eyes, feelings and words unsaid, there amid the sparkling fireflies.

"Shouldn't we go there?" Enrique said.

"Not until I see the Hebrews."

A turn to the left and we stopped at the entrance to the market. "You're going to the Jews like that," Enrique said, "in a priest outfit?"

"I have to; not enough time to change."

I stepped down, passed beneath the tree where I'd first met the Gypsy, and hurried through the market. Gone were the dancers and musicians. In their places was a sense of dread. Those not already wearing red or carrying machetes were bunched up at cutlery and clothing stalls, shouting, pushing, arguing, trying to buy anything red.

The Hebrews were at the same tables as before, all beards, dark hats, black clothing and writing tablets.

The old man gave me a puzzled look.

"It's me," I said. "Remember? I'm here for the *cédulas*?"

"What *cédulas*, Father?"

"Please. I'm not with the Inquisition. Not a priest either."

He sighed, pulled the documents from a leather pouch, and handed them over—one in the name of Captain Gonzalez, a second in the name of the inquisitor-general of Nicaragua, and a third in the fake name I'd created for myself, Don Antonio Arteaga y Flores.

"Do me a favor," said the Jew. "Forget where these came from."

"Forget where what came from?"

We laughed and shook hands. I paid him the balance, hurried back to the coach, and a few minutes later we drove up in front of the military clothing store.

Not wanting to change out of my priest's garments, and not wanting to answer that meddlesome little clerk's questions, I asked Enrique to go in and fetch the captain's uniform I'd purchased.

He jumped out, slammed the door, and marched inside.

Wagons and coaches rolled by. Soldiers on horseback clattered along the cobbled street. The pleasant aroma of street cooking permeated the air, mixing with the more pungent smells.

At last Enrique came out with my bundle. "Get down," he said, hopping into the coach. "That damn clerk followed me out. He's there now, in the door, watching."

I bent low, and stayed low until we rolled out of sight, the driver cracking his whip and yelling at bystanders.

"Damn it to hell," Enrique said. "I should have known this was going to be trouble. He wanted to know who you are, where you're from. Said when you first came in, he suspected you were the heretic, you having a limp and Catalonian accent."

"Didn't he see the governor's poster?"

"He did, but he's still not convinced you're dead."

We drove to the plaza, paid the driver, waited until he was out of sight, and hailed another coach. The streets were as crowded as ever, people dressed in red and carrying machetes.

"Where to now?" Enrique said.

"*Les Belles Haitiens*. It's time to find Molly."

A few more blocks, around a corner, and there it was.

Please dear God, let her be here.

The door was green, just like the door in San Juan Bautista, with horseshoes above it and other symbols of the owner's superstition.

I knocked and waited. It was already past noon. Less than three hours left to find Molly, bathe, change into a cavalry uniform, get to La Casa at two, convince the banker I was Captain Gonzalez, and get back to the landing.

An attractive young woman of color motioned us in with our bags, bolted the door behind us, and led us up a stairway and onto a balcony populated by black cats. Sheets flapped on lines in the courtyard below. Women bent low over ironing boards and wash pots, cats meowed, and if I hadn't known better, I'd have sworn we were back at Green Eyes' place in San Juan.

A door opened, and out stepped a woman who looked a lot like Green Eyes, except older. She looked me up and down in my priest garb. "How may I help you, Father?"

"I'd like to see Molly. She came here last night."

"We have a Desiree, Chantal, Monique, and Anne Marie, but no one named Molly."

"Please, Madam, just tell her we're here. She'll want to see us."

"You also need baths, no?"

"*Oui, Madame*, and I'd like to have this uniform pressed." I handed her the bundle. "We're also in a bit of a hurry. I have an appointment at two by the clock."

"Not to worry, monsieur. Plenty of time to enjoy our accommodations."

We settled on a price, then followed a couple of lovely señoritas into separate rooms that could just as well have been in San Juan Bautista, complete with a copper tub filled with steaming water, candle light, a bunk, and sketches of frolicking nudes on the walls.

"Is someone going to tell Molly I'm here? It's important."

"Patience, monsieur. First we make you clean and handsome."

At my request, they trimmed my hair and mustache to give me the look favored by Captain Gonzalez, then left long enough for me to strip and sink into the tub.

Girls came and went, a parade of scantily dressed señoritas with towels, soaps, robes, buckets of fresh warm water and a platter of fruits and juices. I ate. I drank.

I rehearsed in my head what I was going to tell the banker, and I was getting impatient when I heard Molly's voice.

The door opened and closed behind me. I heard whispers. The door opened and closed again, and then a hand touched my head from behind. Molly's hand. Soft and loving.

"Antonio," she whispered, "what took you so long?"

She stepped to my front, leaned down, and kissed me on the cheek, her long hair brushing my bare shoulder. She was lovelier than ever, her hair damp and smelling like gardenias, and she was wearing the same kind of white robe the girls wore, thin and lacy. She pulled back her shoulders, smiled, and began untying the ribbons, slowly, while looking into my eyes.

"Tell me, Antonio, is this what you want?"

My breath quickened; my excitement grew.

"You know what I want."

"Say it. I want to hear you say it."

"I want you, Molly. I cannot live another day without you."

The robe fell to the floor, and she stood there long enough for me to take in her full beauty—the firm breasts, the flat stomach, the long thighs and white skin where the sun had not touched. An image of the banker flashed through my mind, sitting behind his desk. And yet here was Molly in front of me, nude, moistening her lips with her tongue.

"Will you want me tomorrow?"

"I want you now, Molly. I want you tomorrow and the day after and every day."

"Promise?"

At that moment, I'd have promised her the moon. "I promise."

She sank into the tub facing me. We came closer. Her lips found mine. Hungry lips. Soft lips that tasted of honey. And for the first time in more than a year I discovered love, in a warm tub of water in a bath house in Santo Domingo.

CHAPTER 43

How long we remained in that tub, locked in the embrace of lovers, I do not know. What I do know is I'd never been closer to heaven. And when the water cooled, we came out and did it again on the bunk. And on the table. And it wasn't until the bells tolled for two that I pulled myself away in spite of her objections, got dressed in a cavalry uniform, rounded up Enrique, hailed a coach, and headed back to La Casa.

The coach creaked as if the wheels had not been lubricated for years. The horses shuffled along with their heads down, as if unaware of the concept of hurry. Worse, the driver stopped to chat with an acquaintance. I slid back the partition. "Señor, please?"

He turned back to me, slowly. "In a bit of a hurry, are we, General?"

"It's captain, and either you get this coach moving or I'll get a different driver."

He bade goodbye to his friend and snapped the reins, but still we rolled along as if married to the potholes. Enrique sat across from me in his clean clothes, his hair slicked back, smelling like freshly squeezed lemons.

"If you're going to be a cavalry captain," he said, "you better start acting like one."

"How exactly does a captain act?"

"For one thing, he doesn't say 'Please' to a slow-ass, camel driver. He'd take out his pistol and threaten to shoot the little bastard. And by the way, I don't know what you and Molly did back there in that tub, but you better know what you're doing. She's a pirate's woman. Been passed around. And even if she hasn't, you can bet Billy sank his little wick into—"

"Shut up, Enrique."

The coach drew to a noisy stop in front of La Casa. I pulled on my hat, told Enrique to wait in front, and stepped onto the tiled walkway in my captain's uniform, all crimson and blue with red epaulettes, campaign ribbons, golden sash and shiny brass buttons. Storm clouds loomed up in the southern sky, black and ominous. The scaffold construction was still going on in the plaza, and the usual traffic was going in and out of La Casa.

"God give me strength," I muttered, and strode toward the entrance the way I'd seen Captain Gonzalez walk: at a fast clip, arms swinging, looking straight ahead, forcing myself to scowl.

The sentries snapped to attention. I returned their salutes and clopped through the door like a Roman centurion. Up the marble stairway, down the corridor, past a sign that read, Ships and Licensing, and there it was, Accountancies and Fiduciaries.

The clerk stiffened on my approach. A half dozen or more men looked up from their chairs. I stepped to the counter, stomped a heel on the floor and spoke in a commanding voice. "*Licenciado* Garcia is expecting me."

"Oh, yes, *Capitán*, of course. If you'll just take a seat over there."

"How long is this going to take?"

"Could be awhile. Those other gentlemen are also waiting."

"Listen, *mijo*, I've got a ship to catch."

He grabbed a ledger and hurried toward the back. I pivoted around and turned my glare on the other men. "Military business. Would you *caballeros* mind?"

"Not at all, sir."

The minutes ticked by. I stood at the counter and drummed my fingers on the surface. The other men smoked their pipes and chatted about chupacabras and pirates. One of them seemed to be examining my decorations. "Isn't that the Badge of Courage?" he said, pointing.

"Indian wars," I snapped, wanting to rip off the ribbon before it burned a hole in my heart.

The clock on the wall struck half past the hour. What was taking so long? Passengers at the landing were already loading. Worse, the lovemaking with Molly had left me sore, and this ill-fitting uniform, tight in the crotch, didn't make it any better.

A blast of martial music interrupted my thoughts, all brass and percussion.

I stepped to the window. Men, women and children were running into the square. From the east came a military band, with fluttering flags, guidons and banners, the cavalry on prancing horses.

Could it be? Yes, the survivors from the *Sevilla*: the marines on foot, muskets shouldered, their uniforms rumpled and dusty, followed by wagonload after wagonload of waving crew and passengers. Then a rag-tag group of dancing kids, citizens, and mangy dogs.

"They must be celebrating the sinking of that pirate ship," said one of the other men.

"What pirate ship?" I asked.

"Didn't you hear? One of our warships sank the pirates. Sent them to the bottom."

Billy's ship, I hoped, and was wondering if Molly had heard the news when *Licenciado de Contabilidad* Garcia, stepped out of his office. "*Capitán*," he said, and motioned me inside.

The high collar of my uniform tightened like a noose around my neck. The banker looked me up and down. "I'm told you have a problem with your account."

"A minor problem. Father Menendez told me you'd recommend—"

"That you change the account number and secret code. Absolutely, and if you don't mind me saying, you should never, never share that information with anyone you can't trust—"

"I'm in something of a hurry. My ship sails with the tide."

"It's only five minutes to the landing."

I handed him my travel document and fake *cédula*, told him the account number and secret code—Relámpago—sank into the same chair where I'd sat earlier as Father Menendez, and told him I'd also like to also transfer some of my funds to a certain Don Antonio Arteaga.

He took his time looking over the documents. The music outside grew louder. I felt the sweat underneath my armpits. "Is there a problem?" I asked.

"No, no, it's just that we have to be careful."

At last he took the papers and disappeared into a back room, leaving me alone with my thoughts. Had he recognized me from this morning? I stood and paced the room, tugging at my tight collar, wiping sweat from my face. The commotion on the street was growing louder, the music spirited. Was that the same score they'd played at the burning of the hunchback?

The door opened. "You can rest easy," said the banker. "No recent withdrawals."

I wasn't sure what was important about that and didn't ask. Didn't ask how much was in the account either. Didn't want to know until I was safely away.

"Do you want all of it to go into your new account?"

"No, I want half to go to Don Antonio, the other half to the new account, minus, say, a hundred to leave in the old account. Just in case I need more funds before it clears."

"You'll need a different code for your new account."

"Saraatepe," I said, and spelled the name for him.

Mercifully, he did not ask for an explanation. Instead, he finished the paperwork for the transfer to Don Antonio, did the paperwork for the new account, called in another clerk to witness signatures, and asked me to sign pages and pages of copies.

The signing took only two or three minutes but seemed like hours. Pick up the quill, dip it in the well, sign, blot, and sign on the other page. Enrique was probably cursing up a tempest.

Once the last page had been signed, I stood.

"Not yet," said the banker. "We have to make duplicate copies."

I wanted to curse, to cry out in frustration. Instead, I sat there while he made yet another copy of each transaction. Then he asked me to sign those as well, which required a witness.

Finally, he stamped all documents with an official *sella*, thanked me for my patience, wished me a safe voyage, and escorted me to the door. “Please, *Capitán*, this is important. Don’t ever share your code or account number with anyone else. You can’t trust people nowadays.”

I thanked him, hurried down the corridor, down the stairs, and out the door. Don’t run, I told myself. Don’t trip and fall on your face. Return the salute of the guards.

Where was Enrique?

There, in that coach coming down the street, but clogged in traffic and merrymakers. And that damn band, blasting away with martial music.

I struck off to meet him, pushing around citizens and even people I recognized from the ship, some of them humming and marching to the music, others shouting, “Death to the English!”

Four or five little boys trotted behind, tugging at my jacket and begging for money, slowing me down. Then an old woman grabbed my arm and tried to sell me a shawl. I tore loose, broke into a trot, and hopped into the coach with Enrique while it was still in motion.

He yelled at the driver to get us to the landing pronto, then turned back to me. “Tide’s already going out. It’s past three. We may not make it.”

CHAPTER 44

I stripped off the uniform as fast as I could, stuffed it into a travel bag, and began pulling on Father Menendez's cassock, happy to be out of that suffocating captain's outfit.

"What took so long?" Enrique asked.

"Paperwork." I pulled out my copy of the documents, held it to the light at the window, and could hardly believe my eyes—8,563 escudos, more than a thousand ounces of gold.

Enrique snatched away the paper. "*Por Dios*, Padre. You're rich."

"No, Enrique. This money is tainted. All I want is the four-hundred they stole from me."

"Are you crazy? You earned it for what they did to you."

A pothole almost bounced us out of our seats, splashing mud on the window. I slid back the glass and looked out. The Vera Cruz was midway out on the Ozama, still loading freight and passengers. Other vessels were there as well, but the warships had already weighed anchor and were under sail. Poor Molly. I could picture her sitting inside the waiting room with her bags, dressed like *une femme de coleur libre*, getting more frantic by the minute.

We rolled to a stop in front of the departures building. A crowd had gathered at the fence to see off their loved ones. A green tidal flag snapped and fluttered above the customs house. Green, meaning ebb. Enrique opened the coach door, and just as quickly slammed it shut.

"*Hijo de la gran puta*! It's that damn Captain of Customs."

I yelled at the driver to keep going.

"What about Molly?" Enrique asked.

"She won't leave without us."

"Are you sure? Why don't you go anyway? That captain has the brain of an anvil. He won't recognize you in your priest clothes."

"No, Enrique, I'm not leaving without you."

At the end of the street, where it dead-ended at waters' edge, we turned around and drove back toward the landing. Out on the Ozama, the traffic was heavy with barges, tenders, water taxis, and dugout canoes containing entire families.

"Look," Enrique said. "The captain is leaving."

I ordered the driver to stop. We waited until the captain and his two soldiers crossed the street and rounded a corner, then rolled on, stopping directly in front of the entrance.

Molly was nowhere in sight. We jumped out with our bags and dashed into the waiting room. She wasn't there either, only the ticket master, a cleaning crew, and a greasy little fellow with hair pulled back in a ponytail.

"*Coño*," Enrique hissed. "What the devil is he doing here?"

"Who?"

"The toad, that greasy little shit from the military store."

I ignored him, dashed to the counter and spoke to the clerk. "A woman was here, waiting for us."

"Look around, Padre. If she's not here, she's already boarded."

We trotted out the back and down to the river where oarsmen stood next to their small craft, waiting for latecomers. I rushed to the master of a small boat with a rotting thatched roof.

"Can you get us to the *Vera Cruz*?"

He spat out a wad of tobacco. "It'll cost a *real*."

"Your sign says a half *real*."

"Do you want a ride or not?"

I handed him a one *real* coin.

"Each," he said.

Enrique muttered something I didn't hear and gave him another real. We flung our bags into the boat and were about to board when that greasy little clerk rushed out with a pistol, waving it around like a drunk, slurring his words.

"You're not going anywhere. I know who you are."

Enrique whacked him across the wrist with the cane.

The pistol fired. Powder burns bit into my face. Smoke filled the air, and when I regained my senses, I saw the man on his knees, holding his wrist and crying in agony, Enrique standing over him with his cane. "Enough!" I shouted. "He's drunk."

An oarsman retrieved the pistol, grinned, and stuffed it into his belt. Then we hopped into the boat and pushed off, leaving the clerk still on his knees, cursing and hurling insults.

"What was that about?" the boat master asked me.

"I have no idea. Must be mistaken identity."

A toothless old oarsman looked up. "*Oyeme*, Padre, you're a good-looking fellow... for a priest. Tell us the truth, now. You weren't messing with his woman, was you?"

They all had a good chuckle. I tried to laugh with them, but all I could think about was Molly. Why hadn't she waited? Was she on the ship?

At last, the *Vera Cruz* loomed up before us, passengers staring over the side. I shaded my eyes, looking for Molly. Only four women, but not one resembled her. How could that be? She must be in some other disguise. Yes, that had to be it. She was dressed as a crew hand.

We struggled up the ladder with our bags and were soon on deck, mingling with other passengers. I pushed, shoved, and looked all around, my heart sinking. She was not there. Neither were Samson and Captain Gonzalez. They must have taken one of the other ships.

I lumbered to the railing and stared back at the city, fighting back tears. Had she deliberately stayed behind? Was the secret she shared with Billy more important than me? Were those moments in the tub her way of saying thank you and goodbye?

Bells clanged, whistles blew. The marines herded passengers onto the quarterdeck. Up came the anchor. Sails were unfurled. Then the land and trees began to move, and the lovely city of Santo Domingo with all its good and bad memories slid away to our stern.

CHAPTER 45

I'd grown so accustomed to looming disaster that I did not know how to conduct myself in a tranquil environment. There was no Captain of Customs or nosey little lieutenant to dog me. No inquisitors-general or captain of cavalry. And no wanted posters.

I still looked over my shoulder and suspected every passenger of being either an English spy, agent of the Inquisition, or Vampire Jack. Which is why I barricaded our door at night. As for Molly, I still hoped she was on board and in disguise, and that she'd knock on the door and slip into our cabin with a logical explanation.

She didn't. Not the first day, not the second, and not after five miserable days at sea. Where was she? "Only one thing makes sense," I said to Enrique during a tempest that sent us to our hammocks early. "Someone abducted her back at Departures."

"No, Father, if someone tried to nab her, she'd have put up a fuss. You know Molly. There'd have been blood on the floor. Bodies lying around. There's a simpler explanation…."

"Like what?"

"You'll get angry."

"Look, Enrique. I'm not going to get angry. Just tell me."

He drew in a sharp breath and stretched back in his hammock, hands behind his head. "Here's the way I figure. She's got Billy's treasure. *Verdad*? Billy said as much himself. Probably a sea chest full of gold and precious stones. Maybe two or three chests… doubloons, emeralds, pearls. Buried on some hilltop back there in Hispaniola. She stayed behind to fetch it."

"That makes no sense. She'd have told us, asked for our help."

"No, she wouldn't. She's a pirate. She was playing you for a fool."

"That's absurd, Enrique."

"Hey, do you want to hear this or not?"

"I'm sorry. Go ahead."

"Well, like I was saying, I can see her on that hill right now, digging up her treasure…, dancing around in torchlight, trying on bracelets and necklaces."

He rolled over to face me. "Women are like that, you know. Give them a choice of jewelry or being bedded by a man, and they'll choose jewelry every time. It's in their blood. They can't help themselves."

"Molly's not like that."

"Oh, no, then how come she's not on board with us?"

The steward plodded down the corridor with his nightstick, telling passengers to douse lanterns. Over in the next cabin someone was cursing the turbulence and noisily losing his dinner. I closed my eyes and tried to sleep, but Enrique kept on, speaking in a low voice while timbers creaked and groaned and our hammocks swung back and forth. "It's been a few days," he said. "You should know by now."

"Know what?"

"Whether you caught something from her. You know—the fire piss, the pox, a rash."

"Shut up, Enrique."

The days passed. We lost sight of the other four ships in the convoy. Sometimes we tacked south, other times north, and before long came an announcement that our one-week voyage would take two. The quality of food deteriorated. Our drinking and cleaning water developed a nasty smell. I used the time to write letters to both the bishop and Captain Gonzalez as Father Menendez, attempting to turn them against each other. Then, on the twelfth morning of our voyage, while I was lying in my hammock in that foggy world of half asleep, there came the dreaded cry:

"Sails, ho!"

Footfalls thudded on the deck above us. I struggled up, hurried out of the cabin with Enrique, up the companionway, and onto the quarterdeck with other passengers.

The captain was already there with his looking glass. Above us, the lookout was shouting, "Larboard stern! Three masts. Bearing southeast, same as us."

I squinted my eyes. Could it be the *Vulture*? She had the same profile, her sails brilliant in the early morning sun.

"Is she ours?" yelled the captain.

"Looks English from here."

Groans filled the air. Passengers crossed themselves, and for a moment I was captain again, Molly beside me, bandana around her head, pistol stuffed into her belt, staring across the gunwale.

One of our escorts came into view, a warship, and the mystery ship melded into the horizon.

Three days later, in the murky light of early morning, we dropped anchor in the bay beneath the beautiful port city of Cartagena.

The fresh air was a welcome change from the foulness of our cabin. I didn't realize it was Sunday until I heard the tolling of church bells. Over at customs, beneath the fluttering banners, we could see passengers streaming off other tenders.

"Don't get your hopes up," Enrique said.

"Why not? I'll fancy she boarded another ship by mistake."

"Only a dimwitted fool would do that. Molly's a smart woman."

At last, more than three hours after dropping anchor, we stepped on solid ground. Uniformed officials directed us into queues. The lines crept along. Ahead of us, agents were asking their usual questions. Name and occupation? Port of origin? Destination?

When our turn came, Enrique couldn't resist telling the story about chupacabras he'd related for the governor. I pushed around him and moved to the next table. The agent stamped my travel document and looked up. "You should also avoid Plaza San Pedro."

"Why is that?"

"They've been hanging Wayuus every day. Smells bad."

I thanked him, took my token for surrender on departure, and headed straight to the embarkation window. "When is the next ship leaving for Nicaragua?"

"Who knows, Padre? You have to come each day and ask."

Enrique had drawn a crowd with his story about chupacabras, so I stepped over to a window marked *Postales y Correspondencias* and handed the clerk my letters—one for Gonzalez, another for the bishop. "I'm Father Menendez," I said. "Do you have letters for me?"

He reached under the counter, flipped through a stack of letters, found one, and handed it over.

"Looks pretty important. Got official seals."

It was from the bishop, his response to my report as Father Menendez from San Juan. I leaned against a column, slit it open with my dagger and read his rambling report of turmoil in Nicaragua—mob demonstrations, assassinations, hangings, and burnings.

Please return with Captain Gonzalez. I need your help.

I put away the letter and followed Enrique into the usual chaos, peering into the faces: Carmelite nuns in brown habits, Gypsies with their scarves and jangling jewelry, women of color in slave wrappings, the whores with their rouge and flashy clothing.

I even looked for Molly on the balconies and stood on that muddy street while dogs sniffed at my cassock and children laughed and the clouds brushed the sun as if all were right in the world.

Where was she? It seemed that everything wonderful and bright in my life, everything charming and sweet—light itself—had gone out of me. Enrique came up and laid a hand on my shoulder.

"I'm sorry, Padre. Why don't you come home with me, meet my wife and children?"

"Not today, Enrique. I'll stay at the Colón."

We shared a coach and were soon driving past landmarks I remembered from my first visit—the place I'd almost killed Enrique, the slave auction block, the *Casa de Contratación*, the hated Office of the Holy Inquisition.

"See that fortress up there," Enrique said, pointing. "That's where we put up our defense against the English back in March."

I pretended to show an interest in what he was saying but caught only a few words. "Biggest clash yet in the War of Jenkins' Ear… tide trapped them in the bay… sank fifty of their ships… killed them by the thousands… bodies floating like dead fish."

He was still talking when the carriage drove into the plaza and rattled alongside the rotting corpses of Wayuu captives. And he didn't shut up until we pulled over and stopped near the *Iglesia de San Pedro Claver*. "Why are we stopping?" I asked the driver.

"It's Sunday, Father, the Day of *Las Promesas*. We'll have to wait for the procession."

We climbed down and waited. First came the priests with their crosses and censers, their faces shrouded in cowls. Then the drummers in black, beating out a gloom that matched my own. And finally a single line of waddling, knee-walking "promisers." Most were women, praying aloud, tears streaking their faces, some even flailing their shoulders with switches and leather straps.

Enrique shoved up beside me. "When I was wounded, my wife walked on her knees in that procession, praying for my recovery. It must have helped, because here I am."

I thought about that. God didn't enter into contracts, but if he did I'd promise anything for the safety of my children, or to reunite with Molly, or to put an end to the evils of the Inquisition.

In time, the coach dropped me at Posada Colón, a two-story inn that overlooked the ships in the bay. Enrique promised to look in on me the next morning. I wished him a joyful homecoming, watched his coach roll away, and lumbered into the lobby with my bag, the drumbeat of gloom still playing in my head.

It didn't help when I saw Captain Gonzalez with Samson and three or four other soldiers, sitting at a table with a group of tavern wenches, laughing and drinking in open violation of God's commandment to keep the Sabbath holy.

A minute or two later in my room, with the door locked and barricaded, with my two pistols within easy reach, I washed up at the basin, took a seat on the balcony, and looked down at the bay. The tears welled up. My jaw tightened, and I thought of all the loved ones I'd lost. The hunchback. César the jailer. Saraatepe. My children.

And now, Molly.

Yes, I'd walk a mile on my knees to bring them back. Ten miles. A hundred. What good was all that gold, all that wealth, without someone to share it with?

CHAPTER 46

Cartagena—*Posada Colón*

As if I didn't have enough weight on my soul, I found myself back on the *Sevilla* in my dreams, running from Billy and making fast for the coastline while Father Sebastian berated me for every sin I'd ever committed. "Have you no shame?" he railed, pointing a bony finger. "First you take an Indian into your bed. Now you're pining over a pirate. A pirate girl, Antonio."

The ship plunged into another trough. Reefs rose up around us, ugly and churning. Smoke poured from open hatches, but instead of a tarry smell, it had the nasty odor of wet goat—musky and bitter. Passengers wailed. My stomach felt as if I'd eaten a rancid bone, and somewhere amid the madness, I heard pounding at my door.

"Father, are you in there? Father?"

I sat straight up, rubbing sleep out of my eyes.

"Either you open this door or I'll kick it in!"

I bounded out of bed, grabbed a pistol, and thumbed back the hammer. "Who is it?"

"Cartagena Militia. Open up. We need to talk."

Cartagena Militia, the people Gonzalez would enlist to arrest me.

I dashed onto the balcony in my underclothes, ready to jump. But the land dropped away into a wooded ravine, forty or fifty feet below. Certain death if I jumped. Worse, soldiers were in the ravine as well, with a pack of snarling dogs.

"Father, I'm counting to three."

"Hold your horses. I'm not dressed."

I pulled the cassock over my head, placed one pistol beneath a pillow, stuffed the other into my pocket, and opened the little spy window at the top of the main door. A short, stocky lieutenant and two other soldiers stood outside. Gonzalez was not among them.

"God give me courage," I muttered, and unlatched the door.

They pushed into the room, bringing with them the same repulsive goat smell that had invaded my dreams.

"Are you alone?" the lieutenant asked.

I waved my arm. "See for yourself."

Without asking, they searched the room, looking under the bed and cushions, atop the armoire, in my travel bag, even peering into the chamber pot. The lieutenant picked up my walking cane, remarked how heavy it was, then inspected the flint lock they'd found under the pillow. "Why does a padre carry a loaded pistol?"

"For Wayuu Indians. For intruders who break into my room."

"Patience, Father, please. We're just doing our job."

He released the hammer and tossed it onto the pillow. "What time did you go to bed?"

"Early. Why are you asking?"

"I'm asking the questions. Did you leave this room?"

"No, Lieutenant, I was here, asleep."

"Hear any screams? Anything suspicious?"

"I don't know. I might have, but I thought it was a dream."

He stepped onto the balcony and yelled down to the soldiers with the dogs. "Anything?"

"Nothing, Lieutenant. Only some brambles and a turtle."

He muttered an oath, marched back into the room, exchanged looks with the other soldiers, then said, "What we're looking for are blood stains… also some missing heads."

"Heads?"

"Women's heads, Padre. Two of them. From next door." He motioned with his thumb. "I'm surprised you didn't hear the noise. Some sick bastard chopped off their heads, then lashed them upside down to the bed posts… carved a devil sign onto their chests."

His words fell on me like a blight. Please, dear Lord, not Molly.

"Funny thing about it is the goat smell, like a nasty old *cabro*."

The fear struck deeper. "Who were the women?" I asked.

"All we know is they were passengers from one of the ships that came in yesterday."

"Names, what are their names?"

"We don't give out names, but since you're a padre I can tell you the white one had a French sounding name, Lapierre, something like that; the other was darker, chocolate colored. Couldn't have been more than twenty. Maybe younger."

I headed for the door. "Could I see the bodies?"

"Already wagoned away. They get ripe in this heat."

A darkness flooded over me. I thought of Molly's suntanned arms, her callused hands and white body, her soft breasts.

Molly without a head.

The lieutenant asked a few more questions, thanked me for my time, and quit the room, leaving me in a state of turmoil.

I splashed water on my face, toweled off, and hurried into the hallway. The lieutenant was still there, answering questions from a small crowd that had gathered around him.

"Were those girls violated?" asked a woman with white hair.

"I don't have that information, señora."

I pushed closer, hoping to get into the room and look through the bags, and was at the door when Samson and Gonzalez came trotting up the stairs. Bastards. What did they want?

Back to my room I hurried, then sank onto the bed, trying to think of reasons it couldn't have been Molly. She'd have barricaded the door. Shot an intruder. Screamed for help. But if the dead woman wasn't Molly, why did Jack kill her? Unless he thought it was Molly, saw it wasn't, and killed her anyway for diversion.

It grew quiet in the hallway. I cracked open the door and peeked out. Gonzalez and Samson were gone, so was the lieutenant. Only a few guests remained, speaking in hushed tones. I stepped into the hallway and immediately became the center of attention.

"Father, did you hear what happened?"

"God will protect you," I said, and made the sign of the cross.

A guard barely old enough to shave stood at the victims' door. Inside, a cleaning woman with stringy hair and dark Indian features was mopping up the mess. "Not much to see," the guard said, his face flushed. "They took everything except the stench."

"Who took it, *mijo*?"

"Who knows, Father? You know how these things are… a soldier sees a pretty dress, thinks it looks good on his wife…"

"Who discovered the bodies?"

"I think it was the charwoman…, this woman here."

No one knew anything more, not the guard, not the charwoman, and not the *jefe* who came up for a look. They didn't even know where the bodies had been taken.

At last, no closer to learning the truth, I returned to my room, slammed the door, and dumped the contents of my bag onto the bed. There it was—the torn shirt Molly had worn on the *Sevilla*. It had once been white, with a pleated front and puffy sleeves, and for a moment I could picture her in it, standing on the quarterdeck. Passing along my orders to the crew. Things going overboard, splashing into the water. Molly, holding my hand.

Molly without a head.

I pressed the shirt to my face and breathed in her essence and would have burst out crying had it not been for the knock at the door. "Father, it's me. Are you in there?"

It was Enrique. I put away the shirt, reverently, as if it were a communion vestment, and opened the door. He stood there with a travel bag in each hand. "Damn Wayuus," he said, marching in and dropping his bags on the floor. "They should all be strung up like pirates, left to rot." He paced around, kicked the wall, and finally slumped into a wicker chair. "Is that goat I smell?"

I told him about the murders.

"Couldn't have been Molly," he said.

"Why not?"

"Because Molly's not here. Never been here. Probably in New Orleans with her jewelry. Why can't you get that through your skull? And it wasn't Vampire Jack who killed them either."

"Oh, no? Then how'd that goat smell get in here?"

"Wayuus, Padre. They wear animal skins. You're lucky they didn't take your head as well. You want to hear my story or not?"

"Sorry, go ahead."

"Look, here's what happened. Got home last night. Right? Looking forward to seeing my family. Get cleaned up. Have a good dinner. Play with my kids…"

"What, Enrique? Just tell me."

"No one home. Not even the dogs. Didn't learn until this morning what happened. Seems she took the kids and went to see her mama up in the mountains, near Bogotá. Right?"

"Right."

"But then the Wayuus go crazy. Close the roads. Slaughter settlers. Attack outposts. Hell, they're even chopping off heads."

"Chopping off heads?"

"Heads, Father. Are you hard of hearing? Anyhow, my wife and kids are now stuck in the mountains. It could be months. And that's not even the worst part."

"How could it be worse?"

"I'll tell you how. This morning I stopped by the bank… where I used to work as a guard. Right? They said I'd been gone too long, so they hired someone to take my place. A younger man. Can you imagine? Me, a wounded war veteran, tossed onto the street."

Again he paced the room, cursing, waving his arms.

"Just calm down, Enrique. You've got your own money now."

"Calm down? That's what they told me. 'Calm down, Enrique,' like I was a child. Said I was argumentative, combative, unstable. That one minute I could be like a mad dog, foaming at the mouth. Next minute scared of my own shadow." Again, he kicked the wall.

He slumped back into the chair and buried his face in his hands.

"Where are you going with those bags?" I asked him.

"Going with you, Padre. Cross the Isthmus and get me a ship over on the Pacific, take it down to Cali. From there I can trek up to Bogotá. I figure you could use some help."

He looked at me. “How come you’re not talking? Is that plan agreeable to you?”

“Of course, Enrique, I’m just sorry for what—”

“Oh, and one more thing. Just stopped at the landing on the way up. They tell me *Las Palmas* is repaired and ready. She’s sailing tonight, on the tide.”

CHAPTER 47

Feeling better, I availed myself of the inn's laundry and bath facilities and changed into a clean cassock. Then the two of us headed to the waterfront to book passage on *Las Palmas*. By then, word of the murders had spread, and there were rumors of other murders as well. And pirate landings on the coast. And chupacabras bounding along rooftops. Which explained the presence of soldiers and militiamen on every street corner and in front of public buildings.

"Look," Enrique said. "We should burn it down."

"What?"

"That damn Jesuit bank that fired me, that confiscated your savings." Again he flew into a rage—cursing the managers and wishing a plague on the place.

I agreed with every word. How dare they take my hard-earned money—mine and Saraatepe's—for a crime I hadn't committed. Even if I had committed the crime, those four-hundred escudos weren't the bishop's for the taking.

I slid back the partition that separated us from the driver. "A change of destination. Take us to *La Casa de Contratación*."

Enrique turned to face me. "I thought we were going to the landing for tickets."

"We are, just as soon as I rob the bishop's account."

"Are you crazy? You've already got enough gold for a lifetime."

"I'm not doing this for the gold, Enrique; I'm doing it for vengeance, to destroy an evil man."

The coach rolled to a stop in front of La Casa. Enrique tried to get down with me. "No," I said, and handed him some coins. "Here, go get the tickets, then come back for me."

"What if you don't come out? What if—"

"Stop it, Enrique. I have to do this."

A few minutes later, I was seated in a back office with yet another *licenciado de contabilidad.*

"Let me see if I have this correct," he said. "You're going to purchase a large quantity of land, buildings and livestock from a *caballero* in Nicaragua named Don Antonio Arteaga y Flores?"

"Correct."

"And this is for the Church. *Verdad*?"

"Correct."

"Don't you find this a bit strange?"

"What's so strange about it?"

"A priest buying for the Church. I thought Church property was acquired through donations."

The sweat under my arms trickled down my ribs. "That's usually the case, but what we're faced with is avarice."

"Avarice?"

"Greed of the worst sort. Here's what happened: The original owner, God rest his soul, was most generous. Donated half his property. The other half he promised to the Church upon his death. Right? But when he died, the legalities were unsettled."

"And now his son owns the property."

"Correct, and he wants nothing less than its full pecuniary value."

"Doesn't the Church have… shall we say, other persuasions?"

"We do, but it's more complicated when the owner is the bishop's brother-in-law."

"Ah, so now we come to the heart of the matter."

He examined the fake *cédula* and travel document, wrote down the account number I gave him, and disappeared into a back room, leaving me again to face my doubts. Suppose he knew the bishop by name, and wanted to know why I had the same name?

I stood and paced the floor. Through the open window came the sounds of the city—the clatter of hooves, the rattle of coaches and wagons, the caw of sea gulls.

Please, dear God, get me through this ordeal one final time.

He came back with two ledgers.

"What did you say your secret code is?"

"I didn't, but it's Galileo… like the astronomer, the heretic."

He sank into his chair and mopped his brow with a dirty handkerchief. "Normally we wouldn't have a problem, but this is a considerable sum of gold."

My stomach twisted.

"However, we can crate the gold for you, ship it to Nicaragua. You can pick it up there, where they know you. We'll ship it tonight, on *Las Palmas*."

I breathed again. "Isn't that risky?"

"Not a problem, Father. We give you a certificate of demand. It's paper, but as good as gold. All you have to do is take it to our branch in Granada, where they know you. Tell them the secret word. They'll give you the crate. Then you can either pay off this Don Antonio with gold or you can put it into his account. Makes no difference to us."

He called in another clerk to witness my signature. I signed as Father Diego de Ureña—the same name as the bishop—and tried not to show my excitement.

"How much is that crate going to weigh?" I asked.

He made some notations on paper. "Let's see. You've got almost twenty-four thousand escudos, *Verdad*? Which works out to about three thousand ounces. Now, if you figure sixteen ounces to a pound, you're looking at… oh, a hundred and ninety pounds."

I sat there, speechless, while he wrote out a certificate of demand—payable to the bearer—for 23,863 *escudos de oro*. Could it be? Had I really drained the accounts of all my enemies? Father Menendez. Captain Gonzalez. And now, Bishop Diego de Ureña, the Inquisitor-General.

The clerk escorted me to the door. Enrique picked me up in the carriage. Back at the inn, I changed into the clothes I'd worn on the *Sevilla*, when I'd been disguised as a *funcionario* with La Casa. And a few hours later, well after dark, the two of us boarded *Las Palmas* along with Samson and Gonzalez and a crate of gold that weighed almost as much as El Moro.

I'd boarded many ships during my long ordeal and faced many dangers, but nothing compared with the excitement of setting off on that final voyage. The tears welled up. I trembled with joy and sadness. I breathed in the smells of sea meeting land, and when the boatswain finally sounded his whistle to begin preparations, I thought I'd never heard lovelier music.

The Galician first officer, the man who'd pulled me from the lake back in Ysese, gathered us on deck for a welcoming speech. Then a skinny priest with a high-pitched voice, standing in the glimmer of a low-burning lantern, blessed the ship and led us in praying the Rosary.

I fell to my knees, and was so caught up in my Ave Marias, praying for my children and Molly and a safe passage, that I failed to notice Samson and Gonzalez until Enrique elbowed me. "Since when do snakes pray?" he hissed.

I followed his nod to the gunwale where they rested on their knees, their lips moving in prayer. Gonzalez in his cavalry uniform; Samson in his leather vest, silver chains dangling.

"*Bendita tú eres entre todas las mujeres. Y bendito es el fruto de tu vientre….*"

How could these evil men who thought nothing of slaughtering Indian women and children pray for God's blessings on the Holy Mother? Or on anything?

"I say we bash their heads soon as we weigh anchor," Enrique whispered.

"Hush, before someone hears you."

He brought it up again when the ceremony ended, amid the stir and noise of getting underway, and while the lights of Cartagena were fading in the distance.

"Why don't we go to their cabin? Wait for them."

"That's crazy, Enrique. Don't you imagine they'll fight back?"

"Look, if you don't have the stomach, I'll do it myself."

The debate continued in our cabin that night. And the next morning at breakfast and was still going on when Samson and Gonzalez marched into the galley and headed for the food counter. Gonzalez had on his usual sneer of superiority, but Samson looked long-faced and sad, as if still mourning the loss of El Moro. He also wore a black arm band.

"They don't look so tough to me," Enrique said.

"Would you please shut up? Now's not the time."

"It will be if they recognize you."

"I'm Captain of the *Sevilla*, a big man at La Casa. Remember?"

They sat at the next table, paying us no heed until Enrique noisily twisted around to face them. "Good morning, Captain. Good morning, Samson."

Gonzalez almost choked on his coffee. "You. What are you two doing here?"

"Business in Granada," I said.

He glared at me. "Why weren't you at the governor's meeting?"

"Family is more important than a meeting with the governor."

"Damn right it is," Enrique said. "Let me tell you what happened to my family."

I stood and went for more café, figuring if I wasn't there, Enrique would be less provocative, but when I returned, he was wagging an angry finger in Gonzalez's face.

"That's the reward I get for helping you. No job, no pay, my wife gone. And for what? They killed your heretic anyway, didn't they? Deprived you of the pleasure of seeing him burn."

"You got your ten Pieces of Eight."

"A hundred Pieces of Eight wouldn't be enough for what I suffered. Now I'm hearing the heretic wasn't so bad, that all he did was protect the Indians from fanatics. People like you."

Samson stopped chewing his food. I kicked Enrique under the table, but that seemed to infuriate him more. "The way I heard it," Enrique said, "your men plundered and burned an Indian village, violated the women. What's so noble about that?"

Gonzalez came to his feet. Enrique also jumped up. "Come on, Captain. Fight a real man instead of helpless Indian women."

By then, everyone in the galley was staring—the servers at the counter, the passengers at other tables.

Then a marine guard trotted over. "What is going on?"

Gonzalez pointed a finger at Enrique. "I want that man clapped in irons."

"On what charge, sir?"

"For insulting an officer of the Spanish cavalry."

"Horse *mierda*," Enrique shot back. "I'm a passenger, not one of your obedient troopers."

"Gentlemen, please," I said, coming to my feet. "Let's just calm down. Hmm?"

The guard backed away. Enrique and Gonzalez stood there a moment, facing each other. Finally, Gonzalez said to me, "If I were you, sir, I'd keep that Indian-lover under control."

He took a gulp of coffee, slammed down the mug and stormed out of the galley. Samson glowered at Enrique a moment, scooped up a handful of bread and cheese, and also quit the room.

I waited for things to return to normal, then said to Enrique, "Are you crazy? Don't you realize Gonzalez can arrest us the moment we set foot in Nicaragua?"

"For what cause?"

"He doesn't need a cause. He's the law."

"All the more reason to toss him overboard."

We were still arguing when a clamor broke out on the deck above us, with shouts and a great rush of feet. People hurried out, trotting toward the exit. "What is it?" I asked a server.

"Didn't you hear the lookout? Spotted a ship. Might be pirates."

CHAPTER 48

Aboard *N.S. Las Palmas*

Out the door and up the companionway we dashed, following the other passengers, expecting to see the *Vulture* bearing down upon us, flying the Jolly Roger.

There was nothing to see, only open water, a few clouds, and the first officer speaking to the gathered passengers.

"It's nothing, folks. Nothing to worry about. It's gone now."

I thought little of the incident until it occurred again the next day. Again, the officers tried to assure us it was a Spanish vessel. They didn't explain why the marines were on full alert. Or why we'd changed course to embrace the Isthmus coastline, coming so close to land that sea gulls were alighting in our rigging.

It rained on the fourth day, which deepened the gloom. I heard prayers all around, and endless speculation: The officers were lying. The pirates were playing us like a cat plays a doomed mouse. We'd have to beach on the shoreline–fight hostile Indians.

There were no sightings that day. Only an occasional canoe laden with naked savages, shouting at us, shaking their spears.

On the fifth day, we awoke to the happy news that a *guarda-costa* vessel, the *N.S. Portobello*, had joined us. Word went out that pirates wouldn't dare attack us now. Not with the *Portobello* as escort. She was formidable. Twenty-four guns. A floating fortress. The same kind of vessel that had captured Captain Jenkins, he of the missing ear.

No one mentioned the *Vulture* had forty-eight guns.

There were loud celebrations that night in the galley, everyone boasting about the superiority of Spanish vessels, saying we should cut off more English ears, and were singing *Que Viva España* when a pair of lantern-toting marines marched to my table. "*Perdónenos*," said the stockier of the two, "but the captain wants to see you."

I stood and pulled on my waist coat. Enrique said, "Probably just wants your advice, you being a big man at La Casa."

I hoped so too. But why after dark? Why marines?

I followed them out the door, beneath the low-hanging beams, up the ladder and into the fresh night air.

Wind whistled in the sails. A crescent moon hung low in the sky, shimmering on the water. A sentry challenged us from the darkness. The marines answered back, and we were at the roundhouse door, ready to enter, when a sudden flash lit the deck.

"*Portobello*," someone yelled. "She's fighting the pirates."

Flares arced into the night. The marines took off at a trot, shouting commands. Then the captain burst out of the roundhouse, looking glass in hand, muttering oaths I shall not repeat.

Behind him came Gonzalez in his cavalry uniform, followed by the Galician first officer, the chief mate, a marine lieutenant, and the skinny priest who'd blessed the ship.

I followed them to the gunwale to watch the action. Both ships were about a half mile to front and starboard, their profiles lit by flashes of battle, the cannon booms like endless thunder. Below us and all around, men scrambled to their posts. There were curses and commands, the shrill notes of whistles, men climbing into the rigging, gunners manning their cannons.

"Blow them out of the water!"

"Sink the bastards!"

To add to this chaos, passengers began streaming from the companionway in a panic. The marines tried to push them back. I reached down from the quarterdeck and helped Enrique up the ladder.

"The devil you doing?" a marine shouted at us. "Get below!"

"We're with the captain," I snapped back.

A broadside lit the night, followed by the rolling boom of guns.

This happened again and again, always in a different place, as if the *Vulture* and *Portobello* were engaged in a deadly game of hide-and-go-seek. Each round brought them closer to our ship, forcing us more and more to larboard, taking us so close to land we could see breakers, and the glow of fires from native huts.

"At least we're close enough to swim," Enrique said.

"Better pray you don't have to," said the first officer. "Zambos control that shore."

"Zambos?"

"Escaped slaves and Miskito Indians. Headhunters, mind you."

We were still pondering that unhappy thought when, during one of those slack moments in fighting, the captain laid a hand on my shoulder. "You, sir, I'd like a word with you."

I followed him into the roundhouse, so did Gonzalez, the first officer, the priest, and the marine lieutenant. The captain waved us into chairs, unrolled a chart, and spread it on the table.

Jabbing a finger, he said, "This, gentleman, is Rio San Juan del Norte, the river that takes us into Nicaragua. We're only about, oh, an hour from its mouth. The tide is favorable for us. Normally, we'd never take it at night. But if the *Portobello* loses this battle...."

He turned to me. "I'm told you're with La Casa. What would Don Ignacio advise?"

I breathed again. How silly of me to think he'd brought me here to expose me as the heretic. "Well, Captain," I said, "The first thing he'd ask is the risk of night navigation on the river."

"The usual. Sandbars, obstructions, floating trees, Zambos shooting flaming arrows."

"Don't forget the snakes," said the first officer.

"Ah, yes, snakes. The Zambos fling them from the trees."

A sentry stuck in his head, but his words were drowned by the thunderous roar of a broadside.

"*Mierda*!" the captain said. "They're almost on top of us."

We rushed out of the cabin. By then, both the *Portobello* and *Vulture* were only about a hundred yards to starboard, firing into each other with a terrible fury, so close we could see men running about their decks. Down went a mast.

"Which ship?" shouted the captain to the lookout.

"*Portobello*!"

Groans and curses filled the air. Another mast went down, collapsing in a torrent of sparks. Fire rose up on the *Portobello's* deck, sparkling like Roman candles. Then both ships were ablaze, drifting apart in a lurid sea of red, embers rising like thousands of tiny stars.

"Look," someone shouted, "They're jumping overboard."

A deathly silence fell upon us. We could see them silhouetted against the fires, little dark figures with flailing arms, splashing into the water, individually and in groups.

"Poor bastards," Enrique said. "Most can't even swim."

I thought we'd move in to pick up survivors. Instead, the captain shouted, "Steer to larboard! She'll blow any moment."

No sooner had he said it than the *Portobello* exploded in a blinding fireball, its force slamming us with such fury that I was lifted from my feet and thrown backward.

Darkness came over me. I could neither see, nor think or hear, and had the awful sensation that I was in the water, sinking, drowning, dying. Was this how it would all end, after all that running and struggling to survive?

In time, I became aware of men stumbling about, groaning, cursing, helping others. Then someone pulled me to my feet and helped me to the gunwale.

Shattered glass crunched under my feet. My body felt as if I'd been trampled by horses. And somewhere amid the darkness the priest with the high-pitched voice was reading from John 11:25: "I am the resurrection and the life. He that believeth in me, though he were dead, shall yet live…."

Little by little, my head cleared. I saw the moon, figures around me. But no ships. Nothing but dark water and reflected moonlight. No burning debris either–or survivors.

How could that be? More than a hundred souls gone. In the blink of an eye. And for what? For Jenkins' stupid ear and this stupid war and stupid Billy.

The captain yelled up to the lookout, "Any sign of the pirates?"

"None, sir. Blast must have sunk them!"

"Keep a sharp lookout. We'd best head into the river!"

I stumbled across the deck in the darkness and found the captain as he was limping into the roundhouse. "Listen, Captain, it's possible saboteurs are aboard this ship."

"Yes, yes, I'm well aware of the dangers."

"I'd advise you not go anywhere alone. Take a marine with you."

"Thank you for your concerns, sir, but right now I'm more concerned about savages along the river." He turned to a marine. "Convey this gentleman below. And tell Captain Gonzalez to report with all his men. We might need their help."

I opened my mouth to remind him I was a big man with La Casa, but before the words came out, Gonzalez came trotting out of the darkness and followed the captain into the roundhouse. I tried to go in, but a marine stepped in front. "Sorry, sir, you heard the captain."

The marines escorted us back to our cabin, and there we remained, complaining, pacing around like caged animals.

What was wrong with the captain? Why would he allow Gonzalez and his little band of murderers to run freely about the ship but confine us to our quarters?

A commotion on the deck above us told me we'd entered the Rio San Juan del Norte. I stepped to the porthole, and there it was: my land, my home, the giant trees with vines trailing into the water. I also saw fires on the banks of the river, and people standing around, and an occasional burning arrow soaring through the air.

Yet there were no shots or shouts or alarms, only the creak of the timbers, the smell of burning wood, prayers from the next cabin, and the disciplined chant of the leadsman.

At last I fell into a restless sleep and had the ghastliest dream of snakes slithering through the porthole, of Zambos chopping off heads, and Vampire Jack at the door. I also saw survivors in the water, crying for help, and I was reaching down, trying to pull them to safety, when a loud knock brought me out of my slumber.

I bounded up and grabbed a pistol. "Who is it?"

"Marines. Open up."

I opened the door, still holding the pistol. The stockier of the two stepped inside with his lantern. "*Perdóne, señor*, but you're wanted topside. It's urgent."

"For what?"

"The captain, sir. We can't find him."

CHAPTER 49

Rio San Juan del Norte

Again I followed the marines out the door and up the ladder into the darkness. Enrique stumbled along behind us, cursing, still trying to put on his shoes. Not until I stepped onto the deck and breathed in the dampness of fog did I realize we were not moving.

"Where are we?"

"Four hours upstream… at anchor. Tide turned on us."

"What's the time?"

"Seven bells of the mid-watch. Three-thirty by your clock."

Fireflies flickered all around, turning on and off like little semaphores. Things croaked and shrieked. From the jungle came the slow beat of a drum, as if calling the Zambos to action. Worse, the trees lining the banks were no more than an arrow's shot away, and I got the creepy feeling Zambos were out there by the hundreds.

A sentry challenged us at the quarterdeck ladder. The marines answered back, then we followed them into the gloom of the roundhouse. The place reeked of tobacco smoke. At the captain's table, lit by a low-hanging lantern, sat the Galician first officer, Captain Gonzalez, the marine lieutenant, the priest, and first mate, all looking as long-faced as mourners at a funeral.

Gonzalez glowered at Enrique. "What's he doing here?"

"My bodyguard," I shot back. "Do you have a problem with it?"

"Gentlemen, please," said the Galician, motioning us into chairs. "We've got other problems." He looked at me. "We've searched everywhere for the captain."

"Vampire Jack," I said.

"Vampire what?"

"English saboteur. Name is Jack Swallow."

I related our experiences on the *Sevilla.* Everyone exchanged troubled looks. The priest made the sign of the cross, and that was when something splashed in the water, like a body that had been thrown overboard. "What the devil?" said the first officer.

One of the marines hurried out for a look. While we waited, a flaming arrow soared over the ship, clearly visible through the overhead sky-glass.

Gonzalez sprang to his feet. "*Mierda*, they're attacking!"

I expected to hear shouts and shooting, but there were only the sounds of the jungle, the wash of river against our hull, and the reports of the sentries, saying all was tranquil.

As calm returned, we sat back down and resumed our discussion about Vampire Jack. "He'll strike again," I said. "Don't be surprised if he sets the ship ablaze and jumps overboard."

"That's crazy," Gonzalez said. "If he goes overboard, the Zambos will get him."

"No, Captain, the Zambos and English are friends."

We talked until the ship bells struck eight times—four by the clock. The Galician ordered the marines to challenge everyone, to post guards in the hold, and stand watch at the roundhouse. Then he ordered the marines to convey us back to our cabins.

"Get some sleep," he said. "We'll keep you informed."

Back down the companionway we went a second time, following the marines into the shadows and evil smells, ducking beneath low-hanging beams.

"You smell that?" Enrique said, sniffing the air. "Something's dead, rotting. I also smell goat."

The marines held their lanterns a little higher and were glancing around when from behind us came the shout of another marine: "Corporal Lopez is missing."

The marines handed us a lantern and trotted away, leaving us alone in the shadows. I pulled out my pistol. Enrique took out his door key, reached for the door, and suddenly backed away.

"*Coño*," he whispered. "It's open. Look at it."

I thumbed back the hammer on my pistol and pushed the door.

Molly came into my arms, bringing with her the fragrance of cinnamon and vanilla, her face soft against my cheek, her body warm. Even in that moment, choking with emotion, I could not help but remember the tub, feel the excitement in my loins.

"What happened?" I asked. "Where were you?"

She motioned us inside and closed the door. "He's two cabins down, bottom of the ladder."

"Who?" Enrique asked.

"Vampire Jack. He's dressed as a marine."

Enrique reached for the door handle. "I'll get the marines."

"No," Molly said. "He's not in the cabin. If we sound the alarm, he'll jump overboard. Best to go to his cabin and wait."

"How are we going to get into his cabin?"

She held up a skeleton key. "Same way I got into this one."

We took the lantern, and were going out, pistols in hand, when something thudded against the hull, followed by blood-curdling cries. I rushed back inside and opened the porthole. A large bonfire blazed on the river bank. Savages were dancing and jumping around it, shouting and shaking their arms, hurling rocks and spears.

"Idiots," Enrique said. "One blast of grape and they'll be cut to pieces." No sooner had he said it than they plunged into the river as if planning to attack from the water. Out of the fog behind them came a flurry of flaming arrows. This was answered by a volley of musketry from the marines, and the night came alive.

"Come on," Molly said. "Jack will soon be here, he will."

We crept along the passageway like lions in stalk of prey. The roar and flashes of battle came through the open hatch. The stern cannon fired, then the bow cannon. I heard the unmistakable crank of anchor chains—the crew preparing to drift us downstream—and I could imagine the marines at the gunwale and in the rigging, firing in relay, the crew stomping out flames from the arrows.

Then we were at the cabin. Vampire Jack's cabin.

The stench was discernible even amid the smells of gun smoke. From somewhere came the sounds of praying:

"*Pater in manus tuas commendo spiritum meum....*"

"He's praying," Enrique said. "The bastard is praying."

"No," Molly said. "It's from the next cabin. Jack doesn't pray. Doesn't know Latin either."

I took up position on one side of the door, Enrique on the other. Molly, holding the lantern, quickly unlatched the door with her key and stood back.

"God give me courage," I muttered, and kicked open the door.

Nothing. No movement or gunshots or shouts. Only two hammocks, a faint glow of candlelight, and a sickening stench.

I crept inside, slowly, swinging my pistol left to right. Enrique shoved in behind me. Molly closed the door behind us and held up the lantern. "The hammock," Enrique hissed. "Something's in it."

I yanked away the blanket and stared down at the captain's body. There he lay, naked, his eyes open, his face bearded and bloody, the image of a horned goat carved into his chest. Poor man. Why did he have to be so stubborn? Why hadn't he heeded my warning?

"*Hijo de la gran puta,*" Enrique said behind me.

I swung around. "What?"

"A shrine. Bastard made himself a shrine."

I stepped over to look. There, on the shelf above the chamber pot, on either side of a low-burning candle, rested the putrid heads of the two women from the inn, one white, one black. Flies buzzed around them. Their bulging eyes, open mouths, and shriveled skin made them all the more gruesome. So did the liquid that pooled beneath them.

My stomach revolted. Molly set down her lantern. "He's done this before. They say his mother was a *puta*, that she serviced the men of the fleet, that she beat him mercilessly—"

"Listen," Enrique said. "*Se cabo*. The shooting stopped."

It grew so quiet we could hear the prayers of the man next door. The glow from the lantern cast creepy shadows. I opened the porthole just enough to glance out. No more flaming arrows. No savages either, and it was clear we were drifting downstream.

"He'll be coming now," Molly said. She doused two of the three candles, put them on shelf next to the heads, and closed the privy curtain, leaving us barely enough light to see. Then we crouched in the darkness behind the two hammocks, and were whispering to each other when a faint voice murmured, "Monsignor?"

My heart almost stopped. "*Coño*," Enrique said, "he's alive."

I sprang up for another look. Sure enough, the captain's lips were moving. How could that be? Vampire Jack must have thought he was dead. "Monsignor," he whispered. "Is it you?"

I took his calloused hand. "Hush. You're safe. We'll get you out."

"Down," Enrique hissed. "He's at the door."

I drew out my pistol and again crouched behind the hammock, away from the door. Enrique squatted beside me.

The door swung open, and there he stood: a man in the uniform of a marine corporal. Carrying a lantern. Even in the poor light I could see scars on his face, the sneer, the dullness in his eyes. Like a wolf's eyes. He shuffled inside, stopped, and sniffed the air like a dog.

When he saw us, he flung the lantern and turned to run.

The three of us fired at once, a blinding series of flashes that exploded like thunder in the confined space. The cabin filled with smoke. I lifted my second pistol to put a ball into his head. Before I could do so, he slumped to the deck. Then Enrique was on him with his dirk, cutting and slashing at his throat as if he were slaughtering a pig. Except he kept cutting. And cutting.

I'd seen enough and went to the captain's side. Molly relit the lanterns, hung them in the overhead, and swung open the porthole to let in fresh air. Enrique, his hands drenched in blood, lifted the dead man's head by the hair. "Didn't you say to cut off his head?"

"Fook!" Molly exclaimed. "Fook, fook, fook!"

"What?"

"That's not Jack."

"*Mierda*," Enrique said, "don't tell me we just killed a marine?"

"No," Molly said. "It's Dealy Hobbs. He works with Jack."

"So where the hell is Jack?"

"Overboard by now. I'm sure he was here."

Enrique placed the head on the shelf and stood back to look at it. From the passageway came shouts and the sound of running feet. The man next door was praying as if the day of judgment was upon us.

Then the marines were pounding on the door.

CHAPTER 50

I tried to explain, but they rushed inside anyway and demanded we surrender our pistols. One of them slipped on the blood and grabbed the hammock for support. Another squatted beside the body. "Look, it's Lopez. Bastards chopped off his head."

Curses and accusations flew around like brickbats. A marine shook a fist in my face. Another threatened to skewer Enrique with his bayonet. I pointed to the head on the shelf.

"Does that look like Lopez to you?"

The sergeant took a look, then peeled open the dead man's uniform. "*Joda*, look at that fur."

Another marine bent down with his lantern. "Lopez was hairy."

"Not like this. This creature must have howled at the moon."

At last, the Galician first officer burst through the door. Chaos turned to order. Marines hauled away the captain in his hammock. Enrique and I followed them out, pushing our way through marines, crewmen, the priest, and even Samson and Gonzalez.

I looked around for Molly, but she had vanished, again.

The first officer yelled for everyone to shut up, then demanded an explanation. I backed against the ladder and, without mentioning Molly, said we'd heard groans, found the door unlocked, and went in to investigate. "Hadn't been here a minute before he charged in."

"Why'd you cut off his head?"

"Because he's a chupacabra," Enrique blurted. "It's the only way to kill them."

I rolled my eyes. The Galician and the priest fell into a debate about the validity of his statement. The marine lieutenant said he'd heard the same thing. Gonzalez agreed. Finally the first officer said, "Toss the body overboard. Do it now."

"What about the women's heads?"

"Bag them. We'll give them a Christian burial in the lake."

The first officer asked a few more questions, apologized for the roughness of the marines, and returned our pistols. "We'll finish this up tomorrow," he said. "Everyone back to your posts."

"Wait," I said. "Vampire Jack could still be aboard."

"Not to worry, *caballero*. We're not relaxing our vigil."

Enrique and I lumbered back to our cabin. Molly would be waiting for us, I figured, resting in my hammock. I could hardly wait to see her again, hear her explanation, hold her in my arms.

The cabin was empty. Not a whiff of cinnamon or vanilla.

Exhausted by the ordeal, I crawled into the hammock, and it seemed as if I'd just fallen asleep when the steward knocked on the door with news that it was daylight.

"First Officer wants you in the roundhouse by two bells," he said in his gruff voice. "That's nine by your clock."

We ate a hasty breakfast in the galley—ignoring the stares and whispers—and stumbled topside for the meeting. The day was sunny, with the sweetness of honeysuckle in the air. Giant trees loomed up on both sides. White egrets flew alongside the ship, and here and there we saw caimans at rest on partly submerged logs.

As before, everyone in a position of authority was seated around the captain's table—the first officer, Captain Gonzalez, the marine lieutenant, and that skinny little priest who talked like a woman—everyone rumpled and looking sleep deprived. The first officer, whose eyes were bloodshot, assured us the captain was well, then opened the logbook and looked into my face. "Tell us again what happened. Take your time. I need to get it all in the log."

I again related the story, being careful to not mention Molly.

He made notations. "You said you shot him two times. *Verdad*?"

"That's correct. We each shot him."

"I counted three holes in his body."

"You must have been counting exit holes as well."

"May I assure you, *caballero*, that I know the difference between an exit and entry hole."

"Maybe Lopez shot him," Enrique said.

He paused a moment. "The other mystery is this. Captain says you're a monsignor who he pulled out of the water back in Nicaragua. Said he'd know that voice anywhere… the deep baritone of a singer, the Catalonian accent. Strange, don't you think?"

Everyone glared as if they could see right through my disguise. "Where did you say you're from?" asked the priest.

"Southern Spain, near the village of Jaén. Why are you asking?"

No one spoke. It grew so quiet I could hear the shrieks and roars of howler monkeys. Finally, the first officer made some more notations, blotted them, and closed the log. "Thank you for your time. I'm sure there'll be another inquiry when we reach Granada."

We hurried back to our cabin, expecting to find the place swarming with marines, looking through my bags, but nothing had been disturbed. I sank onto the bunk and waited for my heart to stop pounding. Now what? Gonzalez would almost certainly press the issue once we reached Granada. Unless….

I pulled out Father Menendez letterhead, took out ink and quill, and began writing:

> *Esteemed Captain Gonzalez: I am now in Granada, arguing your case before the bishop. He is not well. Suffice to say Granada is dangerous for you. Therefore, I beg you, upon your arrival, to proceed directly to the barracks. Do not under any circumstances take any actions that would alert the bishop to your presence….*

Which to me meant: don't arrest anyone, and don't ask questions.

I signed as Father Menendez and sealed it with the *sella* of the Holy Inquisition. Then I took the letter topside, slipped into the roundhouse like a thief, and stuffed it into the bag marked *Postales*. With any luck at all it would go ashore before the passengers.

The river grew wider, with more native villages and pleasant smells of wood fires. We drifted past Fortress El Castillo, communicating via semaphore. Word went out that we'd reach Granada by midnight. Molly remained among the missing, and I was sitting in the cabin with Enrique when there arose a clamor from the deck above.

I hurried out, following other passengers topside, and there before us, brilliant in the afternoon sun, loomed the twin snow-capped peaks of Isla Ometepe, the lake island that had been my home for the past thirteen years. Saraatepe's home. Our home.

The place I thought I'd never see again.

I wiped away the tears and imagined I could see her: my beautiful Saraatepe with a red hibiscus flower behind her ear. Leading me to the cave. "Over there," I could hear her saying in her lyrical Choro tongue. "Across the stream. Beneath the trees. In the mist."

Now she was here. In this water. Beneath this ship.

And the man who murdered her was standing at the gunwale only feet away, chatting with the skinny priest who was to be my replacement. I turned away before I did something stupid and almost bumped into Samson.

"You," he said in his coarse voice, "a word if you please."

He glanced at Gonzalez, then motioned me to the gunwale on the opposite side of the quarterdeck. His cheeks were red, his eyes bloodshot, his stubble-covered head slick with sweat, and when he spoke, his words were slurred, as if he'd had too much to drink.

"Watch out for the captain," he said. "He's asking questions."

"What kind of questions?"

"About you, where you come from. Him and that skinny priest."

"Why are you telling me this, Samson? I thought you and the captain were friends."

"Snakes don't make friends. And that's what Gonzalez is."

I wanted to say something, but all I could do was stare at this man who'd chained me to a table, beaten me half to death, and broken my leg. This man I'd sworn to kill along with Gonzalez and the bishop. Could it be that I was wrong about him?

He spat over the side and staggered away, grabbing at the shrouds, leaving me in a cloud of doubt. The boatswain blew his whistle—I thought to lay on more canvas—but it turned out to be a memorial service for the women's heads, for Corporal Lopez, and the lost crew of the Portobello. I watched a few minutes, thinking there should also be a memorial service for Saraatepe, then returned to the cabin and told Enrique about Gonzalez.

He picked up a pistol. "It's not too late to kill the son of a bitch."

"No, Enrique, it'll work out."

"Every time you say that we get deeper into *mierda*."

He shoved his dirk into its holster and stormed out. I rested awhile, prayed my letter would work, and didn't return topside until darkness fell over the ship and word came to gather our belongings for debarkation.

By then, the decks were crowded, everyone dressed to go ashore—all stockings and buckles, scarves and waistcoats, bonnets and powdered wigs, the marines in dress uniforms.

The scrawny little priest was there too, addressing the passengers about the great burdens that lay ahead, raising his voice in the shrill manner of a fanatical Dominican:

"Fellow Castilians, hear my words! You are the burning light of Spain, the soldiers of God, the hammer of heretics. Together we shall drive out the heathens and make the land safe."

"Idiot," I mumbled, and moved as far away from him as possible.

The night air was cool. Stars brightened the sky. The wind carried the fragrance of the islands we were passing—the Island of Lizards where the rebellion had started, the Island of the Dead with its strange rock carvings, the Isle of Thieves, the tiny *isletas*.

And finally, there it was, the port of Ysese, where I'd been pulled from the water by the same Galician who was now yelling to prepare for debarkation.

Torches flared around the customs house. Semaphores flickered. Coaches were queuing up to take us into Granada, and tenders were already approaching us. "How'd they know we were coming?" asked a voice from the shadows.

"The semaphores," said the Galician.

The anchor splashed into shallow water. We fetched our bags and waited amid a crush of passengers. By then, the ship's lanterns were all aglow, and in this light, I noticed people I'd not seen before—old men and women, cripples, people of color, women with babes in arms. But not Molly. Where was she?

The excitement of coming home and the challenges that lay ahead beat through my veins like a Zambo drum. Were my children safe? Would Gonzalez confront us? What had become of Father Paolo, little Mateo, Abuelita, and Rosa Morales?

The first tender picked up the wounded captain, the mail bag, and a wooden crate that I supposed was "my" gold. Enrique and I boarded the second tender, and at last we stepped onto solid ground, beneath the great lakeside trees with their vines trailing into the water, breathing in the familiar smells of marsh and smoke.

I wanted to cry and laugh at the same time. How long ago had it been since César and I dashed across this very soil for our lives, the cavalry charging us from behind, musket balls snapping around us, the oarsmen helping us into their little boat?

Customs men directed us along a shell walk, and we were soon standing in queue at the *Casa de Aduanas* beneath the hanging lanterns with their swirling insects, amid the pipe smoke and noise and grumpy officials at their tables.

"I don't see her," said Enrique, twisting around.

I didn't either and was getting more concerned by the moment.

Gonzalez did not suffer the indignity of having to wait. They waved him through, important man that he was. "Fat bastard," Enrique hissed. "Must have put on twenty pounds."

No sooner had the words left his mouth than the clerk at the window marked *Postales y Correspondencias* began waving a letter at Gonzalez.

"Captain, Captain, here's one for you."

Gonzalez marched over and took the letter. I pulled in a deep breath, and even with panic in my chest, I could picture the words I'd written: *Proceed immediately to your barracks....*

His expression changed from curiosity to agony, as if he were reading about the death of a loved one. He mouthed the word, "*Joda*," then wadded up the letter and hurried out the exit.

And that was when I saw Molly.

CHAPTER 51

Port Ysese, Nicaragua

She stood near the exit, a grin as big as Ireland, dressed in a robe *à la Française*—black and white with frilly decorations, plumed hat, a necklace of pearls, and the kind of low neckline that invited attention. An attractive older woman waited with her. And between them stood a beautiful young girl of four or five, her golden tresses done up with red ribbons.

The stir around me faded away. My mind flashed back to that tub in Santo Domingo. No, I told the customs officer, I was not a resident of Nicaragua. He waved me through. Then I was standing before Molly with my bag.

She smoothed back the child's hair. "You asked about the treasure I was hiding," she said in that accent I'd come to love. "This is my treasure. Her name is Isabella."

I could not have been more shocked if she had introduced King Felipe himself. "Why were you hiding, Molly?"

"I wasn't hiding. I went to Haiti to fetch Isabella. As for this other lady, her name is Annie…Tante Annie, my mom's sister. Speaks French and English. No Castilian."

"And the child?"

"She doesn't speak Castilian."

"That's not what I meant."

"I know what you meant, but why ask what you already know?"

Enrique rushed over.

"That Captain of Customs has taken an interest in us."

Out the door we went—the porters carrying Molly's baggage—pushing through the usual crowd of locals and heading toward a line of waiting carriages.

A low-lying fog hung over nearby marshes, filling the night air with dampness and earthy smells. The carriage in front rolled away. Through its open window I caught a glimpse of Gonzalez.

"*Caballero*!" shouted a voice behind us. "A word if you please."

It was the customs captain and two other soldiers. The brass on the captain's uniform glittered in the torch light. He held up his lantern. "You the man from La Casa?"

Enrique, Molly, and the others kept going, disappearing into the fog. I puffed myself up like the *funcionario* I was supposed to be. "Director of Ship Registry in San Juan Bautista," I said, letting him know my rank was superior to his. "How may I help you?"

"There was a killing aboard your ship—an English spy. *Verdad*?"

By then some of the other passengers had gathered around, all of them babbling about chupacabras.

The captain snapped at everyone to stand back. "Look," I said to the captain. "I'll be making a full report tomorrow, at La Casa. I imagine there'll be an inquiry."

"We make our own inquiries."

"Maybe you didn't hear me, *Capitán*. You want my story, you come to La Casa tomorrow afternoon, office of the director."

I turned and stalked toward the coaches, willing myself not to run. Then, with the captain watching, with my heart racing, I held open the door for Molly. She climbed into the coach with Annie and Isabella. Enrique jumped in on the opposite side, and I was about to pile in myself when another coach rattled up and stopped beside me.

The door opened, and there to my astonishment sat the man who'd financed my escape, Father Paolo himself. "Meet me outside the gate," he said, speaking in Catalán. "*Dóna't pressa*."

His coach rolled into fog and darkness. I climbed into the coach with the others, and by the time we drove through the guard gate I had explained that Father Paolo was an old friend from Barcelona.

"You can trust him," I said. "He'll help us."

The coach stopped. Ahead of us, Father Paolo's coach had also stopped. I could barely see it in the fog. Couldn't see the trees or swamp either. I hopped down, apologized to Molly, and climbed into the coach with Father Paolo.

Mateo was there too, the little shepherd boy from the Island of Lizards. He crawled into my arms, babbling in Choro.

"Is it you, Father? Are you real? They said you were dead."

"I'm not dead, Mateo. I'm here. I won't leave again. Not ever."

We rolled away, two coaches in the night, following the same road through jungle and marsh that César and I had taken back in August. "Tell me about my boys," I said. "Are they safe?"

"They won't be if the bishop finds out you're back."

I breathed easier. Until that moment I wasn't even sure they were alive. "Where are they?"

"At the convent with other orphans." He reached across and laid a hand on my arm. "Not to worry, Antonio, they're not old enough for the bishop. Not yet."

I related some of my adventures on the Spanish Main, telling him how I'd killed El Moro and Father Menendez—which seemed to please him—and when I finished, he said, "I suppose you'd like to clear your name and return to the priesthood?"

"No, Paolo. Father Antonio is dead, buried at sea."

We rattled to a stop at the military checkpoint, behind the coach that carried Molly and Enrique. Soldiers stood around by the dozens, searching and questioning. Father Paolo spoke to the officer in charge, and they waved both coaches through the guardrail.

"How did you manage that?" I asked.

"Didn't you hear? I'm acting fiscál, appointed by the bishop. I speak for him. Even handle his correspondence. That's how I knew you were coming in on *Las Palmas*."

We drove on, Mateo fast asleep, and that's when Father Paolo told me they'd arrested Rosa Morales, madam of the House of Seven Veils, the rouged woman who'd helped me escape.

"She hasn't owned up," he said, "but I'll wager she'll talk when they turn her over to Samson."

The news fell on me like an avalanche. "Why can't you get her out, you being fiscál?"

"I tried, but the bishop wants to hang her anyway."

He related other horrors—burnings, hangings, destruction of native villages, executions without trial. Each story reinforced my belief that the bishop should die a heinous death; and by the time we rumbled into Granada with its red-tiled roofs and cobbled streets, I was boiling with rage. "Did my letters have any effect on the bishop?"

"Scared him out of his wits, especially that one about the Ave Maria ghost."

My anger stirred again when we clattered past the Alhambra where Rosa Morales awaited her fate and where I'd been imprisoned and tortured for the crime of protecting an Indian holy site. Even now, in the plaza in the moonlight beneath the palms, there stood two more stakes and a gallows, awaiting the bishop's next victims.

We drove on around the plaza, past the ancient cathedral with its twin towers, and rolled to a stop directly in front of the bishop's residence. It stood there like a guilty reminder of all that was wrong with the Inquisition. "Why are we stopping here?"

"We're going to the vicarage. It's behind the cathedral."

Everyone climbed out—Molly, Enrique, the girl, Aunt Annie and little Mateo. The coaches pulled away. And while we stood there in the moonlight, gathering our bags, I glanced up at the bishop's home. Bastard. While I'd been rotting and starving in my cell on the other side of the plaza, he'd been living here, in a spacious two-story mansion with arches, balconies and courtyard in the Moorish style, protected by a tall wrought iron fence.

A faint glow of yellow shone through balcony doors.

"Is that his bedchamber?" I asked.

"He's terrified of the dark. Always leaves a lamp burning."

I wanted to hurl a rock through the window. Set the place ablaze. Drag the bishop from his bed and fling him off the balcony. "Do you have extra sheets?" I asked Father Paolo.

"What are you planning, Antonio?"

"I'm going to sing him the *Ave Maria*."

CHAPTER 52

Granada, Nicaragua

Father Paolo directed the women into a large bed chamber. Enrique and I got a room that opened onto the courtyard. Real beds with goose down mattresses. A courtyard with flowering shrubs. A bath house in the rear. The pleasing chirr of night crickets.

After we settled in, I took a lantern and asked everyone to gather in the dining room—everyone except Isabella, who'd fallen asleep. "Before you get started," Father Paolo said, "I've got a couple of surprises." He motioned in two of his servants. "Recognize them?"

I stared into their dark Indian faces.

"Your oarsmen," he said. "The ones who almost drowned with you in the lake."

I shook their hands and slapped them on the backs and was thanking them in their Choro tongue when an old woman in Indian garb shuffled in with a pot of soup. Not until she turned to face me did I recognize her—Abuelita, she of the fever juice.

"You fly away like bird," she said in her tortured Castilian. "Now you fly back like bird."

Father Paolo blessed the food, and as we ate, I told them my plan, assigning a role to each person except Aunt Annie. "There's no time to rehearse. We've got to do it right the first time."

Enrique checked to see that his pistol was charged and laid it on the table.

"Why don't we just shoot the bastard? Bang! Problem solved."

I rolled my eyes. "You don't just assassinate a bishop."

"Why not? The man's a pervert, a murderer."

"Look, Enrique, if we shoot him, they'll blame the Indians. The army will take over… people like Gonzalez. Then we'll get another inquisitor-general, even more brutal."

"So what's the point of this little farce?"

"Point is to scare him."

Father Paolo brought out white sheets. Little Mateo gathered up pebbles and a sack of goose down. One of the oarsman grabbed a reflector style lantern. Molly, Enrique and I stuffed pistols into our pockets—two each. Then, with Father Paolo leading, we crept back along the walkway between the bishop's mansion and the cathedral.

Mateo halted beneath the bishop's window. The rest of us crossed the street and gathered at the edge of the plaza, beneath the palms and mango trees. A half-moon cast ghostly shadows. Orange blossoms perfumed the night air, and a cool breeze blew down from the mountains. Better yet, the night crier had long since quit his post, and there were no sounds other than the cooing of night birds and the distant bark of a dog.

Enrique pushed up beside us. "What if he has guards?"

"We'll be long gone before they figure it out."

"Every time you try to calm me, we get deeper into *mierda*."

The two oarsmen reconnoitered the plaza and reported back that four or five town drunks—*borrachínes*—lay sleeping directly beneath the gallows platform.

"Not a problem," I said. "Let's do it."

Molly, Enrique and I wrapped sheets about us, then positioned ourselves across the street from the mansion, at a spot where the bishop could see from his balcony.

An oarsman placed the reflector lantern on the cobbles to our front. Mateo began flinging pebbles against the bishop's window. The bishop's quarters came alive. There was a cry, a moving shadow, the light changing position, moving across the room.

Drums rolled in my head. Then, with the three of us illuminated in the light, and Father Paolo and the other oarsman in the shadows with their sheets, something remarkable happened. No longer was I

Father Antonio; I was *El Cantante*, standing on a stage before an audience of hundreds with my fellow actors, the lights upon us.

The curtain rose, and I began to sing, *adagio* at first and then *andante*, putting the words I'd composed for this occasion to the music of Giulio Caccini's masterpiece:

Oh, how she cries for the fallen,
And the innocents falsely accused
Ave Maria...

Molly and Enrique joined in, *basso profundo* to my right, tenor on the left. A balcony door opened, and there he stood, the monster himself in nightgown and cap, staring down at three ghosts in the night. Molly, whose singing voice was less than angelic, evoked the spirit of evil by raising both arms to heaven.

"My children," she cried as if in agony. "My babies, my husband. What have you done to them? For shame, for shame!"

By then Mateo had ascended a platform on the cathedral, upwind from the balcony, and began releasing goose down.

Feathers floated over the balcony like snowflakes in the wind, dancing and swirling. At the same time, Paolo and the oarsmen dashed along the street in their dark clothing, white sheets fluttering, chanting at the top of their voices:

"Sharpened stakes! Burning fires! Ropes that stretch the neck!"

"Why?' Molly beseeched, her arms outstretched. "Tell me why?"

The violins in my head cried. Flutes wailed, and I could hear the music of the harpsichord, the strike of the keys. Not since I'd sung for the hunchback from my cell had I been so absorbed:

But in her heart she knows
Heaven will intervene,
Against the evil men do,
Ave Maria...

Birds fluttered up from their roosts. Dogs barked and howled. Candles began to glow in windows. And our fellow ghosts scattered in all directions, still chanting, creating an even more spectral-like scene with their trailing sheets.

Little by little we backed into the shadows, Molly attacking her aria in the B minor of distress, hurling her imprecations like flaming arrows: "*Porque? Digame porque?*" Why? Tell me why?

We dragged out the final syllables. I bowed to our audience of palm and mango trees. The curtain fell. My ears rang with make-believe cheers and applause. We removed our sheets. Molly kissed me on the lips and said our performance was magnificent.

And when we stepped out from the bushes, the bishop was gone, the balcony doors closed, and all that remained was the burning lantern and the barking dogs.

CHAPTER 53

The Ave Maria played in my head all night, and was still playing when the ancient bells of the cathedral jarred me awake. Dogs came to life, barking and howling as if the Moors had landed. Roosters crowed. Worse, street vendors began hawking their products—fresh chicken here, bread there, goats' cheese, and eggs.

Enrique flung a pillow at the wall. I rolled out of bed and headed for the bath house. From the bishop's courtyard, beyond a brick wall too high to climb, came the chatter and laughter of children. Could it be my boys? Would they remember me?

I scrubbed away the lingering filth of the voyage, changed into Father Menendez's cassock, and followed the smell of fresh coffee across the cobbled courtyard to the dining room. Molly was already there with Tante Annie and Isabella, looking as bleary eyed as I felt.

Molly frowned. "Why are you dressed like a priest?"

I explained—or was trying to—when Father Paolo, who'd been summoned early to the bishop's residence, burst through the front door and slammed it behind him. His face was red, and he had the look of a man whose wife had just left him for a fisherman.

"The bishop is an idiot," he said. "Keeps blabbering about demons and chupacabras."

Isabella scampered away and began chasing butterflies in the courtyard. Paolo sank into a chair and glared at me. "He says God is punishing him for not burning enough heretics. Not driving out enough Indians. Says the only way to cleanse the land is do what the Hebrews did to the Philistines—destroy them."

He rang the servants' bell and yelled for Abuelita. I opened my mouth to comment, but he waved his arms. "Hold on, let me finish. He also issued an order for another *auto da fé*… for Sunday morning. That's tomorrow, Antonio. Says to burn or hang every prisoner in the Alhambra. And that includes Rosa Morales."

Enrique stepped into the room. "We should have shot him."

I paced around the room. "What time does La Casa open?"

"Nine," Paolo answered. "Why do you ask?"

"Nine is too early. We should plan on getting there at eleven."

"To do what? What are you planning now, Antonio?"

"First thing is to pick up the bishop's gold."

"*Jesús, Maria y todos los santos*. You took the bishop's gold?"

I explained. He rang the bell again. A minute or two later, Abuelita, Mateo, and the two oarsmen shuffled into the room with breakfast. Paolo blessed the food and asked for guidance. And while we ate, I laid out the scheme I'd been working on for weeks.

"How are you going to haul the gold?" Paolo asked.

"Why not use the bishop's coach? The small one. You're the fiscál. You can arrange it."

Enrique burst into laughter. "What's so funny?" I asked.

"Don't you see the irony? You, the condemned heretic, using the bishop's own carriage to steal his gold and free his prisoners. And with help from an English pirate."

"Molly's not a pirate."

"That's not what it says on those wanted posters."

Molly shot him a murderous glare. Father Paolo sent the oarsmen to fetch the coach. Everyone else went off to get ready. I returned to the bedroom with Enrique and began changing my looks—white powder to my hair and mustache, cotton between my gums and cheeks, a folded towel under my robe to give me a paunch.

Enrique sat on the bed and stared at me. "Why can't you see it, Padre? Just look at Aunt Annie. Scars on her face. And that mean look. A sure sign of pirates. Hell, Molly would be long gone if you hadn't told her about the gold. Now she's latched on like a bloodsucking leech. Got herself all prettied up. Even brought along that little girl to capture your heart."

I opened my mouth to say what I thought of his theory, thought better of it, and instead went out the door and slammed it behind me.

Aunt Annie was sitting on a bench in the courtyard, smoking a pipe and staring at me with those hard eyes. Little Isabella was there too, all dimples, blonde hair, blue eyes and ribbons, plucking hibiscus petals and giggling like the child she was.

My stomach twisted. Would I ever see my boys like that again? Happy. Safe. Laughing. Enrique was right about one thing, though. A girl like that could capture the heart.

"You're as pretty as a princess," I said, and reached out to stroke her hair.

She screamed as if she'd stepped on a snake and dashed for the safety of Annie's skirts. Annie gave me one of her mean looks, whispered something to the child, and off they went.

At the stroke of ten-thirty, the bishop's carriage drove up, all black and shiny and pulled by two spirited horses. A white cross was emblazoned on its side. The drivers—the oarsmen—jumped down and held open the doors. I climbed in behind Molly, who was dressed like a tavern wench in a simple black dress and head scarf, and we were soon rumbling over the cobbled streets.

Enrique checked his pistols again. "What if Gonzalez is there? Or that customs captain?"

"Shut up, Enrique. I need to think."

We rounded the corner where I'd seen Saraatepe, passed the dreaded Alhambra with its massive double doors, and stopped for the guards at an arched entry. A small crowd had gathered in front to read the latest poster, but it broke up at the sight of the bishop's carriage.

The guards waved us through, and we rolled into a narrow alley that separated La Casa from the Alhambra. I'd been down that alley before, more dead than alive, and the one thing I'd never forget was the green door that opened into the Alhambra's torture chamber. It was still marked *PROHIBIDO LA ENTRADA*. My stomach knotted. What poor creature was behind that door now?

We stopped on the La Casa side of the alley, at a platform marked *RECOGIDA Y ENTREGA*. I hopped out, bounded up the steps, and knocked on a heavy door.

A uniformed guard opened the little spy window. "Pickup," I said, and handed him the certificate of demand.

He took the paper through the bars. "This says code protected."

"The code is Galileo."

He closed the window. I waited. The drivers waited. The horses whinnied and stomped their hooves on the cobbles. My fellow conspirators sat in the coach in white-faced silence. Across the alley, the door to the torture chamber remained closed, though I imagined I could smell the sweat and the smoke, hear the screams, the pleas for mercy. Molly stuck her head out the coach window.

"What is taking so long?"

I shrugged, then turned back at the sound of an opening door.

"Father, please to step inside?"

The place reeked of tobacco and smoke. At the counter stood two guards and a banker who looked like all the other bankers at La Casa. On the floor lay an open wooden crate. The banker looked up. "You should be wearing red, Father. Didn't you read the poster? They killed a chupacabra on *Las Palmas*… that ship that came in last night. Gutted three women before they killed it. Said it was all fur and fangs."

I handed him my fake *cédula*.

"Also says the *Portobello* went down with all hands."

He examined the papers, then strode to the spy window and glanced out. "That the bishop?"

"Father Paolo. Would you like him to vouch for me?"

He took a long puff on his pipe. "You and the bishop related?"

"Brothers. I'm in a bit of a hurry."

"They tell me he's not well."

"We worry about him."

"Must be the pressure of the uprising, all them Indians going crazy." He handed back my papers, bent over the crate, and brushed away a layer of straw. "Here's your shipment: hundred and fifty-two rolls of paper-wrapped gold. Manifest says twenty coins in each roll."

He removed a roll, placed it on a balance, and adjusted the weights. "A bit over twenty ounces. Looks newly minted. Never seen such a large withdrawal."

The guards hammered the lid back on. I signed for 23,863 escudos of gold, almost three thousand ounces, and then followed the two guards with the crate out the door and down to the coach, where I watched them secure it on the rear baggage rack.

"Don't forget to wear red!" yelled the banker from the doorway.

I thanked the guards, gave them a half real each, and was about to hop into the coach when that cursed door on the Alhambra side of the alley swung open.

The one marked *PROHIBIDO LA ENTRADA*.

Out stepped Samson with that scrawny little priest from the ship.

Samson wore a vest, black and shiny, along with a chain necklace and earrings. At the sight of him, the two guards and the banker hurried back inside and shut the door. Samson nodded toward the coach. "That the bishop's?" he asked in his coarse voice.

"We've come to ask about Father Menendez."

"What about him?"

"He hasn't returned." I stepped closer. "Where is he, Samson? He was supposed to return last night on La Palmas. With you. You were the last to see him, you and the captain."

"But he told us he was back already. We received his letters."

"What letters?"

"Captain Gonzalez has them. Ask him. He'll tell you."

The skinny priest, no doubt sensing trouble, eased back inside. Behind him, I could see a smoking iron pot, chains dangling from the overhead, and a victim on a table.

"Who is on that table?"

"Madam Rosa. She helped the heretic."

"You get her off the rack. Do it now, Samson."

"Who are you to be giving orders?"

"The new calificadór. Don't tell me you don't recognize me?"

He backed away and stared as if trying to remember me.

"Go, Samson. Do what I say. Then meet us in the lobby in five minutes. You've got some explaining to do about Father Menendez."

I jumped into the coach and slammed the door.

"Change of plans."

CHAPTER 54

A few minutes later, we were in front of the Alhambra, beneath the balcony where I'd sung for the hunchback. Paolo laid a hand on my knee. "Are you sure you want to do this? You've already got the gold. Tomorrow you can pick up your children. Then go away."

"Not without Madame Rosa. I'm going to save her."

"How?"

"Samson. He's going to help us."

"You can't be serious. Samson is so confused he can't decide if he's a hair stylist or the bishop's torturer. On weekends he's a hair stylist. Every woman of means goes to him."

Enrique laughed and made a nasty comment about *maricones.*

"Doesn't matter," I said, and jumped out with my bag. Enrique and Father Paolo climbed down behind me, grumbling and glancing over their shoulders. I directed Molly to take the gold to the vicarage. "Put it where we talked about, then get back here with the coach."

Enrique grabbed my arm. "Are you crazy? She's a pirate."

"Shut up, Enrique. Just shut the hell up."

The coach with Molly and the gold rolled on. Two guards stood watch at the same door through which I'd escaped with Abuelita and César. The guards recognized Father Paolo and bade us enter.

I made the sign of the cross and stepped back into the world of my nightmares. Samson was already there, waiting in front of the alcalde's office with the pinch-faced priest, Father Shining Light of Spain. The priest rushed over and pumped Paolo's hand, asking in his high-pitched voice when he could have an audience with the bishop.

"You've come at a bad time, Father. The bishop is ill."

"I'm sorry to hear that," he said. "I'll lodge at the vicarage until I can gain an audience."

I wanted to put my hands around his scrawny neck and choke him to death—he who wanted to remove the Indians from their ancestral lands. Instead, I said, "You'll do no such thing. I want you to go to the island where you've been assigned. Do it today. Now! Get acquainted with your parishioners. Learn their names. Hear their woes. Then report to us in three weeks."

He looked at Paolo for support.

"Go," Paolo said, and the priest scurried off like a beaten dog.

I marched into the alcalde's office as if I were mayor and motioned Samson to follow. Paulo latched the door behind us. We all sat at the same table on which had rested the alcalde's head, then, with Samson staring, I began removing my disguise and putting it back into my bag—the towel beneath my robe, the cotton between my cheeks and gums.

"Take a good look, Samson. Do you recognize me?"

"*Coño*, you're that man from La Casa."

"No, Samson, look again."

He squinted. He moved his head side to side, examining me, confusion in his eyes.

Enrique leaned forward. "You can't be that stupid. Samson. He's Father Antonio."

Samson bolted up. Enrique just as quickly whipped out a pistol.

"Sit your big ass back down."

Samson eased back into his chair. "But, but, Father Menendez wrote us letters. He said—"

"That I was dead? No, Samson. I wrote those letters. Father Menendez is the dead one."

"You killed El Moro too?"

"It was either him or me."

Tears welled up in his eyes. Samson the executioner, the most feared monster in Granada. "What do you want?" he asked.

"For starters, I want to know if you enjoy torturing innocents?"

"No, Padre. The bishop makes me do it. 'Make them suffer,' he says, 'or I'll make you suffer.' He's got this whip. He lays it on my back like I was a horse."

An image of the bishop lashing Samson with a whip flashed through my head. "I'm going to make you an offer, Samson." I pulled a doubloon from my pocket and spun it on the table. "Here's the first payment, a two-escudo coin. It's worth thirty-two *reales*. That's two-month's pay. Tomorrow I'll give you another thirty doubloons. Almost a thousand *reales*. With that much gold you can go away, set up a beauty shop and stop killing innocents."

He picked up the coin and looked at it. "What do I have to do?"

"How many prisoners are they planning to execute tomorrow?"

"Four. Make it five with Madame Rosa."

"What crimes have they committed?"

"None, other than being Indian and in the wrong place."

"I want you to release them, Samson."

He didn't like the idea. Neither did Enrique and Paolo. The plan was too dangerous. Gonzalez wasn't that stupid. We should quit while we were ahead.

"I'll release the prisoners," Samson said, "but you're crazy if you think I'm going to lay a trap for Captain Gonzalez. He's got cavalry. Two, three hundred men. They'll storm the place. Burn us out."

"Are you saying you won't help?"

"Not for thirty doubloons."

"How much?'

"Fifty. Half now, and the other half tomorrow."

I almost laughed at his audacity. Enrique double-cocked his pistol and pointed it in Samson's face. "I got a better idea. I say we take you to the dungeon. Strap you on the table and bring in Madam Rosa and them savages you were going to hang."

Samson swallowed hard. "It was only a suggestion."

"I'll give you forty," I said, "but not until the job is finished."

He squirmed and nodded agreement. Enrique shook a finger in his face. "Just so you know, Samson, you cross us, and you'll never get on that ship tomorrow."

"Why would I cross you? I despise Gonzalez."

As noon approached, we could hear the shuffle of feet and slamming of doors, people leaving early, calling out to each other to wear red. I turned to Samson. "Now, start calling them in."

With us watching, he called in all the guards and told them they could leave early. The stir continued for another ten or fifteen minutes, and by the time the cathedral bells chimed the start of midday, there remained only echoes and the shuffle of char women with their mops and buckets. "What about the head jailer?" I asked.

"Upstairs. He can't leave his post. We may have to lock him up."

"And the guard at the door?"

"He's a cripple. All he does is let people in and out."

We made a quick survey of the offices, made sure they were empty, and followed Samson up the same stairway I'd descended with Abuelita on the day of my escape.

The jailer, a man with thinning white hair and bad teeth, sat at a table directly across from my old cell. He struggled up at the sight of us, but Samson waved him back into his chair.

"Have you heard about the chupacabras?" I asked him.

"Claro. It's scary. I'm locking the place down tonight, keeping my pistols charged."

"No," Paolo said, "It's best you go home, look after your family. Samson will take over."

"I can't do that. They ordered me not to leave my post, not the night before executions."

"Who ordered you?"

"I'm told it was the bishop himself."

Paolo stepped closer. "Look at me. Do you know who I am?"

He stared at Paolo. "I can't rightly say I do, Father."

"I'm the fiscál, the bishop's second in control. I'm the one who gives the orders."

A look of panic crossed the poor man's face. He scooped up his food bag, stuffed a pistol into his belt, and hobbled down the stairs.

"Get back here by dawn!" Samson yelled after him.

"*Vale.*"

We listened for the sound of the front door closing behind him, then grabbed the keys and lanterns.

Madam Rosa lay in a room that reeked of chamber pot and unwashed body, huddled in the shadows in a filthy dress, her eyes as wild as a cornered dog. How different from that day she'd picked me up in her coach: Madam Rosa of the House of Seven Veils, all rouged up in a Parisian dress and glittering jewelry. Now, her hair was stringy, her nails broken, her arms and face covered with sores.

She sat up. "Is this the end?" she asked in a feeble voice.

I pulled her to her bare feet and tried to explain but got only sobs and prayers. The Indians, who were more accustomed to deprivation, bounded up at the mention of freedom. "Follow me," I said, and guided them to some back stairs that connected with the dungeon.

Unlit torches lined the walls. Every shadow looked like a sentinel. And when we came to the door that led into the torture room, I felt my heart thudding against my ribs.

We shuffled past, followed a long corridor, opened another door, and emerged into the diffused light of the rear courtyard.

The sweetness of orange blossoms filled the air. From the lobby came the chatter of the cleaning women. Samson closed the lobby door. Then we followed him along a row of flowering acacias to a high brick wall in the rear.

"The door's here," he said, "behind those bushes."

He took out his ring of keys and fumbled with the lock. The door opened. And there, at the same street where Madam Rosa had picked me up during the escape, waited Molly, the two oarsmen, and Little Mateo with the bishop's coach.

The Indians gave a triumphant shout and dashed away. I helped Rosa into the carriage and instructed the oarsmen to drive her to the House of Seven Veils.

"Wait," Mateo said. He reached inside the coach and took out a sack and a jug. "Chicken blood and feathers," he said. "Abuelita says you'll know what to do."

"What now?" Molly asked.

"Gonzalez. It's time we come face to face."

CHAPTER 55

We retraced our steps back through the courtyard, entered the lobby, and went back to the alcalde's office. "How are we going to get Gonzalez here?" Paolo asked.

"Simple, write him a message."

"Not a good idea," Molly said. "A letter can get us hanged. That's what the pirates say."

"Pirates are too ignorant to read or write," said Enrique.

"Billy can read and write. He studied the law in London, he did."

"And where'd you learn to read and write—the school of piracy?"

Molly's face flushed crimson. "Why are you acting the fool, Enrique?"

"All I'm saying is you know a thing or two about pirates, you and that so-called aunt. Pirate's written all over her. She might as well be wearing a sign."

"That's enough," Paolo said. "We're talking about Gonzalez, not pirates." He plopped into a chair behind the alcalde's desk and pulled out paper and quill. "I'll write it."

With the matter settled, I stepped into another room with my bag, slipped out of my priest garb, and changed into breeches with knee stockings, buckled shoes, a white shirt, waistcoat, and black tricornered hat. When I returned, Father Paolo read his message aloud:

"Esteemed Captain Gonzalez: By this letter I send word that a passenger known to you from *Las Palmas* has been exposed as an imposter. He may in fact be Father Antonio, the escaped heretic. Please to meet me in the Alhambra at once. Alone."

Molly held her tongue. Samson said it was perfect. I nodded agreement and then we went out the front and employed one of Mateo's street urchin friends.

"This message is urgent," Paolo told the boy. "It's for the eyes of Captain Gonzalez only."

"*Vale*," said the child. He took the note and trotted away.

How long we waited, standing near the front door and trying to remain calm, I do not know. The char ladies finished their task and left the building. A wagon rolled by, loaded with barrels. Then the two oarsmen showed up with news that they'd returned the coach to the bishop's carriage house. At last, Samson pointed across the plaza. "There he comes."

The boy trotted up to us, all grins. "Done. Letter delivered."

"What did the captain say?" Paolo asked.

"He wasn't there, sir. They said he was practicing maneuvers with his men."

"Who took the note?"

"A priest, sir. He promised to deliver it."

"I told you specifically to give it to the captain."

"But I didn't know what to do. The priest insisted on taking it."

"What priest? Describe him, *mijo*. Tell us what he looked like."

"Well, he was skinny as a stick. Not very tall, and he talked funny, like a woman."

I rolled my eyes. Paolo, who rarely showed anger, erupted like a volcano. "That damn Salamanca fanatic. Didn't we order him to the islands? I'll have his head."

The boy scampered away. Paolo was still complaining when Samson pointed across the plaza again.

"Look, it's the bishop's coach."

Paolo frantically motioned us back inside, and again we watched from behind the door. The coach stopped in front. Out of it sprang that scrawny little priest, a smirk as big as the Alhambra.

"We should have killed the little snot," Enrique muttered.

The priest helped down the bishop. And there stood the evil one himself, in the purple and white of his office, complete with pectoral cross, gloves, cape, and a peaked *mitra* as if going to communion. Worse, he flourished a leather riding crop in his hand.

He glared at Father Paolo. "Is it true you have the heretic?"

Father Paolo said "Maybe," and motioned him inside.

We weren't ready for him to see us yet, so those of us behind the door trotted across the lobby and up the stairs—Samson, Molly, Enrique, Mateo, and the two oarsmen—taking the steps two at a time.

Molly tripped on her dress and fell against the railing. I grabbed her arm and pulled her along, and we had just reached the top when the bishop burst through the front door, his voice echoing across the empty lobby. "I want Samson to skin him alive. Make him suffer."

I directed everyone into the places we'd previously discussed—Molly into Madam Rosa's old cell, the two oarsmen into the cell that had been occupied by the four Indians.

Please, dear God, get me through this.

"What about me?" Enrique said.

"Take the rear stairs. Get to the front and watch for Gonzalez."

"What if he shows up?"

"Pray that he doesn't."

He and Mateo faded into the shadows. By then the bishop was on the stairs, coming up with the skinny priest and Father Paolo, breathing hard. "Samson," the bishop cried. "Get your sorry ass down here. Help me up these stairs."

Samson looked at me with pleading eyes.

"Go," I said, pushing him. "Try to delay him."

He trotted away. I dashed into the jailer's office, fumbled in my shoulder bag for the wig I'd brought for this purpose—the wig of a scraggly-haired old man—and put it on.

But where was the hat? There. I put it over the wig. Then I noticed the jailer's tattered jacket on a nail. Why not? I pulled it over my waistcoat and had just stuffed cotton between my cheeks and gums to give me a fuller face when the bishop appeared at the door.

"You there, jailer. Get your lazy ass up. Didn't you hear me?"

His sneer was almost satanic. His breathing was labored, raspy, and even in the poor light I could see his sunken eyes and pallid skin, his skeletal frame and the way he bent at the waist.

"*Perdoneme, su Gracia*, I didn't expect—"

"Never mind with your excuses. Show me the prisoner."

He raised his crop as if to lay a blow on me. I flinched, grabbed the keys and a lantern, and led him into the darkness of the hallway, hobbling like the old man I was supposed to be, praying under my breath for lightning to strike him dead.

Samson and Father Paolo followed. The bishop supported himself on the arm of the skinny priest, his long vestments skimming the floor like a bride at a wedding.

I paused at Madam Rosa's old door and slid back the top partition.

The bishop glanced inside—at Molly sitting on the floor with her arms cradled around her knees. "That's not the heretic."

"No, your Grace, it's Madam Rosa. I thought you'd like to—"

His crop bit into my face without warning. "*Idiota*! How dare you defy the wishes of God's representative on earth! I asked you to show me the heretic, not the town whore!"

I might have strangled him right there, slowly, if Samson had not stepped between us. "Can't you do anything right?" he growled at me in his coarse voice, feigning anger.

He grabbed the keys from my hand, led the bishop to the door of my old cell, and began sliding back bolts. The sounds tore at my insides. My heart beat faster. Would I have the courage to go back into that room? Take the risk of being locked up again?

"Are you certain it's the heretic?" the bishop asked Samson.

"*Sín duda*, your Grace. I spoke to him only minutes ago, heard his Catalán accent."

He inserted the key and turned it. The bishop began slapping his crop in the palm of his hand. His breathing became louder, like a lover in anticipation of ecstasy.

Samson pushed open the door. The bishop swept inside, his robes flapping. I made the sign of the cross and stepped back into the hellhole of my memory.

A flickering candle cast a dim light on the hammock and wooden table. Feathers were scattered all over the floor. And on the wall, scrawled in chicken blood, were the words Molly had written: WHAT YE SOW SHALL YE ALSO REAP.

"*Coño*," Samson blurted, "he must have escaped."

The bishop's eyes widened. He pointed at the writing. He tried to speak. Then he clasped his chest and sank to his knees, gasping for breath. The skinny priest dropped down beside him.

"Somebody fetch a medico. Hurry!"

No one moved.

"What is wrong with you people? Can't you see he's having a seizure?"

Paolo grabbed the priest by both ears and yanked him up. "This is all your fault. We ordered you to the island. Instead you went running to the bishop. Couldn't you see he was ill?"

"But, but…"

"Don't you 'but' me. You better pray he lives."

Paolo turned to Samson. "Take this oaf and lock him up. Throw away the key."

Samson pushed the skinny priest out of the room—none too gently—and I was standing there, watching the bishop turn blue, when Mateo dashed up the stairs.

"Father! Father! It's the captain! He's coming! And the whole cavalry is with him!"

CHAPTER 56

I rushed to the bars to see for myself. Horsemen were coming in at full gallop—thirty, forty, maybe fifty—skirting the plaza to my right, following the same route as the *auto da fé*. Doors rattled. Even the bars shook. Paolo came up beside me.

"*Madre de Dios*. Now what?"

"Get everyone into their places. We'll face him at the front."

"What about the bishop?"

"Lock him in here."

Samson slammed the door and locked the bishop into my old cell. Then we stampeded down the stairs like a herd of frightened horses. At the bottom I handed Molly my shoulder bag.

"Take this to the alcalde's office and wait."

"What about the oarsmen? And Mateo?"

"Just get them out of sight. Now go! *Vete*!"

With my heart in my throat, with my plans collapsing around me, I trotted across the lobby, hurried past the old guard at his desk, and joined Samson, Paolo, and Enrique at the front door.

Samson, seeing his opportunity, said, "I want a hundred."

"I'll make it fifty," I said, realizing how desperate I must sound. I shoved him out the front door and followed him onto the landing in my jailer's outfit. The pistols in my pocket gave me small comfort, but I'd use them if I had to.

The cavalrymen drew to a noisy stop in front, their standards and colors catching the breeze, their horses snorting and pawing. Even from the landing, I could smell sweat and leather.

Gonzalez frowned from atop his mount, looked the building over, and pointed a gloved finger at the bishop's coach.

"Why is the bishop here?"

"The heretic," Paolo said. "The bishop came to see for himself."

Gonzalez turned his gaze on Samson. "Father Antonio is here?"

My hand tightened on a pistol. If Samson was going to betray us, this would be the time.

"*Sí, Capitán*, no doubt about it. It's Father Antonio."

Gonzalez swung off his horse and lumbered up the steps. At the top, he turned back to his men.

"You there, Casado, pick six troopers and come with me."

Paolo held up a hand. "Hold on, Captain. The bishop asked for you and you alone. Send these men back to the barracks."

Gonzalez stood there, hands on hips, scowling.

Father Paolo said, "Are you defying me, Captain?"

"No, Padre, it's just that—"

"Just what, Captain? If you can't give the order, I'll give it myself." He stepped around Gonzalez and spoke directly to Lieutenant Casado. "Send these men to the barracks."

The lieutenant glanced at Gonzalez as if asking his permission.

"You heard him," Gonzalez said.

The lieutenant saluted, and I was praying all would go well when from above came the bishop's voice.

"Samson! Father Paolo! Open this door! Do it now!"

Gonzalez looked up. "What the pox? Is that the bishop?"

"The heretic," Paolo shot back.

He punched Samson's arm. "Go and shut him up. *Vete*! *Vete*!"

Samson took off at a trot. The cavalrymen rode away. Gonzalez, still glancing up, followed us through the door and into the lobby. The old guard at the desk closed and bolted the door behind us, and at last I had the captain where I wanted him. Inside the Alhambra.

Alone.

Enrique, who'd been waiting near the bottom of the stairs, marched over to meet us. "What is this?" Gonzalez said. "How come you're not locked up with the heretic?"

"Because he tricked me as well."

"How can you be that stupid? You were with him on a ship."

"So were you, Captain. If I'm stupid, what does that make you?"

They glared at each other. Paolo stepped between them, and I imagine the matter would have gotten out of hand except for the bishop's voice above us, hurling invectives at Samson:

"You miserable ox! You ugly piece of shit!"

His words ended in what sounded like a slap. The commotion grew louder, with curses and the unmistakable slap of riding crop on flesh, as if Samson had placed the bishop across his knees, lifted his robes, and was giving him a sound thrashing.

Samson the hair dresser.

I grinned at the image. Gonzalez looked as confused as ever. Paolo touched him on the shoulder. "This way, please. The bishop wants us in the alcalde's office."

At our approach, Molly swung open the door.

"Who is this?" Gonzalez asked.

"She's the one who reported the heretic."

Paolo guided the captain into the room and motioned him into a chair. I took a seat at one end, Father Paolo at the other. Molly stood against the wall. Then Gonzalez noticed Mateo.

"What's he doing here?"

"Another witness," Paolo said.

"Witness to what?"

"The massacre on the Island of Lizards. He's the lone survivor."

Gonzalez's face went white and sickly, as if he suddenly realized he'd walked into a trap. He pushed back in his chair as if to stand but settled back when Samson entered the room with the bishop's riding crop. Samson loudly bolted the door behind him, then positioned himself against the wall, arms crossed like a harem guard.

"Enough," Gonzalez said. "Where's the bishop?"

"He'll be down shortly," Paolo answered, "but first we need to ask you a few questions." He fixed the captain with a hard glare. "Do you have a bank account at La Casa?"

"What if I do?"

"Because we've been hearing complaints—shop owners saying they pay you protection money. Prominent individuals saying they have to pay you not to denounce them as heretics. There's also talk that you've taken funds meant for the Church."

"Nonsense. What I have in my account is honestly earned."

Paolo gestured toward me. "Jailer, show him the documents."

"What documents?" Gonzalez asked.

"Bank records. Transactions you made at La Casa."

"Impossible. I haven't been to La Casa in months."

"Show him, jailer."

Gonzalez turned his gaze on me, staring at the welt on my face where the bishop had hit me. At my tattered jacket. At my fumbling hands when I placed the bag in my lap. I took out the papers and spoke in what I hoped was the voice of the old jailer.

"Let me see, hmm. This must be his bank code. Looks like... Relámpago."

Gonzalez mumbled under his breath.

"Speak up?" Paolo commanded. "What did you say?"

"I said since when can that old jailer read?"

I shuffled the papers. "There's an account number too. It looks like...GR866301."

Gonzalez drew in a sharp breath. I reached into the bag again. "Oh, and there's also this—a withdrawal certificate, signed by you. Your account has been closed."

"Closed? What do you mean, closed?"

"*Cerrado, Capitán. Se cabo*. The balance is zero."

Not since I'd plunged a knife into Father Menendez had I seen such shock. For a moment, I thought he'd burst into tears. At last, he struggled up and leaned forward with his hands on the table. And when he spoke, his voice was strained, as if he could barely get out the words. "Where is that damn heretic? He stole my money."

Paolo nodded in my direction. "That's him sitting right there."

I pushed back in my chair and stood, thinking to do the same to Gonzalez that I'd done to Samson—remove the wig and hat, spit out the cotton, and stand before my enemy as Father Antonio. No sooner did I start to peel off the jacket than he struck, charging me like a bull.

A knife came out. I scampered backward over the floor, holding the bag as protection. The knife slashed my leg. I cried out in pain. Molly yelled something that sounded like “Fook.” Then Enrique grabbed the captain from behind.

The knife clattered to the floor, and the fight should have been over, except no one told Gonzalez. He yanked loose, grabbed a chair and swung it in a circle, driving everyone back.

By then I was on my feet, my stocking stained with blood. Enrique whipped out his pistol and aimed it at the captain.

“Stand down or I’ll put a ball into your skull!”

“No,” I shouted. “This is my fight!”

Molly tossed me the brass cane. The one I’d used on El Moro. Then it was just the two of us, a disgraced priest against a cavalryman, a wooden chair against a brass walking stick.

Gonzalez came at me with the chair, cursing.

“Come on, Padre. Stand and fight. That’s what your little whore did. She had more guts than you.”

He pushed forward, holding the chair in front, his black eyes focused. “Know what your little *puta* did? Spread her legs for me. Gave me some of that brown Indian *chucha*.”

He swung the chair. It glanced off my shoulder and splintered on the table. I used the opening to land a blow to his ankle. He yelped. I charged. Then we were rolling on the floor, kicking and punching, cursing and grunting.

It should have been easy for the captain—a trained killer against a wounded padre, but I had hatred on my side, a burning desire to snuff out the light of this man who had destroyed my life. And while he’d spent the last few months whoring, eating, drinking, and putting on fat, I’d been running up and down companionways.

He tried to pull himself up by the table. I kicked his feet from under him. He grabbed another chair and tried to put it between us. I kicked it away. He reached the door, still crawling.

But the strength was going out of me as well.

“Come on, Padre. Finish him.”

With all my remaining strength, I threw my entire weight on him. Then I straddled him the way Father Menendez had straddled me, hands around his neck, choking him.

I shouted and cursed with all my breath, thinking of all he'd stolen from me—my beautiful Saraatepe, my life and happiness, the future of my children—and I was still cursing and shouting when the room flashed as white as if lightning had struck.

The world faded away. The notes of *Ave Maria* filled the room.

And there stood the Gypsy, her arms outstretched in the manner of our Savior on the cross.

"No, Father. Vengeance is not yours alone."

I rolled away, gasping for breath. Samson and Enrique dragged Gonzalez from the room. Molly helped me into a chair and began tending my wounds. My ribs felt as if they'd stopped a cannon ball. My lower lip was bleeding, and I could barely see out of my left eye.

"Why didn't you kill him?" Molly said.

"The Gypsy wouldn't let me. She—"

"You're babbling nonsense. Did he lay a blow on your head?"

A basin appeared beside her, then a pitcher and dipper. Molly helped me drink, and as my head cleared, I realized the oarsmen were cleaning the floor with mops and Paolo was standing over me.

"We've got another problem," he said.

"What?"

"Lieutenant Casado. He and his cavalrymen are still in the plaza."

I took a long gulp of water, and somewhere in the recesses of my head, I heard the Gypsy's voice.

"Speak to them, Father. You know what to do."

Yes, I knew exactly what to do.

"Good," I said to Paolo. "I'd like to speak to Lieutenant Casado and his top officers. But first tell Samson to strip the bishop to his underwear and bring his clothing down here."

Enrique stood up from the table.

"Please don't tell me you're going to—"

"I know what I'm doing. Get out there and relay the message."

Samson returned with the bishop's vestments, which reeked of sour sweat and body odor. I motioned everyone into a seat around the table and explained my plan. No one objected, but no one seemed that confident either. I assigned each person a role, and we were rehearsing our parts when from the outside came the clatter of hooves.

"*Coño*," Enrique said. "They're here already."

CHAPTER 57

Paolo made the sign of the cross, then he and Samson went out to meet them. I retreated into the alcalde's inner office and changed into the bishop's clothing—the purple and white of authority. Molly adjusted the mitra on my head, wiped the pectoral cross with a towel, and stood back to look.

"Perfect," she said. "What a handsome bishop you make."

"Even with a swollen face?"

"They won't notice if you sit sideways."

She and Enrique remained with me in the alcalde's inner office, out of sight. The two oarsmen, who were dressed in livery, took up positions on the conference side of the door, looking like bronze versions of the Vatican's Swiss guards.

"They're coming," Molly said.

From the lobby came the clomp of boots. I closed the door, took a seat behind the alcalde's mahogany desk, and picked up a quill. Then they were in the conference room with Samson and Father Paolo. Paolo told them to sit down.

I dipped the quill in ink and wrote the words, *God, give me strength.* Paolo tapped on the door. "They're here, your Grace." He opened the door just enough for them to see me at an angle, me the pretend bishop, sitting at the desk.

"Who is here?" I answered, trying to imitate the bishop's voice.

"Lieutenants Peralta, Nuñez, and Casado."

"Can't you see I'm occupied? You're the fiscál. You handle it."

"*A sus órdenes*," your Grace."

"Wait," I barked. "The truth. I want the truth. Otherwise they'll suffer the consequences."

"*Vale*," Paolo said, and backed away, leaving the door ajar.

Paolo sat where I could see him. He shuffled some papers. "The bishop wants to know if any of you have an account at La Casa?"

They all answered no.

"Are you aware that Captain Gonzalez has an account there?"

No one knew—or admitted they knew.

He passed around the bank statements. There were mutters of disbelief. Then he began relating the charges against Gonzalez—theft, extortion, bribery, plunder. "He even took funds meant for the Church. It's a serious offense, and you know the consequences."

There were murmurs and nods.

"He's your fellow officer," Paolo said. "How could you not know?"

Lieutenant Casado spoke up. "We heard complaints."

"From whom?"

"Shop owners. They say he charges them a protection fee."

"And you reported him? Right?"

"No, Father."

"You knew he was crooked and didn't report him?"

"He's our senior commander, Father. There's no one to report to."

"You could have reported to me. Or Father Menendez."

The silence that fell over them was almost laughable. They all knew Father Menendez was as crooked as the bishop and Gonzalez but didn't dare admit what they knew.

"Were any of you involved in his affairs?"

Everyone answered no.

I rapped the bishop's crop across the desk. "You tell those officers if they know anything, they'd best speak up now. This instant!"

The room remained quiet. I could almost sense their fear.

"Samson," I said, "are you out there?"

"I'm here, your Grace." He appeared at the door.

"Where is Captain Gonzalez?"

"Downstairs, your Grace. I'll have a full confession before the day is finished."

"Good. I want names. Get me names of associates. Understand?"

"Yes, your Grace."

I waited for him to retreat, then called in Father Paolo.

Paolo hurried to the door. "Your Grace?"

"That report we heard of pirate sightings. Have you sent out a reconnaissance?"

"Not yet. We're waiting for—"

"Waiting for what? For pirates to attack? Get someone out there. Now! Send fifty men to Rivas, another fifty to Ysese. Send those two lieutenants, Petronez and…"

"Peralta, your Grace. Peralta and Nuñez."

"That's them. Peralta and Nuñez. Tell them to report back by tomorrow evening."

"What about Lieutenant Casado?"

"Someone's got to guard the city. Keep him here with fifty men."

By then all three officers were on their feet, ready to run. My only regret was that I couldn't see their faces. Paolo gave the orders, and off they dashed, boots clomping across the lobby.

The door opened and slammed behind them.

I let out a shout of triumph and then flung the bishop's *mitra* against the wall. Molly stepped over and gave me a hug. "That story about pirates," she said. "Is it true?"

"Of course not, but I had to get them out of town."

We all had a good laugh. Paolo said he'd send over to the vicarage for food. "Why don't we just eat there?" Molly asked.

"Can't. Not with an *auto da fé* tomorrow. Priests and brothers are already arriving from the provinces. Nuns too. We'll have to lodge them at the vicarage."

"What about us?" Molly said. "Where will we stay?"

"The bishop's guest quarters," Paolo said. "We'll move you and the women there. Women only." He looked at me. "Do you mind staying here with Samson? Someone has to man this place. We can't leave the bishop and captain here alone."

The prospect of another night in the Alhambra filled me with dread, but I didn't dare show it, not in front of Molly and Enrique.

"Not a problem," I said to Paolo.

Night crept over the Alhambra like an evil fog, bringing with it the bark of dogs and a faint reddish glow from Volcán Masaya. We moved the bishop and Gonzalez into the inner cells, where their cries for help could not be heard. I remained in the Alcalde's inner office and ate the food Paolo sent over, occasionally gazing through the gloom at the stakes in the plaza, and across the trees at the convent where my boys were housed.

Were they safe? Would I see them tomorrow?

How I wished Molly were with me. Here, in a tub of warm water. I closed my eyes and allowed her to slip into my inner being. Molly, clad in a robe.

A door slammed. Samson, I figured, making his rounds. I heard other familiar noises—the clang of a chamber pot lid, the murmur of prayer. Someone crying.

My stomach wrenched. Was it the bishop? The captain? Were they suffering the way I'd suffered for eleven months in this cursed place? A flash of light in the plaza caught my attention. A moving light, someone with a lantern.

Why would anyone be out on a night like this? Didn't it trouble them to cross that cursed plaza with all its ghosts?

Hadn't they heard about chupacabras?

Another door slammed. I heard voices. Then footfalls. Was it Samson? How easy it would be for him to lock me in. Make me prisoner again. Suppose he'd locked it already? Suppose he was conspiring with Captain Gonzalez?

With that terrifying thought, I hurried to the door and opened it.

And there stood Molly.

Her hand was raised as if to knock. In the other she held a lantern.

"Samson let me in."

She stepped into the room and set the lantern on the table, bringing with her the scent of cinnamon and vanilla. Her hair was damp, as if she'd just bathed, and she wore a cape over a white blouse and skirt. "Why are you staring? Do you not want me here?"

I glanced out the door and into the lobby. Samson wasn't there. Nothing but the beat of my heart and a low-burning lamp down by front door. How foolish of me to think Samson would betray us. Not with all that gold at stake.

"Answer me. Do you want me to leave?"

"No, Molly, I'm glad you came."

"You don't look like it."

"How am I supposed to look?"

"Like you're happy to see me."

She came into my arms, and our lips met in a moist, lingering kiss. An image of that tub in Santo Domingo flashed through my mind. Then we were kissing and clawing with the same intensity as that first time in the cabin, and in the tub in Santo Domingo.

"Do you want me?" she whispered between kisses.

"Desperately."

"And tomorrow?"

"Tomorrow too, and the next day and the next."

She swept off her cape, removed the two pistols from her belt, and began unlacing the ribbons on her blouse. First one, and then the other, looking into my face, moistening her lips.

I doused the lantern and all but one of the candles, leaving us in a soft glow. And then we were in each other's arms, whispering the words of lovers in their most intimate moments. There, in the alcalde's office with its all bad memories. In sight of the plaza where they wanted to burn me. One floor below where Gonzalez and the bishop waited in their cells. Oh, to breathe the scent of her, to hear that lovely voice with the strange accent, to feel the silkiness of her most intimate being.

I pulled her toward the inner office.

"Not there," she whispered.

"Where?"

"The table."

CHAPTER 58

When I awoke the next morning and found her under the blanket next to me, breathing softly in her sleep, I allowed myself a moment of joy. Hardly a day had passed since I'd met her that I didn't wake up and wish for this moment. Now she was here, in a hammock beside me, warm and soft and nude.

The rumble of a passing wagon caused her to stir. She ran a hand down the side of my face, letting it rest on my lips.

"Antonio, Antonio, is it really you? Am I dreaming?"

I kissed her on the shoulder and breathed in the lingering scent of our lovemaking. "I think I can never get enough of you," I whispered.

"Then we should not the moment waste."

We came together again. In the hammock in the first light of morning while roosters crowed and dogs barked and the city slept and all that mattered was this moment. And we were still lying there, holding each other, when a loud explosion jolted the room.

She sat upright. "*Que pasó*?"

Doors rattled. Dust filtered down from the overhead. Then came a second blast and yet a third, echoing through town in the early light. My stomach twisted. The old dread came back. An image of the hunchback flashed through my mind.

"I should have warned you. They always fire three blasts before an *auto da fé*."

"All they do in New Orleans is ring the bells."

It grew lighter. The first rays of sun struck the treetops. Then the ancient bell at the Cathedral of Granada began pealing for mass. So did the bells at La Merced and La Iglesia de Guadelupe, and before long the entire village was echoing in chimes.

"You'd better go," I said to Molly. "The jailer will be here soon."

She dressed quickly, pulled a cape about her shoulders, took her pistols, and kissed me. Not just a kiss, but the kind of warm, moist meeting of lips that promised more nights to come.

"Be careful," she said. "I'll be watching from the bishop's gallery." At the door, she smiled, kissed me again, and hurried away.

I put on my sandals, trekked down to the washroom, cleaned up, and came out in time to find Samson and Enrique trying to explain these new developments to the jailer.

"There's been some changes," Samson was saying.

I stepped closer and introduced myself as the new calificadór. "Listen, *Viejo*, we've got new flesh to burn—the heretic himself. This time we're not taking any chances. I don't want anyone in here except me, Father Paolo, and Samson. Understand?"

"*Sí, Padre*. What am I supposed to do?"

"You can help Samson's assistant, outside. Now go. Both of you. Get that kindling piled up."

The jailer grabbed his hat and hurried down the stairs. Samson's assistant pulled on his executioner's hood and followed. Then Father Paolo arrived in his formal dress—a white cassock with dangling cross and decorative red stole. With him were Mateo, the two oarsmen, a basket of food for breakfast, and a jug of Abuelita's fever juice. "What's that for?" I asked Mateo.

"The prisoners. Abuelita says it'll kill their pain."

Samson frowned and turned to me. "I thought you wanted them to suffer."

"That was yesterday. Give it to them."

He took the jug and stalked down to the bishop's cell, but had scarcely entered before there came a crash, followed by the bishop's voice: "*Idiota*! What is wrong with you? Don't you know who I am? I'll have you burned! Skinned alive!"

Something else crashed. There were more curses, things knocking about as if Samson were wrestling with the bishop.

I shook my head, took a few bites of cheese and bread, and went back to the alcalde's office to change into the purple and white of a bishop. Not the smelly garments I'd worn the day before, but the ones I'd purchased in Santo Domingo—buckled *sandalia* for my feet, chasuble, *mitra*, white gloves and emerald ring. I also whitened my face with powder, trying to emulate the bishop's pallid looks, and was dabbing smut beneath my eyes when I heard the blare of bugles.

"Look," Enrique said. "They're coming out."

Bugles blew, drums beat, and out from the great cathedral marched the boys' choir of Granada, a procession of white robes, candles, Cross of Burgundy banners, and effigies of the Holy Virgin. The notes of *Te Deum* crossed the plaza and reached my ears, followed by the boys' youthful voices, high pitched and lyrical, singing in Latin:

Te Deum laudémus. Te Dominium confitémur....

To their front rode Lieutenant Casado and twenty cavalrymen in their dress uniforms, all blue with red and gold trimming.

Behind them came the vicars, prelates, prefects, and even a few nuns in black habits. Then the priests, brothers and friars from the islands and surrounding villages. Hooves clattered, horses snorted and pranced, banners fluttered. The smells of leather, smoke, horse droppings and sweat filled the air.

Paolo joined me in the alcalde's office. "We set up a chair for you at the top of the steps," he said in a strained voice. "Don't come out until the prisoners are firmly lashed."

"You look a bit pale. Are you nervous?"

"All it takes is one thing to go wrong. One thing, Antonio."

"Nothing will go wrong. Now go. *Vete*. Stop worrying."

As soon as he left, I turned my attention back to the plaza. By then it had filled with onlookers—men, women, and children; Gypsies with their drums; vendors with pushcarts; children climbing trees. But no Indians. None.

"Prisoners coming out!"

I stepped into the lobby and watched Samson lead the bishop and Gonzalez down the stairs—two prisoners with sack-like robes covering their nakedness. Dunce's hats on their heads. Hands tied behind them. Gags over their mouths. For a year or more I'd dreamed of this moment, prayed for it. Imagined all the things I'd say to them. Now I felt only pity.

Samson poked the bishop and pointed at me.

"Take a good look, your Grace. There's your heretic, Father Antonio himself, all done up as you. But you, your dishonorable grace, are going to the stake as the heretic. Justice, wouldn't you say?"

The bishop lunged at me, his eyes wild. Enrique held him back, but still he struggled, kicking, muttering muffled curses through the gag. Gonzalez, by contrast, didn't move. Didn't seem to recognize me. Or care. Abuelita's fever juice, I figured.

Instead of lecturing them on the evil of their ways as I'd planned, I stood back and watched Samson and Enrique push them toward the stairs. "Samson!" I called out.

He turned to face me. "Your Grace?"

"There'll be no more taunting. No poking of fire in faces."

"*A sus órdenes*, your Grace."

They trudged down the stairs, crossed the lobby, and went out the door. The crowd erupted in cheers and hoots, followed by the chant, "Burn them! Burn them!"

I shuddered. I still couldn't understand why they wanted to burn me? Me? El Cantante.

Father Paolo lifted his arm to start the drumbeat. Then I picked up that cursed riding crop and forced myself across the lobby and out the door, trying not to trip on my long vestments.

The drums fell silent. The chants faded. Everyone stared as if the devil himself had stepped out of the Alhambra. Father Paolo, standing on the podium where the bishop would normally direct the execution, announced, "Behold, his Grace, the Bishop of Nicaragua."

There were murmured curses and groans of disapproval. The two oarsmen rushed to my side and led me to a wicker chair on the landing as if I were an invalid.

"*Asesino*!" yelled a voice in the crowd. "You should be the one to burn, not El Cantante!"

I ignored the taunt, sank into the cushions, and took in the scene before me—the condemned men lashed to the stakes; priests, soldiers and townsmen gathered around them; the gamers at their tables, still taking bets on whether or not heads would explode; horses on the side street; banners fluttering; residents congregated on balconies. A sea of angry faces still staring at me.

At me, the bishop, who'd probably burned someone dear to them.

An egg whizzed by my head and smashed into the door.

The two oarsmen—God bless them—quickly shielded me with their bodies. Soldiers rushed into the crowd, pushing and shoving, looking for the culprit. Women screamed. Men cursed and shouted. The boys' choir remained where they were, immobile, probably wishing they were somewhere else.

Eventually Pablo restored order, then lifted his arms for silence: "Fellow priests, soldiers of the crown, citizens of Granada. Please. Hear my words. Let us rejoice that our beloved bishop has recovered from his affliction in time to join us."

There were more groans.

"Please join me in a prayer for his full recovery."

Get on with it, I wanted to yell. No one wanted him to recover.

Paolo's prayer seemed to last forever, with the only other sounds being the grunts of the real bishop, the shuffling in the crowd, and the distant hoot of an owl.

From down by the lake came the rattle of musketry. Not just the random shot or two, but an entire volley, like soldiers engaging an enemy. Others heard it too, judging by the way they reacted, and when I turned my attention back to Father Paolo, the prayer had ended and he was reading from pages we'd prepared together.

"First, it pleases me to announce that by the order of our bishop, the edict to remove the rightful inhabitants from the islands is hereby rescinded."

A roar of approval rose from the crowd. The real bishop shook his head in protest. I acknowledged the cheers with a flick of my riding crop.

"Second—and these are the words of the bishop himself—'I am deeply grieved to learn that our trusted military commander, Captain

Bonifacio Gonzalez y Perez, has used his position to engage in the most despicable criminal acts for his personal gain.'"

There were so many boos and hisses that Paolo had to pause.

"Moreover, said captain is found guilty of the most heinous violation of native girls and women under his control… and the wanton slaughter of innocent subjects of the crown…."

"Burn the captain! Make him suffer!"

On it went—a reading of scripture, a recitation of charges, a word about the greatness of Spain—and, finally, "By virtue of the authority vested in the bishop by the Holy Inquisition, said captain is condemned to the most severe punishment allowed: death by fire."

Gonzalez didn't so much as lift his head. Either he'd accepted his fate like a good soldier, or he'd fallen into a fever juice coma.

Was he having visions? Did he see his victims in the crowd?

Did he see Saraatepe?

The thought set my blood to boiling. Bastard.

The musket fire was getting closer. Lieutenant Casado stepped off the podium and went over to confer with one of his sergeants. What was going on? Had pirates really landed?

"Finally, by the grace of God, the escaped heretic, Father Antonio Escofet, S.J., has again washed up on our shores. For his previous crimes, and for his additional crimes while trying to escape the justice of the Holy Inquisition, he too is condemned to death by fire."

No one applauded. No one cheered. Nothing but stony silence. Except from the bishop, whose cries began penetrating the wrapping over his mouth. Worse, he was now shaking his head so violently that his dunce's hat began to loosen.

Please, dear God, no. The priests will recognize him.

Father Paolo, seeing what I saw, nodded to the drummers. The beat renewed, drowning out the bishop's grunts. Paolo raised his arm, held it a moment, and dropped it.

The drums ceased. Samson and his assistant dumped their braziers of fire onto the woodpiles. The brush caught. Flames crackled. Smoke swirled around the bishop. Still he struggled, twisting from side to side, shaking his head, rubbing it on the stake.

"Come on, come on," I said, speaking to the flames.

The bishop's gag finally shook loose.

"*Idiotas*! Can't you see I'm not the heretic? I'm the—"

The band struck up the same martial tune they'd played at the execution of the hunchback. Children danced. Gypsies beat their drums. Flames rose up around the bishop. His protests turned to shrieks. The smell of smoke and burning flesh permeated the air. People backed away. But some of the priests were talking among themselves, pointing at him and glancing over at me.

Had they heard? Did they know?

What happened next may have been spontaneous or it may have been planned. All I know is someone shouted, "*Muerte al obispo*!"—Death to the bishop—and torrents of eggs, mangos, tomatoes, even horse droppings, began falling around me.

"Child rapist!"

"Murderer!"

Soldiers gathered in the street and at the bottom of the steps, forming a protective barrier to my front. The noise was so great I could barely hear Paolo shouting for order. Soldiers tried to restrain individual protestors from storming the landing where I sat, but still they surged forward, some waving sticks and axes, others flinging anything they could get their hands on.

"Padre," said one of the oarsmen, "we should get you inside."

I thought so too, but to retreat now would spoil my final act. So I sat in that wicker chair on the platform with the band playing and things smashing into the door behind me.

Waited until flames had completely enveloped the captain and bishop, and protesters were pressing against the soldiers, screaming for vengeance. Waited until Enrique, Paolo and Samson had pushed through the mob to my side.

And that was when I stood, clutched my chest as if in agony, and in my final act as Bishop of Granada, pretended to fall dead.

CHAPTER 59

The music came to a ragged end. Soldiers rushed to my assistance. Paolo motioned them away. Then Samson, Enrique, and the oarsmen carried me into the Alhambra, past the old guard at his desk, across the lobby and into the alcalde's office, where they laid out my "dead" body on the conference table.

"Clear this room," Paolo yelled. "Everyone out. Go!"

I couldn't see who followed us in, not with my eyes partially closed, but I could hear the voices—Lieutenant Casado, the jailer, Samson's assistant, and others. So I lay there like a dead man, unmoving, praying no one would take a closer look.

At last the door closed. The latch clicked. Paolo tapped me on the shoulder. "You can get up now, your Grace. You deserve a medal."

I rolled off the table, saw it was only the two of us, and quickly washed the white powder from my face and began dressing as Don Antonio, the man from La Casa. By the time I finished, the outside commotion had grown louder, with chants, shouts, and things crashing against the building.

"Has Casado left?" I asked Paolo.

He opened the door a crack and peeked out. "They're in the lobby. I'd better go talk to them."

He eased out and shut the door behind him. I knelt to the keyhole and watched him tell the lieutenant that the bishop was now "in heaven" and that he—Father Paolo—had performed the sacrament of extreme unction. "May God receive his soul," Paolo said.

Everyone I could see made the sign of the cross—Samson, his assistant, Lieutenant Casado and another officer. Then Paolo added, "He died of the fever. There were pustules. Also had the flux. I'm recommending a quick burial. Anyone who touched him could catch what killed him."

The lieutenant looked suddenly ill. "I was in the room with him… yesterday."

"How do you feel?" Paolo asked. "Any signs of fever? Vomiting? The flux?"

The lieutenant took a step backward, shaking his head.

"Then you should go. All of you. Wash up and change your clothing."

They hurried across the lobby as if they couldn't get away fast enough. I didn't see this but heard the clop of feet. Then I peeked out in time to see the old guard jumping up and unlatching the door. Paolo called after the lieutenant. "What was that shooting about?"

"Don't know, Father, but I sent my sergeant to find out."

The door opened. A sudden hush fell over the crowd. The lieutenant—or maybe one of the others—yelled, "He's dead! The bishop is dead!"

Cheers rang across the plaza. The music started again. So did the Gypsy's drums. And in that moment of triumph, I could have cried with joy. Molly would be here any minute. I had a new identity as Don Antonio. I'd slain the beasts of my nightmares.

And I'd soon have my boys.

Paolo went off to confer with the other priests—almost all of whom were still in the plaza—and came back with the news of a memorial service for the bishop that evening. "No open casket and no viewing," he said. He looked at me and smiled. "I also spoke to the mother superior. She'll bring over your boys this afternoon… for potential adoption."

I sank into a chair and let the tears flow. In my mind it was all worked out. Molly and I would stand before the mother superior as husband and wife and adopt the boys.

The oarsmen along with Mateo and Enrique hauled in a mahogany casket, which they draped with a banner of a Burgundy Cross. Samson and Enrique then changed into travel clothing and said it was time for them to leave. I gave Samson the escudos I owed him and was about to see him off when Paolo said, "Wait. Let's not forget that scrawny little priest."

Samson bounded up the stairs and came back with Father Shining Light of Spain, who looked as if he'd just emerged from a dungeon—his cassock rumpled, eyes bloodshot.

Paolo showed him the casket. "Take a good look, Padre. This is your fault. You knew he was ill and yet you went to him anyway, put him under stress. I should have you burned."

Sorrow spread over the wretched man's face. Paolo wagged a finger. "I'll give you one last chance. *Las Palmas* is sailing today, with the tide. I want you on it. You can go back to Spain… or anywhere you want. I'd better not ever again see your face. *Me entiendes*?"

"*Sí, Padre*, thank you, thank you."

He dropped to his knees and tried to kiss Paolo's ring.

Samson jerked him to his feet and pushed him out the door. As soon as they left, Enrique handed me the brass walking cane, told me I needed it more than he did, and shouldered his bag to leave.

"Wait a minute," I said. "I have something for you."

I led him into the privacy of the alcalde's office, opened my bag, and gave him the captain's uniform, the fake *cédula*, and the secret code and account number for Gonzalez's account. "It's a lot of gold," I told him. All you have to do is put on that uniform and go to La Casa in Bogotá. But do it soon. It'll take a few weeks for word to spread that he's been burned."

Tears flooded his eyes. He promised to write from Cartagena or wherever he ended up. We embraced, wished each other a long and healthy life, and he too went out the door—into the plaza where drums were still beating, the band playing, people cheering and singing like drunkards, firing muskets into the air.

I watched him go, trying to contain my emotions, and suddenly thought about Molly. What was keeping her? Hadn't she promised to return to the Alhambra after the burning?

At eleven by the clock, I sent Mateo to the bishop's residence to see what was going on.

He did not return.

I was about to go myself when someone began pounding on the door. Paolo opened it… and there stood Lieutenant Peralta in muddy uniform and dirt-streaked face, looking as if he'd just crawled out of the swamp. "Pirates," he said. "They came out of the forest."

Behind him came other soldiers, pushing a shackled black man. I went out for a closer look. Could it be?

Yes, one of the slaves I'd freed from the burning ship.

"Must have been a hundred of them," said Peralta. "Pirates, Zambos, even women. We killed maybe a dozen. The others took to the swamps. Also found some murdered locals down the road, strung up from a tree. Upside down. Devil markings all over them."

Out the door and across the plaza I raced, past the smoldering stakes and pushing through the crowd like a mad man, trotting, breathing hard, my heart in my throat, my leg throbbing with pain. Please, dear God. Let Molly be safe.

At last, I stood before the bishop's residence, gasping for breath. The wrought iron gate was unlocked. I opened it, dashed alongside the fence, crossed the rear patio toward the guest quarters, and was about to pound on the door when a horrifying shriek rent the air.

Then, as if the gate to hell had opened, a party of savages burst from the shadows, all feathers, painted faces, monkey teeth necklaces, machetes and spears.

Zambos. Billy's confederates.

CHAPTER 60

They circled me like me like a pack of wolves, yipping, barking commands in a language I didn't understand, prodding me with spears, bringing with them the smells of swamp and unwashed bodies.

The shortest of the bunch, a toothless little fellow with white markings around his eyes, yanked away my walking stick and sniffed my clothing as if trying to decide to pee on me or not.

From his smells, I figured he'd been drinking something more potent than Abuelita*'s* fever juice.

He took my two pistols and gave them to his friends. Then he laughed as if I were the odd one, and began shouting in my face, polluting the air with his putrid breath.

"I have no idea what you're saying."

He shouted louder, as if that would help me understand.

"Billy!" I shouted back. "Where is Billy?"

The name seemed to carry magic, as if the wind had spoken.

They conferred among themselves in their strange language, shouting and pointing. Then two of them pushed me into the bishop's guest quarters, down a matted passage, through a pair of doors, and into a large sitting room.

And there, pipe in hand, in the company of Little Mateo, Isabella, Aunt Annie, Molly, and two other pirates, sat Billy himself.

Molly, who held Isabella in her arms, caught my eye and shook her head. Billy stood, bowed as if I were royalty, doffed his hat like an English gentleman, and spoke to me in the French language we shared. "*Bon jour, Capitán.* What took so long?"

Unlike the other pirates, who were as dirty and mean-looking as the savages, Billy looked as if he'd recently visited a bath house. He also had the dashing looks of an English officer, right down to his ruffled white shirt and blonde hair that was tied back with a ribbon.

I glared at him. "What are you doing here?"

"Ah, *Capitaine,* please. *Pourquoi* you ask such question? You who steal my woman."

"She came of her own volition."

"A minor detail. *N'est-ce pas*?"

Molly said nothing. Not since that day when Billy landed on the beach had she looked so miserable. Little Mateo didn't look much better. Aunt Annie, by comparison, didn't seem the least perturbed, sitting there with her scarred face and hard look, puffing on a pipe.

"And worse, when I come peacefully under the white flag, do you treat me like a gentleman? *Non,* monsieur, you shoot my flag bearer. Then you shoot me… here, in this leg."

"One of the crew shot you. It wasn't me."

"*Mais Capitaine*, do you not take responsibility?"

"You want to talk about responsibility? How about Jack. He was under your flag. Do you take responsibility for his depravities?"

"Jack follows the devil's orders, monsieur. Not mine."

He limped to the savages who'd taken my walking stick, took it from them, and barked what must have been an order, because they hastily quit the room. Then he handed the stick to me as if surrendering his sword.

"Here, *Capitaine*, this is the way gentlemen treat gentlemen."

He went back to his chair, motioned me to sit, and took a long puff on his pipe. "In England we have a saying, 'Water under the bridge.' Gone. *Se fue*. Now we must go forward, work out our differences in a cordial manner."

I looked at Molly.

"Please, *Capitán*. It is not the woman I want. Not the girl either." He took another puff on his pipe. "Have you ever heard of the infamous pirate, Anne Bonny?"

"Everyone knows the story of Anne Bonny."

"And do you know what became of her?"

"They say she was hanged from a gibbet."

"Ah, so they say. But, alas, Anne Bonny was with child. She pleaded the belly. Her husband—Calico Jack Rackham—they hanged like a dog. Annie, they spared. Today that child would be oh, twenty or thereabouts, the same age as your sweet Molly. *N'est-ce pas*?"

Molly looked as if she wanted to crawl under the table. I could almost hear Enrique saying, "See, didn't I tell you." I stared back and forth between Molly and Aunt Annie. Was it possible? Molly the daughter of Anne Bonny and Calico Jack, the scourge of the Caribbean back in the year nineteen?

"Makes no difference. What counts is who Molly is now."

"Ah, such noble sentiments. Suppose I told you Molly is a thief."

"What I took was plunder," Molly said. "Things you stole."

"No, *Cheri*, what you took was war booty."

Billy turned back to me. "Here's what happened. A little over a year ago, when we were anchored in the lake, your sweet little Dulcinea ran away. Pit-a-pat, she called it. Not that I cared. *Au revoir*, I would have said. *Adios*, goodbye. Except for the sea chest."

Molly gave me a pleading look.

"All I want is that sea chest. Not Molly, not the girl."

"Give him the chest," I said to Molly.

"Can't. It's buried on the island—Ometepe. We have to go there."

"Which is why we need your help," Billy said. "We should all go to the island, but there are checkpoints. Soldiers everywhere, looking for pirates. Perhaps we can take the bishop's coach to the landing. Rent a boat. Even get your good friend, Father Paolo, to help."

"Why would Paolo help pirates?"

"For the same reason you will."

"And that is?"

He took a long puff on his pipe, blew out the smoke and smiled. "Because, Father Antonio, I know who you burned on that stake…, and it wasn't the heretic."

Billy relit his pipe with infuriating slowness, tapping out the old tobacco, stuffing in fresh tobacco, and then using a candle.

"Just imagine what will happen when word gets out that you and Father Paolo collaborated with pirates to burn the bishop. Usurp his power. Bury an empty casket. Ha, what rascals you are."

A rumble of thunder rattled the windows. Then the cathedral bell began pealing for the noon hour. The mother superior would soon be heading to the Alhambra with my boys. Maybe I could barter with Billy, arrange a swap. I turned back to him.

"What is in that chest?"

"Treasure, monsieur—doubloons, pearls, diamonds, emeralds, sacks of gold coins."

"What's the value?"

"Thirty, forty thousand escudos."

"Not even half that," Molly said.

They fell into a heated dispute, with Molly saying fifteen thousand, Billy saying forty, and the debate didn't end until I said, "Suppose I buy that chest from you."

"You?" Billy said. "A penniless priest? And what, pray tell, are you going to buy it with?"

"Two thousand ounces of pure gold."

His eyes widened. He exchanged glances with the other pirates. "What a canny fellow you are, padre. Make it three thousand."

"I don't have three thousand."

"Three thousand or nothing."

"The most I can get is twenty-five hundred."

He conferred with the other pirates in English. From their expressions, I could see they liked the idea. At last, Billy marched over, smiling, and pumped my hand.

"*D'accord*, monsieur. For the gold, Molly and the chest are yours. Go now, bring me the gold."

Molly followed me to the door, clinging like a woman afraid of losing her man. "Will Billy honor the agreement?" I asked her.

"If he doesn't I'll slit his throat, I will."

She kissed me on the lips, right there beneath the portico in full view of Billy. He smiled as if he approved, showing his perfect teeth.

"Go," Molly said. "Before Billy changes his mind."

I passed through a gate that connected the bishop's residence to the vicarage, slipped unseen into Paolo's bedchamber, and opened the faux bottom of the armoire where we'd hidden the bishop's gold.

I divided it into four piles, each weighing about forty pounds. Then I loaded it in sacks and lugged them one by one to the bishop's residence. By then the savages had gone, rain was coming down, and a coach and four was waiting in front.

Billy, waiting beneath the overhang, stuffed the gold into a sea chest and had his men load it onto the rear rack of the coach.

"Come on!" he yelled to Molly. "Get in the coach."

Before I could protest, the other two pirates grabbed my arms and tried to drag me inside. Not until then did it hit me.

Molly was part of the scheme. What a damn fool I'd been. What an idiot to trust the daughter of Anne Bonny.

But then, adding to my confusion, Molly rushed to my aid, fighting to get between me and the pirates. Billy grabbed her around the waist and pulled her away. She turned her fury on him, screaming and cursing the way she'd done at Jack in San Juan.

"Hush," Billy said. "You're my insurance."

"I won't go. I won't."

"Oh, yes, you will." He yanked out his pistol, cocked the hammer, and aimed it at my face. The other pirates backed away. I waited for the flash that would be the last thing I saw, but Jack lowered his pistol. "Not yet," he said. "I have other plans for you."

Molly rushed back to me. Hot tears ran down her face. "Chair where I sat," she whispered in Castilian. "Behind the cushion. Primed and loaded."

She took my hand and placed it between her breasts. "My heart beats only for you."

"Samson will be on the ship," I whispered. "He'll help you."

Billy dragged her into the rain and toward the waiting coach. The two pirates he'd left behind shoved me back into the residence and into the room where I'd sat before with Billy.

Aunt Annie had already left with Isabella, but little Mateo was still there. Thunder rumbled. I heard the clatter of hooves, and then a door opened and closed behind me, letting in a strong odor of goat.

I swung around and stared into the face of Vampire Jack.

CHAPTER 61

There he stood, this apparition from hell, long greasy hair and eyes as black as Satan. "Why don't you just go?" I said, waving a hand toward the door. "No one will get hurt."

I repeated the words in French, as if that would make a difference.

His lips formed into a sneer. From the looks of the other two pirates, I figured they were as terrified as I was. Jack nodded at them. They separated and began moving toward me. Three grimy pirates with murder in their eyes. Jack in the middle. Ring in his left ear. Red scarf about his head. Dirty fingernails. Pistol in his belt.

Whether they planned to use their dirks, pistols, or bare hands, I do not know. What I did know is I was not going to die without a fight. So I backed toward the chair where Molly had sat, holding my walking cane in front.

Mateo was still sitting on the floor, looking like a scared rabbit.

"Wait for my word," I said in Chorro. "Then run for the door."

He nodded. The rain was now beating against the windows. Thunder crashed and rumbled. The room grew darker still, as if Jack were conjuring up the forces of darkness.

I backed another step. Had Molly really left a pistol? Was it primed and loaded?

Jack feigned a lunge. I retreated behind the chair, wielding the cane in a protective manner.

He laughed at my puny efforts.

"Go!" I shouted to Mateo.

He sprang to his feet and dashed between the pirates, screaming, running for the door.

The youngest pirate took off after him.

Jack turned to see the outcome.

And that was when I tipped the chair backward.

There were two pistols. Two. Bless you, Molly.

I grabbed one, thumbed it to full cock, and fired directly into Jack's chest.

In that second or two before I fired the second pistol, I caught a glimpse of wide-eyed shock on the other pirate's face. In that frozen moment before my second shot tore into his chest.

Down he went, backward, his arms flailing.

Jack was still on his feet, fumbling for his pistol, blood running from his mouth.

Without thinking, I drove the chair into him. His pistol clattered to the floor. I reached for it and was swiveling to fire when he slammed into me from the side. Then we were both on the floor. In the blood. Rolling, kicking, struggling.

Hairy hands closed around my throat.

Blood dripped onto my face. "You can't kill Jack. Jack kill you. Cut your throat. Drink your blood."

The smell of goat alone was enough to kill me. The only thing between me and certain death was Jack's pistol, but it was pressed between us, flat against my stomach. Useless.

The awful sneer on his lips, the dripping blood, could be the last thing I'd see.

"Roll away!" cried the Gypsy.

With all my remaining strength, I rolled sideways. Space opened between us. Not much, but enough for me to pull back the hammer and squeeze the trigger.

There was a flash. A muffled report. Smoke and fumes. Jack released his grip. Then I was on my feet, running for the door.

For my life.

The door was still open, rain blowing through.

Where was the pirate who'd gone after Mateo?

He'd shoot me if I went through the door.

I glanced out. Rain blew sideways, roaring, whipping palm fronds into a frenzy, visibility so poor I could barely see the cathedral next door.

A hand grabbed my ankle.

Jack's hand.

Only way to kill Jack is cut off his head.

I bolted into the rain. Get away, my mind told me. Run.

Into this madness came the third pirate. On a horse. He galloped past me in a fury, lashing his mount. Then he too was gone, fading into the rain.

I glanced toward the bishop's stable. The door was open. And there too stood two other horses, saddled and waiting. Jack's horse. The escape horses. If I could catch up to Billy I was going to kill him with my bare hands.

The horse seemed to sense my urgency, even the direction I wanted to go, and took me down the same street I'd traveled on the day of my escape with Madam Rosa, past the blacksmith and tanning shops with their evil smells, toward the clouds that were getting blacker. Toward the landing.

Billy would probably be there by now, pretending to be a French gentleman with wife and family and a large trunk. No reason for customs to suspect a thing.

Rain bit into my face. Mud and water splashed. The wind howled. Lightning flashed. And I was cold, but the knowledge I'd beaten certain death warmed me.

God's will, I figured. That and Molly's pistols.

Once or twice I caught a glimpse of a rider in front, also at full gallop. Probably the pirate.

Soon we were out of the city and galloping along a country road, fields on one side and a stretch of marsh on the other, the reeds leading down to the lake.

"Halt!" commanded a guard at the checkpoint.

"Coach and four," I said. "Did it pass this way?"

"A while back," he said, and waved me through.

On I rode, kicking up mud, ducking beneath overhanging limbs, urging the poor beast beneath me to go faster, praying the tide had not yet turned. Please, dear God, please.

I said another prayer at the point where César had gunned down Lieutenant Vasquez. And at the gate that entered the landing. The rain was still coming down in sheets, so hard I could barely see the warehouses and the customs house.

It wasn't until I reached the trees along the shoreline that I saw what I didn't want to see: *Las Palmas* in full sail, the wind to her back, going out with the tide.

Molly gone. My dreams shattered. Again.

I tied up at the railing and hurried into the embarkation center.

She wasn't there. Only the cleaning crew, the guards, the customs captain, and a few officials with their pipes, all talking about pirates and chupacabras. Yes, they assured me, the passengers they'd seen boarding the ship fit the description of Billy, Aunt Annie, Molly and Isabella.

The smell of goat tortured me, yet I sat there for an hour or more, trying not to cry, gazing out at the lake until *Las Palmas* faded into the mist.

CHAPTER 62

Granada was in an uproar—soldiers going house to house; cavalrymen galloping off in all directions; even artillerymen guarding the approaches with cannon.

They stopped me twice, and finally escorted me to the Alhambra where I left the horse, stumbled inside, and found Father Paolo in the Alcalde's office, conferring with cavalry officers.

His eyes lit up when he saw me, and he probably would have thrown his arms around me except for my wretched appearance. "Thank God you're alive," he said. "You smell like goat."

I slumped into a chair, still breathing hard, and related my story. Paolo listened, seemed to recognize there was more than what I was reporting, and ordered the officers out, telling them to scour the cane fields and check the passenger list at the landing.

As soon as the door closed behind them, I said, "Billy knows about the empty casket."

"What empty casket? We put the pirate in it, the one you shot."

"I shot two pirates."

"We found only one body."

"Was he hairy? Swarthy? Smell like a goat?"

"No, he was light-skinned. Had a hole in his chest. Anyhow, we cleaned him up, dressed him in the bishop's clothing, and stuffed him into the casket. Even poured water on him to speed up the ripening… just in case someone has a mind to dig him up."

"You didn't find Vampire Jack?"

"I just told you. We found lots of blood, but only one pirate."

I grabbed my hat.

"Where are you going?"

"To see the mother superior. Would you look after my horse?"

"Don't forget the bishop's memorial service. It starts at five."

I trotted across the plaza in my drenched clothing, my heart beating at a gallop. How could Jack still be alive?

Only way to kill Jack is cut off his head.

The convent's massive front door was locked. So I ran to the back, took a shortcut through the stables, and was admitted through a side door and into a sitting room where sat the mother superior in her white robe and habit, all pinch-faced and hostile looking.

She sniffed the air as if offended by the smell.

"Where is your wife?"

I suppressed a curse. What would she say, I wondered, if I told her I'd just shot two men, that pirates had kidnapped my "wife," and a monster called Vampire Jack was still on the loose?

"The storm," I finally answered. "I thought it best to come alone."

She asked a few more questions and finally tapped her cane on the floor. The door behind her opened. A sister in habit marched in. And behind her came two little boys with big eyes and curious looks, all scrubbed, clipped, and dressed like gentlemen in stockings and ruffled shirts.

"This is Elijah," said the sister. "He's four. And this one is Lucas, age six." The mother superior slapped Lucas on the shoulder. "Stand up straight, boy."

They stared at me. At my wet clothes and muddy boots, at my ruffled hair. Not a hint of recognition. My throat tightened. I choked back the tears. How I yearned to wrap them in my arms and comfort them, tell them who I was. Take them away.

I couldn't. Not without a wife. And certainly not as Father Antonio.

So I stood there, dripping water and listening to the mother's speech on the duties of fatherhood, on the necessity to raise the boys as devout Catholics and good Spaniards, and how hard it was to feed, clothe and school the growing number of orphans. And how wonderful it would be if gentlemen like me would be more generous with their purses.

At the end of her speech, I gave her ten gold escudos.

She thanked me and said she'd get the papers prepared for my signature by Wednesday. "Don't forget. No adoptions without a wife in attendance. And one more thing, *caballero*." She wagged a fat finger. "You should bathe and change before you come for the boys."

I left the place cursing Vampire Jack, cursing Billy, and cursing the mother superior. How was I going to produce a wife by Wednesday? One of Madam Rosa's girls, I figured.

There were no tears that evening at the bishop's memorial service. No kind words spoken, not that many flowers either, and only the clergy and cavalry officers in attendance. I sat on the back row, in the shadows, and slipped out as soon as it was over. Then, because the vicarage was still occupied by visiting priests, I spent the night in the bishop's residence. Alone. In the same room Molly had occupied.

One door down from where I'd shot the pirates.

It didn't help that it had stormed all night–or that a tree limb kept slapping against the shutters. I also had bad dreams—Molly lying in Billy's arms, naked, laughing at me, saying how stupid I'd been to believe her story about a hidden treasure chest.

The church bells woke me—loud, quickening peals, the kind that told of dire news. Then a street crier came clattering down the street on horseback.

"*Oigan! Oigan*! Pirates attack *Las Palmas*! Many killed!"

Las Palmas, the ship that Billy and Molly had taken.

CHAPTER 63

I hurried over to the vicarage, hoping Father Paolo had more information. He didn't. I gulped down a mug of coffee, grabbed a chunk of bread and cheese and, along with Mateo and Father Paolo, took the bishop's coach to the Ysese Landing.

The ruts were deep, the road washed out in places, everything muddy and wet, but at length we reached the landing where semaphore officers were waving their mysterious flags.

The customs captain came out and saluted Father Paolo. "Pirates were waiting below the fortress," he reported, "but our gunboats drove them away, swept the river clean."

"How many casualties?" Paolo asked.

"We're getting conflicting reports. It's hard enough when the weather is clear, trying to communicate with flags and lights." He pointed into the lake. "That mist out there makes it nigh impossible. All we know is this: the fortress is sending a gunboat with a report. It should be here by candle-light. I'll send a rider as soon as we hear."

Dinner that evening was as gloomy as a wake. It was only the two of us, Father Paolo on one side of the table, me on the other, candles and Abuelita*'s* food in the center, Paolo quietly relating how he'd written a report about the bishop to the viceroy in Guatemala.

I tried to concentrate on his words, but all I could think about was Molly. Molly with a bandanna around her head.

Molly with pistols tucked into her belt.

Molly floating in the river.

"Are you listening?"

"The gunboat should be in by now. Shouldn't we go to the landing?"

"Didn't you hear the captain? They'll bring the report here." He wiped his mouth on a napkin and leaned forward. "Let her go, Antonio. She's gone. It'll be months…."

A rider came clattering down the street.

Mateo let him in. It was a customs official in blue, breathing hard, his uniform soaked and muddy. He saluted Father Paolo.

"Begging your pardon. Father, but I've got a message for a Don Antonio Arteaga y Flores. They said he'd be here."

I stood. "I'm Don Antonio."

He saluted again. "Message from Captain Cisneros…, that's the customs captain. He wants you and Father Paolo at the landing."

"What's the news?"

"They don't tell me, *caballero*. All I know is a gunboat came in. There's a body on it."

"Whose body?"

"Didn't tell me that either."

Father Paolo yelled for the coach. He also sent Mateo running to the barracks for an escort. Within minutes Lieutenant Casado showed up, saying he wanted to ride with us. I grabbed my hat and pistols—Molly's pistols—and a few minutes later we were racing for the landing.

Down that same dismal road I'd traveled so many times before. In the darkness. Swamps and forest and fog on both sides. Insects chirping. Frogs croaking. Low hanging limbs brushing the overhead. Cavalrymen in front and back. A light rain falling. Questions rattling around my head like loose pebbles: Whose body was on that gunboat?

Why had they sent specifically for me?

At last we rolled through the gate and right up to the pier. Bolts of lightning streaked the sky. Waves slammed against the breakwater. Men in lanterns came out of the customs house, one of whom I recognized as the Captain of Customs.

"You Don Antonio?" he asked, holding up a lantern.

"I am."

"Come with me."

He led us along the pier to a gunboat that bobbed in the water, its lanterns all aglow. A crewman helped me into the boat, down a ladder, and into a cramped and shadowy cabin.

Paolo, Lieutenant Casado, and Mateo pushed in behind me. The air was foul. Not the tarry smells of a sea-going ship, but the familiar smell of death.

I crossed myself. Please, dear God, not Molly.

The captain hung his lantern from a beam. And there on the deck before me lay the body, wrapped in canvas.

"Who is it?" I asked the captain, dreading his answer.

"We were hoping you could tell us."

He nodded to a crewman. The crewman bent down and began unlacing straps. The smell of decay rose up to meet me. My stomach convulsed. I turned away, drew in a breath of fresh air, and said another silent prayer. Please, dear God, please.

When I turned back, the canvas had been drawn back and the body exposed.

The captain took down the lantern and held it next to the body, directly over the face.

I couldn't speak. All I could do was stare.

Mateo pushed around me. "*Coño*, it's that damn pirate."

At last I found my voice. "They call him Billy," I said. "An Englishman. Captain of the *Vulture*. There's a price on his head."

"His papers identify him as a Frenchman. Are you sure it's him?"

"*Sín duda, Capitán*. He kidnapped my wife and daughter."

"He was clearly murdered. Notice the knife wounds in his chest and neck?"

"How could it be murder? He's a wanted man. Dead or alive."

"You were here yesterday, weren't you, all gloomy looking?"

I nodded.

"Why didn't you report it then?"

Paolo stepped forward. "He reported to me. What else could he do? The ship had sailed."

We went topside. The night air was cool and fresh. The rain felt good on my skin, but the captain's avoidance of my question was an ominous sign. He led us into the customs building, past the tables, and down the corridor toward his office.

At the door, he stopped and faced me.

"So you're saying the woman is your wife?"

"Yes, Captain. What happened to her? And our daughter?"

"What else did the pirates take from you?"

"What do you mean?"

"Like, for example, a shipment of gold."

Father Paolo spoke up behind me. "Listen, Captain, that gold was church gold. Don Antonio was donating it for the building of new churches on the islands. *Verdad*, Antonio?"

"Every centavo."

"Good, you'll find the gold in my office, along with your wife and daughter."

Before I could absorb his words, the door to the captain's office burst open, and there stood Molly *sans* make-up, her clothes rumpled, her hair a mess.

No ornamentation either, but she was the most beautiful sight I'd ever seen.

She flew into my arms, crying, saying she'd thought I was dead, that Jack had killed me.

The captain left us alone in his office, in the light of a low-burning lantern. Isabella was there too sleeping on a sofa.

Aunt Annie was nowhere in sight.

I tried to speak, but all I could do was hold Molly in my arms, cry with her. Little by little, I learned Samson had been the one to knife Billy, but Molly confessed to it, saying he was the infamous Captain Billy, so they pulled her off the ship at the fortress.

"I wasn't going to kill him at first," she said, "was going to wait and run away, come back here, but then he told me about Jack. I didn't know Jack was there until he told me. Said he'd left orders to string you up the way he did the others."

I told her about my encounter, how her pistols had saved me, and how I'd put two balls into Jack's chest. "They didn't kill him. He must have crawled off somewhere and died."

"Only way to kill Jack is cut off his head."

I laughed. I'm not sure why because if they didn't find Jack's body I'd spend lots of restless nights with doors barricaded and pistols next to my bed. "Where is Aunt Annie?"

"Still on the ship. She wants to return to New Orleans."

"Is she really Anne Bonny?"

She put a finger to my lips. "Hush."

In time the captain came back and announced we were free to go, and that Molly could apply for the reward. "We'll need a full report of exactly what happened," he said. "Give it to Father Paolo. In writing and send me a copy."

They loaded the chest with the gold in the coach. I took Isabella in my arms, and on the way out said to Molly, "That treasure you took from Billy. That you buried on the island. Is it really there, or were you making up the story?'

"Do you have a shovel?"

"I can get one."

"Good. Let's go dig it up. Maybe we can hide it in the cave you're always talking about."

About *The Heretic of Granada*

In *The Girl in the Glyphs* (Peace Corps Writers 2016) a young archaeologist's translation of a 1740s manuscript by a heretical priest leads her to discovery and fame.

The Heretic of Granada is the manuscript she translated.

Although *Heretic* is a work of fiction, the historical backdrop of Caribbean piracy, native uprisings, superstition, colonial rule, the Spanish Inquisition, the hostility between Catalonian and Castilian Spaniards, and the brutal war between England and Spain (the War of Jenkins' Ear) is authentic. Most of the cathedrals, fortresses, convents, seawalls, and other colonial structures depicted in this work—including those of *La Casa de Contratación*—are still extant.

The plaza de armas of the beautiful colonial city of Granada, Nicaragua, was the site of numerous hangings, burnings, garroting and other executions in the time of the Inquisition.

In spite of reports that date the origin of chupacabras to the 1960s, stories about a furry, goat-sucking beast with horns and fiery eyes date back to the period of the conquest.

The basic currency in Father Antonio's time was a silver coin known as a Real de Plata. A larger eight-real piece, was commonly referred to as a Spanish dollar or Piece of Eight. Gold

Escudos (3.38 grams) was equivalent to sixteen reales.

The powerful Casa de Contratación (Royal House of Accounting) regulated Spanish commerce in the colonies, enforced the monopoly on trade, licensed ships and captains, and provided banking and many other services for colonial rule. It shared power with the military and church and answered only to the crown and its viceroys.

The Spanish Inquisition was officially abolished in 1834.

About the Author

DR. DAVID C. EDMONDS was raised in Louisiana and Mississippi and is a former Marine, Peace Corps Volunteer, Senior Fulbright Professor of Economics, and academic dean. He studied at Louisiana State University, Notre Dame, Georgetown, and American University, and has spent considerable time in Latin America as both a US government official and scholar. His previous books have won more than a dozen prestigious literary awards.

Acknowledgements

The Heretic of Granada would not have been possible without the support, encouragement and critical eye of many friends, associates, fellow writers, former students, and family members.

In Cajun country, I am deeply indebted to my good friends in the Writers' Guild of Acadiana, as well as Karen Burlet, Jessy Ferguson, Bea Angelle, and Cynthia Thomas.

Among my Chile IV Peace Corps friends who listened, read my chapters or otherwise shared their thoughts are George Pope, Bill Callahan, George Wildman, and Karen Mitchell.

In Florida, I am no less grateful to the Tarpon Springs Library Writers' Group for listening, reading, and critiquing *Heretic* in its early days—Bob Dockery, Georgia Post, Rebecca Roberts, Claudia Sodaro, Sonia Linke, Stephanie Geddes, Susan Ingold, Carol Gilardi, Gwen Hamlin, Meg Skinitis, Brian Roth, Joseph Mendonca, and Dexter Jerome.

Ditto for my writer friends in the Fiction Writers' Group of Tarpon Springs. Thank you, Gino Bardi, Mark Turley, Laura Kennedy Bell, Liz Drayer, Ken Dye, Lee Blimes, Jean Gogolin, Beth Hovind, Donna Lengel, Shannon O'Leary-Beck, Eleni Papanou, Elizabeth Indianos, Dorte Zuckerman, Laurie Cottrell, Debbie Browne, Bill Frederick, Bill Ciaccia, Belva Greene, Tina Forcier, Linda Rodante, Louise Michalos, Annalisa Bardi, and Micki Morency.

The TS Library director, Cari Rupkalvis, deserves credit for putting up with us over the years.

Thank you, Terri Gerrell, for accepting me into your family of talented writers at Southern Yellow Pine (SYP) Publishing. Thanks also to my dear friends with a St. Petersburg College connection—Barbara Glowaski, Diane Ronspies, Susan Parchetta, and Dr. Vilma Zalupski.

And my friends and associates at the Tarpon Springs Rotary Club who either read or offered encouragement—Joan Jennings, Ramona Pletcher, Alleyne Newcomb, Joan Tobin, Sue Thomas, Anne-Todd Eisner, Bill Grantham, and Bill Vinson.

A BIG special thanks to Pamela Lopez and Kim Duncan, who put a gallon of red ink on the pages. And my Barcelona friend, Mayte Careaga Gioia, who taught me a thing or two about Catalonian culture, history and language. *Gràcies molt, la meu amic gitana català.*

The love and encouragement of family always makes my job easier. Thank you, Chris, Julie, Alex, and Davy Edmonds, and Mark, Leza, Isabella, Juliana, and Alina Ries, and all my Montes and Nieves relatives from the beautiful island of Puerto Rico.

The popular novels of the period—Daniel Defoe (*The Adventures of Robinson Crusoe*), Jonathon Swift (*Gulliver's Travels*), Voltaire (*Candide*), Samuel Richardson (*Pamela*), and Henry Fielding (*Tom Jones* and *Shamala*)—were an enormous help in my attempt to capture the language, logic, culture and thinking of a 1740s individual.

Finally, there are no words to describe the love, encouragement, and support I received from my bride of twenty years, Maria Nieves Edmonds, and the sadness I feel at her loss.

www.ingramcontent.com/pod-product-compliance
Lightning Source LLC
Chambersburg PA
CBHW031102030726
47496CB00002BA/349
9781596160651